GLOWING **LIGHTS**

GLOWING LIGHTS

ON STAGE TRILOGY
BOOK TWO

NAMIAR TOPIT

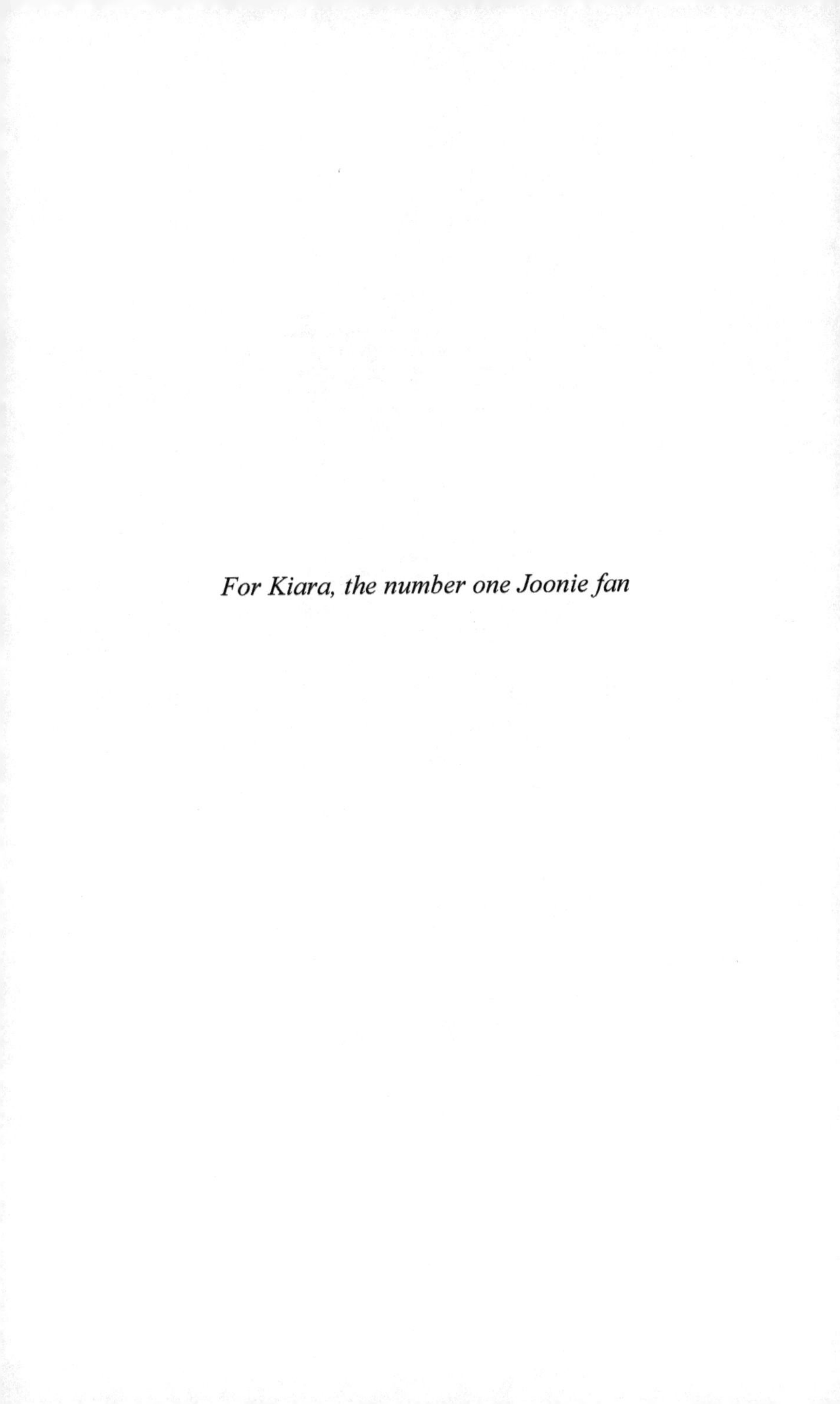

For Kiara, the number one Joonie fan

PROLOGUE: The Night of Confessions

Tae's Point of View

"So…me and Do, we're together. Like, *together* together. Just for your info," Minjae stated from across the table after downing a shot of soju.

Finally. There you go.

A small smile tugged the corners of my lips. It wasn't like this turn of events was a surprise for me. Though, it was nice to know beforehand, since surprises weren't really my thing. As a leader of this chaotic group of delicate, unpredictable artists, unpredictable events didn't sit well with me. Also, it was kind of my job to be on top of these things. Knowing Do and Min, it wasn't even a possibility in the first place that they could keep something like that a secret. Their natures were way too chaotic for that—the exact opposite of me.

I glanced around the table. Chris and Joonie didn't seem surprised in the slightest. But Jiwoo clearly did, as she had completely frozen beside me. The silence dragged on. Thankfully soon enough, Chris was the one to break it. "Ugh, we know. No need to make a statement."

That, still, didn't wake Jiwoo from her petrified state. So, after another silence, it was Do's turn to get fed up.

"So yeah, that happened," he said with a somewhat strained tone. Well, who could've blamed him for that...?

That statement, finally, broke through to Jiwoo. It was almost like she was waiting for Do to confirm it himself. As it turned out, she didn't really mind and to everyone's relief, everything went back to normal. Personally, I was just glad it was over and done with. For once I didn't have to be the one to break the "bad" news to Jiwoo by myself.

Unlike the rest of them, I wasn't much of a drinker. Apart from the shot I'd downed earlier, I had been on my first beer for ages. Dragging it on so I wouldn't be harassed with endless questions of why I wasn't wasted. The others though, drank like there was no tomorrow with the inevitable sorrow of hungover. It amused me, in some weird way, knowing that I'd have fun tomorrow morning when all of them would be wallowing in misery.

After Do and Minjae disappeared into Do's room to do things I'd rather not think about, the night turned into a night of confessions faster than one could say "the gayest boy band in history." Jiwoo was whining about being jealous of the relationship between Do and Minjae, whereas she had been single for ages. She stated that men couldn't handle strong women—though in my opinion, she just had way too high standards.

Chris told us that he hated the cutie image he had and wished to change it but didn't know what else he could do instead. I guess he couldn't see all the possibilities and all his talents. Joonie admitted he was gay, which we pretty much knew already. In other words: no surprises. Good.

Once they all had dropped everything they had weighing on their shoulders, they turned their alcohol influenced, glassed up gazes towards me. Clearly expecting me to contribute on the subject. I couldn't help but roll my eyes. Yes, even though I knew from experience that the gesture would give away my sober state. As they just continued staring me down, like I couldn't be here if I didn't confess something, I finally broke the silence.

"I like pineapple on pizza."

Jiwoo glanced at Joonie her eyes all squinty and sharp, while pouring a shot of soju. Joonie just nodded, took the shot glass, and swayed his way towards me—nearly tripping on his own feet along the way, I might add.

"Tae, you are way too sober," he whined when he reached me. He plopped to sit down on my lap and shoved the shot glass in front of my face, spilling half of its contents all over my chest. "Just live a little," he continued, slurring and barely even able to balance his drunk ass to stay on my lap and not fall to the floor.

· Reluctantly, I downed the shot. It burned my throat, as I wasn't really used to strong alcohol. After tossing the glass to the table, I wrapped my hands around Joonie. It was only to prevent the very possible accident that was just inches away from happening when he staggered on my lap. But of course, Chris got some humor out of even that little gesture.

"Aw, that's so sweet! When exactly are you two coming out of the closet?" Chris cheered, grinning, and raising his glass to us. Jiwoo burst laughing out loud. Joonie was practically purring, noticeably satisfied with the reaction that one question had on everyone. Naturally, I couldn't resist taking it a bit further.

"We never were in the closet in the first place," I joked and gave Joonie a light peck on the cheek.

That much was very usual for Joonie and I. We were close, had always been. After years of fanservice, that much came straight from my spine. In real life though, I wasn't even sure I'd be capable of romantic feelings at all. Love was never really my thing. I had always been insanely focused on my career; I was way too busy to even think about those kinds of things.

Besides, love was messy and complicated; business was easy to handle and straightforward. Love was unpredictable, whereas surprises didn't exist in the business world. GRiD was business to me, first and foremost. A family too, but that came only after the business.

My thing was to be on top of things and adding another person to that equation was hazardous. And, unlike Do, Min and Joonie, I was pretty certain I was straight. After all, I wasn't completely made of stone, and women were just more attractive in general. Like Jiwoo, with her long, fiery red hair and the body of a goddess with a brain of a true intellectual. But she was just a friend and a co-worker, not someone I had romantic interest in.

Joonie probably didn't think anything of the little kiss on the cheek too since we had always acted this way around each other. He just giggled for a bit and continued drinking as if nothing had happened. He did stay on my lap, though. As he was light as a feather, it didn't bother me much, and I let him stay.

When his eyes started to droop, I decided he had enough alcohol in his bloodstream. "Alright, it's time for you to go to bed."

Chris and Jiwoo nodded, so I lifted Joonie up, surprisingly without hearing even one complaint from him. Bridal style, I carried him straight to his room. He clung to my neck, hiccupping adorably a couple of times on the way.

Joonie's door was open, so I was able to lay him right on top of his bed. He was well on his way to passing out when I covered him up with his blanket. His hair had spread all over his face, which he kept trying to blow away. Obviously, it didn't work very well. Chuckling under my breath, I helped him a bit and brushed the hair aside. For a brief moment, I got mesmerized by his face that could only be described as unnaturally pretty for a guy.

Now if he was a woman...

Joonie grabbed my wrist, interrupting the thought before I could even finish forming it.

"I love you, Tae," he mumbled, half asleep.

"I love you too. Now go to sleep," I replied with a smile lingering on my face.

Again, this was something common for us. But what took me off guard was something Joonie said after that. Tightening his grip on my wrist, he forced his sleep weighted eyes to open and looked me dead in the eyes.

"No, I'm *in* love with you. Why can't you just see it already?" he slurred. At the same time he gave up on trying to stay awake and downright passed out on me.

It took a while to digest what Joonie had said. But when I did, the first thing that came to mind was that maybe he was joking or something. Then again Joonie wasn't like that. He would never say something like that as a joke.

I was so sorry for him. It was hard to breathe for a second. Almost like someone had knocked the air out of my lungs and turned my world upside down. Then, the pity hit. It wasn't fair. No one should've fallen in love with me. Especially not Joonie. He was my rock, the only other sane person in this household. I had always counted on him to be there, and now I was going to break his heart.

My head felt light, but for some reason, I kept staring at his sleeping face like a creep. A random, very out of place thought crossed my mind and took me by surprise: If I were to ever be gay, he'd most definitely be my type.

Seoul Searching

"Miss, we are about to land, you need to shut down your phone."

"Sure," Jiwoo muttered under her breath and pocketed the phone, without even sparing the poor innocent flight attendant an apologetic nod. "How amazing that the humankind has managed to invent a flying metal box, only for its weakness to be one lousy phone during take-off and landing. The Wi-Fi was finally steady…"

"Relax," I said, and glanced at Jiwoo across the aisle. "It's not like you can't obsess over the ratings and news once we've landed…" I glanced at my wristwatch. "…in like less than an hour."

"True."

"Besides, their 'Mad Love' performance was amazing last night. I'm sure the true fans at least will be okay with them…being together. Publicly I mean."

Jiwoo exhaled a long sigh and leaned back in her seat. "It sure looks like it."

We both turned our attention to the two lovebirds—Minjae and Do-hyun—bickering over chips in their seats ahead of us on Jiwoo's side of the plane. It was as if things had finally returned to normal. The whole DoMino scandal…it was really over, right?

Right.

It only took five months of intense media circus and working our assess off on the tour, but it really looked like things were about to calm down.

Stretching out in the seat of the airplane was almost impossible for a tall person like myself, even if it was first-class. It was my personal hell. My eyes began to get dry and irritated because of the recycled air. My legs were practically numb, and my lower back hurt from all the sitting, but thankfully it was almost over.

Suddenly there was extra weight on my shoulder. Looked like Joonie had finally lost his hours-long battle against sleep. He was out cold, leaning against my shoulder. He looked adorable, his pouty lips—

Nope, I was not about to go there.

Still, everything came back to me as a rush from the night of confessions. Especially Joonie's confession. The private one reserved for me, that had made my whole world go upside down until the whole scandal came and I was able to drown myself in work. It was getting harder and harder to push the thoughts to the back of my mind each passing day, though.

I had only once made actual effort to think about the whole thing. The morning after the...incident. It felt like I had been falling off the cliff, spiralling into something unfamiliar and scary. Something I was not in control of. And I hadn't liked the feeling one bit. I still didn't. It was a surprise in my surprise-less world, and that threw me off my game. With just that one sentence on the night of confessions, Joonie left me utterly and completely stunned.

I was suddenly second-guessing everything about myself. I genuinely thought I knew myself. A control-freak, a workaholic, and the leader of a successful idol group. There was no time for feelings. And most definitely: I was completely straight. But back then...there had been an undeniable, tiny spark somewhere deep in my chest. Admittedly, I got scared and buried the whole night in the back of my mind.

There was nothing I wished more than that we could get back to how things were before. Or rather, that *I* could get back to how *I* was before, since Joonie acted like he always did. It was me who was acting all awkward. For a moment, I speculated why he hadn't confronted me about it. Even if he didn't remember anything about the night of confessions, he should've noticed I had been avoiding him.

I didn't want to lose Joonie either and that's what made it all so complicated. First of all, I couldn't afford to lose Joonie since he was a crucial part of GRiD. We wouldn't have a lead vocalist without him. Plus, he was very good at keeping all of us sane. The one that kept the schedule on point. Kept us fed and away from fast food. My rock. The one I could lean on when everything started to get too much for me to handle on my own. "Friends" wasn't the right word for my thing with Joonie, but neither was a *relationship*. I had to have him by my side. Couldn't we just stay platonic soulmates forever?

It didn't even make any sense. Why would he even fall for me? I had never led him on. Nevertheless, I felt so incredibly sorry for Joonie and was angry at him for making things unnecessarily complicated at the same time.

However, I did realize that we could never go back to the way we were. I didn't really want to, as hard as it was to admit. Still, I had no idea of what I wanted, exactly. Hell, I still didn't even know if I could be gay or bi or whatever.

But soon was my chance—my time-frame to figure everything out. We were about to have a month-long pause on the world tour, for shooting two music videos to be released with the repackaged album and to have a brief promotional period for the said album. But also, it would give us a bit of a breather.

Joonie would be stuck with me for the first week, because he was the only one who could make me learn the choreography. Yes, I was many things, including an award-winning producer, acclaimed songwriter, rap-artist, and the leader of GRiD. One thing I was not, however, was a dancer. I had two left feet, but I made do. Mostly because of Joonie being an extremely patient teacher.

We were also going to be home for a whole month. As nice as the luxury hotels were, they were still just hotel rooms. There was nothing else like home, sleeping in your own damn bed, surrounded by your own damn things. Not to mention you could make your own damn breakfast, damn lunch, and damn dinner. Or rather, I'd make the breakfast while Joonie would be in charge of the rest. That was the way it had been for years. Except for the time spent in the army, of course.

Slowly, my mind started to form a plan. I loved my plans. Plans made me feel like I was on top of things. I needed to start over, completely from scratch. That meant I'd have to face my own feelings, figure out if I would even be able to have romantic feelings. After that, I'd have to determine if I could be sexually attracted to a man, as I was most definitely a sexual person otherwise. Then, finally, I'd have to confront Joonie about his confession, figure out if he still felt that way towards me.

I'd had to make every day of the whole month at home count. I planned to finally walk out of that whole mess with a clear head and sorted out feelings. Who knew? Maybe that would result in a new relationship. Maybe not. But I sure was going to figure that one out. Even more for Joonie's sake than my own though, as I owed him that much after he had been my rock of support for years with this...hazardous group.

For him, I had to at least try.

Another smile made its way to my face when I glanced at Joonie again. Hell, I smiled like an idiot. Right there, at the seemingly comfortable first-class seat, when the plane started inching closer and closer to ground. When the staff announced that they were going to start preparing for landing, I shook Joonie's shoulder lightly to wake him up. He stirred at first before fluttering his eyes open.

"We're home?" he asked with the traces of sleep making a rough edge to his normally smooth voice.

"Soon," I said softly and turned back to look outside the window to the lights of Seoul—home—below us.

With a deafening screech from the tires hitting the ground and a few light bumps, our plane eventually touched down on the landing strip of Incheon International Airport. After the safety belt light turned off, I stood up and fished my cap and sunglasses from the overhead cabinet and headed out after Joonie. He was wearing a cap too, paired with huge sunglasses and a black mask. The air pollution levels weren't supposed to be that high today, so I guessed it was to hide his face from the cameras.

After we made it through customs and collected our luggage, Joe gathered us to the exit. With him leading and the other security personnel surrounding us, we started to slowly make our way through the crowd. None of us were in the mood for the cameras and fans—who would be just after a long-ass flight? I never understood the thing about hanging randomly at an airport only to get a photo of us. It never made any sense. It wasn't like we would be doing anything stupid or newsworthy here.

With our enormous amount of luggage, we all had to ride in separate cars. It was, at least, a short ride and another chance for me to think. To be honest, the hardest part was already behind me—admitting that Joonie's words had affected me. Due to finally letting myself think about it, I had finalized my plan. No matter what, I was going to figure things out.

A month. A month of brutal honesty. A simple, one-month solution to all my problems. Just one more night, then maybe it was time for some soul searching.

And day one was for observation.

Attractive in General

I spotted Minjae as soon as I hit the kitchen at 6:30 in the morning. Apparently, Minjae had had one of his bad nights, since he was already up and brewing coffee when I arrived, despite it being his day off.

"Good morning," I said while starting to hunt down ingredients for breakfast. "Bad night?"

"Yeah, jet lag." He continued staring ahead with a glassed-up gaze, waiting for the coffee to brew.

"Alright, but please try to get some more sleep tonight," I always worried about him. It would be bad if our main choreographer and dancer wouldn't be able to keep up.

He rolled his eyes at me and continued staring at the coffee machine. It looked like he was trying to make it brew faster with sheer willpower.

Joonie appeared a bit later, but I hadn't started my mission yet, as we had company. I wanted to wait until we were alone downstairs. For once, I couldn't wait to start a dance practice, although I knew I'd be bruised up by the end of the day, because I was always messing up and tripping to my own damn feet.

Everyone else had already learned the choreographies for the new songs by themselves, so they got a day off. But I was scheduled to have a private training session with Joonie on that very first day back home. I would've felt bad for making him do it, but I made an exception. I needed to start figuring out this thing between us. Preferably as soon as possible, so I could focus on work again.

The two caffeine-addicted men practically ignored the whole breakfast I had laid out on the table. Instead, they just nibbled on fruit and ate exactly one boiled egg each. Other than that, they solely focused on their coffees. Weird.

"What's with not eating, huh?" I asked.

Both of them lifted their gaze precisely at the same time and gave me an incredulous look.

It was Minjae who eventually cleared it up for me, staring me straight in the eyes with one eyebrow cocked up. "Music videos. Diet. Add up."

Right. Suddenly, I didn't feel like eating the bread and noodles anymore, either. Carbs. To be honest, with everything else going on, I'd completely forgotten we were all supposed to diet. I lowered the bread slowly back to the plate, thinking I seriously needed to get a grip of my own damn life.

Minjae chuckled. "Hyung, it's not like you're gonna be in the spotlight that much. So, by all means, ignore us and finish that damn bread."

"Besides, you'll need those carbs for what I'm going to put you through today," Joonie added, giggling along with Minjae to my apparent stupidity. Sometimes I wondered exactly how the hell I became the leader, since Joonie would have been better suited for the job. Maybe it was because I was the oldest? I really couldn't remember.

Chris came to my rescue just in time, piling up his plate with all the greasy and carb-filled stuff he could find on the table. All of us looked at him like he was insane, although we all knew none of that would show on his body in any way. He was one of the lucky few that had the extremely good metabolism to take care of those for him.

"What?" Chris asked when he noticed us all looking at his plate like it was something out of this world.

"Nothing," Minjae said, grabbing an apple and scurrying off. "I'll take this to Do," he hollered from the threshold before disappearing to the hallway.

"Oh, I see. You're all starving yourself again. Well, more food for me." Chris scooped more noodles into his bowl.

Joonie just shook his head disapprovingly but didn't elaborate. Instead, he turned his gaze towards me. "I think we should head downstairs."

I agreed, and we left Chris to take care of the cleaning for us.

As soon as we hit the dance studio, Joonie explained to me that he'd show my whole part of the choreo once, for a recap, and then we'd break it apart.

"Pay close attention," he said as I plopped down to sit on a floor pillow and glued my gaze to Joonie through the mirror. Perfect. I couldn't have possibly planned a better way to start my mission of observation.

He started to dance. Even though it was my simpler part of the choreo, he made it look exquisite. I couldn't have shifted my gaze from him if I tried. I was completely and utterly mesmerized by his movements, too distracted to even start analyzing. There was something sensual and graceful about the way he moved, about the way he spoke when describing the parts of the choreo, and even in the way he passed glances at me occasionally through the mirror.

For the first time ever, I allowed myself to give my full attention solely to his looks.

Of course, I knew Joonie was attractive in general. I'd have had to be blind not to notice that. He was world-famously beautiful, in fact. His overgrown, bleached hair dyed with whatever bright color he was into each time he visited the hairdressers had some natural waviness to it. At the time, that color had been bubblegum pink. He had a heart-shaped face, wide brown eyes paired with some thick, long lashes, beautifully rounded, plump lips, and smoother than smooth, unnaturally light skin for a Korean.

His body was delicately framed, beyond thin. He even highlighted that slim body of his with loosely fitted clothes. As the most fashionable one out of us all, even including Minjae, he was addicted to weird, avant-garde accessories. As the most feminine looking of us all, he could surpass most female idols in terms of being beautiful. And that was saying something.

But there was more to his looks than you could see just by the first glance. His bottom lip was a bit chapped, as he had a habit of chewing it whenever he concentrated hard on something or got distracted. Back in the day, he had been a bit insecure with his feminine features—now he seemed like he had accepted himself and rocked his looks. His every movement oozed healthy confidence. He even emphasized his feminine traits in subtle ways with his clothes and the makeup he wore, even when he wasn't on stage sometimes...

As if all that wasn't enough, he had the widest vocal range of us all. He could hit notes higher than some highly established female artists and still could go lower than Minjae ever would.

Even in comfy, homey clothes, bright and early on Monday morning, he looked stunning. He rocked those hot pink, skinny jeans of his, paired with an oversized white jersey—combination I could never pull off.

Compared to my totally boring looks, Joonie looked like a real celebrity. I didn't bother to keep up with the changes in the fashion industry like he did. I didn't care about designer clothing. My natural brown, bland hair didn't attract nearly as much attention as his frequently changing one. I had a strong jawline, small eyes, and my face, in general, didn't really fit the impossible Korean beauty standards.

Frankly speaking, even I couldn't figure out what he saw in me.

Maybe I needed to worry about that instead. Since clearly, we already established that I could, very much so, be attracted to him.

Two Left Feet

"If you're not going to pull yourself together and start paying attention," Joonie scolded, staring me down and judging my sorry ass as I tripped to my own feet for the 100th time that morning, "you're gonna have to get Minjae to teach you this."

"No! That's like throwing me to the wolves!" I laughed, but honestly, I wasn't sure if Minjae wouldn't kick me out of the whole dance studio after ten minutes of trying to teach me.

While Joonie glared at me relentlessly, I rubbed my sore ankle which got more twisted with each fall. It hurt like hell. Joonie didn't seem all too sympathetic about it. I was in charge of many things, but when it came to dancing, Minjae was a tough taskmaster and Joonie knew it. Minjae had no mercy whatsoever. I wasn't about to deal with that on my first day back home. Shutting my mouth, I heaved myself from the floor for what must've been the 100th time.

"Whatever, let's just get to it." *And this time I won't be distracted by you. Definitely.*

"Now that's the spirit," Joonie replied with that annoyingly light and not-at-all winded voice of his and turned to face the mirror.

Reluctantly, I nodded and tried to concentrate. But damn, it was hard being trapped in a room with a god. Goddess? Whatever, man. I was done with genders anyway. Then I could shamelessly think Joonie was beautiful without meaning I suddenly turned gay or developed feelings for him. Right?

Right.

Keeping that in mind, I was finally able to focus. Somewhat. Barely.

Two hours, four forming bruises, and an even sorer ankle later, we finally got the chorus part down. It wasn't perfect, but the last time we went over it, I didn't trip. That counted for something.

Every muscle in my body hurt, my lungs were on fire, and I was on the verge of blacking out. I swear there were black spots in my vision.

"See, that wasn't so hard," Joonie said, not even breaking one tiny bead of sweat. He was still breathing at a normal tempo and moved so graciously, as if he was still dancing. Very much unlike me.

I rolled my eyes at him while picking up my towel. I plopped down on the couch and attempted to toss the towel onto my shoulder. It landed on my face. I didn't even bother to remove it.

There was one thing about dancing I completely detested: it didn't matter how many choreographies you mastered, how many hours you danced, every damn time you started learning a new choreo, you'd find muscles you hadn't used before, and it made them ache like a motherfucker. And I was fit. I hit the gym almost every morning. We sometimes spent whole days there with Do, and sometimes with Joe too. That was nothing compared to the agony after a dance session.

The couch dipped down a bit on the other end.

"I don't get it. It seems like you're not even sweating while I'm dying over here. How do you do it?" I muttered through the towel still covering my face.

"Maybe if you'd practice on your own like the rest of us, this wouldn't happen," Joonie said, disapproval seeping through his voice.

A "hmph" escaped me. The thing was...I did practice. For hours on end. It was the sole reason I could learn this shit so fast. Well, fast for me. I had the choreo memorized alright; my body just didn't do what my brain told it to. But that was something I wasn't going to admit to Joonie.

"Yeah, yeah..."

"Look, I'm gonna make lunch. See you upstairs in 30 minutes. Try and get your shit together, because we're continuing right after lunch," Joonie said, and his weight lifted up from the couch.

Soon, the door closed and Joonie was out of my hair. When my breath finally evened out, I pulled the towel away from my face. I glanced at the digital clock on the opposite wall beside the door—it was 12:04. I'd have around 25 minutes of break before lunch, so I heaved my heavy ass off the couch and headed to my room.

My mood got ten times better as soon as I opened the door. My room wasn't anything fancier than the others. In fact, it was exactly the same layout with a huge main room that acted as my home office and bedroom, with an ensuite bathroom and an enormous walk-in closet.

But it was not the dance studio. And it wasn't a damn hotel room. It was all my own place, a place I could call home.

I stood in front of my bathroom door for a while contemplating if I should take a shower just to ease my sore muscles. Eventually I decided it wasn't worth the trouble since I was going to get sweaty all over again. Instead, I threw my sweaty shirt to the laundry bin, washed my armpits over the sink, and splashed some cold water to my neck and down my back too. After drying up with a clean towel, I sprayed on some deodorant. Good enough.

So shirtless I was, with the new towel carelessly thrown over my right shoulder. While humming the track to the choreography, I exited the bathroom…only to spot Joonie entering the room precisely at the same time.

My eyebrows shot up in a surprise. "Oh hey! What are you doing here? Weren't you supposed to make lunch?"

Joonie didn't answer anything. His glassed-over eyes traveled over my naked chest, then headed "downwards" as he bit his ever so plump lower lip. Glancing down on myself, I noticed I had missed this one tiny bead of water while drying, which travelled down my body in sync with Joonie's gaze.

Clearly, I had caught Joonie by surprise. Now if my face wasn't as extraordinary as Joonie's, my body certainly was. Even I knew that much. Gathering all my confidence, I took a step closer to him to test my waters and let the corner of my mouth turn up into a slight smirk.

Joonie started to chew his lip even harder, and his eyes were still glued to my torso. It was good to know I wasn't the only one getting distracted. Hell, even if I didn't turn up gay after this little experiment, it was nice to know I had this effect on him. On anyone, really.

Clearing my throat finally woke him up from his trance, and he blinked a couple of times before finally managing to get his eyes focused again. He even visibly gulped.

"Umm, what did you say?" he asked, a slight blush creeping up on his neck. His eyes drifted everywhere except back to me.

"I asked, weren't you supposed to be making lunch?" I held in a chuckle.

"I, umm, Chris took over the kitchen and was already making it when I got there. I figured I'd hang with you instead, but uh, maybe it's better if I go look over him. We both know he can burn anything," Joonie blabbered as the blush reached his face. He turned on his heels and scurried off like a scared animal.

I was left looking at the closed door in awe.

The behavior was, by no means, usual for Joonie. He had always been the blunt one. The one that didn't take any bullshit and said his opinions out loud. Just like on the night of confessions. Joonie had no shame, and he rocked his confidence. But apparently even he could get flustered over a little exposed skin every once in a while.

After having looked at him move all gracefully to the choreography while I had only managed to trip on my ass, it was nice to notice I could get that kind of reaction out of him.

I let out the small chuckle I'd held in while shaking my head slightly and made my way to my walk-in closet. After putting on a clean, grey t-shirt to match with the equally boring sweatpants of mine, and checking my emails, I headed to the kitchen.

When I entered it there was a whole lot of chaos going on.

A phone was ringing on the counter, loudly, but no one paid attention to it. Joonie was trying to save whatever was aflame on the frying pan, laughing his ass off, while Chris had his hand under the faucet with a pained expression on his face.

"Just what is going on?"

"Nothing," Chris grunted while Joonie laughed even harder.

"I told you we shouldn't let Chris in the kitchen alone," Joonie said and handed me the frying pan. "This is unsalvageable. Can you deal with it? My phone's ringing."

At least Joonie had recovered quickly. Nice.

"Sure," I said, flashing a half smile his way before starting to scrape off the blackened...whatever it was supposed to be...off the pan with a spatula. I wasn't very successful. If I said it was cemented, it would've been an understatement. It was as if—

"Stop calling me!" Joonie yelled behind my back.

"Who was that?" I asked, turning.

"Ugh, no one," Joonie said and tossed his phone back on the counter. "Just a telemarketer."

Odd. My eyebrows knitted together. We all had secret numbers; how would a telemarketer get them? "You sure?"

"Yeah," Joonie said with a dismissive tone and glanced at the frying pan I was still scraping. He snatched it from me and said, "Forget it. Just throw it out."

As soon as our skin touched, I jolted back as if I had been electrocuted. "Sure…"

Spill the Tea

Day two of my mission started slightly less...appealing. Jiwoo had sent me a text saying she was going to borrow Joonie for the day. Apparently, he'd been booked last minute to fill in for someone that was supposed to model in some commercial photos but got sick. Back in the day, we had participated in those kinds of things a lot.

That became less and less as there weren't that many companies that could afford us. The question became, who could afford it? I opened the email Jiwoo had sent me for further info. A huge mistake.

It was a tech company. To be more specific—GJ Electronics Inc. The commercial was going to promote their latest launch which looked like some kind of a smartwatch. The worst part? The logo of the company looked familiar. Too familiar. *Oh, joy.*

My own damn father had stolen Joonie from me for the day. To be fair, he probably had nothing to do with it. Those kinds of things were most likely handled by the marketing department. There was a huge possibility that my father didn't even know about it. Dad had his pride, which certainly didn't include using GRiD for advertising his own stuff. It was the very thing he had not approved of me doing, to the point of cutting me off financially. Well, jokes were on him since I probably made more money in a year than he'd made in the previous five years combined.

Seemed as if I was going to have to practice by myself. I dragged my feet through the morning routine. No one except Chris showed up to breakfast, so I got to eat in peace. I took my time, just loitering around, because my muscles were all sore from yesterday…and I wasn't exactly thrilled to practice without Joonie. He was basically the only one who had enough patience for me.

I admit: I missed him. Besides, how was I supposed to continue with my plan if he was not here? I hated when my plans didn't work out the way I wanted them to.

When I eventually dragged my body to the dance studio downstairs, I was met with a very annoyed-looking Minjae.

"Hyung, you're late."

"Yeah, and? What are you doing here?" My mood suddenly sunk to the floor.

"Filling in for Joon. Obviously."

Do-hyun was also there, leisurely sagging on the couch. The lucky bastard. Didn't have to rehearse.

"And you, what are you doing here?" I asked, crossing my arms over my chest.

"Oh, you know. The usual. Having a nice day off... Hanging with my boyfriend... Making sure you keep your paws to yourself while I'm at it."

Both Minjae and I rolled eyes. Somehow, Do still hadn't forgotten the teeny tiny moment I did some very minor fanservice with Minjae. It had already been ages since then, and clearly, I had no feelings whatsoever towards Min. Then again, Do had always been like that. It shouldn't have come as a surprise.

"Enough with the chit-chat," I stated and went to the PA system, thinking I might as well get to it if I was facing a day of torture.

"Yeah, show me what you got so far," Minjae said with his signature soft voice, but it still felt like doomsday.

Nevertheless, I needed to get to it. And I knew Minjae would whip me into shape. As much as I hated the thought, it was necessary.

To my complete and utter surprise, I didn't mess up the chorus that bad. I didn't even get a full-on scolding from Minjae, even though he did have a slight frown going on between his eyebrows the whole time. He corrected me in a few places, and then we spent the next hour with the first verse. Thankfully that only looked complicated when Minjae did it, but it wasn't nearly as hard as the choreo. The second verse was mostly me and Do rapping, so no choreo there if we weren't counting some freestyling.

I slowly got a grip on the routine. Even the hardest part, which was the bridge before the last chorus, I got somewhat down in the following few hours. I had only had to endure two lectures from Minjae, which was a huge relief. And probably some kind of a record. We even started and got the second choreography—the way easier one—down for the most parts.

But when noon arrived, my legs were shaking, and Minjae called it quits. I immediately collapsed to sit on the floor. I didn't care that it was hard; my legs burned enough for me to not feel the pain in my backside.

What a torturous morning. And no Joonie in sight.

"Hyung, no offense but I don't know how Joonie puts up with you," Minjae said, pinching the bridge of his nose, the other arm crossed over his chest. "But I must admit, he's done a good job with you in just a day. You're not nearly as hopeless as he made it sound."

Panting hard and trying to focus on breathing properly, I nearly missed the praise that was hidden somewhere in Minjae's statements. But when I did, I raised an eyebrow, slightly amused. Was he getting soft on me?

"Did I just hear a compliment?" I asked, or more like whined since I was still a bit winded from the workout.

Do chuckled from the couch, though I wasn't sure if it was for our conversation or whatever he was looking at on his phone.

"Absolutely...not. Don't forget, you still have plenty to work on..." Minjae started and continued straight on to pointing out all the mistakes I had made and all the problems I was having.

Apparently, there was something wrong with my starting pose. I also needed to think about the live performances—like how I was going to add a microphone to the equation, especially a handheld one. And I couldn't just stay still whenever there wasn't choreography going on, etc.

"You done?" I asked when I was sure he had been going on and on for at least five full minutes.

"Not even remotely, but I have to head out soon. I have a meeting with the backups." He glanced at the clock.

Do took notice and got up from the coach. "I'll tag along."

"I could drop by my office too if you can wait long enough for me to hit the shower first?" I said.

The two lovebirds glanced at each other before nodding simultaneously. It still gave me goosebumps to see them communicate wordlessly. It happened more and more each day. Communication seemed to really be the key between those two; before, they didn't even realize they had feelings for each other even though literally everyone else—including our fans—sensed the chemistry.

After gathering my things, I followed suit. I was not in the mood for practicing alone, so I took the chances of getting out of the house gladly. After heading straight to the shower, I threw on some random jeans, a t-shirt, and a comfy hoodie.

Minjae and Do were already waiting for me at the downstairs garage when I arrived. They were both leaning against the car and tapping their feet for having to wait for me but stayed silent.

Joe drove us to the company premises with our SUV. In no time, I was sitting in my office chair with some music blasting my ears through the headphones. At first, I blindly stared at the blank screen of the computer. Then I glanced over the keyboard at my right. Then to the left, where my mic for testing and freestyling purposes were.

Now what?

I hadn't planned much further than that. I just wanted to get out of the dorms and avoid dancing. I wasn't really in the mood to work on any ongoing projects, and I certainly didn't feel creative enough to do something new.

A knock on my door startled me. Do walked through before even bothering to wait for my response. We worked together so much he knew the door code for convenience reasons, which I mildly regretted telling him as I wasn't exactly in the mood for company. Immediately after letting himself in, he plopped on the couch like he always did and dug his phone up.

Sighing, I took the headphones off and turned to face him. "What's up?"

"Minjae threw me out of the mockup. Figured I'll keep you company instead."

"Too bad I'm not in need of company," I replied, hinting that he might as well get lost.

He didn't really get it. Or rather, he didn't care either way. "Oh, come on... Just let me stay. I'm bored out of my mind."

"Fine..." I started, giving up and heaving myself on the couch too. "So, everything good between you and Minjae?"

"Yeah, yeah. Apparently, I'm just too much of a distraction for Min," he said with a smirk on his face.

Poor Minjae. Poor LBR staff. Whatever Do-hyun did to him downstairs was probably something I'd rather not see or think. Now that they didn't have to hide even the least bit, they had this unbearably sweet, lovey-dovey atmosphere surrounding them. I had already gotten somewhat used to it since I had to live with them, and in private they had acted that way for a while now...but to the staff, it was all new.

"Ugh, can't you tone it down a bit? Also, that reminds me, why don't you two get your own place?"

"We thought about it. But why bother? It's not like we spend a whole lot of time at home anyways."

"Makes sense."

"Duh..." he said, leaned back with a devious smile spreading on his lips and looked up from his phone. "Anyway, what's going on between you and Joonie?"

Well, that took me off guard. "W-what?"

"Ha! I knew it!" he nearly yelled with his voice sounding like he'd won the Olympics. "You stuttered."

"You knew what?"

"That there's something going on. You two are not on top of the fanservice game anymore like you used to be. So, spill."

Internal Crisis

Aish, those guys missed nothing. It was basically the same thing Jiwoo had said. But unlike her, Do just might've been able to help me, considering he had probably gone through similar stuff with Minjae. So, somehow, I ended up recapping the whole situation to him, as uncomfortable as it was since usually, I was the one dishing out advice, not asking for it.

Do listened to me rant and whine, not interrupting me even once.

"...so basically, how do you even know if you're gay? How does that even work?" I concluded, finally cutting to the main problem.

Do was silent for a long while. There was a frown between his eyebrows while he thought everything through.

"Tae," He finally replied, "you don't need to figure out if you're gay or bi or whatever. At the end of the day, the label doesn't even matter. Why don't you just figure out if you like Joonie or not? I mean, I wasted so much time figuring out that shit myself—though a few years earlier than you—and look how much that helped me. I only ended up hating myself for a long time. Then I ended up projecting that on Minjae who did not deserve it one bit. Don't repeat my mistakes.

"In fact, I'm gonna make this easy for you. Gimme your phone."

"Umm, what? And why?" I pulled my phone closer to me. How was my phone supposed to help in any damn way?

"No questions, yet. Just hand me your phone," he commanded again, this time a bit more impatiently.

Reluctantly, I handed it to him. He typed something on it while getting up from the couch. I followed him with my gaze. His lips turned up to a slight smirk when he finally found what he was looking for.

Soon enough, he tossed the phone back. "Look, I don't know about Joonie. But I swear, some similar videos about Min are better than porn. Watch it, and if your dick doesn't so much as twitch, then forget it and move on. If there is...a reaction...you've got your answer."

Heat rushed to my face and my eyes widened after just barely glancing at the title of the YouTube video. *"GRiD's Sweet knowing he's hot for 10 minutes straight."*

"I'll be next door if you have questions...later," Do said at the threshold and slammed the door shut behind him. The lock clicked.

I kept staring at the title and the thumbnail (Joonie winking) more speechless than ever before in my life. Right until the screen went black. This whole thing was absurd and stupid enough that I tossed the phone to the other end of the couch. How could one possibly determine if he's gay by just watching one damn video? One couldn't. Right?

Right.

Then again it, kind of, sort of, sounded like a plan. And it couldn't hurt to just watch it and see what happens. The outcome didn't need to be final.

So, I did the unspeakable. With slightly shaking hands, I picked up the phone and hit play before giving myself a chance to second guess my values and life-choices. There was even a disclaimer that the video wasn't meant to sexualize Joonie, but I just fast-forwarded it because...

Yeah, right.

After the video finally got to its point, I couldn't turn my eyes away even if I wanted to. And I most certainly didn't want to. It started with a dancing clip from our "Contrast" performance at our comeback concert, continued straight away to the music video, showing a collection of Joonie's parts in it. And damn had he been able to fit in so many fanservice parts. Licking his lips, biting his lips, winking, etc. Or maybe it was just the skilful edit that made it seem like it was a lot.

Then there were random clips from our Twitter, our VLIVE, some selfies. Some of them were slow motioned, some shown twice with a different focus on each. In one clip, Joonie licked a pink lollipop seductively. A fucking lollipop. How cliché. And yet, *so* unbelievably satisfying to watch. I couldn't even remember when that clip was taken or where it was from, but damn was I glad it was included.

By the end of the video, I was out of breath and my dick was rock hard—almost painfully so—pushing against the zipper of my jeans. I could've stopped watching...but I didn't. Instead, I let the player continue straight away to the next suggested video. *Some "Sweet's Sexy Moments," "Best Sweet focused fancams of all time," "Joonie Being Rude,"* and a few other similarly named videos later...my dick was already aching with pure and raw need.

Clearly, there was a reaction. *The* reaction. Reaction of all reactions. In fact, I had never been that turned on in my entire life.

My mind was basically blank. Honestly, I wanted and needed some friction. Any kind of friction. Pretty sure I could've nutted in my pants by just shifting my position on the couch. But, as that would've been devastatingly embarrassing, I stayed still. Letting it pass. I clicked the screen shut and tried to think just about anything but Joonie.

A debate started in my head.

This doesn't mean anything, a voice whispered in my head.

Yes, it does, another countered.

I'm not gay!

That ship sailed ages ago...

I shook my head slightly and suddenly remembered what Do said before. *"The label doesn't matter."*

Around fifty deep breaths later, I managed to get myself somewhat calmed down. Calm enough to get curious. What else was there in the deep wasteland of YouTube? Keeping up with social media was Minjae's job before the scandal, and Chris had handled most of it since. And, of course, the publicity team. I, personally, had no idea what else I'd find.

Trying very hard to not pay attention to the thumbnails, I scrolled down the list of videos popping up after typing in "GRiD." Most of it was just our official content—music videos and some other stuff we'd made specifically for YouTube. But after I scrolled even further down, the fan-made content appeared. There was much about Do and Min, understandably so. But one particular video, titled "JoonJoon/TooSweet Is Real," caught my attention. The thumbnail was Joonie and me, smiling at each other at a concert.

Hesitantly, I tapped play. To my ultimate relief, it wasn't anything sexy this time. Just sweet moments of us, put together. Maybe it was, again, the editing or just seeing all the clips at once, but I had never even realized how couple-like we acted. It looked real. Too real. For the first time ever, I completely understood why some people at fan meetings and such, called us the eomma and appa of GRiD. We looked like domestic husbands for fuck's sake.

There were numerous clips, from Chris most likely, of us in our kitchen, just fooling around while cooking. Or rather, me hovering over Joonie when he was cooking. Of course, all of the fanservice was added too, from the music videos and concerts. Even from past documentaries about us. But even those seemed so unbelievably real despite it being strictly fanservice, I couldn't help but be surprised.

It was a lot to take in. Clearly, I wasn't fully straight. I could bend a little...a lot...for Joonie. Obviously, there was chemistry between us; I could see that now. There just wasn't denying that I might have some feelings towards him, and maybe they had been there longer than I had thought. At least, based on how I looked at him on all these videos I hadn't even known existed...and even more importantly, how he looked at me. I could've blamed it on the edit and stuff, but I didn't. It was time to look the truth in the eyes and just live with it.

And I needed help. Lots of it.

So, with heavy steps, I made my way next door to Do's office. After entering the door code, the lock clicked open, and I made my way in.

"Hey! That took a while. Had fun?" Do greeted, barely even lifting his gaze from his weird-looking activities. He was sitting on the floor, cross-legged, cutting some posters to smaller parts. He was practically surrounded by discarded pieces of paper. A weird sight, yes, but as I had some more pressing matters to discuss, I plopped down on his couch and ignored it for the time being.

"So... I might be the teeniest bit gay. Apparently."

"Great, join the club," Do said nonchalantly from the floor, not even bothering to stop whatever he was doing with the posters. Seemed like the asshole couldn't care less about the biggest internal crisis I had ever had.

"Now what?" I asked impatiently.

"That's entirely up to you." He stopped whatever he was doing with the posters and glanced up to the ceiling. "Or just go for it and see what happens. Again, don't repeat my mistakes. Besides, you already know he likes you back."

I nodded. Yes, Joonie had said he was in love with me. That ought to count for something, right? Even when he said that while drunk, I believed he meant it. Joon wouldn't say something that serious without meaning it. He said it because he wanted to, I was sure of it. He had always said whatever he damn well pleased.

While I was in my own world, Do got back doing whatever he was doing with the posters. Well, until he abruptly stopped, making me snap back to reality.

Staring ahead, having a somewhat amused look on his face, he muttered... "And now Min owes me a car."

"What? Why?"

He glanced at me and smirked. "I won the bet."

I frowned. "What bet?"

"Nothing. Just this tiny bet about whether you end up with Joon or not"

"You two made *a bet* over my barely existing love life? Over a car?!"

"It was not just any car. It was *the* Aston Martin Vanquish," he said the grin only growing.

They were both absolutely batshit crazy. I knew next to nothing about cars but that sounded expensive, even for us. "You know, I haven't ended up with him yet..."

Do acted like he didn't even hear the statement and started to hum some random tune, getting back to his weird task. I looked around, finding the whole mess a bit amusing. "What are you doing?"

"I'm glad you asked," Do said, grinning and holding up the huge poster of GRiD which was now cut so it was just him and Minjae left. "I raided the storage room earlier and now I'm redecorating." He proceeded to tape the poster to the wall, which I only then noticed was already filled with posters and photos of him and Minjae together, or of Minjae alone. There was even a life-sized cardboard Minjae.

"Do...I think you should see a shrink. That's downright creepy," I said, slapping my face with the palm of my hand.

Do just laughed. At me. Weirdly enough. "Hyung, just wait. It's amazing what love does to a man."

I shook my head at him, utterly and completely speechless.

Then Do started opening and closing the drawers on his desk. "Which reminds me...let me see… it should be here somewhere..." When he finally found whatever he was looking for, he tossed it to me.

It was a small bottle of lube.

"Seriously?" I rubbed my temple with the other hand, just barely hanging there by a very thin thread, trying my hardest to not smack his head against the wall to try and force some sense into that thick skull of his.

"Hey, I'm only trying to help! You might or might not want to use that whenever—uh—things get heated. Males don't work like females, I'm sure you're aware of that."

Well, I am now.

Don't Ask Don't Tell

A delivered take-out lunch and an hour or two of mindless blabbering later, we headed home, but not before I had to witness a lover's quarrel over Do's redecorated wall. Who would've guessed Minjae wouldn't jump for joy over it? Certainly not Do-hyun. It miraculously came as a complete surprise to him.

On the way home, my phone buzzed in my pocket with a text from Joonie on our group chat telling us that though he was done with filming, dinner would be late. Great. I'd have to face the man from the videos in person. I wasn't sure I was ready for that…

Not that I hadn't lived with the guy for years. It felt quite a bit different after watching sexy videos of him online. Let's not even mention the guilt that had started to dwell on my stomach.

To my relief, Joonie hadn't arrived home by the time we had. Cowardly, I made up a lame excuse and holed up in my room. Door locked and all. Of course, I'd have to face him sooner or later, but maybe over dinner or something where there would be others present. I wasn't ready to face him alone. Yet.

Seeing the damn videos was the main problem. Yes, those somewhat cleared things up for me, so I didn't completely regret watching them. Still, the reality was an entirely different matter I had no idea how to handle.

On the other hand, I was tempted to let nature do its thing. Let the chips fall where they may, so to speak. But that wasn't me. I'd never done anything like that. Everything in my life up to that point had been calculated and planned to the slightest details. Just letting things go wildly out of control, willingly, was a terrifying thought.

Besides, even though I now knew what I wanted—which of course was something with Joonie—that didn't mean I knew what Joonie would think of all this. Maybe, that drunken confession of his was just it—a drunken confession. Nothing less, nothing more. Maybe I'd let the whole thing spiral out of all possible proportions.

I needed a distraction from the never-ending cycle of over thinking, and I sat cross-legged on my armchair with the intention of losing myself to a game on my phone, or something. But as soon as I plopped down, I felt the damn lube bottle in my back pocket. At first, I tried to ignore it, but obviously it didn't work. Cursing under my breath, I gave up, heaved my ass off the chair, and tossed the bottle to the deepest and darkest corner of my nightstand's drawer. After slamming the drawer back shut again, I plopped back to the armchair.

I started scrolling some news with my phone absentmindedly. There weren't that many news articles about us anymore, not even on the more scandalous news sites. The small ones I found were all positive. Knowing we'd gotten over the storm just fine brought me a smile.

The phone buzzed in my hand.

My heart shot through my chest, ripping me out from being lost in some pointless article.

A sigh escaped my lips. As if I wasn't down enough, my mood sunk even lower in a fraction of a second. The caller was my dear father—an almost stranger named Gang Jae-sung—the CEO and founder of GJ Electronics Inc. He had a reputation of not accepting a no for an answer. Sadly, I'd have to admit that reputation was based on reality. Ignoring the call or dismissing it wasn't an option. Dad would just continue calling me as long as it took for me to answer. Not to mention that he'd be more pissed off with every call he'd have to make.

I tapped the small green icon and lifted the phone to my ear.

We exchanged the sickeningly formal greetings he always expected us to go through. He didn't really sound like he even cared. Typical. It didn't take him long to get to the point. "You're back in Seoul? How was the flight?" he asked.

"Yes, I'm back. The flight was long," I stated, mimicking the disinterested tone he himself had.

"Don't give me that tone," he said, with what I assumed was supposed to be a fatherly tone. I didn't even bother replying, so after a brief pause, he added, "You should visit your grandma now that you're in the country."

Well, true, but…

It took a lot from me to not snort at that statement. Dad himself nearly never visited Gran, so I was sensing some hypocrisy in the air. I, on the other hand, visited her every chance I got since I was practically raised by her. She was the only person I genuinely loved from the bottom of my heart. She had kept me fed when I was younger. She had supported me with my dreams of becoming a musician. She had always been there for me. I respected her more than anything in this world.

Meanwhile, Dad had drowned himself at work after Mom left. When he finally did get back in the picture, it was only because his trophy wife number three wanted to play "happy family." So no, Dad didn't exactly have the grounds to scold me for not visiting my grandma.

"Of course," I wanted to call him out on his hypocrisy, but I had a different weapon in my back pocket. "So, I heard our Joonie was at your commercial shoot today. How did he do? It has been a while since we've done any ads, so we could use some feedback."

Now, I was pretty sure Dad wouldn't know anything I was talking about. In fact, I counted on that. But the man surprised me: "He did good, so we wrapped it up nicely despite the unfortunate cancellation. He fit in the concept quite perfectly. The ladies at the marketing department were all swooning over him, though I'm not sure why. The guy looks like a female doll."

I couldn't help but let a little chuckle slip before replying. "That's part of Joon's charm. Glad he did well though."

"I guess. The whole thing made me think that maybe we could do some business together. I'm starting to see the opportunities and must admit you're doing something right in the 'branding yourselves' department."

My jaw dropped. Was this the reason he called? Could it be possible that he would finally acknowledge the value of GRiD? Would he finally admit this was good business too?

It took me a while to answer. "Y-yeah I guess," I said. Well tried to say, but somehow the words were still half-way stuck to my throat. "If you can afford us," I added when I got my shit back together.

"Now you're finally talking like my son. I see you've made this...'music' thing a good business. Now, how was the US?"

My mood sank. I could already sense where this new topic would lead.

"The US was nice. Despite...well, everything." Surely, he knew all about the scandal. It was probably the real reason why he called. He always waited some time passed so he could rub salt in the wounds with the maximum effect.

As predicted, he took his chance to plunge right into the topic he had clearly been waiting to discuss.

"It's true then? They're gay?" he asked with a tone that could only be described as disgusted.

Even though Dad acted like a modern man in every other part of life, he couldn't stand anything gay. One of the main reasons he didn't want me to pursue a career in the music industry had been that, to him, it seemed *too gay*. He had told me that a lot when I was young.

"Yeah, it's all true," I replied, not even bothering to hold down the urge to roll my eyes.

"Told you. You know, I still have a nice open vacancy for you at GJ Electronics. With that brain of yours, you could climb the ladder pretty fast too and have my position as the CEO in no time.

Besides, would do you some good to get away from them before you turn gay too."

I was not in the mood of listening to his bullshit any longer. I mindlessly blurted out a question I already knew I'd soon regret. "I'm pretty damn sure you can't turn anyone gay... But what if I was 'turning' gay?"

There was a long and strained silence. I waited patiently, toying with the hem of my hoodie. There was absolutely nothing he'd say that would shock me at this point. The man has practically detested me and my life-choices from birth anyway. It honestly wouldn't be anything new if he disowned me for good after that. When silence continued, I started to think that maybe I had finally managed to shock the poor man enough to leave him speechless. Unfortunately, that wasn't the case.

"Careful now, son. We'd never talk about it. After all, I'd hate to lose a son."

The line went dead.

Don't ask, don't tell it is, then.

I dropped the phone on my lap. The day had been way too much. It wasn't only that Dad was being an asshole—he had always been an asshole and he probably always will be. No news there. Though that might have been the last drop, so to speak. I was exhausted because I just couldn't get the choreography right. I was exhausted because every single one of my muscles was sore from the workouts some crazy people called dancing. I was exhausted because I still had no clue of what to do with this whole Joonie thing. There was no way I had the emotional bandwidth to face Joonie that day, as cruel as it might've sounded.

So, I chose to be a coward for a moment. I texted the group chat I'd be skipping dinner to work on something and put the phone on silent. In reality, I just crashed to the bed and slept. Everything else could wait until morning.

Starstruck

Waking up late wasn't my thing. Unfortunately, that happened to the best of us sometimes.

I had forgotten to set my alarm. It was seven in the morning when my internal clock finally woke me up, and I fluttered my eyes open. I jumped up the bed like it was on fire, my heart beating way too fast. The room was spinning. Or was it my head? Whatever. There was no time for a shower, so I just threw on some workout clothes. I was already on my way out with my hand on my door handle when my brain started working, and I froze.

I'd have to face Joonie. I'd be stuck with him the whole day, as I still didn't have my parts of the two choreos completely down. The next day we were scheduled to start with the group rehearsals in order to be ready to shoot the music videos the next week, so I couldn't possibly escape. I took a deep breath and turned the handle, stepping to the corridor leading to the common area of our dorm and most importantly—the kitchen.

Tae, you can do this. You can face Joonie. Just act like you just didn't watch a bunch of hot videos about him on YouTube yesterday... And an image of Joonie from one of the videos flashed before my eyes, where he looked seductively straight to the camera with the damn lollipop on his lips.

Oh great, now I'm sporting a boner.

Thankfully, there wasn't anyone in the kitchen. At least I didn't have to explain the tent that had formed to the front of my sweatpants.

As I was running late, I didn't do anything fancy for breakfast. Just the usual. And I brewed some coffee since Minjae hadn't woken up yet. Though they did emerge from their rooms with Do soon enough, to my relief. I still couldn't quite forget the one time I had gone and tried to wake them up on tour. Let's just say seeing them cuddling buck naked at Minjae's hotel room wasn't something I looked forward to seeing again anytime soon. I certainly learned to knock.

Chris also came in, stuffed his face with food and then was out the door as fast as he had appeared. Minjae and Do-hyun followed right after him as they all had a packed schedule today to make room for the group rehearsals. Joonie, however, was nowhere to be seen. Figuring he'd emerge soon enough; I took a cup of coffee—black—and got immersed with the newspaper someone had left on the bar top.

Apparently, I had zoned out pretty good because I didn't even notice Joonie until his greeting made my heart skip a beat. I nearly knocked my mug and spilled the contents all over the table. Slowly, I turned to glance at the way-too-pretty-for-his-own-good man, who had somehow successfully sneaked up on me.

"You're jumpy today," Joonie said with a chuckle when he topped up his own coffee mug and sat right beside me. Way, way too close.

After grunting out something probably very unintelligent, I turned my gaze back to the newspaper then proceeded to take another sip of coffee. Though, not without sparing a side-glance to the pink-haired man sitting right there next to me.

Damn. I nearly got starstruck. Seeing the man live, right there, at this proximity was an out of this world experience. Even with his hair still damp and disheveled, not even a hint of makeup on his face...he looked unrealistically beautiful. His long hair shone under the lights. There wasn't a single imperfection on his face. It was like staring at the sun after being in the dark for so long.

Also, he was close enough that I could've easily touched his arm with my own by just leaning one inch to the right. In fact, I felt compelled to do just that. So much that my arm twitched a little closer while I tried my best to resist the weird pull.

I hadn't even realized I had stared at Joonie before he spoke again, glaring at me with a dubious look in his face, "Seriously, what's wrong with you today?"

After clearing my throat and gluing my gaze to the surface of the table, I replied, "Nothing, just forget it."

He narrowed his eyes at me but ultimately let it drop. It was weirdly quiet for a while when we silently finished our morning coffees. And I was painfully aware of the fact that, yes, we were alone. How rare must that have been? I started to get what Do meant with all the whining about not having any alone time.

Eventually, we headed to the dance studio downstairs. We only worked on some details since Minjae had pretty much whipped me in shape the day before, surprisingly enough. At some point I relaxed and started to act a bit more normal around Joonie. When lunchtime came around, we ordered some take-out, as Joonie wasn't feeling like cooking for just the two of us—since the others would eat on the road or during their scheduled activities.

So, there we were. Sitting at the dining table upstairs, with our bowls of bibimbap in front of us and, of course, some kimchi on the side. I had to admit it was domestic as hell, but I liked it. I liked it a lot. A lot more than I was comfortable to admit, even.

As I inhaled my food, unable to stop myself with the unsatiable hunger I'd built up dancing, Joonie's phone rang, but he didn't answer it. Instead, he briefly glanced at the screen, silenced the phone, and shoved it right back to his pocket. At first, I didn't give much thought to it, but then it happened again. That time, as soon as the call ended, Joonie did something with the phone for a while before shoving it back to his pocket.

"Why aren't you answering?" I asked, admittedly a bit curious.

"It's nothing...I bet he'll leave a voicemail anyway," he said with what was probably supposed to sound like a disinterested tone, but something told me there was more to it.

"He?" I asked with a weird feeling setting in my stomach. I had to tell myself I was only curious, and not getting jealous at all. Not even one bit.

"It's really nothing, hyung, just forget it," he said, and I shrugged the nagging feeling off.

But when it happened the third time, Joonie's shoulders slumped, and I snapped. "It's clearly something so start talking. Now."

Joonie rolled his eyes at me but did elaborate. "It's just some random dude who keeps calling me and leaving these weird voicemails. I'll just block him. It's nothing, I promise."

Now that got me worried. "Doesn't really sound like nothing. In fact, it sounds awfully stalkerish to me. Here, let me listen to one." I reached for his phone.

"Seriously, just drop it. I'll just change my number or something," Joonie huffed.

But I wasn't going to let it slide.

I snatched the phone out of his hand and held it far enough for him to not reach it. "If it's really nothing, you might as well let me listen to one."

With a defeated face, he crossed his arms over his chest, sulking, and leaned back on his chair. "Fine."

The first voicemail I listened to was already creepy as fuck. Indeed, it was just some random dude...with a device that changed the sound of his voice, swearing his eternal love for Joonie. Disturbingly creepy already. But the second one I listened to, got even more disturbing. It was more or less a death threat.

An actual fucking death threat.

And Joonie said it was nothing? Nothing my ass. This guy sounded like he was delusional and unstable. Only the gods know what else.

"Joonie, this is serious. Why haven't you reported this? To the police? Or at least to the security staff?"

He rolled his eyes at me once more. "It's always just such a hassle...totally not worth it. I bet it's just some lonely guy who has too much free time in his hands."

"If you're not reporting it, I am. This is a *death threat.* It's supposed to be a hassle."

"Fine," he snapped and snatched his phone back, finally reaching it.

He dialed a number immediately, to my relief. With just a few words, he had got his point across. Probably to Joe. "There. Happy?"

"Not even close. But I will be when we've taken at least the usual precautions, the others have been informed, and that bastard has been caught and put behind bars...or a mental health institution."

Joonie muttered something that sounded something like "overreacting much." I couldn't have cared less about whether I was overreacting in his mind or not. Whenever something like that happened, I couldn't take it lightly. As the leader of the group, I couldn't ignore something potentially dangerous. There was always the possibility of *what if.*

A tiny little voice in my head also told me that maybe there was an instinct somewhere deep inside me that wanted to keep him safe from all the world's evil.

Gay Awakening

It only got worse.

Even started to freak me out how much I suddenly wanted to lock Joonie away to some missile proof bunker until the creepy voicemail dude had been caught. Trying my hardest to not turn into a creep myself, I shoved that thought right to the deepest and darkest corner of my mind and ignored it. Instead, I tried to focus on dancing after we headed back to the dance studio for the rest of the day.

As I had gotten better with both of the choreographs, we were practically just fooling around when the day started turning into an evening, maybe, *occasionally* fine-tuning some level changes and transitions. Even with my worries over Joonie, and my two left feet, the dancing part was starting to be kind of…fun…instead of just straight-up torture. And that's how I always knew I'd finally gotten a choreo somewhat down.

My mood brightened more and more every passing second. Maybe it was because for the first time in ages, I stopped overthinking and let loose. So what if I didn't fully know what was going on? After all, Joonie was still Joonie. And me? I was still me. Sort of. Just maybe a bit gayer.

Eventually, we gave up rehearsing and sat on the floor. Joonie used me as his support, sitting between my legs with his back against my chest. I had to peek over his shoulder every time he wanted me to see whatever meme he was showing from his phone.

For a short while, I was comfortable. It wasn't awkward; it wasn't weird. It was just like old times, when we had been close friends who'd done fanservice for years and thus were used to the closeness.

After a while though, I started noticing strange things...like how well he fit there, almost like his body was meant to be right next to mine. Like how much I wanted to wrap my hands around his waist whenever I leaned my chin to his shoulder when he showed another pic from his phone. Like how his hair had this faint scent of strawberry shampoo that made my head spin every time he moved so much as a few centimeters and a new wave of the amazing scent blew on my face.

He turned slightly to glance at me, and I saw his side profile. His lashes were so thick and long they cast a barely noticeable shadow under his eyes. From time to time, his loose t-shirt dropped from his shoulder, and I could get a glimpse of his beautiful collarbone. The skin on his neck was no less than perfectly smooth, making me want to touch it softly with my fingertips...just to find out if it would feel as smooth and velvety as it looked.

By that point, I had a hard time focusing on anything he said. Especially when he shifted a bit to try and find a better position, and he accidentally brushed against my crotch with his perfectly round butt. Blood rushed to his face as he laughed and apologized. The faint blush painted his cheeks with the exact same rosy shade that his bottom lip had. The same one he started biting.

When he released his perfectly round lip from the hold of his teeth, I got consumed by this crashing wave of pure need to kiss him. Before my mind could even keep up with my body, I had wrapped my hands around his waist, turned him a bit so I had full access to his lips and pulled him even closer. When his eyes got a bit wider in surprise and his lips parted invitingly, I threw all the possible remains of caution to the wind and went for it.

My eyes closed involuntarily right before I reached my target. My lips just barely touched Joonie's incredibly soft ones...but it was all it took for my heart to start beating weirdly loud, almost like the muscle only now realized it was alive. It took me by surprise and made me hastily part ways with him. What took me even more by surprise was the immediate longing that started right after my lips were no longer in contact with his.

Then the panic crept up on me. I didn't have the slightest idea why I had just kissed him. It wasn't supposed to happen, at least not yet. I certainly wasn't there yet, with my plans. What would Joonie's reaction be? When I didn't feel him moving at all, not even an inch, let alone running for the hills, I finally dared to open my eyes.

I was met with an amused looking Joonie, who had a slight smile on his lips but a questioning frown between his eyebrows.

"What was that for?" he asked with that soft, angelic voice of his that suddenly sounded like music to my ears.

I didn't know what to say. "I don't know... I—" I stuttered, let my hands drop to my sides, and gave him a bit more space by leaning back. I probably should've at least asked before randomly kissing him. "I'm sorry."

"Is this why you've been acting weird lately?" He interrupted me before I could even finish whatever I had started. Didn't matter though since I had already forgotten.

"Yeah...I guess. This whole gay thing has been on my mind a lot lately...I guess just wanted to see how it would feel." I trailed off, not being able to put my million thoughts into words fast enough.

Joonie turned his back on me again and looked the exact opposite way. Hugging his knees, he hung his head down low, to hide his face from me.

"Tae, as much as I love you, I'm not going to be some sort of gay awakening of yours. I'm not interested in being an experiment," he said with that same tone he had used "I love you" before the night of confessions. Warm, but platonic.

It made me want to throw up. Clearly, he didn't remember ever confessing his love for me. The one love that felt real, not this bullshit. It made me wonder if he ever even meant that. And that hurt. Like hell. Like all of the five months of avoiding this exact conversation, questioning my sexuality and my whole fucking being had been for nothing.

With just that one sentence from Joonie, my ego shattered into millions of tiny pieces. Someone had punched the air out of my lungs. I dragged myself a bit further away from him, hanging my head. Clearly, he wanted some space. And I couldn't look at him.

"That's not what I meant," I said softly.

Joonie lifted his head and turned half-way towards me. His face showed a wide range of emotions, but the most prominent one was anger. Clearly, he was hurt. He had clearly twisted the whole thing inside his pretty little head all upside down.

"Then what did you mean, Tae?" Joonie started, raising his voice more and more by every word he spat out. He turned to fully face me. "And don't you dare to start another five months of radio silence on me."

"You noticed?" I asked, as if I already didn't know. Of course, he had noticed. Even I could see that. But at this point, I was just stalling for time, trying to figure out what I'd say to not make this whole thing turn to worse.

"Of course, I noticed. Was it something I said? 'Cause I can pinpoint this whole thing to one particular night, and it's bugging the hell out of me. For the life of me, I can't remember anything after you carried me to bed. Is it because I said I'm gay?"

Shit. I guess there's no avoiding this talk then.

"No, I have no problem with you being gay." Far from it, actually. "But you kinda did say you were in love with me."

There was a long silence when I tried to look everywhere but Joonie's face before he spoke. "That's it?"

I had no other choice than to look at his face again. Instantly, he looked straight in my eyes with his eyebrows raised.

"What do you mean 'that's it?'" I asked. Needless to say, it was a gigantic deal for me, and he only asked... *"That's it?"* What the actual...?

Joonie shook his head. "I can't believe you've been avoiding me for five months just over that. I hope you realize how much of an egotistical little prick you are," he stated and got up.

I grabbed his wrist before he could storm out of the whole damn room. "Just sit down and let me explain."

Surprisingly enough, he listened to me and got comfortable again. Well, not before another eye-roll. "Then, explain."

"First of all, did you even mean it?" I asked. I just had to know. There was no way I was going to make myself even more of a fool in front of him if he hadn't even meant it.

Another silence. But I wasn't going to give in even one inch if we were having this conversation. I stayed silent. Patiently waiting for him to either confirm it or deny it. Bracing myself for the worse.

"Yeah..." he admitted eventually, averting my gaze.

It was almost funny how much that simple confirmation affected me. At first, my heart skipped a beat, and then it started to race.

"Right..." I scratched the back of my neck nervously, trying to find the right words to not piss him off again. Then I gave up on that and just decided to be honest and say the weird thought I was having out loud. Come what may. "Honestly, I haven't fully figured out what I think about all that yet. Look, I know I'm slow. And I'm sorry about that. It's just I only figured out I might not be...as straight as I thought. Like yesterday. So, I might not be able to give my answer to you yet, but please don't be mad at me."

At some point during my word vomit, Joonie shifted his eyes back to mine and narrowed them like he didn't fully believe me. But I could see he did hear me out and even gave it some thought. So I dared to continue. No, scratch that. Beg would be more like it.

"Just give me a chance at this, please?"

He sighed and got up again. I didn't try to stop him this time. Disappointed, I watched him walk to the door. But just when he was reaching for the door handle, he stopped.

"Fine. But no more acting weird around me or I'm calling it quits. Come find me when you want to 'try' this whole gay thing again," he practically spat and walked out the door.

Eternal Traumas

One thing I hated more than anything, was being woken up before my alarm. That morning it was Jiwoo calling me to tell me that she couldn't reach Joonie, and there was a major change in his schedule for the day. Apparently, the stylists had moved their meeting with Minjae and Joonie to this afternoon instead of the next day due to unforeseen circumstances.

It was supposed to be about our clothes and concept for the music videos we would be shooting next week, so it couldn't be moved ahead. With a sigh, I promised Jiwoo that I'd get the message delivered and headed to shower, reluctantly skipping my morning gym, I might add.

As I was in a hurry, my shower didn't last long. In no time, I was dressed and headed out, dragging my feet down the hallway past Chris' door, straight to the last door on our side of the hall—Joonie's room. I was going to knock but his door was cracked open already. I knocked anyway but opened the door further, peeking in.

"Hello?" I called hesitantly from the doorstep and stepped in carefully.

"Yeah, just wait somewhere. I'll be done in a minute!" Joonie yelled back from his bathroom. Or that's what I assumed based on the direction his voice came.

The door to his bathroom was wide open, and that was exactly where I found Joonie. His hair was still wet, tangling down his back and dripping water. He was stark naked too, except for the towel that hung low on his waist, which seemed to me like it was the size of a postage stamp.

It wasn't like I hadn't seen Joonie less than fully clothed before, but somehow it was different now. Damn nearly shocked me. I couldn't take my eyes off him, so I just kept staring in awe. If my mind wouldn't have turned into a mess, I might've wondered how I never saw him this way before. I had missed so damn much I nearly got angry at myself for not opening my eyes sooner.

My eyes immediately found his perfectly shaped collarbones and started traveling down. Right across his chest and lingered on his abdomen for a moment. It wasn't like he had a defined six-pack as I did, but he certainly was in shape. I couldn't stop myself from tracing my stare down the faint, barely visible happy trail that disappeared behind the towel. I didn't even notice that there was a lump forming in my throat before I had trouble swallowing it.

The tables had certainly turned since the other day when he had walked in on me being shirtless. All of a sudden, it was my turn to not know how to form complete thoughts. Let alone speak in complete sentences. I wondered if this shit ever happened to Minjae and Do-hyun.

When I finally snapped my eyes back to his face, I noticed he was staring at me. Looking quite a bit amused, I might add.

"Like what you see?" he asked, with his eyebrows arched slightly. Clearly, he was mocking.

Typically, I'd have had some witty comeback to that, but my brain froze. Half of his face was covered with white foam, and he had a razor on his hand. It didn't really shock me or anything, but still unable to think of something good to say, I just said, "You're...shaving."

"Yes, Tae. I am a male. Newsflash, I do have to shave," Joonie said, before faking a shocked gasp. "You do know I have a dick too, right?"

Well, that was a mistake.

"Hahaha. Real funny," I muttered with faked a laugh and turned on my heels.

I heard him chuckle as I plopped down on his red couch and started going through my email. And soon enough, he emerged, still wearing just a towel, rubbing his wet hair with another towel. I just barely glanced at him and focused on my phone again since I certainly didn't want to repeat the embarrassment that happened a minute ago.

"What did you actually come here for?" Joonie asked on his way to his wardrobe.

"Jiwoo called. They moved the concept meeting for the MVs to this afternoon."

Joonie sighed and closed the door behind him. "It's gonna be a packed day then," he hollered from his closet, already sounding exhausted. Judging by the noise, he was rummaging through his clothes.

"Yeah..."

I wondered what he'd wear today. He always had some interesting fashion choices. Shaking my head, I focused back on my phone for the time being. Joonie was done exactly at the same time I had gotten through the emails and replied to a couple of the more urgent ones. The rest would have to wait until breakfast. I stuffed the phone back into my jeans' pocket and lifted my eyes up to Joonie, who was now fully clothed, to my ultimate relief.

As always, his outfit was...interesting. He wore some black, pinstripe dress pants paired with a black and white button-up and a colorful scarf loosely fitted in the tie's place. He had a matching dress jacket folded across his arm.

"You gonna practice like that?" I arched my right eyebrow, amused.

He just rolled his eyes again. "Of course not." He pointed to a black bag that he had tossed beside the door.

"Right..." I said, trying my hardest to find a change of topic fast. Luckily, there *was* another reason for me being here too that I had almost forgotten. "Oh right, I forgot. I've scheduled extra safety training for us. We're cutting the dance practice an hour shorter to make time for it."

His face fell magnificently, and he growled. "Do we really have to?"

"Yes," I said sternly and headed to his door. "Look, you have to tell the others about the threat too."

"I know," he replied, sounding defeated.

"Good. I'll see you at breakfast."

He headed back to his bathroom, slamming the door. I heard a blow-dryer go off. Clearly, he was pissed at me. I *had* put him through a lot the past day.

It always complicated everything whenever these kinds of things happened, and we would have to take extra measures in terms of safety. As if it wasn't a lot in a normal setting too. But I couldn't just ignore it. Death threats—or any kind of threats— weren't a thing you could take lightly, even if nothing had ever happened before. Even when safety was one of the things one would have to sacrifice up to a point if pursuing a career this public. But I sure as hell was going to do everything in my power to try and prevent anything serious from happening.

As soon as I reached the kitchen, I was pleasantly surprised. The breakfast had already been laid on the table by Chris, and there was a steaming hot mug of coffee in my regular place. Nearly drooling, I plopped down to sit on the stool and took a sip before I took a glance around the table, and surprisingly, everything looked edible.

Chris chuckled. "Good morning to you too." He sat next to me with a huge pile of food on his plate.

"Yeah, yeah, same. And thanks for the breakfast. But how did you manage to not burn anything?" I asked, half-impressed and half-joking. Maybe Chris was good at everything else, but in the kitchen, he was usually a nightmare.

Chris shot me an ice-cold glance and made a face. "You're welcome. Aren't you supposed to be going to dance practice or something?"

Instantly my mood sank, and I sighed. Truth to be told, I still wasn't very confident with the choreographies, even though I did get them somewhat down. "I don't know...I think I still have trouble with footwork. Can't keep up..." I answered honestly, trailing off.

Chris' eyes softened. "I have a hack for ya; just wear your Timberlands for the practices."

"What, why? They're very heavy."

"Indeed. Now when you get used to dancing with those shoes on, it's gonna feel super light and easy wearing just about everything else."

Chris might've been onto something. "Right..."

"Trust me on this, hyung," Chris said, winked, and took a sip from his latte. "Now who's gonna wake up Do and Min? Not me for sure. I have eternal traumas from the tour."

"So do I. Let's just get Joonie on it." I chuckled and winked back.

"Get me on what?" Joonie asked from behind me. I might or might not have jumped a couple of inches up.

"For fuck's sake, don't sneak up on people," Chris said, clutching his t-shirt in his fist on his chest. "I damn nearly broke your arm off."

I might've chuckled, but in reality, Chris' threat held some serious meaning behind it since he had trained several types of martial arts for ages. Joonie, however, just laughed his ass off at our expressions and made his way to the coffee maker. He chuckled right up until the point Chris informed him that we had decided it was his turn to wake the two lovebirds up.

Uneasy Feelings

Joonie had clearly realized that he had advantages over me after the kiss, as he kept teasing me the dance practice.

The way he swayed his hips seductively whenever he noticed me staring at him made me damn nearly lose my mind. The way he glanced at me from time to time through the mirror with a look that promised all kinds of things made my heart beat uncomfortably fast. The way he *accidentally* brushed his leg or arm against me every time we passed each other, made my pants feel a bit tight. Certainly, I was glad I had opted for some jeans that hid my half-boner fairly well.

After hours of endlessly getting side-tracked watching Joonie dance and trying to keep up, afternoon swung around. We finished filming the dance practice video for YouTube, and everyone started to pack up their things. But I knew that the surprise safety briefing was about to begin and didn't move to pack a thing. Sure enough, I spotted Joe on the other side of the glass door leading to the room where we were rehearsing. I gave him a small nod to let him know I knew he'd arrived.

Turning back to face the others, I cleared my throat. "Not so fast guys. I think Joonie has something to say."

Three curious sets of eyes turned towards Joonie, who started twirling the strands of hair that had escaped his messy bun.

"There's this stalker case. And a DT," Joonie said, hesitating between every word.

Everyone understood what he meant at once, even with the abbreviation and what it would mean for them. They groaned almost simultaneously. Joonie eyed me with an expression on his face that said "I told you so" quite clearly. I narrowed my eyes at them all, in hopes of having at least a little bit of authority over the hazardous handful of artists. Even if nothing had happened in similar situations before, it didn't mean that they all shouldn't have all been taken with a certain level of seriousness.

"Guys, seriously. Just deal with it. It isn't your first time on the rodeo, so let's not act like amateurs," I said and waved for Joe and the other security staff to join us.

As the new owner of the security company we used, Joe walked in and started lecturing us about the basic safety precautions.

"Don't disclose our dorm's location on social media, don't disclose which hotels you stay in, never go public without a guard, change your phone number regularly…" And so on. In addition, we were supposed to take some extra precautions as long as the guy with the threats hadn't been caught. For example, we would transfer to separate cars to and from airports and concert venues, as well as have empty decoy cars leaving at the same time to make it even more difficult to follow us. They were also adding more staff to ensure our security. Joe apologized for the inconveniences that might cause, but at the same time he emphasized how important it was to be prepared.

Then it was time for some recap training together with the security staff about walking in formations and such. Together with Joe and Seong-gi, we performed a simple formation used when moving individually in crowded places as an example. The guys were paired up with the security staff and they began practicing while Joe and I supervised. I noticed some new guy was walking pretty close behind Chris and let out an almost silent chuckle, earning Joe's attention instantly.

"What's funny?" he asked.

"Oh, nothing much. Just that your new guy is about to get his arm or some other limb broke, that's all," I said and nodded towards Chris and the new guy.

Joe followed my line of sight just in time. Sure, Chris was cute, small, and adorable, but somehow he had learned to use that to his advantage. In a flash after Chris noticed the guard was walking too close to him, he had him in a nice little package on the floor. Writhing in agony as Chris had his whole arm twisted in a way that seemed painfully unnatural. He tapped the floor in a sign of surrender and only then did Chris let go and hissed that he should be keeping his distance.

"Impressive. The small one has some spice in him," Joe said in a sudden wave of awe. "When did he learn that?"

"Remember that airport incident he had back in the days that got a bit out of hand?"

"The one where he got that scar on his earlobe?" he asked, referring to the small scar his right ear from when a fan had forcibly yanked an earring off. "Only remotely. I was just a trainee then."

"Well, he was advised to take some self-defence classes after that. He...got a bit carried away. I believe he geared towards martial arts in the army too. We are the only ones that can get close to him nowadays." I explained, chuckling.

"That's actually pretty impressive. I wonder if he'd need a sparring partner..." Joe said, trailed off, and continued to watch Chris with an awed expression on his face.

It seemed like Chris had just made a new fan. If I hadn't known any better, I'd have said he had a similar look to that which I had while I watched Joonie on the fan-made YouTube videos.

I trained my eyes back to Joonie. He was walking around the room with a bored expression, doing exactly as he was told to by the two guards hovering close to him. One was his regular, a man named Choi Yoo-suk. The other, I didn't recognize.

"Who's the new guy with Joonie?" I asked Joe who reluctantly shifted his gaze away from Chris.

"Oh. That's Lee Min-ho. Still in training, so he's just gonna be an extra for the time being. Though he's supposed to be Chris' new reg 'cause Won's going to step down soon."

"Right..."

I never really understood the thing with regular guards. I just used whoever was available at the time I personally needed one. Which was not that often. All the others had a regular though. Joe was still stuck with Do, Minjae had Seong-gi, Joonie was usually with Yoo-suk, and Chris had been with Mr. Won for forever and was apparently changing to this Lee Min-ho guy.

"Wait, why's Mr. Won leaving already?" I asked. The guy was like, in his early thirties or something. And fit. It's not like it was time for him to retire or leave due to physical reasons like they usually did.

"His wife's pregnant. They figured he'd change to something not...as time-consuming and dangerous as this job. I respect his decision. Even gave him a boring nine-to-five job at the office."

Right. Regular people had families.

Joe sighed and rubbed his neck. "Truth to be told, there's been a lot of resigns and changes in our company after Mr. Kim retired and I stepped in. We're kind of short-staffed at the moment. It's hard to find good replacements so I'm hoping these new guys turn out to be even remotely useful, or I'll have to start the recruitment process from the start. This threat to Joon-seok isn't making things any easier, that's for sure."

I nearly winced, sympathizing for Joe. "Sorry..."

"Well, it's not like it's any of you guys' fault. Let's just hope the police get the bastard caught and put behind bars soon."

"Oh, has Joonie filed the report already?"

Joe shook his head. "Nope. But I did. With Joonie's permission of course. Which reminds me, I'll have to take his phone and take it to the station as soon as we're done here."

"It's alright, I have a spare one at my office Joonie can use. The label has a stash of back-up numbers too, so it's not gonna be a problem."

Joe nodded stiffly and turned his eyes back to Chris, but small but heavy ball of worry settled in my stomach.. With all the recruitment trouble, I could only hope the new guys were trustworthy. Reflexively, I turned my gaze back to Joonie, joking with the new guy and Yoo-suk on the other side of the room. Apparently, they were already done. As soon as Joonie glanced my way, I signed for him to join us.

For once, he obeyed without any complaints or eye-rolls. Zigzagging past the others, he made his way in front of us and eyed me curiously.

"Joe needs your phone," I stated.

"Yeah, I filed the report. The police need your phone in case the guy calls again, and you know..." Joe said apologetically and drifted off.

Joonie went for his bag he had laid on the floor and fished the phone from the side pocket. He handed it to Joe who then dismissed the practice, and the security staff was out the door in mere seconds. Probably heading for lunch since we didn't need them there at the HQ where there were company guards and surveillance systems. I still couldn't help but see Joe and the others leave with the uneasy feeling lingering on my stomach.

Kissing Test

After changing in the locker rooms and showering, we all headed for lunch in the HQ cafeteria as well. Joonie and I stopped at the info desk at the lobby and asked for a new number for Joonie. The intern girl on the other side of the counter blushed epically while handing Joonie a pack holding the sim-card. I wished her a nice day, winked, and offered a bright smile. She nearly started hyperventilating, the poor girl.

"Stop teasing the new ones," Joonie hissed under his breath when we turned around and headed to the cafeteria on the other side of the lobby.

"I'm trying! Just can't help it. Their reactions are priceless." I struggled to hold down a good laugh.

Joonie just shook his head with a faint smile lingering on his damn perfect lips. We both ordered food on the counter and when our meals were handed to us, we headed to sit with the others near the window. They had taken an enormous table for just the five of us in the filled-to-the-brim cafeteria.

And speaking of new people, I spotted a group of six young boys eyeing our table curiously with trays in their hands. There were no other free tables, and I recognized a couple of them as members of this newly formed idol group by our label, so I waved them over to join us. They hesitated.

Eventually, one of them braved up and started walking towards us, with the others following closely behind. The bravest one bowed slightly. "Annyeong haseyo."

"Ye. Annyeong haseyo," I greeted back and waited for a second for the others to reach us.

The second one of them reached our table and asked stiffly, "Is it okay for hyungs if we'd join you?"

"Please," I said and gestured to them to sit down.

The others scooted over to make room for the new guys, and for a moment, it was a hustle of greetings and awkward polite bows. Chris looked like he was getting hilariously uncomfortable by them calling him "hyung," probably because he had gotten used to always being the maknae. The youngsters introduced themselves, but honestly, I forgot all their names as soon as they said them. I figured I'd learn soon enough anyways.

When it quieted down a bit and we all resumed eating, I eyed each of our group's members in a way that hopefully told them to play nice. It would be beneficial to both groups if we got along nicely. It would be fun—and maybe even a bit nostalgic—to do something together with the newer groups of our label. Not to mention highly profitable. We had been toying with some ideas already with the company board.

As soon as we had chomped the food down, we apologized that we had a strict schedule and left. Chris and Do-hyun headed to the mockup stage that was being turned into a set for our music video shoots. They were supposed to have a meeting with the director there. Minjae and Joonie were supposed to head to the meeting with the stylists and concept designers to finalize the outfits for the same videos, but I asked Minjae to go ahead as we still had to get Joonie a new phone. Joonie promised to join them as soon as possible when we parted at the lobby and headed to my office.

"The new guys already sounded way more professional than we ever did," Joonie said with a smile while we were on the lift heading to the upper floors.

"Yeah, they do train them well these days."

"I just wish they knew what they signed up for, exactly," Joonie said, whispering while avoiding my eyes.

Had this whole stalker thing actually affected him despite the carefree demeanor he had been projecting? I touched his chin, turning him to look at me directly before cupping his cheek.

"Joonie, it's okay to be scared sometimes," I said softly while gazing deep in his eyes, only noticing then that he was wearing bright blue contact lenses.

I swear his beauty took my breath away every other minute.

He just stared back at me silently, not muttering out a single word. Once again, the urge to kiss him washed over me and I couldn't help but lean closer with my heart trying to bounce right out of my chest. Joonie fluttered his eyes close and parted his lips invitingly.

"Can I kiss you?" I blurted out. before I could stop myself.

Oh well, at least this time I asked.

The lift stopped, and the doors opened. We parted so fast I almost hit my back against the wall. I shook my head to clear it and stuffed my hands in my pockets to prevent them from grabbing Joonie's wrist and dragging him straight to my office to continue where we left off. Instead, I calmed myself and we walked to my office at a normal speed. I guessed Joonie was a bit shaken too, since the atmosphere got strangely silent.

When we reached the door, I hastily typed in my code and the lock clicked open. We entered the room, still silent. After hunting down the spare, brand new phone I had in my drawer for emergencies, I turned around and handed it to Joonie. He just thanked me and headed for the door. This wasn't over. I beat him to the door, slammed it shut, and spun the surprised Joonie around.

"Did you really think you'd get away that easily after teasing me the whole day...? And just now at the elevator?" My mind grew foggy while I traced the smooth skin on his soft cheek with the back of my hand.

Joonie just stared at me, still in shock. His mouth even hung slightly open as he inhaled as if he had forgotten how to breathe. When he didn't say anything or pushed me away, I asked: "Can't I test the kissing thing again?"

He was still frozen to the spot. I leaned a bit closer to his neck. Inhaling the sweet strawberry scent his hair emitted to the air. I almost couldn't help but press my lips softly to the hollow spot just below his ear. The skin there was so smooth. My lips turned to a smile as soon as I heard Joonie take another sharp breath.

Worried I'd gone too far, I glanced at his face. He had his eyes closed. Breathing heavily while biting his lip. Apparently, he didn't mind. Getting braver, I moved the collar of his shirt out of my way and one short peck on his collarbone.

"Is this okay?" I still asked, wanting to be sure.

Joonie only inhaled sharply before nodding.

I trailed more soft kisses heading back for his neck. Joonie started squirming in my embrace. I teased him a bit more, laying soft kisses all over his neck, his jawline...but not to his mouth. I wanted him to beg for it after teasing me the whole damn day.

When I nibbled his earlobe, Joonie finally surrendered and lost it.

He breathed out a small, "Yes."

"Yes, what?" I muttered against his neck.

"Yes, you can..." he started but gasped as I gently bit the delicate skin on his neck. "You can try the kissing thing again."

After letting go of his neck, I straightened myself. Joonie was now biting his lip and gazing me straight in the eyes under his lashes. He was just a few centimeters shorter than me, but just enough so I had to look slightly down to meet his eyes at our proximity.

I cupped his cheek softly and searched his eyes for consent even if he had just said I could try. When he didn't move so much as an inch, I softly trailed his lower lip with my thumb. That made him release his lip from the hold of his teeth while I leaned closer...this time aiming for his lips.

My world turned upside down when my lips met his. Turned out, the small peck back at home had been absolutely nothing in comparison. Because this time, Joonie kissed me back.

Joonie was a good kisser. Great, actually. The way his lips moved perfectly in sync with mine sent shivers down my spine. As revenge, he bit my lip in a soft, teasing manner. That's when I felt my body melt against his even warmer one, and I couldn't help but press him even tighter between me and the door. I almost got scared of my own thoughts that tried to ruin this moment by straight-up yelling in my head how wrong it was. I made my head shut up and continued because kissing Joonie certainly didn't feel wrong. It felt completely and utterly right. It felt like I belonged. It felt like I had found my home, even though he had always been there. I cursed myself again for not noticing.

When Joonie grabbed my waist and gently rolled his front against my very prominent hard-on, I gasped and almost growled against his lips. The sound of my surprised breath intake made me wake up, and our lips parted. After taking a few more breaths and shrugging the initial surprise off, I leaned in for another of those world-turning kisses.

But this time, Joonie gently pushed me and shook his head, smiling. "As much as I'd like to continue this...experiment...I'm already late. Besides, it kinda hurts to do this with you when you clearly haven't decided yet."

Immediately I released him from my embrace and took a step back. "Yeah, sorry. I kinda got carried away."

At least I had made him ask for it. Kind of.

"So, how was it?" Joonie asked, smirking.

"How was what?" I asked, slightly confused. Or just still a bit out of it because that kiss had been so damn powerful.

"The kissing test. Wanna stick your dick up my butt yet?" he asked, and I practically choked on my own saliva. "'Cause we both know I ain't gonna top."

So, he was still making a joke out of this.

"Joonie, I'm extremely serious about this. Hell, I'm extremely serious about you. Why can't you just see it and stop with all that extra bullshit?" I asked. But before he could mutter out a single word, I calmed simply from getting that off of my chest. I continued with a softer tone. "But you're right. I don't think I'm there yet." I turned around, unable to face him as I admitted it.

Joonie let out a small, sort-of-but-not-quite chuckle. "Relax, I'm just messing with you."

"Right." I pressed my palms against the table and tried to breathe. The whole thing was way too much for me to handle all at once.

"Look, I'm sorry. But I'm seriously late, so let's continue this talk in the evening, alright?"

I nodded, and then came the sound of the door opening and closing behind me.

It took me a while to calm down completely. But when I did, I sat on my couch, head spinning. I didn't know what to think. Of course, I knew why Joonie was acting the way he was—I had been kind of a douche towards him because of my own damn problems. But it annoyed the hell out of me that he didn't take me seriously at all. Well, now that I finally realized I was dead serious with him. It hadn't been a lie, what I had yelled at him. I was completely under his spell. Whipped thoroughly.

My eyes wandered across the room, eventually landing on the old, discarded recording mic. I had set it up next to my table for freestyling and composing purposes, since it was too old for serious recordings.

Might as well vomit all my confused thoughts on tape.

It was kind of a habit of mine to get the thoughts out of my head and to tape them so they might make more sense. So, absent-mindedly, I browsed through my music library for some of my beats for freestyling.

I settled for a slow guitar instrumental beat. It was somewhat easy to work with and did have a vibe I was going for. I pressed play, the beat set on repeat, and cleared my throat. Getting used to the beat, I just listened for the first few bars. When the bass kicked in, I let go and started spitting some random words that came to mind.

The rhymes I could think of from the top of my head ended there. As there wasn't any theme I was going for, my mind skimmed through everything I had been thinking. From experience, I knew it would just be easier to throw it all on tape and sort it out later. Yes, the control-freak in me got messy when making music...but music kind of required it. Too bad life didn't work that way.

To make it all fit, I took it up a notch. Doubled up, so to speak.

The way you're biting your lips, swaying your hips
First, you're teasing me, then next you're leaving me
I'm losing my sleep; you're making me scream
Caught myself begging 'please,' but you keep ignoring me, b—

As I was practically shouting, spitting all my anger and frustration to the tape, my breathing got winded. I ignored my dragging breaths and continued with a softer tone.

Yet while I'm losing my mind, misbehaving, then letting you go
Mind me, I'm coming around, slowly I'll be over my mind
Just give me some sign, and I'm yours in no time
'Cause secretly, I might be hoping you'd someday be mine

That last bit somehow surprised even me. The words just blurted out, like I couldn't help it. The words just emerged from somewhere deep inside me without me having to even think about them at all. *Probably nothing.*

I turned the first verse into some kind of chorus and stopped the tape. For a moment, I stared ahead, my mind completely blank.

In the end, I did just that one verse and the semi chorus-like part. Didn't matter though. I saved the audio file to my discord folder, naming it with only the date. The folder was already filled with previous word vomits, similarly named with just a date and that's it. Never, *ever*, did I delete anything I'd recorded—I just tossed them all there. The good and the bad. Most of them never saw sunlight again. Sometimes, I'd pick one of the better ones and I'd finish it together with Do. Rarely, they ended up as tracks on GRiD's albums.

Something in Between

After my little rant, my mood got way better. But that also meant I soon got bored out of my mind. For a while, I just leaned back on my chair and stared at the blank ceiling of my office. There was an entirely empty afternoon ahead of me and dealing with boredom was not my thing. At all.

There was no point in joining Minjae and Joonie in their meeting with the concept designers and stylists since I knew nothing about fashion. Besides, I'd just get distracted with Joonie there anyway. I wasn't in the mood for joining Do and Chris downstairs for their meeting with the music video director.

Normally, I would've worked with some unfinished tracks in these moments, but this time I wasn't in the mood for that either. It felt like I had already used up all my creativity for the day. I could've held a solo VLIVE, but I couldn't think of anything I'd like to talk about with the fans.

Basically, it was my turn to ditch work. It wasn't like the others didn't have a lazy day or two, even when they did have work to do. And I didn't have anything at the moment. Besides, my visit to Gran's had been long overdue.

In a haste, I fished out my phone from my pocket and called Joe. Thankfully, it only took only a couple of beeps for him to answer.

"Tae?" he asked in a questioning tone.

"Yes, Joe. Anyone available for two to three hours?"

"Well, technically I'm free until Do's done here. Heard it might take a while."

"Good, let's meet in the parking hall."

"Alright, see you there in ten."

Hanging up, I scurried out the door, taking my jacket and the training bag from the couch on the way out.

Joe was already waiting for me. After I explained what I was up to, we decided to take his BMW. The others would fit better in the SUV whenever they were ready to go home, and Joonie had the spare key. On the way, I called this flower shop that was near Gran's apartment and asked for a bouquet. They said they'd have something ready in fifteen minutes.

She lived like half an hour away from the HQ, and the traffic was pretty light, so it was the perfect timing. As soon as we reached the flower shop, I was ready to hop right out of the car, but Joe stopped me.

"Additional safety precautions, remember?"

"Right," I muttered back and handed him a couple of bills from my wallet.

Even though we had been on high alert before, it still felt kind of weird to have someone else pick out your fucking flowers. I liked to do things by myself. Even when I was living with my parents—before Mom left and Dad cut me off financially—I never asked the servants to do anything.

Oh well, I technically couldn't complain since it was me who had insisted on the extra safety measures.

Soon enough, Joe appeared and handed me the flowers. The bouquet was nice; it had some light pink roses and lilies. Well, as far as I could tell, they were roses and lilies. I wasn't exactly an expert on flowers.

It took us another five minutes to reach Gran's apartment. The building was high, crowded, and in the not-that-sophisticated part of the city, which was not nearly as extravagant as she deserved. I would've bought her a new place ages ago, but the damn stubborn lady didn't let me. Nor my father. She insisted on staying, pleading that she liked the neighbors and the location and that she didn't need anything more.

After Joe parked the BMW, we both headed inside. I knew the door code, so we didn't have to use the buzzer. We took the lift and soon were at Gran's doorstep. As soon as Joe spotted the armchair outside Gran's apartment, he plopped down and opened a newspaper from the pocket he had inside his suit jacket. Apparently, he didn't want to come inside.

Whatever. Suit yourself.

Shrugging, I rang the doorbell on Gran's door. I could hear some commotion from inside before the door opened. Except it wasn't Gran who opened it. Took me by surprise as well, because the person who did open the door was Dad's trophy wife number five or whatever. What was her name...Ye-jin? Ye-rin? Ye-whoever.

The bimbo number five, brunette, blinked a couple of times before a smile broke onto her face. "Tae-joon! How nice to see you," she beamed, unbelievably loud I might add, and moved to the side to let me in.

"Annyeong," I greeted the brunette while walking inside, not knowing what else to say. I had only seen her at their wedding...three years ago? She had lasted exceptionally long.

"Ye-rin dear, who is it?" I heard a yell from the living room.

Ye-rin it is then...

"It's Tae-joon," Ye-rin yelled back at Gran, and we both headed towards the living room.

Smiling on the way, I wallowed in the familiarity of the overly decorated apartment. Every wall's surface was filled to the brim with pictures, mostly of me, Dad, or both of us. There was even Dad and Ye-rin's wedding photo on one wall, surprisingly enough. Even Gran hadn't been able to—or hadn't wanted to—keep up with all the wives and the weddings. Before Ye-rin, anyway.

When I entered her room, my heart broke into a thousand little pieces. Gran looked older than ever. Weaker than ever. Apparently so sick she needed a wheelchair. It didn't look like she was paralyzed, or that she had something broken...more like something was withering her body down from the inside out, making her weak.

"My favourite grandson!" she exclaimed when she saw me.

For a moment, I couldn't mutter out a single word back. The thought went round and round in my head. Had I been away for that long? When was the last time I had seen her? When was the last time I spoke with her on the phone? Being so damn preoccupied with work, I hadn't even noticed. Only her eyes shined just as brightly as before, and that was the only thing that kept me sane at that moment.

I shook myself out of it and hastily handed the flowers to Gran, saying, "I'm your only grandson."

She took them happily as Ye-rin scurried to the kitchen. Before I could blink, she came back with a vase, filled with water. I placed the flowers in the vase and on Gran's end table as silence settled in the room.

"Ye-rin dear, could you go by the market and bring us something to go with the coffee?" Gran said, breaking the stagnation.

Ye-rin just nodded and headed to the door, and I sat on the couch beside Gran in her wheelchair.

"Gran, what happened?" I asked with the smallest voice, surprising even myself of how broken it sounded.

"My ears aren't the same anymore, so I have no idea what you just said. But based on that face you're making; you're wondering about the wheelchair."

I couldn't do much else than nod.

"Oh, it's nothing, dear. You must not worry," she said with a warm smile. "My body may be letting me down but at least my mind's just as pristine as ever. Now tell me, what have you been up to lately?"

Pulling myself back together, I shrugged the guilt off and tried to speak as normally as I possibly could. "Mainly work. You know, with half of the world tour having had happened and all."

"It would've been nice to see one of the concerts. Too bad you never play around here anymore," she said, narrowing her eyes at me.

"We do have one gig here before we head back to the tour. It's a showcase really...in a smaller venue. I can get you a ticket. Front row."

"That would be wonderful, dear. Don't forget to get one for Ye-rin too. I'm sure she'd like to come."

"Oh right! Now, what is her deal? Why's she here?" I asked.

"Ye-rin's different from the previous ones. Such a nice lady. Been helping me around the house quite a lot lately..." She subtly glanced towards the wheelchair she was in.

The guilt stung my chest again.

"That's good, I guess." *And surprising.* Not one of the previous wives of Dad's had even visited regularly.

The front door opened—Ye-rin arrived from the convenience store and told us she'd brew some coffee. I wheeled Gran to the kitchen, cursing the crappy apartment on my way, since I had trouble wheeling her over the doorstep. The kitchen was just as small as I remembered, mostly filled with the gigantic dining table that was dominating the left side of the room. One of the chairs was missing, though. I figured that was where she usually sat, so I wheeled her there and headed to sit on the opposite side. All the while Ye-rin and Gran gossiped about some dude Ye-rin had bumped into at the store, apparently one of Gran's neighbors.

Ye-rin handed us our coffee cups filled with fresh coffee and then placed the cupcakes and cookies and everything else she had brought from the shop in the middle of the table, before plopping down to sit beside Granny with a bright, mischievous looking smile plastered on her face.

"Now tell us all about the DoMino scandal. We've been dying to know the real deal," Ye-rin demanded from across the table as I stuffed my face full of the cookies.

I choked, hard. While I tried to cough up the cookie crumble that had suddenly invaded my airways, I heard my grandma laugh. Loudly.

"Yes, I know all about that," she said eventually when I had finally calmed down and could breathe properly again. "Ye-rin has shown me how to use that thing." With a twinkle in her eyes, she gestured to the laptop she had set up on the other end of the dining table.

It seemed like I had completely forgotten how Gran practically lived for the gossip. And tabloids. To think she now had access to the internet...from now on she would be unstoppable. I winced and carefully asked, "So what do you think about it?"

"It's...entertaining, I guess. Now tell me, is this one of your publicity stunts, dear? It seems a bit cold to play with people's love lives, don't you think?"

"Oh, how I wish it was just a publicity stunt. They're just so nauseatingly sugary and sweet nowadays that it isn't even funny anymore. It has become nearly impossible to live with them," I huffed, toying with the handle of my coffee mug.

Gran let out another little, chiming laugh. "They're in love, dear. Which reminds me..." she started and downright scolded me. "I'm worried about you. You're nearly thirty, and I've never seen you with anyone. You're going to end up old and alone if you don't do something about it soon."

"I'm...working on it," I said, maybe a slight blush creeping up on my neck. Clearly Gran didn't have anything against gays, but that didn't mean she would jump up and down with joy for me being one.

Gran glared me straight in the eyes for a while before diving headfirst to a long, scolding speech filled with old people's wisdom. "Honey...just don't take too long. Life cannot only be about work. You're so young that you might think you have time, but all our days are limited. It's better to have a partner to share those days with. Be it a man, woman, or something in between." Then her eyes softened. "And don't mind that stubborn son of mine—or your so-called father—he'll come around eventually. He always does."

All the while Ye-rin nodded enthusiastically beside her.

Fair Enough

As soon as I got home from the most awkward visit to Gran's ever, I spotted Joonie sitting on the living room couch, playing with his phone. I planned on ignoring him, sneak over to the kitchen to grab a drink, and then head to my room at least until dinner. Joonie had other ideas though.

"Tae!" he greeted and jumped up from the couch, sounding and looking suspiciously entertained and... Amused? Happy? "You have to try these outfits on so the team will know if they need to be tailored." He grabbed a couple of garment bags from the sofa table.

"Ugh...Joonie, I'm tired. Plus, don't we usually do this at the HQ?" I asked, not the least bit interested in some damn clothes. Let alone in trying them on. The day had been weird enough as it was, and while I was still planning on having a serious chat with Joonie, I would've preferred to do that after dinner when I had some food under my belt.

He downright grinned at me, like he knew what I was thinking and didn't care. "No, it can't wait. We need to fit them now so we can return them tomorrow morning, and then they can be ready by Monday," he explained, still sporting that huge and famous grin of his that seemed to brighten the whole room.

"At least after dinner?" I pleaded to no avail.

"No. Now," he said and proceeded to push me down the hall and towards my room.

I sighed in defeat, walked over to my door, let him in, and followed suit.

Joonie was hyped up about this for some reason. His mood was contagious, and while he was laying the bags over my king-sized bed, I couldn't help but smile at his enthusiasm. Well, at least for a whole two seconds—right up until he opened one of the bags, and I could see some black leather. Now *that* never meant anything comfortable.

"Joonie..." I said, the distress showing clearly in my voice. "What are those?" Not that I particularly even wanted to know the answer, to be completely honest.

"Relax, it's just some leather pants. Nothing you haven't worn before," he said and proceeded to pull them out.

They looked extremely tight. Not to even mention that they were so low waisted I was pretty sure I'd show more hair from down there than just my happy trail. I swear the damn zipper was like an inch and a half. Maybe. With a stretch.

I gulped. "No."

"Oh, come on. You're gonna look so hot in these."

"No! No fucking way. How am I even supposed to fit...my parts...in there?" I asked and waved my hand vaguely over the part where my junk was most likely supposed to go.

Joonie just let out a loud laugh, pushed me inside my closet, tossed the leather pants to my hands, and slammed the door shut.

"I'm waiting," he said from the other side.

I guess I have no choice. How the hell was I supposed to do this? Whatever. I just went for it.

And man was it a damn struggle. There definitely wasn't any room for underwear, whatsoever. So, yeah. I skipped those. Then I started wiggling the leather pants on. The hardest part? Getting them over my fat ass. But eventually—with some yanking and pulling—I managed to get them somewhat on. It was only the zipper and the top button left. My balls had already been squished somewhere I didn't even know, and I hoped I could somehow fit the rest of my manly parts somewhere too. Trying to hold my dick somewhat in place, I started to carefully pull the zipper closed. To my ultimate relief, it didn't get stuck on anything. After getting the button done, I sighed in relief. They fit. Somehow.

"You're taking awfully long time in there, Tae," I heard Joonie say from the main room. He even snickered.

"Just a minute," I muttered back.

I glanced at the mirror on the very back of the closet and got a bit surprised at how good I looked in the damn pants. They snugged extremely close and emphasized every muscle on my legs. Still totally not worth the trouble though. While cramming some stray pubic hair under the extremely low waistline, I realized I'd so have to shave some time before Monday too. Fuck.

Taking my time to pull in a deep breath, I eventually stepped out. Joonie was sitting on my couch, opposite of the door, and stared at me bluntly before letting out a low whistle. A wide smile spread on his lips.

"Not bad," he stated, sounding disinterested but I could see he was basically eye-fucking me.

"Not bad? Not bad?! I'm hot and you know it," I said and smirked. "Now please tell me there's a top and I don't have to be half-naked again?"

Joonie's eyes started to twinkle. "Oh yes, there definitely is..." he said. He immediately stood up and pulled out something black, very thin, and see-through from the same bag where the leather pants had been. I groaned, the sound making it clear I was now desperate.

"That's see-through."

Joonie rolled his eyes. "Oh, just suck it up. At least you get to wear a shirt."

"What do you mean?" I asked. Curiosity got the best of me. Joonie without a shirt? Yes, please.

"You'll see," he replied dismissively. I knew from experience that if he didn't want to reveal something, he wouldn't, so I let it drop.

Instead, I pulled the see-through 'shirt' over my head and thanked the gods that it was a bit loose on me. I glanced at the mirror. The top thing still clung to me, but at least it didn't squeeze the living shit out of me as the pants did. Then I gasped.

"I'm not expected to dance in these, right?" I asked, eyes widening when I turned to face Joonie who was now back at the couch.

Joonie just gave me a smirk. "You are going to dance in those."

Another groan escaped my throat. "No fucking way."

"Yes, fucking way."

"I can barely move!"

"Hey, it wasn't my idea, so don't shoot the messenger. Though I do like the look," he stated, sidled up next to me, and turned me back towards the mirror. He wrapped his hands around my waist from the back, rested his chin on my shoulder, and stared me dead in the eyes through the mirror. "Just wear it, please... It would make my day," he said softly with the look on his eyes piercing a hole right through my heart.

Joonie had used that tactic before, but only now I noticed how powerful those damn puppy eyes actually were. And to be honest, the outfit wasn't *that* bad once my eyes got used to it. It was extremely hard to move in, let alone dance. I wasn't really looking forward to it, but I'd do it for Joonie.

As I looked at the two of us through the mirror, I realized I had always done everything Joonie asked. I was whipped. Had been for ages. I just hadn't seen it. To top it off, we looked fine together. Even when I was wearing something that disturbing and Joonie wore only simple black skinny jeans and a loose satin button up.

"Fine," I sighed, closing my eyes, and tilting my head back against Joonie's shoulder. "These are for 'Mad Love' right? What's in the other bag?"

"That's just a suit. Nothing too weird. Though you should try that one on too."

Joonie let me go and went back to the bags, and I headed towards the closet once again. He hadn't lied; the suit wasn't nearly as bad as the first outfit. The jacket was dark red and had some black embroidery on it. It was paired with a vest and pants made of the same fabric. Joonie told me I was supposed to wear a simple black button-up underneath and, of course, my own shoes.

I was pretty much used to suits by now, so I felt way more comfortable in them.

By the time I was done dressing and stepped out of the closet, Joonie had disappeared from my room. I went to the door to check for him in the common area when it opened and Joonie nearly collided with me. I chuckled and when he recovered from the surprise, he handed me a thick paper bundle.

"Here, the screenplays and concept illustrations," he said and shoved the stack to my chest.

"Right, thanks," I muttered and started to flip through the papers while heading back to the main room.

There weren't many lines in the sheets about "Mad Love." Only a couple for Minjae in the beginning. But there were a lot of descriptions of expressions for all of us, including me. Yikes. I had never been great at wordless storytelling. The second pile of concept sheets was a lot shorter since the concept for that was way simpler. We were basically supposed to dance the choreo in front of a green screen and that's it. The rest would be in the hands of editors.

The concept photos were a bit disturbing. At least for "Mad Love." There was this madhouse scene for Minjae and Do, and a huge sequence for Chris all by himself. It made sense since we had decided to give him a lot more screen time on both new music videos than usual, in hopes of getting him more exposure. And then there was a scene for me and Joonie in some weird setting. Joonie had been drawn to be suspended with some ropes and shit from the ceiling in the picture, while I just stood there and touched his cheek with my right hand.

As I sat ono the couch, still flipping through the concept photos of the second music video Joonie interrupted my thoughts. "Aish! You can't get this wrinkled," he scolded.

""Geez, just calm down." I rolled my eyes and tossed the screenplays and the concept illustrations to my table to turned to face Joonie. "But what do you think?" I gestured to the suit.

"It does fit perfectly. And the color suits you," he said, smiling.

"What are you wearing for the second video?"

"The same suit but in navy blue. Minjae has it in dark purple, Do has an almost black grey...Chris is going dark green, I think."

"Ugh, we'll look like a rainbow."

"Well, that would be the point..." Joonie smiled and glanced at his watch. "But I'll need to start with the dinner soon," he continued and headed for the door.

I grabbed his wrist lightly to stop him. "I kinda hoped we could've talked like you asked earlier..."

"Tae, I know I said that but honestly...I don't think there's anything to talk about before you make up your damn mind," he said and sighed, still facing the door.

I let go of his wrist. "Fair enough," I said, disappointment pulling my shoulders down.

I knew Joonie was right. I couldn't keep toying with him before I'd be one hundred percent sure of what I wanted with him. I *had* been playing with the idea of having an actual relationship with him in the past couple of days. But before that, I'd have to make peace with myself to go further with him than just kissing. Joonie had made that extremely clear in my office earlier.

"Great. I'll see you at dinner," he said and closed the door behind him.

Plenty of Time

After a long night of thinking things through, tossing and turning in bed, Friday arrived. The last day of dance rehearsals, thank all that's good in the world. Once again, I had gotten distracted by Joonie countless times during the day, but eventually we got the dance routines pristine. Yes, even I was able to keep up, mostly thanks to Chris' tip with wearing heavy shoes in the beginning. We were supposed to get ourselves familiarized with the scripts over the weekend...but other than that, the weekend was supposed to be somewhat free. The shooting would only start on Monday.

Maybe that's why everyone was in such high spirits to get the rehearsals done. Because of that, we finished early, just before 5 p.m. Minjae and Do were out the door of the studio in a flash, apparently heading for a date. Minjae was thrilled since, now that they were out, it didn't matter if they'd be caught by the paparazzi. Of course, I had approved, since even if they would be in tabloids the next day, it would probably be in a positive light. I doubted we'd see Do and Minjae before Sunday, and Chris was heading to visit his family for the weekend…

Which all meant that I was probably facing the weekend alone together with Joonie at the dorm.

Joonie had been awfully distant the previous night and through the day, but I couldn't really blame him for that. But the night had somewhat been a turning point for me. I was nervous to spend the weekend alone with him, but at the same time, I was determined to get the next part of my plan rolling: to see if we could be in a relationship. No longer I doubted my feelings. Surprisingly enough, I was determined to see where it would go. I wasn't saying I was already in love with Joonie, but I knew I was heading there. Fast.

Through the night I had thought a lot about what Gran had said, and I realized every word of hers was true. Life was short. I couldn't fill it with just work. I had thought a lot about what Do had said earlier too. It didn't matter if I had fully sorted out my feelings towards Joonie yet, as long as I was willing to take the fall, whatever happened afterwards, it shouldn't matter.

"Do you have any plans for tonight?" I asked, navigating through the streets of Seoul towards our dorm behind the wheel of our SUV.

"Nothing in particular. Why?"

"You up for a movie night?"

"Movie nights with no snacks are an abomination..." Joonie stated silently. My mood sank.

I had forgotten—again—that we weren't supposed to stuff our face with just about anything carb related until Monday to prevent any swelling. I had no back-up plan whatsoever, and a movie would have been a great way to set the mood for the talk I had in mind.

"Right..." I said and frowned.

But before I could figure out anything else, Joonie continued. "But I've been wanting to see that new movie Park Jeong is starring in."

I smiled. "It's settled then."

The rest of the way home was somewhat a silent one. My heart started racing and my palms started to sweat once I parked the car in our underground garage. After the previous night I knew I wanted to try a relationship with Joonie and was determined to make that happen as soon as possible. Only there was this one "but." And that was Joonie.

Yes, I knew Joonie had said he was in love with me like five months ago and then admitted it again when asked. The actual problem was me. I had sure taken my time to get to this point.

Though then again, we had kissed and for the second time, he had even kissed me back. So technically, I had nothing to worry about.

The damn "what if" whenever there were other people involved just got me on edge.

After changing into more homey clothes, it didn't take us long to make ourselves comfortable on our huge couch. Joonie took over most of the couch, seeming to fully enjoy the fact that there were just the two of us, and he could have his space. He barely left me the divan part. I didn't mind though; it was more than enough. We rented the movie Joonie had mentioned and settled to watch it. Or more like he started to watch it while I tried to think about how I'd tell him I seriously wanted us to be a thing.

Apart from the occasional comment on the movie, we stayed silent. But the whole time I was painfully aware of his presence on my right side. Every time he shifted his position or just moved his arm, I sensed it, my body aching to touch him. I didn't though, as I was determined to have the talk first.

Half-way through the movie, I noticed that Joonie's eyes started to droop. Little by little, his body started to tilt towards me. Eventually, he was fully leaning on me, with his head resting on my shoulder. My heart raced and my palms sweated, but I didn't dare to move. Let alone wake him up—he must have been exhausted. He normally never fell asleep during movies.

It felt like the movie was over in a flash, and I had gotten exactly nowhere. The end credits rolled in, and I stretched carefully. Joonie was sound asleep, still leaning on my shoulder. Clearly, it wasn't the day I'd get anywhere with my plans, but that didn't bother me as much as I had thought it would. We had plenty of time, right?

Joonie fluttered his eyes open and yawned when I propped him up and shook his shoulder.

"Whoa, I fell asleep?" he asked softly with a husky voice while rubbing his eyes with the backs of his hands while slowly falling back to lean on me.

I chuckled under my breath slightly. "Yeah, about half-way through."

"Mmhm, might as well continue sleeping then," he mumbled, closing his eyes as he nuzzled against my side, wrapping his hand around my waist. My heart melted. he was so cute half asleep.

I was very much tempted to let him sleep there and bear with it for the night. It didn't seem like a good idea though, so reluctantly, I shook him again. "You'll catch a cold if you sleep here. Let's get you into your room," I said and started to try to heave him up.

He put up a fight though.

"No!" he mumbled sternly and tightened his grip around my waist. "I want to sleep right here."

I sighed. This was impossible. "Yes, Joonie. Now get up, I can't leave you here."

"Only if you carry me," he whined.

Rolling my eyes, I picked him up. He weighed nothing, so I really didn't mind. He clung to my neck the whole way, giving me some damn weird flashbacks to one particular night over five months ago. It made me realize how much things had changed after that.

It was a hassle to get Joonie's door open while still carrying him, but miraculously I managed to do it. But as soon as I laid him on top of his bed, he yanked my hand with a surprising amount of force. Losing my balance, I stumbled and landed right on top of him.

As I propped myself up a bit and glanced at Joonie's face, fully awake and grinning. His eyes sparkled.

"You tricked me, you son of a..." I started, though grinning exactly as wide as he was.

"Just shut up and kiss me," he interrupted, sneaking his hand behind my neck and yanking me down.

My lips crashed with his and in an instant, I was in another world together with Joonie. For a brief moment, I was sure it had been me who had fallen asleep during the movie and was now dreaming, just because it had happened so fast my rational mind couldn't keep up. My brain shut down and I kissed him back, hoping to transfer all the words that had been left unsaid this evening. For the first time in a long time, or maybe for the first time ever, I let myself get lost in the moment. And right then, it didn't even matter in the slightest. Losing my constantly nagging brain activity felt good. Way better than I had ever imagined.

It still took me by surprise how damn good kisser Joonie actually was.

Joonie wrapped his other hand around my waist, and I was suddenly hyper-aware of his body under me. His lips felt incredibly soft despite him getting them chapped by biting them all the time. His body felt warm against mine, but thinner than ever, halfway sunk to the soft mattress. I didn't particularly like the idea of crashing on top of him with my full weight, so with our lips still intact and doing their own heated dance of passion, I rolled us over and pulled Joonie on top of me. He gasped because of the sudden movement but recovered in an instant, and I felt his lips curve into a smile just before he bit my lower lip in a teasing manner.

Right then I realized I could never watch him bite his lip again without thinking back to this moment.

I gasped and our lips parted—the moment was over. Joonie rolled off me, chuckling, and I let him. So, there we were, side by side, catching our breaths. My head felt light, and my heart raced like I had run a marathon or something. Not to even mention how hard my cock was.

When I recovered enough, I turned to my side to face Joonie, propping myself up with my elbow. He had his eyes closed, but as soon as he felt me moving, he fluttered them open, turning his face right towards me and stared me in the eyes. To my relief, I didn't find anything that even hinted at him regretting that kiss on his face. He just smiled at me boldly with a spark in his eyes.

"What was that for? I thought you wouldn't want to do this before—your words—'I'd make up my damn mind,'" I asked.

"I thought so too," he said, his smile turning into a smirk in a nanosecond. "But then I thought I'd help you make up that damn stubborn mind of yours."

Little did he know I had already made up my mind. Probably right back on the night of confessions over five months ago...I just had taken a bit longer to realize that myself. I felt my own lips turn up into a smirk.

"Well in that case and while we're at it...let's keep making up my mind," I said and leaned in for another kiss.

We continued right where we left off.

Cheesy Blanket Thief

My well-trained internal clock woke me up bright and early on Saturday morning. There had been a couple of nights I hadn't slept that well at all, mostly because of overthinking. It was way too early for a day off though, so I tried to get some more sleep in by squeezing my eyes shut tighter. Didn't help much. I kept my eyes shut tight anyway, way too reluctant to get up yet. Instead, I stretched on the warm and super soft bed with the intention of falling right back to sleep.

The bed, however, felt way too soft for being my bed. Besides, why did I suddenly sleep so well? Still a bit out of it, I groaned and opened my eyes, just barely to peek.

I wasn't, in fact, in my own bed. I wasn't even in my own damn room.

My head spun when I jerked upwards to sit. The layout was exactly the same as in my room. But there was art on the walls while I kept them bare. In the far corner was a piano instead of my laptop plus keyboard and mic setup. The couch beside the piano was carmine red.

Right.

I was in Joonie's room. And apparently in Joonie's bed. Slowly and carefully, I turned to look on my right side with my heart racing and a cold sweat pushing through my skin. And yep, there was one peacefully sleeping Joonie right beside me. He had his back towards me, and he was clutching the blanket as if his life depended on it. I glanced down on myself and instantly felt an immense relief wash over me—I was still fully clothed. And that's when last night finally rushed back to my consciousness with full force and I felt a smile make its way on my face.

For a second there, I actually thought that the insane sexual tension got the better of us last night. It was a relief that it didn't, as I was still not quite comfortable with the whole concept. It wasn't necessarily that I didn't want to have sex with Joonie, but more like how the hell that was supposed to even happen? It wasn't like I didn't know what to do in bed; it was just that well...uh...I had gotten used to very different kinds of parts.

Apart from all that unnecessary thought processing, last night had been one of the best nights of my life. It was right up there with the night when we made our debut over seven years ago. And we had done nothing but shared a few kisses—though very nice and hot kisses—until the pure exhaustion got the better of us and we fell asleep.

Trying hard not to wake him up, I slid down again and snuggled under the blanket. I wasn't fully successful as he stirred a bit in his sleep, turned sides, and faced me. I practically didn't breathe or move as much as an inch until the frown between his eyebrows evened out, and he was breathing steadily once again.

Sleeping Joonie was a beautiful sight. Mesmerizing, even. The long faded pink hair had spread to the pillow and halfway over his face. His face was completely calm, looking like he didn't have a care in the world. Even the usual barely noticeable frown between his eyebrows was all but non-existent. I was so close that I could see that his long and thick eyelashes were tangled together in a couple of spots. His pouting lips were slightly parted, inviting me to continue last night's activities. It became hard to resist the urge.

I don't know how long I just stared at his face—but I could see the exact second when Joonie woke up, although he didn't even open his eyes. His eye lids twitched, and the corners of his mouth turned into a small smile.

"Why are you staring at me?" he asked softly while slowly opening his eyes to meet mine.

I stared right back at his deep brown ones with a smile still lingering on my lips. "You're beautiful, you know that right?"

In an instant, he hit my face with his pillow. "Shut up, you cheesy blanket thief."

I removed the pillow from my face, chuckling, and cupped Joonie's cheek. I couldn't hold back the urge to kiss him anymore. I placed a light peck straight on his lips and pulled him close against my chest. He buried his face to the nook of my neck.

For a long while, we embraced each other tightly like that, with our legs in a tangled mess under the duvet. At some point, I started trailing his back with my fingertips. He was still wearing the same loose white t-shirt from the day before—the fabric felt soft under my touch and was so thin I could easily feel every lean muscle he had on his back. The hand that was under Joonie was getting numb, but I endured it as I didn't want to move. Ever.

Joonie's stomach grumbled loudly, effectively ending our little moment.

"Breakfast?" I asked.

"Yes, please," he mumbled, still sounding a bit sleepy.

But when I tried to untangle our limbs, Joonie clung to me even harder. "I thought you wanted breakfast?" I asked after several unsuccessful tries to get up.

"Mmhm, but I'm too tired to move." He mumbled. "Carry me."

Based on the strength in his grip though, he was far from *too tired*. So, I sighed. "Fine."

His grip loosened in a nanosecond, and he practically hopped on my back as soon as I got up.

I staggered a bit, finding my balance. "I'll have to carry you everywhere now?"

"Yes," he said bluntly while wrapping his legs around my waist.

I rolled my eyes, but it was only a habit...I didn't actually mind. I'd carry him anywhere. He giggled the whole way to the kitchen, his hands wrapped around my neck and his chin resting on my shoulder. I was in his happy bubble too and couldn't help but grin from ear to ear. I was surprised by how familiar the closeness felt. It was almost like I had missed him for five months and now we were back together. As if we had been like this before.

In a way we had been Though now I knew what Joonie felt for me. And even further, I was certainly catching on to those same feelings. The sparkle that had started a small five months back was growing into something bigger in my chest. Surprisingly, it didn't even scare me that much anymore.

I laid Joonie on one of the bar stools and headed for the coffee maker first. Joonie sat on the counter, and I hustled around the kitchen—a very familiar scene. Except this time, I felt Joonie's eyes on me the whole time. While I made us some breakfast, and we chatted about the weather and other unimportant matters, I still felt weirdly giddy and... genuinely, completely, and simply happy.

In that moment, it didn't matter that we were superstars. Or that we had just gone through a huge scandal with Do and Min. Or that they still hadn't caught Joonie's stalker. It didn't even bother me that the world tour was continuing soon, and we'd be busy again next week with the music videos and stuff. It was one domestic as hell breakfast, and I couldn't have been more comfortable. I wanted the moment to last forever. Or at least for the day.

With that in mind, I tried hopelessly to figure out some sort of excuse so that I could spend the rest of the day with Joonie. No questions asked.

I tried thinking about anything that involved work so I could easily demand his company. I even considered faking that I'd want another dancing lesson, as much as I detested those. Then again, it would totally evaporate the whole concept of a rare day off, so I quickly tossed anything around work out of the window. But then I was left empty-handed.

Am I really this boring? I thought, watching Joonie already finishing his presumably last cup of coffee for the morning.

Then it finally hit me. If I would just ask, straightforward and honest, there wouldn't be a need to scheme anything. For once, I flat out refused to be that boring guy whose life revolved around work. My heartbeat started accelerating at a very alarming speed when the plan came together in my mind.

"Let's go on a date," I stated nonchalantly. Well, it was supposed to come out as a question, but something weird happened between my brain and my vocal cords that completely changed the sentence. Hoping Joonie wouldn't get pissed at me, I carefully lifted my gaze up from my coffee cup to meet his eyes.

There was a brief silence while Joonie emptied the rest of the coffee down his throat and glanced at me with a questioning expression before turning his eyes down to his hands which began to toy with the mug. To me, the silence suddenly seemed to last forever, but I let him take his time.

"Will it help you decide?" he asked with a very small voice that nearly broke my heart. I had completely forgotten that he was still waiting for me to make up my mind. After all, I never got around to having the talk.

Little did he know, I had already decided. A date started to sound like a better and better idea every passing second. It could even be a break from the insane sexual tension that still hung in the air, and to which I just didn't feel comfortable enough to surrender. Yet.

"Yes," I replied simply.

"Then sure. What do you have in mind?"

Private Event

"Just let me handle everything. Dress in something warm and give me..." I started and glanced at my watch. It was only just past ten in the morning, so we had plenty of time. "...An hour, maybe?"

Finally, a small grin spread to his lips, and he nodded. "I guess I'll go change then," he said and scurried off towards his room.

I knew exactly where I wanted to take him. There was this abandoned amusement park from the '80s located on the outskirts of Seoul where we had shot a music video once, way back when. It was not too far away, so we wouldn't have to waste the whole day just traveling, and it was also secluded, away from prying eyes. Joonie liked photography too, and that place was made for that kind of stuff. Granted, it was also a bit creepy, especially upon nightfall, but I counted on it not being that bad during the daytime.

The area was owned by this cheap old chap who charged 5000₩ as an entrance fee for photographers and such, based on my brief internet search. Cash only. I found his phone number on the same website, so I gave him a call to see if I could talk him into a private visit.

The guy was greedy, claiming he made an obscure amount of money with just that 5000₩ entrance fee on weekends. Though after dropping a large enough figure, he agreed to keep the place empty of other folks for one day. With even more money, he was on board with me on the surprise I had in mind for Joonie. We agreed to meet at the old entrance in a couple of hours.

As Joonie's stalker was not caught, I gave Joe a call too. Unfortunately, he was still stuck with Do, Min, and Seong-gi at Daegu, but he promised to give Joonie's regular—Mr. Choi Yoosuk—and the new guy a call. Sure enough, he texted me in five minutes that they'd meet us downstairs in half an hour or so.

The weather was supposed to be mainly clear, despite being a bit chilly. But I knew it could change in a hot minute as it was early spring, so I packed some extra clothes. There were some clouds lingering on the horizon, but hopefully, it wasn't going to rain, and if it was, it would probably come down as snow. It was still early March after all.

As I was packing some sandwiches, fruits, and other pre-made meals I found from the fridge—to hell with the damn diet for one day—my head started to feel light, and my mood got even brighter. I took a significant amount of cash from a small safe in my room and put it in my wallet. It almost seemed like the world was with me as the pieces fell in place that easily. It only took me like a solid 45 minutes to get everything packed and ready to go.

A new tune, lighter than in a long time, stuck in my mind. After getting changed to some jeans, a t-shirt, a cardigan, and a warm wool jacket paired with my trusted Timberland shoes, I took around five minutes to scribble the notes down on my notebook. Humming the tune under my breath, I put the two bags that held the food, the extra clothes, and a thick picnic blanket to our apartment's door. At the last minute, I grabbed a bottle of wine from the cupboard and tossed it to one of the bags. Ready to go, I headed to Joonie's room.

Oddly enough, the door was locked.

"Hello? We can head out soon if you're ready?" I called after knocking.

The lock clicked and the door opened just slightly. "I don't know what to wear."

So that's what was taking him so long. After excessively rolling my eyes, I pushed the door open and forced my way in. Joonie was dressed in just some stonewashed jeans, Timberlands, and a t-shirt. Oddly enough, we kind of matched.

"Just wear anything as long as it's warm. It's not like we're going anywhere public anyways," I stated, eyeing at the mess. There were countless pieces of clothes laid on his bed, the red couch, and even over the piano. "What the hell happened here?"

He completely ignored me and picked up two jackets from the bed and held them up. "Which one?"

One was a black, long-ish trench coat. The other was slightly shorter and light grey, but otherwise incredibly similar. "Umm, anything that looks good in photos I guess?"

"Photos?!" he exclaimed and hurried towards the mirror that hung on the wall over his table. "I barely have any make-up on!"

I took a deep breath and shook my head slightly with a smile lingering on my lips. He was being impossible and at the same time a bit adorable. Normally, I probably would have gotten annoyed, but for some reason, Joonie acting this way had never bothered me. "You have enough."

"Fine," he said, scrunching up his nose. "Though that makes it easier to decide as black is a hard color for photos. I'll take the grey coat."

I knew next to nothing about photography, so I only nodded to that.

He opted for a darker grey cardigan under the jacket and a matching beanie. While Joonie was dressing into those, I shoved a pile of clothes to the side and plopped on his couch to wait and text Yoo-suk that it would take us a bit longer than I thought.

"Can I take my own camera or...?" Joonie asked when he was dressed.

I nodded again. "That would be the point."

He hurried to one of his drawers and started pulling out some objectives. "What lens?"

"I don't know. Something that works outside," I said, getting a bit antsy to go already since it was getting hot in the warm clothes while we were still inside.

"Alright then," he said and packed three different lenses together with his SLR camera into a big ass camera bag, along with a small tripod. "I'm ready."

"Good, let's go." I headed to his door.

Joonie followed me out, and together we headed to the garage downstairs. Yoo-suk and Min-ho—were already waiting for us there. We greeted each other, plopped the bags to the trunk, and hopped to the backseat while Yoo-suk headed to the driver's seat and Min-ho took the front passenger seat. Yoo-suk curtly nodded when I handed him the piece of paper I had written the address on, and we were off.

"You're not even going to tell me where we're going?" Joonie asked with one of his eyebrows shot up.

"It's not a secret. It's nothing special, and you've been there before," I stated, shrugging. "You don't need to know, but I'll tell you if you really want to know."

Joonie seemed to ponder my words for a moment. Then he shrugged too. "I guess I'll find out soon enough."

Aish, I knew this man way too well. If I'd been in his place, I would've demanded to know the destination first thing before even considering going. And here Joonie was being perfectly fine with not knowing a thing. It amused me that he could be so easy-going. Well, except when he was deciding what clothes to wear, apparently.

Thankfully there wasn't any traffic to speak of—at least on the Seoul scale—so we were close to the place in about an hour. The scenery started to look somewhat familiar. Soon enough, Yoo-suk curved right in front of the old and rusty gate of Yongma Land— the once fully functioning amusement park closed after some more accessible and modern parks were built, like the famous Lotte World.

Joonie followed me out of the SUV with an amused look on his face.

"I remember this place!" he exclaimed and basically jumped up from pure excitement. I could practically see the gears turning

100

in his head, trying to digest the endless photography opportunities he knew the place held inside. "I've always wanted to visit this place after the music video was shot here, but never got around to..." he continued with his eyes sparkling nearly as bright as the sun that had started to peak through the clouds.

"I know," I said, holding in another chuckle and heading to get our bags from the trunk.

Joonie was already walking toward the gates in a trance-like state when I got the bags piled in front of the SUV. I was contemplating just letting him explore and follow right after.

But just then an old, grumpy looking man appeared out of nowhere and stopped Joonie at the gates.

"Hey! No entrance today young man. We have a private event."

Joonie's face fell magnificently flat while I tried my hardest to not burst laughing out loud at how hilariously disappointed he was. I touched his back lightly in a soothing manner while passing by to meet the old chap.

"Annyeong haseyo," I greeted, tilting my head respectfully to the older man. "I believe it's our private event. I called you earlier." I opened my wallet and dug up a significant pile of notes.

The man eyed me first and then Joonie, and I could see judgement flashing in his eyes—probably because we were both male and this was clearly a date. Especially when he knew my plans for the sunset...but it passed by as soon as he glanced at the money pile I was holding out to him. Narrowing his eyes, he took the pile of cash and without saying a word and started to walk towards the old ticket booth on the right side of the gate.

Yoo-suk darted inside the park, and after fifteen minutes he came back. He nodded to signify that the place was safe and headed to sit on the picnic table just outside the entrance with Min-ho, and they started to play cards. I spotted they had a small cooler in tow; apparently Joe had informed them it could take a while.

Joonie had already set up his camera, and he was feverishly taking photos of the entrance. I couldn't help but feel a bit excited too; the place looked awesome. Even more so than I initially re-membered.

Capturing possibly every single angle of the entrance, Joonie eventually made his way inside the park. I didn't dare to interrupt him, so I just followed him inside silently. The park wasn't that big, so you could practically see all of it with just one glance around from the edge of the centre square. But based on the rate we were moving ahead with Joonie photographing everything, from multiple angles, I no longer doubted at all if we could spend the whole day there or not. We most definitely could. And would.

The most impressive sight was the old, nostalgic, vintage carousel in the middle of the square. Surprisingly enough, it was one of the most preserved things in the whole park. Most of the rides had at least collapsed, except for the ride called 'Space Fighter' which looked like it was straight from the '80s. Nature had taken hold of most buildings. There were a couple of cherry trees, but sadly they weren't even remotely blossoming yet.

The paint had chipped off from the figures, and asphalt was cracked here and there. There was trash everywhere, and a couple of the walls had some impressive graffiti on them—many new pieces I hadn't seen before. Some things that were easy to take had been stolen. All in all, it was a crude sight, but at the same time so incredibly beautiful.

I was still staring at the old carousel, wondering if it had working lights, when Joonie hugged me from behind. I tried to turn to face him, but he didn't let me. Actually, he didn't even let me look at his face. He had buried it on my back and wasn't giving in. Eventually I gave up and enjoyed the moment, stuffing my hands inside the pockets of my coat to try and warm them up a bit. The air was, indeed, chilly.

"Thank you. It's the best date ever," Joonie whispered.

I smiled. "We only just got here."

Moments Lost

Time started moving incredibly fast. I thought I'd get bored, but surprisingly, it never happened. I was very much entertained by just watching Joonie do what he loved to do.

Sometimes Joonie would have difficulties with the camera settings because the weather was a bit unpredictable. He even cursed under his breath a couple of times, completely immersed in capturing the beauty of the place.

One moment it was full-on sunshine, and the next second a cloud would block the rays. Apparently the sudden changes made capturing the atmosphere a bit harder. Or that's what Joon told me. I knew next to nothing about photographing with manual settings. He rambled on about things called "aperture" and "shutter speed," which all blew right over my head. I did make the effort to try and keep up with him as we explored the amusement park, though.

We found a lot of interesting things on our way.

There was an old, crooked piano, left to rot out in the open. Surprisingly enough, all the keys were still intact. Well, somewhat intact. The sight pulled my heartstrings; it would take a very cold person to mistreat a musical instrument that badly. Joonie tried to play a little, but the sound was horrendous and many of the keys didn't work or got stuck.

I got a heart attack when we were exploring the castle-like building in the far corner of the park, as my foot went through the rotten wooden floor. I tried to convince Joonie to get out of the building as it clearly wasn't safe, but he just laughed at me. Then he leaned to one of the walls and it gave in, so he finally listened to me and we agreed to stay out of the buildings.

When we had gone around the park once, it was already a little over two o'clock in the afternoon. While Joonie was photographing the old carousel, I picked up our bags where we had left them at the main gate. Yoo-suk and Min-ho were still at their card games and only nodded to me as I passed by. Apparently it was slow around here.

After picking out the best-preserved picnic table over at the main square, I hunted down some pre-made salads from our cooler and set them on the table together with a couple of bottles of soda. I practically had to rip the camera out of Joonie's hands and drag him to the table, in order to get him to focus on eating, at least for a moment.

For the whole time, Joonie gabbed on and on about the pictures he had already taken, how awesome they were. I couldn't help but get excited together with him when he showed me some pics. Now, even if I knew nothing about photography, I could still recognize a great pic. And to me, every single one of his photos were downright masterpieces. Call me biased if you want, but they really were good.

When he asked if he could photograph me, my heart sank. But as I had already predicted that would eventually happen, and I'd get to photograph Joonie in turn, I gave up with just a few complaints. Besides, the results could be great content for our Twitter and Instagram accounts.

Joonie was super hyped up. He chomped down the lunch and dragged me to the carousel in the middle of the park. He made me do some insane poses and all, but as he was having so much fun I couldn't help but have a great time myself.

We continued to circle around the park for the second time. This time, though, we were taking turns on photographing each other. A couple of times we even used the tripod and a remote shutter to take some photos of the two of us together, fooling around on the rusty, fallen apart rides.

By the time six in the evening rolled around, exhaustion hit me, and we still had a lot of food in the cooler. Thankfully, Joonie agreed when I suggested we sit and eat. We plopped to on the same table we'd used for lunch and started eating the sandwiches. Joonie went through the pics he'd taken again, occasionally showing me one or two.

When we finished eating, the sky had a thick blanket of clouds, not even a single ray of sunshine getting through it. And it started to darken, slowly but steadily. The old chap who owned the park, lurked around in the corner of my eye. He nodded curtly when I met his gaze, and I knew it was time. I smiled at the thought that this clearly wasn't his first time on the rodeo.

"Joonie...I want to show you something," I said softly.

He lifted his gaze from the preview screen of the cam. "What?"

"Just come here for a moment. And leave the camera behind."

He nodded, though reluctantly, left the cam on the table, and stood up. I took his hand and dragged him to the dead center of the main square. When we stopped, he raised his eyebrows at me questioningly but kept his mouth shut. Gently, I turned him around to face the carousel and covered his eyes with my own.

"No peeking," I whispered to his ear, and he shivered lightly.

Everything around us lit up. There were even more lights around than I had ever dared to imagine. Every single one of the light bulbs on the carousel worked, but that wasn't the only ride that had working lights. The bushes and trees all around us had lights too, which I hadn't predicted or noticed at all.

I was mesmerized by the sight that momentarily, I forgot Joonie wasn't watching yet. I quickly took my hands off his face and stuffed them into my pockets. Wondering what his reaction to the lights would be, I stepped to his right side and glanced at his face.

He was staring at the lights of the carousel with widened eyes and mouth hanging agape.

"It's beautiful," he said when he recovered enough.

"I know."

He glanced around, first to the left and then to the right. His eyes were glistening, and if I looked close enough, I could see a teardrop stuck to his lower lashes. He quickly blinked that away when he noticed me staring and turned his gaze down.

"What exactly do you want from me, Tae?" he asked with such a quiet voice I nearly didn't hear it.

I lifted his chin up with my hand and waited for his eyes to land on mine.

"I want all of you. I want to call every single inch of you mine. Sometime in the future, I want to wake up right next to you every morning, just like today. I want to take you on dates, buy you gifts for your birthday, and travel the world together.

"I want to be on stage together with you and our fans. I want to write songs to you, and I want you to sing them right back at me with that out-of-this-world voice of yours. I want you to be there with me when we receive awards, and also when we're inevitably going to flop. And then I want you to be there with me when we get back up. When we're old, retired, and have our own place, I want us to hang all the pictures on the walls of our home we've taken together starting from today's pics."

A single tear rolled down his cheek, which I wiped away with my thumb and smiled, hoping it was a tear of joy instead of sorrow.

"You've decided then?" he asked after a long and strained silence of staring each other in the eyes.

"Joonie, I think I already decided five months back. I'm sorry it took me so long to realize it."

He sighed and then chuckled. "Yeah, it took you long enough. And for the record, I've been yours from that day forward...though you'll need to work on the blanket stealing habits before I let you anywhere near my bed ever again."

I laughed out loud before grabbing his waist and pulling him close. A lone snowflake landed on his nose, and we both looked up for a brief moment to watch the beginning of a snowfall. I swear the air contained some kind of magic that sizzled around us, making my heart pound annoyingly loud in my chest. A fluttering feeling settled to the bottom of my stomach when I turned my gaze back to Joonie's face. A little while longer he lowered his eyes too. I cupped his neck and pulled his face closer ever so slowly, and he parted his lips invitingly while closing his eyes. Just before my lips reached his, I opened my mouth to speak. "Joonie, I think I'm in l—"

"Hey, guys! It's getting dark and cold around here. I think we should head back," Min-ho yelled somewhere from behind the carousel, effectively cutting me off.

We jumped away from each other, and the magical moment we had, came into a sudden halt. I took a deep breath to get my annoyance of the interruption in check. Just as I was starting to yell at the guy that I didn't give a fuck, Yoo-suk appeared, hit him to the back of his head, and dragged the guy right back towards the entrance, shouting apologies to our way.

Didn't make any difference whether he apologized or not. The moment was lost.

Taken for Granted

In the distance, I heard Yoo-suk go on lecturing the new guy about not disturbing the clients if it wasn't absolutely necessary. Joonie went unfazed. He danced and laughed and ran for a short while, enjoying the slow snowfall to his heart's content. Well, before he remembered the camera and started to take more pictures. I followed him from a short distance, smiling.

Sure, I was pissed that the perfect moment for saying what I had in mind had been cut short...but the day had been so perfect otherwise, that one little mishap couldn't possibly ruin the whole thing. I'd get plenty of other chances to say the words to Joonie.

The air got chillier every passing second. My fingers started to numb and rubbing them together didn't help. When the little clouds that formed in the air when we exhaled grew thicker, I decided heading back home wouldn't be such a bad idea after all.

"Joonie, wanna head home?" I hollered, making him stop in his tracks.

It took me by a bit of a surprise that he immediately agreed to it. After gathering our things, we headed to the main entrance together. We both had a smile on our lips, and it was absolutely and utterly perfect.

As soon as we reached the gate, Min-ho apologized to us formally and bowed his head, while Yoo-suk stood beside him and supervised.

"It's alright, we should head home anyway," I said, though I did want to ask the guy if he was sure he had chosen the right profession. If just a few hours of waiting was beyond him, this would soon become a very boring job. Because it could get worse. And often was. That was the reason we were paying them huge amounts of money. Well, okay, maybe for the risking their lives factor, but that rarely ever actually happened.

Joonie just nodded curtly and scurried inside the SUV. Yoo-suk and I put our things in the trunk; I left a few more bills for the old chap who looked after the place. One by one, all the lights of the old amusement park shut down, and the air became thicker.

It was eerily silent when we started our trip back home.

Joonie was oddly quiet, too, on the backseat next to me. He was staring out the window, trying to warm his hands by rubbing them together. There wasn't exactly that much to see in the dark.

"What's wrong?" I asked softly.

He turned to look at me with a sad look on his face but then turned his gaze right back out the window when his eyes started glistening for the second time that night. "Nothing... I—I just wish I could tell my mom about today."

Right.

Joonie's parents were both dead. They died in a car accident a few years back. Actually, it was six years back, almost to date. I remembered how broken Joonie had been for months after the accident, as if it was only yesterday. He never talked about them much, but I knew they had been close. And he was an only child too, so he didn't have any relatives left around since his parents had moved from China before he was born. I guessed that, for Joonie, GRiD was more than just a group of friends making music together. It was his only family. But we didn't make him miss his late parents any less, understandably so.

I remembered the funeral too, since it had been just Joonie by himself, letting the wind pick up their ashes and carry them to the Han river. I had been there, but only as a driver. I remembered watching him from a distance, while he stood by the riverbank for two hours straight before finally letting them go.

It was way before we got huge. Looking back, I realized we had taken it for granted, being able to be in public so freely.

"Well, they live in the Han river now, right? Maybe we could stop there on the way home?" I asked.

Joonie continued to stare out the window. After a while, I started to think it had been a mistake to even suggest such a silly thing. But eventually, Joonie finally spoke. "That would be nice."

Yoo-suk glanced at me through the rear-view mirror. I nodded, and he nodded back. Shortly after, he curved the SUV close to a bridge and we hopped off together with Joonie and Min-ho. Yoo-suk went ahead and parked the car close by and followed us. We walked the short way to the riverbank, and I stopped at the first bench that we encountered beside the sidewalk.

"Do you want me to come with you, or is this private?" I asked, when Joonie didn't answer, I added, "I don't mind either way."

"If you don't mind waiting, I think I want to do this alone..." he said, smiling apologetically. "It won't take long."

"Alright."

I sat on the bench together with Yoo-suk. When Joonie got out of the hearing range, he stopped, but he was still well visible so Yoo-suk didn't need to follow him. Min-ho paced around for a short while but eventually settled down as well and started playing a game with his phone.

My mind started to wander. I missed Gran. She was aging pretty fast, and I sensed she wouldn't be with us much longer. No matter how much she insisted she was fine, I didn't buy it. Not one bit. There was something withering her body from the inside out, and it made me anxious. I pulled out my phone and dialed her number. I had a few minutes to kill.

"Hello, it's Gang Eon-ju speaking," Gran answered after a few beeps, sounding awfully formal.

"Hey," I started. I had forgotten to give her my new number apparently, as Joe had decided we all had to change numbers. "It's Tae-joon."

"Oh, hello dear, what's on your mind this evening?" she asked with a soft and fragile sounding voice.

It broke my heart, but I played along. "Nothing much. I went on a date today."

"That's wonderful. You finally found someone?" She sounded so happy for me. Cheerful, even.

"Yeah. Though I found this person a while ago. It took me a while to see it, though." My mind kept repeating all the beautiful memories I made with Joonie that day. Even I started to wonder what took me so long to notice the spark between us.

"That's great. It's that beautiful boy—Joon-seok I believe was his name—right?"

I froze in shock and couldn't mutter out a single word. My mouth hung agape, and my heart stopped beating.

"Hello? Are you still there Tae-joon dear?" Gran asked after a short while.

"Yeah...yeah, I'm still here," I managed to choke out just barely. "And yes, I was on a date with Joonie."

Gran let out a chiming laugh on the other end of the line. "No need to get so shy, Tae dear. It's not that hard to see the connection. I have the internet now, remember?"

Right. Fanservice.

"Not all the things you see in there are true, you know?"

Gran just laughed at that. "Well, be sure to take him here one day so I can meet him in person. Sometime soon, I don't have that much time left, you know."

My heartbeat kicked up. Was she finally going to admit there was something wrong? The line remained silent, so I had to ask, "Why would you say that? Is something wrong?"

"Oh, no. Don't you worry. I'm as good as ever. I've got to hang up now though—Ye-rin's here. Bye!" Gran said and hung up abruptly.

I stared at the phone in my hand for a long while, dumb-founded. If anything, Gran avoiding the topic made me even more suspicious. The damn woman had always been too stubborn for her own good. Unfortunately, I didn't have the power to do much else than hope she received the best treatments for whatever illness she was clearly suffering from.

My thoughts were cut by the sound of approaching footsteps. A smile curved my lips upwards as soon as I lifted my eyes and was met with Joonie's grinning expression.

"You ready?" I asked.

"Yes, let's go home."

I loved the whole concept of going home with Joonie wholeheartedly.

Unfortunately, Chris was already there when we arrived. It meant that my date with Joonie was officially over. With a wordless agreement that only took one glance at each other, we decided we would keep quiet about us for now.

Joonie didn't seem to mind though; he just started shoving the pictures he had taken on Chris' face, still excited about the place. Chris promised to put some of them to our Twitter and Instagram accounts sometime.

All the intimacy and closeness between Joonie and me was completely gone as soon as we arrived home. But the sparks that seemed to surround us both neither faded nor disappeared. Joonie made us all some light snacks, and after we had chatted a bit with Chris, we both headed to our own rooms.

As soon as I closed the door behind me, my phone notified me of a new text. A huge grin spread to my lips when I opened it, and it was from Joonie.

Thank you for today. I had a great time.

After a long shower and a few minutes of just scrolling through the news, I fell asleep with a smile on my face I couldn't have erased even if I wanted to.

Lip Biting Thing

Sunday went by in a flash. Minjae barged in the kitchen early in the morning, panicking about the choreos for the music videos. Cutting short my nice and quiet breakfast with Joonie, I might add. Minjae was known for the last-minute rehearsals, so by no means did it came as a surprise to us. Still sucked, though.

Plus, this time, it was way worse than ever before. He had decided to make a last-minute change to the already complex bridge part before the last chorus of "Mad Love." While I admitted it looked way better than the original choreography and thus didn't complain, the whole day was hell for me. At least I wasn't alone in struggling with the dancing, for once.

When we finally got it down enough that Minjae was happy about the outcome, around nine in the evening, I was pretty sure I wasn't the only one that crashed straight to bed and fell asleep in a nanosecond. I was so exhausted I didn't even have any dreams.

My alarm clock woke me up at six in the morning. A quick breakfast later, Joonie drove us out of the house. It was barely seven.

The ride to LBR Entertainment's headquarters was a very quiet one. I didn't trust myself behind the wheel, as I still felt completely worn out, so Joe drove. Minjae looked like he hadn't slept one minute during the night. Do was practically sleeping the whole way, as was Chris. Joonie yawned every five minutes while his glassed up eyes looked out the window, but I bet he saw nothing.

Once we reached the HQ, Joonie ushered us downstairs to the mock-up stage hall. I was too tired to even glance at the props. Instead, I just followed Joonie like a zombie to one of the locker rooms which had been turned into a temporary dressing room. Complete with two separate changing cubicles and stations with gigantic vanity mirrors, two tables, and armchairs. Minjae, Do, and Chris went to the locker room next to ours, which I predicted looked somewhat the same.

I practically slept through the whole hair and make-up ordeal. Loitering on the armchair, only opening and closing my eyes whenever the make-up artist auntie asked. The brush swipes near my eyes irritated the hell out of my eyeballs, but I tried my best to ignore the discomfort. The stylists and concept designers barged in around an hour through that and started suggesting changes that would go well with the concept of today's filming: "Mad Love."

When I was told I was somewhat ready, I opened my eyes and nearly didn't recognize myself. They had made my eye make-up dark and my skin tone one or two tones lighter than it normally was. I didn't get to admire the hard work of the noonas for long, even though they had miraculously turned my face more handsome than I had ever thought was possible, as the stylists instantly ushered me to one of the changing cubicles along with the dreaded garment bag that had been hanging at one of the racks beside the back wall.

Unable to spot Joonie anywhere, I assumed he was already dressing at his cube right next to me. Behind my own curtain, I stared at the clothes for a full five minutes, gathering strength to start making my way into the tight leather pants that I *so* hadn't been looking forward to wearing. I heard the others started to gather their things to move them somewhere, probably closer to the props for the purpose of having the equipment at hand for touch-ups during the filming.

I sighed and started to change into the clothes. After all, I had promised Joonie I'd wear them, as disturbing as they were. It took me forever, but eventually, I made my way inside the pants. Internally, I praised myself for remembering to shave Saturday evening as I didn't need to worry about the hair getting stuck to the zipper. I only had to carefully stuff my dick and balls somewhere in order to get the pants closed. After yanking the barely existing shirt on top, I exited my cubicle with a long and relieved sigh. There was no one else left other than me in the room, and Joonie, who sounded like he was frustrated with something over at his own cubicle.

When I walked closer, Joonie asked, "Tae, are you done?" His voice showed great distress.

"I guess. What's up?"

"Mind helping me for a moment? I can't reach some of the buckles on my back."

I yanked the curtain of Joonie's cubicle open. "What buckl—" I started, but immediately froze to the spot with my eyes widening to the incredibly hot sight in front of me.

Joonie was wearing similar leather pants like me...and damn the pants snug close, enhancing the perfect curves of his behind. To top it off, he didn't have anything covering his upper body. Well, in the normal sense anyway. Instead of a shirt, he was wearing some kind of leather harness that covered absolutely nothing. The thing was held together by buckles on his back, and he had gotten the bottom two and one from the top buckled, but he couldn't reach the ones that were supposed to be closed between his shoulder blades.

I gulped involuntarily at the sight. Was this man about to be the end of me?

My dick twitched inside the extremely tight pants. It almost hurt because there really wasn't any space inside the pants for any kind of movement. I had a hard enough time just swallowing.

My eyes met Joonie's through the mirror. He was holding one of his eyebrows up. When my eyes moved to his lips, he bit the lower one. And that right there was the only thing that made me go over the edge, right to insanity. In my sudden lust-filled haze, I shuffled my way inside the small cubicle, turned him around, and backed him against one of the makeshift walls before yanking the curtain shut behind me.

"You have no idea what that lip-biting thing does to me..."

Joonie just smirked at me and the next second his lips were on my lips. My lips were hungry as they had waited to kiss him all the way from Saturday when we were interrupted rudely on our little date. Joonie's lips started to move with mine just as feverishly. He rolled his groin against mine, and I felt a low groan erupt from somewhere deep inside my chest...then there was a sharp pain on my lower lip, as Joonie bit it.

I was so ready to do much more than kiss right then and there, but (un)fortunately, I snapped back to reality when the sound of the door cracking open reached my ears. Both Joonie and I froze to the spot, trying to breathe evenly, even though we both were panting.

"You guys ready soon?" Chris asked from the door.

Joonie looked at me with wide eyes, but I shook my head at him since I didn't trust my voice. He rolled his eyes at me, cleared his throat as silently as he possibly could and hollered back, "Yeah, I'll be done in a minute."

As soon as we heard the door close, we both let out a long breath of ultimate relief. I stepped out of Joonie's cubicle and rubbed my head to clear it a bit. He still needed to get the buckles on his back done, so trying not to look at anything other than the buckles, I somehow managed to get them secured without starting up our make-out session all over again.

We both needed a long minute to calm down, and I couldn't even look at Joonie's direction if I was going to face the others. I needed to have a serious talk with Joonie about his habit of biting the damn perfect lower lip of his. After getting somewhat calmed down, we slowly made our way to the hall where the props were put together. The others were already doing some warmups since we were starting with the choreographed parts. We quickly joined them.

The props looked a bit weird. There were some green screens here and there, and the rest was just some concrete walls. The place kind of resembled a parking hall…which it was supposed to be…but only barely looked it with all the weirdly placed green screens.

Jiwoo was supervising the whole ordeal on the side lines. My eyes lingered on her like they had lingered before, her bouncy red curls, tiny waist… Yet, I wasn't even nearly as mesmerized with her looks as I had been before. I followed her gaze and it landed straight to Kim Nam-gi, the photographer. I assumed he was here to take some concept photos. Wait. Didn't she mention they were dating? I seriously needed to catch up with Jiwoo sometime soon.

While I warmed up and stretched—well, as much as I could in the leather pants—I glanced at the others' outfits. They were all wearing some very disturbing clothes. The only thing that brought together our styles was the tight leather pants that everyone wore, but we all had different kinds of tops. I had the nearly non-existent top, Joonie had the harness, Minjae was wearing something that resembled a straitjacket, Do was wearing a studded leather vest, and Chris had absolutely nothing covering his upper body. Not even a harness.

This "Mad Love" was certainly different from the delicate one that Minjae and Do had performed at the Citi Field back in New York. Yeah, we had made the music sexy, but even the concept team had outdone themselves this time for the music video.

The whole day after that was pure torture. And it wasn't even the fact that it was just dancing the whole day, going over the choreographs at least a million times per each set. Or even the fact that the leather pants weren't even remotely comfy wear, not to even mention the sweating in odd places. I also had to watch Joonie in that damn sexy harness the whole day. No wonder he had hinted that I was lucky to at least have a shirt to wear.

I had a feeling the week would turn out to be extremely long.

Pure Torture

And long the week was. Extremely long. At first, it was three full days, from 6 in the morning to 9 or 10 at night, of pure torture with the filming of "Mad Love." Let's just say it was...interesting. Watching Joonie all-day-everyday wearing next to nothing. Particularly that one scene, where they suspended him from the ceiling, the spotlights making him seem otherworldly beautiful. Thankfully, my awed expression ended up being exactly what they wanted, so it was done in one take.

Then it was a couple of days full of filming Joonie's former solo that turned into a group piece. Thankfully, the second one was slightly easier to bear since Joonie was all covered up with the suit, so I no longer had to worry about sudden hard-ons during the filming.

Every night we were all so exhausted that we ate something light and collapsed into bed.

By the time Friday afternoon came around, and the director finally announced wrap, the wave of relief that washed over us all was intense. Do instantly unbuttoned the top two buttons of his shirt. Minjae shrugged off his jacket and tossed it to the corner of the last prop set. Chris popped open a bottle of champagne while Joonie and I shared a longing gaze.

Speaking of whom, Joonie bit his lip as soon as our eyes met.

Fuck, here we go again, I thought as my cock twitched. The lip-biting thing was getting old and fast. I, too, loosened a couple of buttons on my shirt. It was getting kind of hot. And not only because of dancing for the whole day.

Chris handed me a glass of champagne, and we toasted together with the whole staff before heading to shower and to change into our own clothes. We were all done in record time and straight away headed home with the SUV. Joonie ordered a whole bunch of all different kinds of carb-filled takeout with his phone on the way. Do-hyun asked Joe to raid the liquor store as well, so there was a short pitstop. Apparently the after party was taking place at our dorm.

When we finally arrived home, we gathered at our dining table. Waiting for the takeout to arrive, I handed everyone their preferred bottle of poison. Beer, soju, wine...you name it. Picking out a beer for myself, I made my way next to Joonie.

As exhausted as I was, the party mood still got to me pretty fast. Contrary to my usual reluctance to get drunk, I downed my beer in record time and instantly popped open another one. Then, I proceeded to stuff my plate full of all the greasiest foods I could find from the takeout containers that had arrived.

The dinner dragged on and was as loud as ever. Someone turned the music on, and then it got even louder. Minjae, Do, Chris, and Joe with some of our other staff were already well on their way of getting drunk by the time the clock hit eight and all others had left, but surprisingly enough Joonie stayed somewhat sober with me.

Instead of getting drunk, he had found something else to entertain himself. And that was torturing me. At first, he was only brushing his foot against mine under the table, so lightly I thought it wasn't on purpose. But when I moved my leg and his followed, I knew he was up to something. He masked it well though. When I glanced at his face, he was confidently sporting a poker face and focused on a calm, collected conversation with Chris and Joe.

I tried to focus on my beer, but it was nearly impossible. I even jumped a bit when Joonie's hand landed on my thigh under the table.

"Hello? Earth to Tae-hyung?" Minjae suddenly asked from my left side and even waved his hand in front of my face. Another heart attack.

I blinked a couple of times to pull myself back to reality. From the corner of my eye, I noticed Joonie smirking. Trying to ignore him, I turned my attention towards Minjae. "Yeah?"

Minjae just shook his empty glass. I rolled my eyes at him before pouring him a new cup of soju and reached over the table to give him another beer too. I nearly dropped the bottle though, because right when I was handing it to Minjae, Joonie's hand on my thigh moved up an inch. Minjae raised his eyebrows at my weird behavior but thankfully forgot it as soon as Do distracted him by taking him to the couch to cuddle. I took a deep breath and closed my eyes for a second to try and relax, but Joonie had—again— some other ideas, as his hand "slipped" an inch higher once again. It was now dangerously close to my already swelling cock that was practically pulsing with pure need.

Fine. Two can play this game I suppose.

Though Joonie had teased me through the whole damn week, this time, he had gone too far. He sure as hell wasn't getting away with it any longer.

I glanced around. Everyone else was distracted with their own activities. Minjae and Do were still on the couch, and Chris was practically passing out at the other end of the table. Joe was leaving, not even bothering to try and fake being sober as he staggered towards the hallway, Min-ho in tow. Faking to stretch, I moved my right arm over Joonie and slipped it under his loose white shirt on his lower back while taking a sip of my beer with my other hand. Joonie gasped and shot me a stabbing glare before squeezing my thigh again. But as I was prepared for that this time, I just tugged my fingers under the waistband of his jeans and let them rest casually on his perfectly, perky ass cheek.

Joonie blushed and chewed his lower lip with eyes hazing up.

"You have to stop with the lip biting," I whispered softly to his ear.

He shivered. "Yeah?"

"You're such a tease...I hope you know how dangerous that could potentially be." I had no shame in smirking at him. He took a sharp, shaky breath and turned his darkening eyes down so low his long eyelashes casted a shadow. I may or may have not let my lips hover near his ear a second longer; it was absolutely necessary to get the point across.

Joonie...he didn't buy it though. The damn shameless bitch—my shameless bitch—turned to look me dead in the eyes and made a point by biting the damn lip. Slowly.

Everything around us disappeared.

At that point, I didn't give two shits about if anyone found out about us or not. They were wasted and wouldn't most likely remember a thing come tomorrow morning. So, I just grabbed Joonie's wrist and dragged him straight to my room. After opening the door wide open, I practically pushed him inside and followed suit. He giggled for my impatience the whole way...well, up until I slammed the door shut behind me, pushed him against the wall, and shut him up by smashing my lips against his.

We both lost it. I let my hands start to roam on his feverishly hot skin underneath the loose shirt. Having craved for it the whole week, my body demanded to feel more, to taste more, of him. Getting greedier every passing second, every passing touch, I let loose.

Joonie's response was immediate. Urgent, even. Vaguely in my lustful haze, I felt his fingers that started fiddling with the hem of my shirt, trying to tug it out from under the jeans' waistline. I might've helped him if I hadn't been so busy trying to get his shirt off at the same time.

Finally, I came into my senses right when he started yanking my belt open.

"Wait!" I grabbed his wrists to stop him meddling with my belt and put some distance between us.

"What?!" he hissed back, stepping closer again.

Taking another step back, I held him at an arm's length away from me, otherwise I would not have been able to hold myself back. And there was a conversation we had to have before going any further.

"Uhh...it's just that—um—I've never done this with a guy before," I admitted. Not that he didn't already know that, but just to kind of apologize, for not knowing shit about this whole thing.

The wicked smirk he gave me was amazing. "Where did all that confidence disappear to?" He crossed his arms over his chest when I released his wrists.

"Well, what if I hurt you or something? I have no idea how this works. Sue me!" I nearly yelled back, probably fueled by my horniness and frustration for not knowing what the hell I was doing.

He looked like he was holding in a good laugh while he raised one of his eyebrows and looked at me with an amused expression. "You won't hurt me."

"How can you be so sure?"

"I *have* done this before," he said, rolling his eyes once again.

"Right..." I said, my brain having a hard time comprehending what he had just said. "Wait, what?"

"You heard me."

I didn't say anything and just continued to stare at him, getting a bit sceptical—I mean let's face it, when on earth would he have had time to find a gay person in Korea to have sex with, apart from our little gayest-boyband-in-history? And I highly doubted he'd done it with Chris and DoMin had been a thing forever.

Joonie wasn't fazed. "Did you really think I could walk into the army, looking like this"—he gestured towards the wholesome finesse that was himself—"and walk out, still a virgin? So many deprived and eager men around..."

"Huh..." Now that sounded hot. And reckless. So I scolded him while leaning closer to him again, pressing him between me and the wall. "You could've ended in prison. A bit risky, don't you think?"

"Maybe I like to live a bit dangerously," he said and wrapped his arms around my waist. "Now, how about we continue where we left off?"

There were no excuses left. No reasons to hold back. So, when I kissed him again, it got a little rough, but Joonie kept up with me magnificently. In fact, it seemed like he enjoyed it. A lot. At least based on the small whimpers and moans he let out while I devoured his lips...sucking, biting, teasing...

There were no sparks around us this time. No weird fluttery feelings in my stomach. No small tingles going up my spine. All of that felt absolutely nothing compared to these new, almost explosive, feelings.

It was like we burst into scorching hot flames, together.

On the way to the bed, we stumbled into the discarded clothes that were flying everywhere as well as to our own damn feet. But eventually, we made it naked and next to my bed. After briefly admiring each other's naked bodies, we were all over each other again, eager to get to the point. It was clear not one of us wanted to prolong this any longer.

At one point, I intended to brush my hand through Joonie's hair, but it got caught and I accidentally yanked his head back. At first, he gasped, but then a loud moan escaped his lips and his eyes closed. It seemed as though he actually did enjoy a little roughness. It wasn't just my imagination. Testing the theory, I wrapped my other hand around his waist to keep him still, and then fisted a bunch of his long hair and pulled ever so slightly harder. He moaned louder and grabbed my hips for support, his hard-on pressing against mine.

A wide, wicked grin spread to my lips. It was a triumphant moment when I realized I had found out something new about Joonie, something I bet not many people knew. And it turned me on even more to suddenly possess the knowledge that he, undoubtedly, wasn't as vanilla as I had initially thought. Though admittedly, I should've guessed it…

"Now would be the right time to bite that lip, or else we're going to get an audience based on how loud you're being," I muttered against the soft skin on his neck before sucking it.

He let out another gasp, but he held back a moan this time. I let go of his hair and his waist. Losing the support, he staggered a bit before falling on the bed. I climbed on top of him, and we continued the impatient dance of passion, both trying to feel everything at once.

It was a lustful mess of tangled limbs and rough touches, both trying to get the upper hand of pleasing the other. Joonie used some dirty tactics, such as making me distracted by biting his lip, then straddling me or going for my groin either with his hands or even with his wet mouth.

As I was way stronger than him, I could pry his hands away, flip us over, pin his wrists over his head, and watch him squirm while I brushed my fingertips over his sensitive nipples before gliding down, eventually reaching his shaft. Now *that* I knew how to operate—I had one of my own.

All in all, we were pretty equal.

I lost the last bits of patience as he whispered my name, almost pleadingly, right to my ear. Letting out a groan that I could no longer hold back, I reached over at the nightstand. But as I had no control whatsoever over the movement, the whole box ended up falling to the floor with a loud bang.

Joonie and I froze for a nano-second. But, as the music was still on and the volume so loud it reached my room, we both shrugged. Besides, now that the box was on the floor, it was way easier to grab the lube and a condom.

To top it off, the whole ruckus made my head clear up a bit to realize I probably couldn't just...shove it in and hope for the best?

I glanced at Joonie and then the condoms and the lube bottle in my hands, probably looking a bit lost. He just smiled at me while getting up to sit, before wrapping his hands behind my neck.

"You'll need to stretch me for a bit beforehand," he whispered. "You know...with your fingers."

That was clear enough for my dumb brain, instead of the vague things Do-hyun had told me the other day in my office what seemed like ages ago. I slowly laid him back on the mattress. After a few kisses over his neck and that incredibly sexy collarbone, he turned himself over under me. I showered his back with small pecks, but as I was already just so beyond aroused at that point, I quickly gave up with foreplay.

Joonie's whines that were begging me to "get to it," stopped at once and turned to silent whimpers as soon as I slid one of my lubed up fingers down his ass crack and started teasing his pucker. He started squirming under my grip, but I held him still easily. He gasped when I pushed the finger all the way in, with one swift movement, right past the tight ring.

Intrigued by his strong reactions to everything I did, I moved my finger inside him. Somehow, probably with just pure luck, I found this one spot that made him push his behind even harder against my hand. His eyes squeezed shut and he bit his lip harder than ever before. I pulled the finger back so I could hit the spot from a better angle and then pushed it back in, putting more pressure on the spot. He could no longer hold back a moan, but he muffled it by biting down the pillow.

Interesting.

I let go of his hand which I had been holding against his back to keep him still to check if he was uncomfortable, or if it was beginning to be too rough. But instead of squirming away or cursing me to the deepest pits of hell, he just tugged his hand under the pillow and arched his back, lifting his behind a bit upwards to give me an even better access. I took it as permission to continue and inserted another finger. He clutched the pillow harder and the moan that erupted from his throat was music to my ears.

While stretching his ass like that a bit longer, occasionally brushing against the magic spot that made him squirm, I rolled a condom on and lubed up my cock with my other hand. It was a hassle, but I got it done. After all, it wasn't my first time with sex, just first time with...Joonie. He whined when I took my fingers out of his hole but quickly caught on what I was planning when I knelt between his legs and lifted his hips up. He got upon his knees as I lined my cock with his entrance.

Thankfully, Joonie took control from there. After I wrapped my hand around his waist to keep him steadier, he started gliding down on my dick at his own pace. He gasped at the exact same time I did when my cock's glans made it past the tight ring. I practically saw stars when all of his tight ass squeezed my dick just right, sending a fierce wave of pleasurable vibrations through my whole body.

He let himself get used to the size of me for a little while. I took it as an opportunity to kiss his neck and shoulders, while teasing the ever so perky nipples of his with my fingertips. Then when he started moving—carefully at first—I tried to move in sync with him. We found the best rhythm in no time, so slow and steady we rocked towards our goal. I buried my face to the nook of his neck, supporting his weight with my body as much as I could while he leaned back.

I was getting closer and closer to the edge, and I tried to slow down a bit to make the absolute bliss last longer. Joonie had other ideas though, as he grabbed his leaking cock and started bouncing on mine faster. Wrapping my arms around his tiny waist and closing my eyes, I tried to slow him down a bit, honestly just to hold back as long as I could. Needless to say, I was failing miserably. Thankfully Joonie came all over his hand just when I was about to cum and his spasming muscles around my cock made me fall over the edge together with him.

Both panting hard, we separated and crashed to lay on our backs, next to each other. The tips of our fingers touched, like in a silent agreement that we just couldn't separate completely, even though both of us were thoroughly spent. Closing my eyes, I tried to catch my breath and calm down my racing pulse after getting rid of the condom.

A small eternity later, I felt like I got a grip on my life again. Opening my eyes, I turned my head to face Joonie. He was staring right back at me, and we both started laughing when our eyes met.

"Well, that was some messy-as-fuck sex," I said when we had both calmed down. "I promise I'll get better at this."

Joonie just chuckled at me in response, closed his eyes, and nodded. I kept staring as I couldn't rip my eyes off his beautiful face. Joonie was way wilder in bed than I had ever even dared to imagine. I loved it.

It would've been awkward if he had been completely inexperienced while I had fucked around quite the lot in the past, though with the opposite sex. That, however, had shown me I wouldn't need to fuck around again with anyone else, as I already sensed he would be all I'd need from now on. And probably more.

Even though I had evolved completely from a straight, no-romance kind of guy to a lovesick, definitely-bending kind of guy in such a short time span...I still pretty much felt like myself. My mind started to make new plans and set new goals. This time over, they all had everything to do with Joonie.

I was eager to find out exactly what got him going, in hopes of someday being able to make love with him without being rushed and messy…and just generally impatient. I wanted to know exactly what made him feel good, both in and out of bed.

I loved every inch of his body. He was just the right fit for me. I couldn't understand how I ever thought having sex with someone who also has a dick would be weird. I had been more turned on than ever in my life, counting the wet dreams of my youth. I couldn't understand how I had once thought that only women were attractive, as Joonie was the definition of an attractive person. And he had been right there beside me the whole time.

Still, I couldn't hold back an eye-roll when he bit his lip again.

"Can you please stop that now. You already got what you wanted," I said, but felt a smile make its way on my lips. "Plus, I already warned you it's dangerous."

He opened his eyes and turned to look at me straight in mine. "And I already mentioned liking dangerous things."

I felt my already spent cock to twitch back to life in a hot second. Bewildered, I turned to my side to have a closer look at his smirking face.

"You seriously can't be ready to go again, right?"

"Oh, trust me handsome...we've only just started." He pushed me to lay on my back, reached out for another condom and ripped the foil open with his teeth before straddling me.

Perfect Breakfast

The satisfaction lasted until morning. Even as I leisurely flipped some American-style pancakes in our kitchen the next morning and felt a pair of hands wrap around my waist from behind.

"Good morning," Joonie said, tightened his grip and laid his chin on my shoulder. "That smells wonderful."

I leaned against him and tilted my head back, closing my eyes. "Yeah? Well, they're gonna smell burnt in a minute if you keep distracting me," I said and flipped the pancake over. "Why don't you sit somewhere and wait while I finish these?"

"I'd rather stand, thank you very much." He chuckled, while he let go of my waist and turned around to get some of the coffee I had already brewed.

I grinned. "Rough night?"

"You could say that," he said nonchalantly, though there was a slight smile on his lips.

I lifted the pancake I was frying with a spatula and placed it on top of the others before pouring some more batter onto the pan and turning to look at Joonie over my shoulder. He was only wearing one of my loose black button-ups. It was way too big for him, as it hung off one of his shoulders and reached halfway down his thighs. I wondered if he wore anything underneath.

"Too rough?" I asked, forcibly turning my eyes back to the pan and flipped the new pancake over.

"Nah, it was just perfect," he said, and I heard him tiptoe beside me. "I like it rough."

"Do you now…" I glanced at his face. How far could I take this next time? "Do we need a safeword?"

"Oh, you want to do something real twisted then?" Joonie replied and laughed. "Fine. I'm up for it. How about…hmm…red?"

"You know I was kidding, right?" I said, smiling, and added another pancake to the plate.

"I was not." Joonie winked. He landed a quick peck on my cheek before laying a mug of steaming hot coffee with just a hint of milk on the counter and scurrying off.

I was left looking after him, dumbfounded. Not going to lie, I loved his boldness. So much I damn nearly forgot I was frying pancakes, until one of them started to burn and the smell reached my nose.

Soon enough, I lifted the last pancake from the pan. Taking another plate from the cupboard, I piled up some of the pancakes and poured a lot of syrup on top. Pancakes weren't a complete experience without milk, so I topped two glasses up and arranged all of that on a tray together with some utensils and my refilled coffee mug. With all that in tow, I headed back to my room.

Joonie was laying on my bed, back resting against the headboard. He was scrolling his phone with one hand while holding his coffee mug up with the other. He lifted his eyes from the phone right when I laid the tray over his lap. After putting the mug down on the tray, he carefully folded out the two stands that held the tray conveniently a bit above his lap so he wouldn't have to worry about knocking it over.

I sat down on the bed next to him, right in time to snag a bite off his fork of the chunk of pancake he'd carved out and was about to pop in his mouth. He just smiled at me and stuffed the whole thing in my mouth before carving another bit which he quickly popped in his own mouth.

We continued that way through the whole big-ass pile. I snagged every other bite, and while he stuffed some to his own mouth I focused on my coffee. In between, we sneaked in a couple of sweet kisses.

It was one of the most perfect breakfasts to ever exist.

That is, until my phone went off on the bedside table with Ye-rin's name flashing on the screen.

I completely froze. It couldn't have meant anything good if she was calling me. She'd never called me before, even though Gran made us exchange numbers the day I visited.

"What is it?" Joonie asked, his perfectly shaped eyebrows drawn together.

The trance of the perfect morning was broken. "I gotta take this."

I tapped the screen and lifted the phone to my ear with my hand shaking.

"Hello, is this Gang Tae-joon?" Ye-rin asked as soon as the call connected. Her voice broke midway. It couldn't possibly have been a good sign.

"Yes. Is Gran okay?"

Ye-rin sniffled almost inaudibly. "No. I think you better come to the hospital."

Unsolicited Advice

With my heart trying to pound off my chest, I rushed through the disinfectant smelling hallways as fast as I could without running. At least the receptionist said Gran had been moved from ICU to the ward already. That had to be good, right?

Right.

"Gang Eun-ju, Gang Eun-ju," I muttered under my breath.

I was trying to speed read the names on the sides of the doors while I passed. It felt like eternity before I reached a door that actually said, "Gang Eun-ju," along with three other names. Why didn't they give her a single room? They should've given her a single room.

One deep breath and I barged through the door. The room smelled like death—or maybe it was just me because none of the elderly ladies looked dead. They were all up and about, chatting loudly like women their age tend to do. The TV was also on, adding its own annoying noise into the mix.

The only irregularity in the whole room was Ye-rin who sobbed quietly in the corner next to Gran's bed.

"Tae-joon dear, what on earth are you doing here?" Gran asked once she spotted me.

I walked over to the side of her bed and took her hand in mine. It felt fragile and small inside my suddenly huge looking claw. Her skin was paper thin and pale. "Ye-rin called. How are you?"

Gran shot a pungent glance towards Ye-rin, who only started sobbing more loudly with her shoulders shaking and all.

"Did she now? I told her to not panic but I guess I should've known. One hysteric woman, she is."

"Don't try to avoid the topic," Ye-rin cried in between her sobs. "You've gotta tell him at this point!"

"Tell me what?"

Gran downright rolled her eyes. "Fine. Tae dear, let's take a walk in the garden, shall we?"

I couldn't do much else other than nod and grab Gran's wheelchair from the corner and help her sit in it. Ye-rin brought us a quilt, folded it on Gran's lap, and we were off.

The whole way to the inner yard was spent in silence, other than Gran giving me directions since I had no clue of where to wheel her. It broke my heart to notice that Gran knew the hospital so well, considering a few weeks back I hadn't even had the slightest clue that she was sick in the first place. My head was too numb and too frozen to even start asking all the questions that circled in an endless loop in my head.

What was happening? How sick was she? What could I have done to help her?

The garden was beautiful, adorned with lush green trees and bushes filled with beautiful flowers. A path going through it all led to a small artificial pond with a bench on the side.

I wheeled Gran next to the bench facing the pond. Gran ordered me to sit too, so I did while taking her hand in mine. It was cold.

"Are you receiving good care?" I asked to end the silence.

"Yes, yes…" she said dismissively. "I just collapsed, it's not that big of a deal."

"So, what's going on? When are you going home?"

Gran sighed and laid her other hand on top of mine. "Dear…I'm not going home again."

"Why not?" My voice cracked at the end.

"They're entering me to hospice care."

"What does that mean?" I couldn't even look at her face.

Gran, however, made me look at her by tugging my chin with her cold, shaky hand. She smiled a sad smile, one that was meant to console but what actually made me feel worse.

"It means it's my turn to go."

A single tear escaped the corner of my eye before I could stop it. I wiped it away aggressively and kneeled in front of Gran on the ground.

"Isn't there anything we can do?" I asked. There had to be something, *anything* I could do, other than just accept it like that. I grabbed her hands and squeezed. "I can get you the best doctors in the whole of Korea. Hell, I can even get you overseas if I have to. Let's just not give up yet, right?"

"Please, just stop," Gran pleaded. "I have aggressive bone cancer. There's nothing we can do, and quite frankly I'm tired. I'm ready to go."

I burst into tears, the wave of emotions crashing through me with such a force I collapsed to Gran's embrace and wept. I wept so hard I was shaking. All while Gran brushed my hair with her hand, muttering, "It's okay. You're going to be alright."

It must've been like five agonizingly long minutes before I could collect myself enough to stop shaking and wipe my face. I looked up at Gran who was still smiling down at me, staying strong through it all. At that moment, I knew I needed to stay strong too, if not for me then for her.

"Is there anything I can do to help you?" I finally asked. "Do you want a better room? I can look up facilities for...um...patients...at the end of their journey."

"Oh honey, thank you for that thought, but I have already chosen and they're moving me there tomorrow morning." She brushed my cheek with the back of her hand. "But there *is* one thing you could still help me with."

I didn't hesitate a second. "Anything."

"I would like to meet this Joonie you have been talking about."

By the next afternoon, I sat in the back seat of an SUV with Joonie beside me. He rubbed his hands on his jeans to remove the nervous sweat.

"It's going to be fine," I said.

"I know. It's just...isn't this kind of soon? To meet your family?"

Well, considering we only started dating like a week ago, yes. But... "It's not like we have a choice, if you want to meet her at all."

Joonie winced. "I'm sorry, I didn't think."

I took his hand and laced our fingers together. "It's okay. But I will say this: I'm glad you're here. I don't think I could do this without you in the first place."

Joonie smiled and squeezed my hand reassuringly. The gesture was everything to me. I was constantly *this close* to falling apart.

I had decided to stay strong for Gran, but I felt like I was going to fail miserably. I was almost at the brink of tears before Joe even curved the SUV to the front entrance of the hospital.

It was much better than the hospital in the city. Smaller, and on a beautiful little hill with an enormous park on the side. Still, my feet weighed a ton when I tried to get them to move towards the reception. I had never imagined having to visit a place like that. To be fair, no one probably did.

The nurse at the reception area pointed us to the park as soon as we asked to see Mrs. Gang Eun-ju, so we headed right back outside. It didn't take us long to spot Gran under a cherry tree. She was in her wheelchair, accompanied by a nurse and looking into the distance.

"Are you ready?" I asked Joonie, who nodded beside me.

"Sure," he said. "Let's go."

I shifted the rose bouquet to my other hand and took Joonie's hand in mine, earning a curious glance. But he never said anything, so I tugged his hand, and we walked the short distance to Gran.

She smiled as soon as she spotted us. The sight of the IV catheter in her hand made my stomach drop. Nevertheless, I handed her the bouquet which she laid on her lap and thanked me.

Joonie let go of my hand and bowed formally. "Annyeong haseyo, Mrs. Gang."

Gran laughed from the bottom of her heart. "Oh please, no need to be so stiff with me. I assume you're Joon-seok?"

"Yes," Joonie replied simply.

"Well, aren't you quite the sight, and just as beautiful live as on TV."

Joonie's eyes widened. "On TV?"

"Yes, I watch all of your concerts. I've seen a couple live as well, but my seat was very far away so that doesn't count."

"*All* of them?" Joonie asked and shot me a very panicked glance. "I hope you don't think I'm like that...off stage."

Gran laughed full-heartedly again. "Yes, all of them. Now, Tae dear, can you get us some coffee from the cafeteria? I'd like to get to know him better."

Joonie stared me down as if to say *"don't you dare leave me alone with her"* but Gran's wish was my command, so I left. Besides, the panicky look on Joonie's face was hilarious. I guess there were at least some situations where he wouldn't be as confident as usual. I loved to see that side of him too.

It didn't take me long to get the coffee, but I didn't return right away. Instead, I watched them from a distance for a little while. The nurse had left, and Joonie was pushing Gran around with the wheelchair. Looked like they got along very well after all.

I wondered if Joonie would one day win my Dad to his side just as easily. Better not to get my hopes up, though.

We spent the whole afternoon outside. I was only reminded of the fact that Gran was dying twice when the nurses brought her more painkillers. The doses were...quite something. I guess overdosing didn't matter much at that point.

Holy crap, that was a dark thought.

Oh well. At least it didn't look like she was in pain.

Eventually Gran started to look a little tired, so we wheeled her inside and found her room. It wasn't big, but at least it wasn't as impersonal as a regular hospital room. The nurses had even put the roses I'd brought in a vase in front of the window.

Once I had lifted Gran on her bed and covered her with a warm looking blanket, her eyelids started to droop. I would've spent the whole evening there if I could, but honestly it started to look like Gran really needed some rest instead of visitors.

So I said, "I guess we'll go for today."

Gran nodded. "Yes, I think that would be the best."

Then she turned to face Joonie and smiled. "Can I talk a little with my grandson, alone?"

Joonie gave her one of his famous big grins. "Of course. I'll wait outside."

I watched Joonie walk out the door before turning my attention back on Gran. Her eyes were gleaming.

"I like him," she said.

I smiled. "Of course you do. Everyone does."

"He's a good person."

"Yes, he is."

"And beautiful."

"I know. Get to the point, will you?"

There was a brief pause before Gran spoke again.

"I'm old," she started. "Which means I have the grounds to give you some unsolicited life advice. Plus, I'm dying."

"Please don't joke about that."

Gran let out a chiming laugh. "Now, *that* is where you're wrong. At this point in my life, I can do whatever I want."

Well, true. "Fine."

"But all jokes aside, I want you to take really good care of Joonie. No matter what, do you hear me?" she asked and pinched my cheek. "The path you've chosen won't be the easiest by default. But given your very public line of profession...I'm worried."

"Don't be. We'll be fine." I wondered how it was possible for Gran to make me smile even considering the...circumstances. But she did. Easily, even.

Gran, however, continued on as if I had said nothing. But with a more serious tone. "And I don't want you to come visit me here anymore."

I frowned. "Why not?"

"Because I want you to remember me how I was. Trust me, it'll be better this way," she said. "I'm going to be out for half of it and drugged into oblivion."

"Are you sure?"

"Yes."

There was a sudden lump in my throat I had a hard time swallowing. "I will miss you so much."

"I know, and I will miss you," Gran said, squeezing my hand. "But you have other people to keep you company. Fine people, like Joonie, even. That gives me peace."

I wiped the corner of my eye. "Yeah."

"I'm so proud of you, I hope you know that."

"I know."

My body had never felt as heavy as it was when I forced it to walk to the door. I couldn't help but take one last glance at Gran's fragile figure at the threshold. After all, I was never going to see her again. The thought alone broke me into a thousand little pieces.

Nice Reminder

If I had been able to fake being okay for Gran's sake, that facade didn't last long once we arrived back home. In fact, I completely collapsed in Joonie's arms right at the threshold. The poor thing had to haul my ass into a bed. Thankfully it turned out to be his bed. I wouldn't have had it any other way.

There I cried. Sobbed like a baby against Joonie's chest. For how long, I wasn't so sure. I completely lost all sense of time. I think the sun rose behind the sheer red curtains on Joonie's window once or twice.

When the tears ran out, I became numb. I could no longer cry, but I couldn't do much else either. My face was swollen, the skin around my eyes ached—the pain being a constant annoying reminder that I was not unconscious, unfortunately. Drifting in and out of sleep, I still registered that Joonie brought me food and forced me to eat, even if it was only spoonful at a time. Or forced me to drink. Had me change clothes.

I loved him. I loved him so much it hurt.

And I owed it to him to get my shit together. So slowly, I regained my sanity by watching him sleep, like a total creep. The way his plump lips glistened in the dark, the long pink hair spread all over his face…it was mesmerizing. His hand squeezed mine reassuringly every now and then, though he was in deep slumber.

I sighed, disentangled our limbs and hands, then forced my stiff body to sit, my back against the headboard. My eyelashes were all clumped together and crunchy when I rubbed my eyes, trying to force them fully open. Taking in my surroundings, I noticed my phone was on the bedside table, charging through the embedded wireless charger. The fact that Joonie had even thought about that swelled my heart to double its size.

The date on the screen told me I had been out for about three days. It was time to get moving. The showcase concert date was only a couple of weeks away. Surprisingly, there wasn't much else going on in my phone, only one single notification: a message from Jiwoo. I guess Joonie had informed everyone I was out of the picture.

But before I tapped the message open, Joonie stirred in his sleep.

With the hand that wasn't occupied with the phone, I brushed his hair back, away from his face. I was still waiting for the best moment to say the all-important words, but a word for lovers came to mind. "Good morning, jagi."

Without opening his eyes, Joonie smiled and hugged my gray sweatpants covered thigh. Adorably. "Keep talking like that, and we'll get caught. You've already camped in my room for days."

"I know." I didn't care much. Without all the shit going on in my life, I would've probably told the others about us by now, if Joonie had agreed. I wasn't one for stalling. I wasn't one for hiding. Especially home. I shook my head, not very willing to let my mind start to think too much and finally clicked Jiwoo's message open.

What would you like to do with Eun-ju's and Ye-rin's tickets? Resell?

For a moment that I personally thought was only a fraction of a second, I only stared at the screen dumbfounded and frozen. Apparently though, it was long enough for Joonie to get worried.

"What's wrong?" he asked, sitting up and rubbing his eyes.

I put the phone in Joonie's hand. "Jiwoo's asking about Gran's tickets."

"Gods, that woman has no tact, whatsoever," Joonie mumbled.

"It's okay. I wondered about that myself." I actually hadn't thought about that at all, but I certainly did now. "What would you do?"

Joonie shrugged before climbing on my lap. "Why not just leave them empty? You know, kind of like a tribute."

"Deal," I said, typed a message to Jiwoo and tossed the phone back on the nightstand. Looked like Joonie was my brain again when my own was useless. And when I gave it a short thought, the showcase concert wasn't about profit anyway—we usually barely broke even with them with such a small venue and huge production. Two tickets wouldn't make much of a difference. I did want to honor the influence Gran had on my career in music, somehow, and that seemed like the perfect way. I wrapped my hands around Joonie's waist and pulled him closer. "Good thinking, love."

At once, Joonie blinked and turned his gaze to the wall behind me, quickly biting that plump lip of his in a nervous manner. "Aish, I hate blushing."

"Nevermind the blushing, it's that lip biting thing that we need to do something about," I murmured, toppling us both over so that Joonie fell on his back, and I hovered on top of him.

But just when my lips were about to reach his awaiting ones, there was a loud bang in the hallway and we both jumped apart. After a moment of catching our startled breaths and realizing no one was entering the room, Joonie huffed, "Ugh, I hate sneaking around at home."

"Yeah…" I couldn't have agreed more. "Though they probably know about us already. Did you know Do-hyun and Minjae have a whole bet on whether we end up together or not?"

Joonie glanced at me with one eyebrow raised. "They do?"

"Yeah, and the prize is some kind of a ridiculously expensive car."

A short but ringing laugh escaped Joonie. "No way."

With sudden inspiration to be more spontaneous—it had worked surprisingly well with Joonie after all—I stood up and pulled Joonie up from the bed with me. "Let's tell them."

"Wait, now?" he asked as I dragged him towards the door.

"Yes, now. When else?"

"Uh, sure…"

I stopped at the entryway, realizing I should probably make sure it was really okay with Joonie. "Unless you don't want to?"

"I want to." Then he thought for a little while—I could practically see the gears turning inside his pretty little head. "But just so we're clear, just for the rest of GRiD and maybe Jiwoo later on. I'm not sure I want to go entirely public."

"Yes, that's what I thought," I said and trailed some circles to the back of his hand with my thumb, hoping to reassure him. "Besides, some of us need to stay seemingly single…you know, for the fans to have their daydreams."

Joonie slapped my shoulder but was also grinning. "You only ever think about profit."

"Sorry, it's a habit."

"It's alright. It's why we're here and live this comfortably."

A little peck landed on my cheek, right before I exited Joonie's room for the first time in three days.

We found Do-hyun and Minjae in our living room. Minjae was sleeping, resting his head on Do's lap. Do was leisurely browsing a magazine—ironically enough, one about cars.

"You look like hell," Do-hyun stated as soon as he spotted us, barely even looking up from the stupid car magazine. "Well, even more like hell than usual. You good?"

"Take a guess, will you?" I shook my head and sat beside him, pulling Joonie down as well. I didn't let go of his hand. I loved the feeling of his fingers interlaced with mine. Sadly, I had to move my attention from our hands back to the other couple on the couch, so we could get this whole ordeal out of the way. "Look, I'll get to the point. I'm sure you two already know, but we're a couple."

The grin that spread on Do's lips was…wide. To put it mildly.

"Yeah, but it's nice to get the official memo." He lightly pat Minjae's forehead with the spine of the magazine. "You heard that?"

"Nope," Minjae said, crossed his arms on his chest and squeezed his eyes shut tighter. "I heard absolutely nothing. I'm sleeping."

"Bullshit," Do-hyun said and turned to a page that had a silver car circled with a bright red marker before holding it barely five centimeters from Minjae's face. "Deal's a deal."

"Ugh, fine. Let me see that." Minjae grabbed the magazine, squinted sleepily at the marked page and sighed. "Aish. There goes my retirement money."

"Hardly." Do-hyun laughed and tapped the page with his index finger. "Oh and I want it as Quantum Silver, please."

"Wow, you weren't kidding about the bet," Joonie said, before squeezing my hand a little tighter. There was still a smile on his face which was all that mattered.

"Yeah. Though, not our problem. Shall we find Chris?"

"Sure."

Chris was in his room, sitting on his armchair, absentmindedly playing his black acoustic guitar. He only nodded at us to acknowledge that he noticed us but otherwise didn't even greet us. I went straight to the point.

"We're dating."

Chris stopped plucking the strings and scanned me from head to toe.

"No, the hell you're not."

Excuse me? I crossed my arms across my chest. "What do you mean?"

"You are definitely not dating Joonie on my watch. I mean look at yourself…you look like a homeless person. At least take a fucking shower before sprouting out such nonsense. You stink."

I took a step aside and sniffed the neck of my t-shirt. "That bad?"

Joonie snickered but pulled me back beside him anyway. "I mean…kinda."

"Crap."

"Come on, let's get you in shower," Joonie said and pushed me back to the hallway.

"Only if you join me." I stopped him right there, out in the open in our dorm, and swept him off his feet to carry him. A nice reminder of how all of this started—me carrying him to his room. Only this time he wasn't drunk, and I wasn't straight.

Joonie wrapped his arms tightly around my neck and shoulders. "Deal."

Holding Back

Indulging myself strictly with work and on my newfound relationship with Joonie—in and out of bed—did wonders to my mood. Though admittedly, sometimes the work got the better of me which annoyed Joonie to no end. I got a good reminder of that one night at my office at the HQ—my headphones were yanked off so abruptly I was momentarily scared that my ears fell off with them.

"Come home," Joonie pleaded. "It's midnight already."

I rubbed my ears and glanced at the clock on the screen's bottom right corner—Joonie hadn't lied. It *was* midnight. Huh. It was incredible how fast the time ticked forward so much faster when I drowned myself in work. My office in the headquarters of LBR had become my escape from thinking. And missing…people. *Her.*

Yeah, nope. I was not going to go home, yet. I wasn't exhausted enough to fall right into a dreamless sleep. It was the only way I would survive the agonizing wait for the inevitable announcement of Gran's…passing away. *And* maintain a semi-presentable state of appearance.

"But I wanted to finish this track…" I said and tried to pull my headphones back from Joonie's death-grip.

I was not successful. Joonie tossed them right across the room and climbed on my lap, facing me, and forcing me to look at him directly. "At this rate you're going to work yourself into an early grave."

Deflating like a balloon, I circled my hands around his waist and buried my face in the nook between the collar of his loose white dress shirt and his smooth, shaved jawline. The mere scent of his strawberry shampoo and the warmth of his body against mine was already almost enough to make me forget the rest of the world. Almost. "I know. I just—I miss her."

"I know, love. And it's okay to miss her. It's okay to grieve. It's okay to be angry about how it turned out. But this…this indifference…it's not living, Tae. This is only *surviving*. I cannot stand seeing you like this. It has been going on for days now."

And that right there made me sorry for Joonie too. We had only just started dating and I'd barely acknowledged his existence in the past few days. Well, except for railing him into next Wednesday a couple of times when his teasing had gotten the better of me, and I'd had a weak moment. Though even that was barely enough for him—and man was he *demanding* when it came to sex.

Although, I should've known. It was Joonie after all. He knew what he wanted and demanded for it in all aspects of life—why would sex be any different? And I wasn't really complaining. He was just sometimes…a lot for me to handle. He had even made us go through *safewords* and *limits* the other day. And not in a light-hearted manner like the first time safeword was mentioned. He was serious.

Nevertheless, I felt bad for drowning myself at work. Must've been the first time in my entire life, but that didn't change the fact that Joonie didn't deserve it. He deserved someone who would give him the attention he needed.

Yet there he was, consoling *me*. "I'm sorry."

"Don't be sorry…it's just…Eun-ju wouldn't want this either."

I sighed. "I know."

Joonie's hand dove under my t-shirt, his touch burning on my cold skin. For a moment, I absolutely hated how my body instantly reacted to his touch. How my heartbeat accelerated, and my dick very much jolted to life. But Joonie didn't seem to care about my conflicted, sudden stillness, as he continued to trace the small of my back with his soft, warm fingertips.

"Besides, I know a lot better of a distraction…" he whispered into my ear, his velvety smooth voice at once waking up something primal inside me. Something that I was a little scared of. Something that wanted control and authority over Joonie. Something that burned in such a high intensity within me whenever I even thought about having sex with him, that I was completely and utterly afraid I'd go way too far beyond all boundaries.

"…a lot healthier distraction," Joonie continued.

Here we go again. "Look, I don't think I'm in the right mindset for—uh—this," I said, grabbing the hand of Joonie that was exploring my back under the shirt and pulling it out, before pressing my lips briefly on his knuckles. "It's not that I don't want to, but…"

"Look, if you really don't want it, I'll leave you alone. Obviously," Joonie huffed, leaning back in my embrace, possibly to give me some space. "But if this is *again* about 'going too far' or whatever, we've already *had* this conversation. It's *why* we have a safeword. It's *why* we talked about the limits. I trust you. It would be nice if you trusted me, too, to tell you if things go wrong."

"I do trust you," I said without even a hint of hesitation, and looked him deep in his eyes. I caught a strand of hair and moved it out of his face. "I really do."

I did trust him. But myself, I wasn't so sure. At first, I had been curious; how far could I take the roughness, the physical and mental power I could have over him that he so clearly enjoyed, before it was too much? But once we talked about it the other day, and I realized that his limits existed somewhere far beyond what I'd done with anyone else before or even what I had dared to imagine…the curiosity turned into an all-consuming *craving.*

The fact that *I* wanted it too, completely freaked me out. It was one more surprise in my surpriseless world. I had always been taught to cherish, to handle the things I loved with uttermost care. As if they would be made of the finest, most fragile glass that could shatter any moment. It was one thing for Joonie to ask for it because it was clearly his preference—but a completely different thing for me to *want* it. One shouldn't *want* to be *that* rough when handling the love of their life, right?

Right.

But Joonie…he had this tendency to bring out the deepest, darkest passions from somewhere deep inside me, right to the surface.

"Then what's the problem?" he finally asked after a long silence of us just looking each other in the eyes and me trying to think things through. Then he leaned forward, starting to toy with the hem of my t-shirt, slowly working it upwards. His teeth trapped his bottom lip in a tight hold, the familiar sight melting away the last of my hesitance.

"I—I'm…" I gulped, trying to form a complete sentence but failed.

"I know you want it," he whispered, in that awfully breathy tone that caused more blood to rush directly into my crotch area.

"I do."

"Then shh…" Joonie hushed and planted his index finger on top of my lips while raising the hem of my shirt even higher with his other hand. "…and let me make you feel good."

My mind hazing up, I no longer objected when he pulled my shirt all the way up. I even raised my arms to help him. By the time his warm hands landed on my chest, I was already filled with burning temptation.

"Fuck," I hummed, my voice already betraying me by having turned coarse.

Then Joonie's lips found my neck, so feverish, slick, and skilful in what they were trying to accomplish—my losing the rest of my mental restraints. I knew that they were going to dissolve any second now, but the last of my fears were still trying their hardest to hold me back.

My hands balled into tight fists when Joonie dropped to his knees in front of me, then brushed his tongue down, leaving behind a slick wet trail that still managed to set my skin on fire. When his hands reached the button of my jeans, my hips raised almost automatically…he had no trouble pulling down both my jeans and underwear.

I could only watch, gripping the handles of the office chair like my life depended on them, when he pulled out a condom from his back pocket. With a wicked glimmer in his eyes, he ripped the foil open and tossed it on the table.

"We should get tested so we can get rid of these," he said, toying with the condom.

Before I managed to reply, he had already rolled the condom on my incredibly hard cock…and then took it inside his mouth. Momentarily, my vision was filled with black spots, and I was pretty sure I was going to pass out from immense pleasure. With a growl ripping free from my chest, I had lost the rest of my mental barriers, and I grabbed a fistful of Joonie's hair and pulled—just how I knew he'd like it.

I got a very nice moan vibrating down my cock as a reward from him as he took almost every centimeter of me in his mouth, struggling against my grip on his hair. At that rate I was not going to last for very long at all. My balls were already aching for release. Fuck. An all-consuming urge to shove my cock down his throat made my hips jerk up.

Reading my body like the expert he was, Joonie did it voluntarily. He literally choked on my dick. At that moment I was so close to filling up the condom already that I had to yank his head back. It took everything in me *not* to cum.

After closing my eyes for a brief second and taking a deep breath, I looked down. I was met with an out of this world gorgeous sight—Joonie looking up at me, his eyes half closed, cheeks flushed to a rosy color, a small drop of drool starting to run down from the corner of his mouth. In between heavy breaths, he licked his lips.

"Finally, we're getting somewhere," he said and wiped the corner of his mouth with his thumb, a dreamy haze clouding his eyes.

That was when I realized I was still pulling his hair, hard. So hard in fact, that his neck was bent all weird and it looked extremely uncomfortable. Yet, Joonie didn't seem to mind. Quite the opposite, in fact, since he started palming the significant hard on that was tenting his pants.

Holy shit.

Something clicked to its rightful place in my brain. If this was what Joonie wanted, I would totally give it to him. I could be rough with him if I let myself. I *wanted* to, anyway. I wiped half of my desk clear with the hand that wasn't entangled in Joonie's hair, a couple of pens and a whole lot of papers flying right down on the floor. I didn't care. I was positive I could sort them out later.

With one swift lift from his armpits, I had Joonie sitting on the edge of the table. It didn't take much more than a prompt pull to have his shirt open, the least secured buttons shooting out into every direction. A surprised sounding wince escaped Joonie, but I shut him up with a kiss and pulled the shirt down his shoulders at the same time.

Joonie quickly caught up with me and his lips started an urgent, sloppy duel with mine. We only broke it briefly when he had pulled my t-shirt up and off with one firm motion. At some point I kicked the pants that had gathered on my ankles to the side. But when my hand dove under the waistband of Joonie's jeans, my fingers met with a material that felt both familiar to touch but at the same time something I hadn't anticipated a man would wear.

I broke the kiss.

"Lace?" I asked, my voice barely audible through all the heavy breathing.

Joonie smirked, hopped down from the table, and slid his jeans off, before kicking them to the side where my pants already were. Underneath, indeed, were some incredibly snug fitting black lace panties.

"You like them?" he asked, then instantly bit his lower lip and didn't let his eyes meet mine.

"Like them? I love them," I stated and released his lip from the tight hold of his teeth with my thumb. "But you know you don't have to do this for me, right? You're beautiful in any clothes…and especially without clothes at all."

He quickly glanced at my eyes before casting them down. "I know, I just wanted to surprise you. Besides, *I* like them."

"In that case, we're keeping them on." A smile tugged one corner of my mouth up and I pushed him to lay on his back.

Joonie took in a surprised sharp breath between his gritted teeth, his naked back hitting the desk's wooden surface with a bit of a thump. I didn't let him recover, but instead locked his wrists above his head with a tight grip so they weren't on my way and started sprinkling kisses on his chest. Alternating between soft pecks, some little nibs, and a whole lot of sucking, I tried to cover as much of his delicate, delicious skin that I possibly could. The moans that Joonie let out were music to my ears. Spending extra attention to his nipples earned me a full concert. Good thing it was past midnight. We didn't have to worry about others hearing.

Gradually, I made my way down, far enough for me to let go of Joonie's wrists. I'm not sure if he even noticed, though, since he kept his arms above his head. Eyes half closed, back arched and chest raising in tune with his dragged breaths, he looked totally out of it.

Taking my time, I ran my fingertips along the edges of the lace panties, but deliberately didn't go anywhere near his dick. I could see it annoyed him, as he kept raising his hips to try and meet my touch, but that only entertained me. Enjoying the teasing quite a lot, I strayed further away every time he moved. He learned to stay still rather quickly.

"Tae, I need you—" Joonie almost sobbed, at the same time precum started leaking from his dick, a wet circle darkening the front of his lace panties.

It was what I had been waiting for—him desperate enough to start begging me.

"Bend your legs up to your chest," I murmured while sliding the panties half-way down his thighs, releasing his stiff cock. "And hold them there."

Without a moment of hesitation, he obeyed, desperate enough to do anything I asked. It was a whole power trip. Enough to make my head light. And the sight was quite something under the panties too, especially in that position, his most intimate parts perfectly exposed to me. He had even shaved. He looked like artwork.

My patience completely running out, I squeezed whatever left-over lube I could from the condom pack, directly on Joonie's crease and tossed the foil to the side. It wasn't much, but it had to do. I was still super careful when I inserted the first digit into the hole, but Joonie took it well. Starting to fondle his shaved balls with my other hand, I inserted another finger, without much difficulty at all.

He'd loosened up nicely it seemed.

Only when I gave up with the almost useless prepping and lined my cock up with his entrance, before pushing right in, did I get a reaction from Joonie.

He bit his lip, hard. Drawing his eyebrows together.

"You hurting?" I asked, to which Joonie instantly rolled his eyes.

"As if," he said. "Just—"

I didn't let him finish that sentence. Instead, I made him shout out an actual proper whimper by pushing his legs even tighter against his chest and pulling my dick almost all the way out before plunging back in with more force. Served him right. He wanted rough, and I was hellbent on giving it to him.

But the look on his face, it was something I had a hard time dealing with, yet I couldn't turn my eyes away. The way he bit his lip to hold his moans back when I pressed into him over and over again was about to end me any moment. Paired with the pressure and tightness of his hole around my dick, I was soon incredibly close to my own release. Thankfully at least based on the rate of the precum that leaked as a continuous stream, pooling on his abdomen, he wasn't far from orgasm either.

With one last push as deep as I could inside him, I drove him over the edge and followed right after myself. I crashed hard on top of him, giving exactly zero shits about his cum making things extremely messy between us. I realized…that I wouldn't need to fear hurting Joonie with this. Not in a million years. It was actually Joonie who was in charge. Had been the whole time. If I had to trust someone to be clear about his limits, it would be Joonie. How on earth had I ever even thought that the bluntest, most shameless man on earth would've held back on me?

I decided that I shouldn't hold back on him either from then on.

Violent Love

Soon it was the evening of the showcase concert. It was supposed to be a fun one. And I tried my best. I really tried. But damn it was hard. Honestly, it was the hardest concert I had ever had to pull through.

The scorching hot spotlights burned my skin more than they usually did. The small stage felt cramped. We had trouble fitting the larger choreographies on it, and there was no room for backup dancers, so they had to fill in wherever they could. The audience was closer than ever—we could actually see them for the most part. Right from the stage. Though the spotlights still made it hard to spot any one individual.

Whatever. It wasn't like I hadn't been on small stages before. Back in the day, there had been no backup dancers. The spotlights were always bright and hot as hell.

The one thing that got to me more than anything was the seat in the front row. Its emptiness settled an uneasy feeling to the bottom of my stomach. I couldn't bear to even glance in that direction for fear of breaking down in the middle of the concert. It made performing a hellish experience.

The smiles didn't come naturally. The light-hearted songs didn't feel right. The darker ones nearly made me tear up. I couldn't focus on dancing, making a hell of a lot of mistakes. My rap didn't flow. My throat felt sore after the first fifteen minutes.

It took a lot of experience, knowledge, and stamina to pull through the show. But somehow, I did it, letting out a long sigh of relief as we bowed to the audience one last time after the encore.

Only then, I finally dared to spare a glance towards Gran's seat. Which was supposed to be empty...except it wasn't.

There was a man on that seat. Right next to Ye-rin, who held the said man's hand. It took me a short second to recognize him.

The man was Gang Jae-sung. Some might've called him my father. Others would call me his son. The one person that was supposed to be close to me, but who had never come to see our shows, was suddenly there. And I could already guess what that meant.

Multiple things happened at once: the lights switched off, right as my knees betrayed me and made me crash to the floor. I saw Dad smiling at me, and just when our eyes met, he nodded ever so slightly.

I doubled over and performed a full bow to his direction, out of a pure and raw, sudden, wave of respect. Right on time for the curtains to close. It was Joonie who, again, picked up my pieces, put me back together, and started dragging me backstage. I barely even noticed that someone from the staff ripped the mic wires off my back while we staggered towards our dressing rooms.

Completely exhausted and spent, I crashed down on the couch. A couple beads of sweat formed on my forehead. I barely had the energy to wipe them off with the back of my hand. Joonie sat next to me, took my hand in his, and started trailing soothing circles with the tip of his finger to the back of my hand. We were alone. As if the others had sensed something was wrong and knew it needed to be Joonie there with me.

My mind was empty at first. I just tried to catch my breath. There was no usual adrenaline rush after the gig was over. It was just me, tired, barely holding myself together. Unfortunately, after my breath evened out, the black spots faded from my vision, and I could see clearly, my mind also started to work again.

There was only one reason Dad would ever come to see our live performance, and the fact that he had been in Gran's seat confirmed it. I felt it, anticipated it. Just knew it. But I refused to think about it. I could almost feel my heart dying, even as I refused to believe it. It hurt so damn badly I nearly couldn't breathe. The fact that Joonie was there beside me, was the only thing that kept me from falling apart.

A knock on the door ripped me back to reality. Do-hyun called through, telling us he and Minjae could take the first two rides back to the dorm, as they were ready to go. I nodded and got up. The faster I got home, the faster I could fall apart in the privacy of my own damn room, hopefully with Joonie still by my side.

But another knock on the door interrupted me as I started to change back to my regular clothes. This time it was Joe, informing me I could take the next car back home with Mr. Choi or wait till the last one and go with him. After glancing at Joonie—who nodded slightly—I replied to Joe that I'd take the next car in ten minutes.

Just as I had wiggled my way out of the skinny jeans and to some way comfier sweatpants, there was a third knock. Joe, again.

"There's a man requesting access backstage, uh, your father, perhaps? Gang Jae-sung?"

I groaned. All I wanted was to plop my heavy ass into a car and get home as fast as possible, so I could sleep until the next century. But of course, Dad wanted to have a fucking chat now that he finally dragged his ass to one of our shows.

"Umm...I can tell him you left already or something?" Joe asked, probably in response to the distress on my face.

"I don't know. It's usually better to deal with him right away..." I started, even though I was still tempted to escape. I turned my eyes to Joonie. "What do you think?"

"I think you should talk with him. Do you want me to stay?"

I gave it a good thought. But the night had been exhausting enough to deal with Dad's homophobia on top of everything else. "Would you mind if I talked with him alone?"

"Not at all. I'll take the next ride, you come with Joe later. That ought to give you two a good twenty minutes."

Joe nodded and closed the door once again. In an instant after the door clicked close, I wrapped my hands around Joonie and squeezed his body against my chest tightly.

"I'll see you at home," he said. To which I nodded, before letting him go.

We didn't even share a kiss.

Reluctantly, I watched Joonie gather his things, go through the door, and disappear into the hallway, joining Chris who was headed in the same direction. Hastily, I changed the rest of my clothes and plopped down on top of the table to wait for Dad to appear.

It didn't take him long. Joe escorted him right to the still open door, and then there he was, looking lost and out of place, just watching me at the threshold, and his dark brown hair styled as neatly as ever. Not even a single wrinkle on his pristine suit. His dark eyes glared at me sternly.

I didn't have the energy to even ask "what's up," or to invite him inside. But I didn't need to, as he stepped in anyway, as if he owned the place. To be fair, though, he probably did.

There were no greetings. No polite bows. I was too exhausted for all that. I just stared at him, waiting for him to open his mouth. And he finally did after a long, long silence.

"There's black smudge on your eyes." Those were the first words he said to me.

I rolled my eyes at him. "It's called stage make-up."

He pulled his shoulders straighter with a "Hmph."

I wasn't about to start arguing about stage make up with him. "So… how was the show?"

He shrugged. "Wasn't that bad. At least it was entertaining to watch you screw up. I'm surprised you pulled through the whole thing."

"Yeah, it wasn't my best night."

He looked past me, at the wall. As if to avoid looking directly at me. There was another silence.

"I could come to see another gig sometimes," he said.

This weird feeling of respect washed over me again. I never knew I had wanted his acceptance of my career so much. At that moment, I realized it was something I'd wanted for years.

It was terrifying, overwhelming, and nice at the same time. To think that after years of rebelling against him, we were approaching the same page.

After a brief but careful consideration, I stated, "I'd be honored if you did."

There was yet another awkward silence. Dad cleared his throat and toyed with his cuff-links for a bit. I was too exhausted to fiddle with something of my own, but it was strange for me too. Hanging backstage with Dad. I never thought we'd be there.

That didn't change the reason why he was there.

"She's gone, isn't she?" I asked. "That's why you are here."

He took a deep breath before he spoke. "Yes, she has passed."

Hearing the actual confirmation hurt like hell. "When?"

"Thursday. She slipped away peacefully in her sleep. They...they told me there wasn't any pain. I would've called earlier but uh...Ye-rin insisted I'd tell you in person, and it didn't seem like good timing just before the show. Anyway, the funeral's next Saturday, as there's no autopsy as per her wishes. She had it all planned already..." He blabbered on, which wasn't typical for him. I guess it had affected him as much as it had affected me.

I had a hard time swallowing a heavy lump in my throat. I could feel the tears burning behind my eyelids, but it was the wrong place for them to spill over. I wanted to fall apart at home.

"I'll see you at the funeral then," I managed to say.

"There's more." He avoided my eyes.

What more could he possibly have had to tell me? I said nothing as I patiently waited for him to spill out the rest.

"It's just me and you left, son. Got me thinking...actually, I hoped that we—uhh—that we could try to get along a little better in the future. You know, at least we could meet sometimes. Other than at funerals and weddings."

The words downright shocked me to the core. They were so out of his character, that my voice stuck in my throat.

I managed to say, "Sure" and we exchanged awkward goodbyes as he left.

I don't know how long I sat there, doing nothing, my thoughts going round and round in endless circles in my head before Joe appeared. I was forced to snap out of the shock. He asked if I was ready. I was. I wanted nothing more than to leave. There was a huge crowd of fans to see me off, the label's security staff keeping them at a safe distance. With the last of my energy, I forced out a half-smile at them, hoping it was enough.

When I was finally sitting on the leather backseat of the company Mercedes, I watched the streetlights of Seoul go by, wishing they'd go by faster as I was anxious to get back home to Joonie. My Joonie. The shameless pop-princess who I had grown to respect over the years, and then learned to love over just a few months. Some could say, in just a couple of weeks.

Those feelings were just a delusion designed to hide the true meaning of love.

Love, actually, is much more painful than that.

Because before that night was over, I'd come to understand what it truly meant to love someone as much as I loved Joonie. I'd come to realize being in love wasn't just about dates, buying gifts on birthdays, or waking up next to each other. It wasn't only the fluttery feelings that settled in my stomach every time I was close to him. Or the sparkles that hovered in the air every time we kissed. Not even the scorching hot, explosive fire that consumed us every time we had sex.

It would feel like you were being ripped apart until there was nothing left but a hollow shell. And then, that shell would be filled with pure agony, overwhelming worry, and all-consuming pain.

It would rush to my conscience like a crashing wave and make me fall on my knees on the hard asphalt upon seeing the scene that was about to rip my heart wide open. It would be clear in my mind when I'd swallow my pride at dawn and crawl to my dad's place to crash as I'd have nowhere else to go. It would bang my head like a hammer a few days later, when I'd sit at Gran's funeral reception, ready to give up everything just so Joonie could've been beside me.

Intervention

Chris' point of view

"See you in a bit," Joonie hollered to the crowd, smiling, just before entering the black company Mercedes.

A few similar cars left the premises at the same time, all heading to different directions in accordance with the new safety precautions. As soon as their taillights disappeared from my view, Min-ho walked through the door. "We should head out too."

I proceeded to walk to my car with him with that fake, cute smile that I had practically trademarked plastered on my face. It fell as soon as the door closed after me, and I was safely hidden by the heavily tinted windows.

The car shot forward. I clicked my tongue at Min-ho's impatience—it wasn't like we were being chased or anything. I very much intended to keep my mouth shut though, as I didn't want to kill his enthusiasm. Instead, I fished my phone out of my jeans' pocket and started scrolling our Twitter. I couldn't really focus on that either, since the showcase hadn't gone very great at all with Tae being so out of it the whole time. Yes, he had a good excuse with his Gran in hospital, but it didn't make the disappointment disappear.

The car lurched, and my phone flew out of my hand. The screen cracked as it landed at my feet.

All right. That's enough. I thought as I lifted my eyes to scream my aggression at Min-ho.

"What the f—" But the rest of it stuck to my dry throat as I saw Min-ho's expression through the rear-view mirror.

His eyes were immensely focused and pitch black. I got actual chills. His eyes met mine through the mirror, just briefly, before he rammed the gas pedal all the way down, accelerating the car to an even more terrifying speed. His neck got rigidly stiff as he steered the heavy-ass car through the streets like it was merely a small bullet.

Something was seriously wrong with this dude.

My head went into some overdrive beast mode. It wasn't like in the movies when time slows. It was more like an adrenaline rush that made my mind work faster. I watched the road whizz by faster and faster. He was on a mission. Of that much, I was sure.

All my worst fears were confirmed in a nanosecond as the tail-lights of Joonie's car grew closer and closer, and he showed no signs of slowing.

His mission was crashing, right into Joonie.

It was too late to stop it.

There was nothing I could do.

My racing mind forced me to brace for impact, and not a second later, we collided.

Our car met with Joonie's at an angle that sent our car spinning across the road. There was another hit to our car's rear right when the spinning had stopped, sending us spiraling again

I lost consciousness for a length of time I couldn't measure.

When I regained it, the first thing I noticed was how still everything was. It was hard to breathe, and there was glass and other shattered trash everywhere. Min-ho wasn't on the driver's seat, which couldn't have meant anything good. Hastily, I yanked my crooked door open, but only went half-way. With strenuous effort, I managed to squeeze my bruised body through the small opening.

As soon as I dropped on all fours to the hard asphalt, I started coughing my lungs out. I never thought I'd be thankful for the immense physical training from the army. It was the only thing that helped me fight through the pain and look up.

I was met with an out of this world sight. There were clouds of black smoke everywhere, and through that, I could see the outline of Joonie's wrecked car. It was completely totaled against a street-light. Mr. Choi was long gone on the driver's seat, lifeless eyes staring ahead and a thick dribble of blood slowly pouring across his face while his limp body leaned on the steering wheel over the flattened airbag.

Joonie laid on the miraculously intact backseat, his body slouching in a weird position. Tears blurred my vision. I started crawling towards him with the last ounce of strength I had in me, hoping from the bottom of my heart he wasn't dead.

But Min-ho beat me to it by far. All I could do was watch as he dragged Joonie's body out of the car and laid him to the ground gently, bawling his eyes out.

This was his fault! Why the fuck was he crying?

Rage replaced tears in eyes and my head buzzed. My vision practically turned red as I staggered upwards, gaining strength I shouldn't have had in the moment.

Thankfully Min-ho had his back towards me, focused on Joonie, while I approached him. I grabbed his shoulders, yanked him off from over Joonie, and landed a hard punch to his face. It was powerful enough to send him falling on his back.

I straddled him and lined up another good punch. I held it, hand shaking, ready to let it fly if he didn't answer my question the way I liked. "What the fuck is wrong with you?"

"Is he dead? I don't know if he's dead." Was all Min-ho said, eyes not even on my threatening fist, but on Joonie. "I don't want him to be dead. He can't be dead."

"Then you shouldn't have driven you're crazy-fucking-ass into his god damn car!" I couldn't hold back. I slammed my fist into his face. It hurt so much more to hit his face against unmoving asphalt than it had in the open air, but I didn't so much as wince.

Min-ho spat blood as he cried harder. "No. That was supposed to be Tae's car. I would never hurt Joonie. Tae, this is his—"

I didn't even hear him finish. Reality hit me harder than the crash itself. Min-ho had been trying to kill Tae. Not Joonie. He wept for Joonie.

He was the fucking stalker.

I entered a trance, and I lost control as I started landing hits after hits after hits to his pathetic face. Each hit deformed his face further, but I kept pounding it with all the strength. He couldn't do a thing under my ruthless attack.

The piece of shit.

Seong-gi appeared out of thin air and yanked me away from the guy.

"What the fuck?!" I screamed, trying to crawl back to finish the job. "Let me go! he's the stalker!" Seong-gi's grip on me loosened, and I was able to break free. "Help Joonie!" I commanded as I rushed to continue my attack. Seong-gi listened and ran to aid Joonie.

But, before I reached Min-ho, he managed to grab a handful of glass and gravel. The grains hit my face, dust blinding my vision and bits of glass cutting the skin on my face.

When my vision cleared, a piece of glass swung at my face. I dodge with less than a paper's width between the sharp edge and my nose. But Min-ho was quicker than I anticipated, and he swung again before I was ready, landing an easy hit across my face. I lost the last of my focus, and he was able to slash another cut across my cheek and the corner of my eye.

I staggered off him, the pain reaching my senses with a bit of a weird lag. Seong-gi was still focused on Joonie, dialing someone on his phone and not noticing that I was losing to Min-ho. With a single punch from him, I fell backwards.

When my back hit the ground, I could only watch Min-ho stagger away as all the pain from the collision and the fight finally wore my body completely down. Having burned all the possible strength of my body and the very last drop of adrenaline in my blood, I couldn't move a centimeter. Or even lift a finger.

As hard as I tried to fight it, my eyes fluttered shut.

Wrong Accident

Joonie's point of view

Pain.

That was the first thing that came to mind when my consciousness returned. But I didn't exactly feel pain. I just knew, somehow, that I was supposed to be in pain—in a lot of pain. My mind was a big mess. My thoughts were all tangled together. Something weighed me down, making me feel tired. Except I wasn't. What the hell happened to me?

"Joonie, it's time to wake up," someone on my left side said with a soft, velvety, even tone.

It sounded kind of like Tae's voice, but not quite. This voice sounded somehow...deeper. And very distressed. I frowned and tried to open my eyes, but it was hard. The damn tiredness all over again, weighing my eyelids down.

While I struggled against the total darkness, someone grabbed a tight hold on my right shoulder.

"Don't worry, he's already coming around," a calm, woman's voice assured on my right side. The unfamiliar voice finally made me force my eyes open—which I regretted as soon as I did it.

Everything was too bright. Hurting my eyes bright. Headachingly bright. I couldn't make out anything in my sight while the room spun so fast. The only thing that grounded me to reality was the hold on my right shoulder by the stranger.

The next sense to wake up was the sense of smell. Unfortunately. The lingering scent of latex and disinfectant filled my nostrils—the nauseatingly sterile smell of hospitals. I hated it, detested it, but had no clue why. What was I even doing there?

Damn nearly puked from the smell. Though puking wasn't an option, as something blocked my throat. There was just something, err, *extra,* that didn't really belong. I could still breathe, oddly enough, though it sort of felt like sucking air through a long tube.

"Joon-seok dear, you have an intubation tube, so you can't talk right now. I'll take it off as soon as I can confirm you're breathing on your own," the woman said.

An intubation tube? What the hell? Why did I have to be intubated?

I tried to relax, or prove I was breathing fine. Meanwhile, I tried to make my eyes focus on something, to anything, really, but the room was stubborn and didn't stay in place. An immersive relief washed over me when I managed to wiggle my toes just fine. At least I wasn't paralyzed. I could move my fingers too.

When my eyes finally focused, I turned towards my left to see if it was Tae whose voice I had heard. There was a man beside me who sort of looked like Tae, but...somehow weird? Older. Maybe it was the weird haircut. The awful mullet was gone—thank heavens—and he had some highlights.

The man smiled at me. I tried to smile back. He looked kind of nice—handsome even, in his own weird way. Just like Tae. Though I had no clue why that man was beside me. He squeezed my hand reassuringly, for which I was grateful.

Wait, how long was I out?

My mushy thought process was cut off by the woman, apparently a nurse, who explained to me that she was going to take the tube out from my throat. I tried to nod my gratitude, but my neck was super stiff and hardly moved.

Before I managed to register anything more, the woman had already pulled the tube out with one determined, prompt pull. I was waiting for a gag reflex to make me puke or something, but it never happened. I just let out a single cough, and that was basically it.

Once the nurse had put away the tube and whatever, she turned to face me. "How are you feeling today, Joon-seok?"

"Like I got hit by a fucking truck. Twice," I croaked with my voice surprisingly coarse and harsh. A shiver ran down my spine.

The man that looked like Tae, let out a suppressed chuckle. "Close enough."

"Yes, there was a car accident," the nurse confirmed.

A car accident.

Some weird flashbacks flooded my mind. I could remember my parents—Mom was in the front seat. Dad was driving. But the memories were all cloudy, complicated, and… not in any sensical order. With a furrow deepening on my forehead, I tried to fit the pieces together, but I wasn't very successful. Not that I had long to focus on it, as the nurse lifted the head-side of the motorized bed, sending loud rattles and clanks through the room.

She also started quizzing me while pointed a bright light straight in my eyes Then she asked if I could move this and that part of my body.

"Everything is looking good," she said. Apparently, I passed the tests.

When I looked down, a plate of food covered the previously empty table over my bed. I honestly hadn't even noticed someone had bought it. Porridge and ice cream, though. What a strange combination.

"Try to eat something," the nurse said and pointed at the table. "We arranged something easily digestible since you might not be able to handle anything solid yet."

A rumble in my stomach told me she was right; I needed to eat something. But as hungry as I was, the only thing that looked even remotely edible was the cup of ice cream. So, I took the cup, which felt awfully heavy in my hands despite it being just a paper cup with a small scoop of vanilla ice cream. I popped a spoonful into my mouth.

There might've been a slight moan that erupted from my chest, as it tasted heavenly sweet. The man that looked sort of like Tae chuckled to that, making my eyes snap to his. He smiled, but that didn't hide the pretty darn dark circles and bags under his eyes. The poor guy must've been awake for quite some time.

"Uhh, hyung, maybe you should go to sleep?" I asked, again getting surprised by how coarse my own voice sounded.

Something weird flashed on his eyes before he glanced at the nurse, who nodded ever so slightly. It looked like a wordless agreement to me. But as I was still waiting for the guy to answer something to me, I just stared at him. It took him a long time to answer So long I started getting a bit antsy.

"It's been a long time you called me hyung..." he eventually muttered.

What did he mean? He was older than me so, of course, I called him hyung.

When I didn't reply to anything, he continued. "Don't worry Joonie-ssi, I'll get some sleep as soon as we're done here." He smiled down at me before dropping to a weird, pained expression. "Uhh, this is a weird question but...do you even recognize me?"

What a loaded question. My brain went into overdrive. Yes, the guy somewhat looked like Tae. And sounded sort of like Tae. And the only one that ever called me Joonie was Tae. But he couldn't be Tae, could he? He looked just so different. I couldn't have been out long enough for him to get a haircut and age a few years...

Or...had I?

"How long was I out?" I asked, intentionally avoiding the proposed question.

The nurse on the right side of my bed sighed before answering. "Just a little over a week. You hit your head hard, so we kept you under as long as the swelling on your brain leveled down. I'm gonna go get the doctor, so just stay put for a moment."

I tried to nod again, but the sudden pain that flashed all through my neck and between my shoulder blades made me wince instead.

168

I turned my gaze carefully towards the familiar-looking man. I had to know if it was really him.

"Tae?" As a non-deniable relief washed over his face, I dared to continue. "You're Tae, right? Only you look a bit...uh..."—*old*—"Different."

He looked down at me with pity in his eyes. "Yeah, it's me."

"Figured. You're the only one who calls me Joonie."

He nearly chuckled, and a grin spread to his lips. "Uhh, actually everyone calls you Joonie nowadays."

What? What did that even mean? Who was everyone?

The nurse returned and sat down on one of the chairs near my bed. A doctor followed just after.

"Annyeong haseyo, I'm Dr. Han. Nice to finally meet you Joon-seok. Well, awake, that is," she said and grinned.

I greeted her back with a nod out of habit and regretted it again when the pain stabbed me in the back like a scorching hot knife straight through a vertebra.

"Can anyone give this man some painkillers? Chop-chop," the doctor said after just one glance on my probably extremely pained face.

"Thanks," I managed to croak.

"No problem. Though before we connect that, I have a few questions. And I need you sober for that," she stated before diving into some medical jargon about areas of the brain, memory, and yada-yada. I couldn't keep up. I did try as I wanted to understand, but I was already too confused by that point.

The only thing that I could figure out from her speech was that they were guessing there was something wrong with the memory part of my brain. Which I had figured out already—thank you very much—as everything was a blur.

Eventually, the doctor got to the actual questions part. "So, all things considered, what *do* you remember?"

My temples starting to ache, I tried to remember what had happened. They had talked about a car accident, so I started from there. "Uhh, Dad was driving..." I started. The memories were tangled up in my head, but they were there. I tried to remember as much as I possibly could. "Mom was in the front seat. I think they were driving me back to the dorms...I was supposed to have a shift at the restaurant in the evening. Suddenly everything just went upside down and Mom screamed." My chest tightened and my eyes watered. Tae squeezed my hand reassuringly. It was the only thing that kept me from losing it.

"And what happened then?" Dr. Han asked softly.

I tried to remember something more, but I couldn't. "I don't know, I woke up here...where's Mom?" I asked, with a small voice, already afraid to hear the answer. Tears soaked my face as I couldn't hold them back any longer. Tae's grip on my hand tightened.

The doctor glared at Tae. "Is that accurate?"

"As I recall, yeah..." Tae replied to the doctor, before gulping visibly. "Only...it's the wrong accident."

I frowned. "What do you mean 'wrong accident?'"

"Joonie, that accident, with your mom and dad...was over six years ago."

Dimple

"But...you just said I was out for around a week?"

"Well, you better fast forward six years because there was another car accident around a week ago, which led you here," Tae stated, waving his hand towards the rest of the room.

What. The. Actual. Fuck?

Yeah, I knew that my mind was fogged up...but by that much?

While the nurse set up a new liquid bag to the stand on my left and connected it to the drip, a million thoughts shot through my mind.

Then the most heart crunching question dawned on me: if the accident with Mom and Dad was six years ago…what happened to them? It wasn't like I couldn't already guess that it had ended badly, based on the fact that Tae was here and not them. I still needed confirmation. It took a while to find the courage to say it out loud. A new set of tears already burned behind my eyes.

"Mom, she's gone right?" I finally asked.

Tae squeezed my hand but otherwise his face remained stoic. It was confirmation enough.

"Dad?"

He hung his head. "I'm sorry."

The tears pushed through despite all my resistance and started rolling down my cheeks as an endless stream.

I couldn't breathe. I couldn't think. My vision got all blurred up by the tears. I wished I could have just gone back to sleep and pretend I'd never woken up at all.

Thankfully, the painkillers started to take an effect pretty fast, and I felt my body and mind go numb. The doctor ordered me to rest both my body and mind for the time being. Soon after, the nurse and the doctor exited, telling me to use the call button if I needed anything.

Tae stayed. When the drugs started to seriously droop my eyelids, he smiled down at me and started stroking soothing circles on the palm of my hand. My mind drifted off, back to the dreamlands.

The next time I woke up, Tae was still there. He was sleeping in the worn out mushy green armchair over in the corner. The shadows in the room had gotten longer, last sunrays coloring the whole room golden. A different nurse stood by my right this time. He shushed me, pointed at Tae, and then gestured to the table that had been once again turned over on top of my bed. The half-eaten ice cream cup had been replaced with a new one, and there was no porridge this time. I smiled back at the nurse and kept my mouth shut, as it had seemed like Tae needed the sleep.

The nurse replaced the drip with another drug bag as I munched down the small ball of ice cream.

"You should sleep, too." The nurse whispered as she clicked a few buttons on the panel controlling my IV fluids. I drifted off again, tired to the core.

That night, I woke up many, many times. There usually was a nurse by my side when I woke up, who would tell me to get some more sleep and assure me I could deal with everything else in the morning. My brain needed sleep to heal. I embraced the numbing effect of the drugs, glad to ignore the confusion that awaited me a bit longer.

Tae was always there when I woke up. The first two times I woke up, he was still sleeping in the same chair at the corner. The third time, he had moved beside my bed.

He had rested his head on top of his arms, with his messy brown hair had spread half-way across his face. Though the wrinkle of worry still lingered between his eyebrows, he looked way more peaceful in his sleep. Somehow, seeing him stay by my side made me feel more safe. That calmed me down.

Tae's mere presence just made me feel all warm and fuzzy inside.

Eventually I knew I was going to have to be able to get back to sleep without help from the drugs. But without the dreamless state the drugs gave me, I started having nightmares. Very vivid ones that repeated the same pattern. There was always the car accident—the only one I remembered. Each time it ended a bit differently, yet my family ended up dead in every single one.

After one particularly creepy one, I woke up out of breath, my forehead soaked with sweat and the corners of my eyes burning from all the tears that had already flooded over. My hands shook while I tried to muffle a scream that erupted from my lungs involuntarily but wasn't very successful. My sounds startled Tae awake. He fluttered his eyes open and grabbed my wrist instinctively.

I hadn't even realized I was bawling my eyes out before Tae wiped my cheeks with a paper towel. I grabbed the towel and tried to wipe off the mess on my own, but the tears kept coming. It wasn't one of the beautiful cries you see on TV either. More like the kind where the lower half of my face got covered with snot and my eyes literally started to ache.

"Shh, it's okay," he said with a super soothing tone and started to stroke the back of my hand with his fingertips.

Tae's voice was calming and his touch even nicer, but it didn't change the fact that Mom was gone. As was Dad. Nothing could wake me up from that nightmare.

"I have no one left."

I shifted my eyes to my lap on the plain blue sheet, ignoring the pain that spread on my neck My hands gripped the soaked paper towels tighter. Tae still held my arm, drawing circles on my skin.

"That's not true," Tae stated with that calm and super soothing voice of his. I snap my eyes up to meet his. "You have me."

The warm and fuzzy feeling came back to me with a rush. With a deep inhale, my breathing steadied, and my tears let up. "Promise?"

His fingers traced circles on my arm both faster and gentler at the same time. "Yeah, I'm here for you. That's a promise. And I'm not even the only one. You'll always have Minjae, Do-hyun, and Chris, too."

I cleared the last tear from my cheek and relaxed fully back into my bed. Some things changed drastically in my missing six years, but it seemed some things didn't. "Grid's still a thing?" I asked.

"Yeah, very much so."

That was, by far, the best thing I'd heard since waking up in this horrible place. Even the corners of my lips pulled up the tiniest bit. "Did we ever make it as big as we planned?" If we really stayed together all six years, surely we'd gotten at least a little break.

Tae let out a small chuckle. "What, you doubted us? Of course, we made it big."

Thank gods. "Cool. So I don't have to wait tables anymore?"

"You haven't had to in years now, Joonie," Tae said with an amused look lingering on his face.

"Good," I said, yawning.

There was something oddly relaxing in Tae's presence. Something that felt almost magical.

With him by my side, I made it through until morning without the need for those vicious drugs. Even as the morning light filtered through the window and I stirred enough to twinge my neck, forcing me to let out a loud groan.

Tae popped right to my side and took my hand. "You want me to call the nurse?"

"Nah, I can deal with it. The drugs make my head all fogged up."

Tae plopped to sit back down on the chair he had dragged beside my bed, rubbed his eyes, and stretched his back.

"Feeling any better at all?" he asked.

174

"Yeah, somewhat..." My body hurt less each day, but the clouded parts of my mind never cleared. The more I forced myself to think, the cloudier it got and the more frustrated I become. "I still can't remember shit, though."

Tae looked down at his hands. "They told me the damage to your brain was somewhat severe and in the area that involves memory. We kinda anticipated that. I didn't really understand half of what they've been telling me, so you might want to hear it yourself."

"Wait, why do they tell *you* these things?" I asked, without considering how rude it probably sounded. Truth be told, even with my parents gone, Tae was just my band-mate. There was no reason for him to be there with me each and every day. "I mean uhh, not that I don't appreciate it or anything... It's just why are you the one taking care of me?"

Blood rushed to my face. Wait…was I blushing? Why did I blush? I never blushed.

Tae rubbed the back of his head nervously before he answered. "Well, uhh, when your parents passed away, you made me your next of kin on paper... I—I'm practically your legal guardian as long as this whole thing gets sorted out."

Well, okay…that *did* make sense. He had been the leader of our group back in the days, and probably still was. Maybe I still had no life besides GRiD.

A nurse barged in—the same nurse as when I first woke up.

"Good, you're awake. Good morning!" she said with an overly enthusiastic tone and walked briskly beside my bed. As I just smiled at her, she continued, "How are you today? Any pain?"

"Yeah, my back and neck hurt when I move," I stated honestly. "But I don't want more drugs. I want to know what's going on."

"Alright but give me a call when it gets too much to handle. What would you like for breakfast?"

"Coffee," I croaked. There was nothing I wanted more. "One—" I started, but Tae interrupted me, smirking.

"One sweetener and lots of milk, please."

"Coming right up," the nurse said and scurried off while I glared at Tae with narrowed eyes...so he knows how I like my coffee, huh?

"Sorry, it's been the same for ages," Tae said, with a shrug. He sported a lopsided grin that showed off a faint dimple in his left cheek.

I wondered why I had never noticed that dimple before?

Retrograde Amnesia

The nurse came back with a steaming cup of coffee in her hand and the doctor from the day before in tow. As soon as the nurse handed me the mug, I forgot all about Tae's strange knowledge of my favorite coffee type and took a steaming-hot sip. My taste buds were brutally awoken by the bitter taste, but as it was toned down by lots of milk and some sweetness, I didn't really mind. It tasted like I was alive. And I loved it. It was perfect.

"So, Joon-seok, I heard you'd like to know what's going on?" Dr. Han asked with an easy-going smile on her face.

"Yes, please," I said, dragging it out and taking another sip of coffee.

"Well, body-wise...you're miraculously fine, considering the severeness of the accident. You just sprained your neck and some muscles on your back badly. That's why you're still in pain. Apart from that, there's some bruising here and there. The worst of that is on your neck and chest because of the seatbelt. Which—by the way—probably saved your life."

I nodded to that out of habit, ignoring the pain that stabbed me on my back again. "And my uhh...memories?" I asked.

"Now that's another question entirely," the doctor said and rubbed her temple, before diving headfirst into the medical jargon. "To put it bluntly, it doesn't look very good. When you came in, there was some severe swelling on your brain caused by the hit on your head. You were in a medically induced coma for the last 8 days, as we waited for the swelling to level down. We took an MRI just before deciding to wake you up, and while the damaged area is somewhat large, it'll heal completely. In fact, it has already started to heal quite nicely.

"When it comes to your memory...it's harder to pinpoint the exact problem and make a solid recovery prognosis. It's already hard because science doesn't know a lot about how memories work in the first place. On top of that, in your case, the retrograde amnesia is most likely a combination of trauma-based and physical-based.

"What concerns me most is that your brain has reverted right back to the previous accident with your parents involved. That must've been a traumatic event for you, and I'm sorry for your loss, but medical-wise, the healing process of your memory might associate this new accident with the previous one. Which means your mind might subconsciously choose to erase the memories in between the two accidents completely."

Tae took my hand again and squeezed reassuringly, as I gulped. "So in short, there's a chance I might not remember the past six years...like ever?"

Dr. Han nodded. "Yes, that's a possibility which I want you to prepare for. However, it's just as likely that you'll recover all the memories just fine. I'm just letting you know the possibilities and what we do know at the moment."

There was a tiny sliver of hope. "And if they do recover, do you have any idea how and when?"

"It's impossible to know. It might be tomorrow or years from now, could be never. As for how, the best I can do is offer some information of previous similar cases to yours where the memories *have* returned. Some people have gotten memories back little by little, both triggered by an event or on their own as the brain slowly heals. Some have come back all at once, also both triggered and on through healing. If you get them back, there is no way to know which way you will until it happens."

I took another sip of the coffee hoping it would ease the headache pounding in my skull. At least I knew what was happening to me…for whatever little relief that was worth.

"So, what happens now?" I asked carefully.

"Now, we just take it slow and easy. Your physical rehabilitation begins as soon as possible to reduce the damage done with the accident and by lying in bed for over a week. Try not to think too hard as your brain cells need time and rest to heal."

My headache, very much caused by thinking too hard, raged harder. "Easier said than done, that last part."

"I know. Just try and take it easy for a few days. I'm sure Tae can fill you in for the most part as I gathered you've been living together for the past years. Just remember, no mathematics or any other sort of brain exercises, no overthinking this memory loss thing, no wallowing in misery. And sleep. A lot."

"And you seriously need to rest your voice too," Tae added. Oh right, he was still there. Why was I blushing again? "No excessive talking. In fact, I brought you this." He handed me a small whiteboard with a marker attached to it with a cord.

I raised an amused eyebrow, took it, and wrote three big letters: WTF. Then I held it up so they all could see it.

They all laughed.

Tae was the one that recovered first. "No, seriously. Your voice is practically a national treasure. Bringing billions of Won to our economy. As well as to your own pockets. Suck it up champ, you'll get over it."

"Umm, I'm sorry, what?!" I yelled as loud as my still sore throat allowed me.

That earned me a scowl from Tae. The nurse and the doctor watched our staring contest, visibly amused. Tae, however, didn't say anything to me and kept eyeing the whiteboard. The wordless fight went on for a while, and I regret to admit it was I who gave up first. Angrily, I scribbled a question mark at the end of "WTF," underlined it a few times, and turned it towards him.

"You heard me. I told you we made it big. Well, we really made it *big*-big."

It didn't convince me, so I turned my eyes towards the nurse and the doctor, who both still looked at us.

"He speaks the truth." The nurse admitted. "You were famous before, but you all blew up after the big comeback…and especially after the DoMino scandal."

Um. Excuse me? What? I grabbed a paper towel from under the coffee mug and erased the text on the whiteboard, before hastily scribbling three words to it: Comeback? Domino? Scandal?

"Right, uhh...the comeback. We all went to the army at the same time. We were in different divisions, so I can't really tell what it was like for you. And the scandal...well, I think you can find all about it later. Let's just say Do and Min are finally together, and that didn't really go down as smoothly as we would've wished."

Ahh, I had seen their chemistry right from the start. It made sense. Though they sure had taken their time, it seemed, based on Tae's expression while he emphasized the word "finally." And I had already gone through the army? Well, that one was another relief.

"That reminds me," The doctor began. "It seems like you two are already doing fine, but I'd like to remind you that, while it's okay to go through the past six years, it would be wise not to drop it all at once on Joon-seok. And you two must be completely honest with each other. Tae, if he has something to ask, and you know the answer, you'll have to be honest about it. It's a must. And Joon-seok, if you feel even slightly overwhelmed, you'll have to ask for a break. And if you'd like to know something, you'll have to ask, as nearly any information can be a trigger to get your memories back. That is, if you want your memories back."

I did most certainly want my memories back. Based on the information I had gotten since waking up, I had lost so damn much. But exhausting it certainly was, and as much as I wanted more, I also needed to obey the doctor if that's what it took. I wrote the word "break" on the whiteboard and leaned back on the bed.

I heard the doctor discuss some things with Tae, which I ignored completely. Instead, I stared at the mushy green wall behind them, seeing practically nothing. I was way too exhausted to keep up. Eventually, the neck pain started to creep up on me again with its full force, making a slight frown between my eyebrows. The nurse asked if I wanted some pain meds to which I just nodded and soon there was another drip attached to my arm. I welcomed the numbing effect of the drugs with open arms and eventually drifted off to sleep.

Hurry Back

The pain medication took care of the nightmares. But the nurses didn't let me sleep for long—maybe for two hours or so. Then it was lunchtime. Apparently, they worked some kind of a schedule at the hospital, which didn't really care for my beauty sleep.

Almost still asleep, I started munching down the bland tasting vegetable-mush soup they put in front of me. My neck made eating a bit difficult. Thankfully, using the remote I found on my right side, I could prop myself more upwards with just a push of a button.

Tae was nowhere to be seen. My pulse gradually started to rise the longer he was gone, the annoying chart on the machine making sure I'd noticed. My hands got clammy too. I had no means to contact him—or anyone for that matter. My only communicating tool was the damn whiteboard that was no use in this situation. I glanced at it anyway as if it would've helped. Only then, I noticed a note that was not in my handwriting.

The note was short. It simply said: "Running errands and need a shower. Will be back asap. -Tae" but that was all that was needed for me to calm down. It was kind of cute, to be honest.

Also *shower*…that sounded heavenly. I ran my fingers through my hair to feel the damage done by staying—for who even knew how long—in that bed with no pampering. As my fingers brushed the back of the right side of my head, there was a large patch with an alarming lack of hair.

Needless to say, I smashed the nurse call button immediately. Maybe a few more times than was absolutely necessary. And then a couple of times more just in case. I was panicking, okay? Sue me.

It didn't take long for a nurse to barge in, asking what was wrong. It was an older lady I hadn't seen before, sporting a somewhat sour look on her face.

I opened my mouth to speak but thought about that "billions of Won" my voice was apparently worth. With the sleeve of my ugly green hospital pajamas, I wiped my whiteboard clean and wrote just one word in all caps: *MIRROR.*

The nurse walked next to my bed and nonchalantly passed me a handheld mirror from the drawer beside my bed. Hands shaking, I grabbed a tight hold on the handle and lifted the thing in front of my face.

Thankfully, I didn't look that much older than I had anticipated. What did take me by a surprise though, was that my hair was freaking pink? Faded, but it was still enough to shock me. And yes, a part of it was shaved off, but it wasn't as bad as I had feared. Still, I pointed to the bald spot on the side and raised my eyebrows to the nurse.

"It had to be shaved in case we had to perform a surgery," the nurse stated with an uninterested tone, before adding something along the lines of *"it'll grow back, punk"* so silently I wasn't even sure she had said it.

Honestly, it wasn't even that bad. I could ask a barber to make it an undercut or something. For a moment, I was just glad I looked somewhat like myself. Apart from the pink color of my hair, that is. As far as I knew, my hair was supposed to be brown. Maybe bright colors were an in-thing. It wasn't like there wasn't anything in my reflection that couldn't be fixed with a visit to a beauty salon. And a good shave wouldn't do any harm either.

Right. I still needed that shower. I asked the nurse if it was possible with the whiteboard.

She nodded and told me she'd get someone over soon. To be completely honest, I was just glad it wasn't her who'd help me through it. She looked like she was basically done with life and especially her job.

The nurse from the morning came to help me. It was a bit of a struggle to get up from the bed as my back still ached like a motherfucker, but somehow, I managed with the nurse's help. It was honestly devastating when she reached for my dick to remove the gross condom-thingy that gathered my pee. I planned on never having it back. Ever.

Relieved to get out of the bed for a change, I slowly walked like an old man over to the bathroom that was attached to my room. For the first time, it dawned on me that I had a room all to myself. That couldn't have been common? Did the label pay my medical bill or…?

Even the bathroom was way bigger than the one we had back at the dorms. Or...*had* had. Did we even live in the same place? The two-bedroom apartment I remembered had been crowded. Minjae, Chris and I had to share one damn bedroom. And even that was an improvement from the first dorm with the freaking tiny bunk beds. If it was really true that we were now successful, surely we wouldn't live there now? Then again, the doctor had said something about us living together...so maybe we did have a dorm?

With all these questions circling on my mind, and new ones popping up endlessly, I showered with the help of the nurse. And boy, it felt good. Eagerly, I scrubbed every part I could reach, twice, while the nurse handled parts I couldn't.

It was awkward as hell, but as I gathered, I wasn't the first male she'd seen naked, I tried not to be bothered. Too much. The nurse tried to make it easier by chatting about the weather and other un-interesting things. For that, I was grateful.

When we were done with the washing part, I leaned on the wall and just let the warm water run on me. The nurse turned her back to me out of courtesy. Another thing to be grateful for.

I let my mind wander. There were just so many things I wanted to know more about, making me eager for the time that Tae would be back. I even considered starting a list of the questions I had in mind but didn't really get very far.

Eventually I decided I had taken up enough of the valuable time of the nurse and carefully stepped out of the shower. After she helped me dry myself with a towel, I gulped and forced myself to look at the full-length mirror on the other wall.

The sight wasn't pretty. My whole upper body, especially my chest was practically covered in halfway healed cuts and ugly bruises. Some were still dark, others yellowed on the edges.

It hurt to even look at the reflection, so I quickly turned away and let the nurse walk me back to the main room. She handed me a fresh set of bland, green hospital pajamas and even helped me put them on. While I climbed back to the bed, I noticed someone had changed the sheets while I was showering, and I couldn't have been more grateful for anything in my whole damn life.

As if I knew anything about my life.

The nice nurse started to comb my hair because I couldn't lift my hand that way without wincing. Body worn down and exhausted, I leaned back and huffed, feeling completely useless. But the nurse didn't seem to mind. Instead, she started humming a tune, which sounded somewhat familiar. Though, I was sure I hadn't heard it ever before.

The tune struck a chord within me, making my heartbeat in a certain recognizable way. I wondered…was one of our songs?

Maybe she'd done it on purpose to trigger some memories?

I didn't dare to ask. For a while, I was hopeful to regain some memories, but it seemed like an impossible task—the more I tried to remember, the bigger the nothingness grew in my head.

Realizing I didn't even know the nurse's name and she had already seen me naked, I grabbed the whiteboard and started scribbling.

"My name is Meiling," she said with a soft tone, even before I got to the end of the question.

We talked for quite some time. She spoke out loud of course, and I wrote everything to the board. I found out her favorite color was red, her favorite artist GRiD—to which I chuckled; never in a million years would I have thought I'd show my dick to a fan. And she was a morning person. I also found out that she was my designated nurse, whatever the hell that meant. But it was nice to know she'd be there most of the time if I needed assistance.

We were laughing together at a dumb joke I made up about being mute when there was a knock on the door. After asking me if it was okay, Meiling let the visitor in as it was visiting hours. A man, looking my age—or actually looking the age I had been six years ago—walked in.

He looked all familiar, but at the same time not familiar at all. He was smiling...or rather smiling as wide as the brutal, still healing, angry red, stitched cuts allowed him to. Involuntarily, I kind of winced at the sight—it was admittedly a bit hard to look at his face. In my defence, there was a part of it missing. Just where the cuts crossed on his cheek.

It wasn't until he opened his mouth to greet me when I fully recognized him by his unique voice.

"Chris!" I croaked, and instantly slapped my hand over my mouth, as Tae's voice nagged in my mind to me for not being able to stay quiet. I started scribbling on the whiteboard, explaining to Chris I wasn't supposed to talk.

Chris laughed as he sat in one of the chairs on my right. "You look...alive," were his first actual words to me.

I wasn't sure if I should scold him or laugh. How was I supposed to act with him these days? Were we buddies? Just...what? I mean, to me it was just a few days ago when I had to do his laundry because he kept ruining his clothes.

"I heard you don't remember much," Chris continued when I failed to respond.

I narrowed my eyes but ultimately decided to let go of the lack of using honorifics this time, as I had no clue how to handle him in the first place.

Yeah, they've told me I've lost 6 years, I wrote.

"That's a lot," he grimaced. "Want me to fill something in for ya?"

Nah, I think my brain's gonna fry if I have to process more, I scribbled down, to which Chris smiled stiffly. *Anyway...what happened to your face?*

His face fell instantly. "Uhh, you know nothing about the car accident?"

You were involved? I asked, to which he nodded. I couldn't help but wince again.

There was a short silence before Chris eventually did open his mouth. Looking a bit uncomfortable I might add. "Actually, it wasn't an accident in the traditional sense. My driver collided with the car you were in, um...intentionally. Only he thought it was Tae's car. It's complicated, but the guy practically wanted Tae dead."

My jaw dropped, and the air was knocked out of my lungs. It made a whole lot more sense why Tae had been sitting by my bedside religiously all this time.

"Uhh, we're all alive, so I guess that's all that matters," he continued with a bitter look spreading on his face.

I guess... I wrote to the board. *Why Tae though?*

There was a long silence where I avoided looking at his face and he stared at mine intensely. He never replied to my question, but I didn't press. Maybe it was best for me not to know until I could handle it. Eventually, Chris sighed and got up.

"Actually, I just came to see you—awake—before I head out. I get to leave this place today. But give me a call if there's something I can help you with," he said and started heading for the door.

I had a feeling I wouldn't see him for a while, something in his eyes told me he was definitely going through some shit on his own. I was worried, but at the same time I barely even knew the guy. At least six years back, which was my reality.

Waving him a half-hearted goodbye, I leaned back on my bed with my eyelids getting heavier again. The nurse excused herself too, and I was left all alone again. Tae still wasn't back.

If only I'd had a phone to text him that he should hurry back to me.

Wait, what?

With that last, lingering, confusing thought, I tried my best to fight the drowsiness that threatened to pull me under again.

I failed miserably.

Code Red

That night, the nightmares weren't only about my parents. There was a faceless man too, laughing at their dead state. A lunatic with empty eyes. I tried to fight him, failing every damn time. Every time I failed, I got more and more frustrated.

The next thing I knew was someone shaking my shoulder to wake me up and my whole body breaking a cold sweat. Fluttering my eyes open, I was instantly met with a worried gaze on Tae's face…at a very close proximity.

"It was just a nightmare," he whispered, his face just a few centimeters from mine, and his hot breath fanning over my face. The scent had a slight minty edge that reminded me of toothpaste.

His sudden closeness shifted my whole state of mind from terrified to...something else? My heart still pounded super-fast and my breath stuck to my throat, but this time it wasn't an entirely uncomfortable sensation. Just weird.

As soon as Tae was convinced that I got back to reality fine as my eyes focused, he moved away, which made me feel even weirder. Like my body wanted him to be that close.

I closed my eyes for a brief moment then propped myself more upwards on the bed.

"Just a nightmare..." I muttered to myself, repeating Tae's words for my own reassurance.

"You know, the 'being quiet' thing is only for like...a few days," he said disapprovingly, but I could see a smile linger on his lips—damn delicious looking lips, that is.

Whoa, wait what? Since when have I ever felt that way about Tae's lips? I couldn't help but sink my front teeth to my own bottom lip. Something dark flashed on Tae's eyes at that exact instant, and he averted his stare from my face. The whole thing made me curious, so I started to ask with the whiteboard, but I didn't even get to the end of it before he noticed what I was after and replied.

"Just don't bite your lips... It'll make them chapped," he said, still avoiding my eyes.

It's a habit, sorry, I wrote to the board, not one hundred percent convinced by his reasoning but ultimately shrugged it off. I had some more urgent things to discuss. *I want to know things.*

Tae waited patiently for my questions. After a while of total silence, he moved to sit on the chair, and started burning a hole in my face with his stare. I almost got lost in his dark eyes while trying to figure out what to ask first.

I wanted to know the basic outline of my life for the past few years and simultaneously didn't want to know any of it. Besides, two years of that I had spent in the army and based on what Tae had told before, he didn't really know about those times. And then, I wanted to know more about this not-accident. Why would someone, anyone, would have wanted him dead? Or me, for that matter?

I wanted to know what my relationship with the other members of GRiD was like, since we apparently still lived together. I wanted to know what I was like these days. There was just so much I wanted to know, and at the same I wanted to remember the things on my own, rather than get told what happened by someone else.

It left me overwhelmed, so I didn't know where to even start. But as the doctor said, every piece of information could be the trigger to make the actual memories come back, I was determined to begin somewhere.

Chris came by. Told me the car accident wasn't really an accident? I eventually wrote to the whiteboard, my heartbeat accelerating with each syllable.

Apparently, the topic wasn't something Tae particularly wanted to talk about. I could tell when he froze and started rubbing his temples in a tired manner. He even squeezed his eyes shut, his expression getting angrier and angrier every passing second before he somehow managed to breathe steadily again.

As far as I could remember, Tae had always had this stoic, almost emotionless face. Which he then tried to overcompensate at photo shoots, for example, making his poses awkward as hell. Yet that one question had affected him deeply. All the world's emotions could be read clearly on his face. The change was so drastic and sudden to me that it seemed surreal. Then again, in between was the six years I knew nothing about, and people changed.

"It started around a few months back, as far as I know," Tae started. "You started getting some super creepy phone calls and voicemails from a stalker. You finally showed them to me when they turned threatening."

The frown I had on my forehead was probably so deep my eyebrows knitted together. I had a stalker? Me? A mere waiter aspiring to be an accomplished singer one day? Through the whirlwind of emotions that one revelation caused me, I had to remind myself to focus and remember we were supposed to be famous now.

Tae continued. "I... we did everything we could to prevent anything from happening but no one would've guessed the stalker was one of our own damn security staff."

We have security staff?

"The guy found out about how we were—uhh, nevermind. Well, anyway he got angry at me. Then a lot happened at this showcase we had, and we ended up switching cars. The guy apparently thought he was aiming for me, as far as what I heard from Chris. He basically saved your life, you know."

Now that was some actual information right there. Tae probably thought so, but I didn't miss that hesitation about something we were doing that made my stalker angry. But I decided to ignore that for the time being and focused on the latter part, which seemed more important.

Chris saved me? I asked.

"Yeah, that brat is one hell of a fighter nowadays, you know," he said with a half-smirk lingering on his lips, an amused one.

I shrugged and wrote, *His face though...what happened?*

Tae's laughter died. "From what I heard from Seong-gi— Minjae's regular guard who reached the crash site first—Chris tried to keep the guy down. Unfortunately, the guy got in a couple of good swings."

Okay, my respect for Chris might've skyrocketed.

"It's pretty bad." Tae continued. "Knowing Chris, he might just go MIA on us because of this. Thankfully, he's still trapped here."

Wait a minute...hadn't Chris said he'd gotten out that morning? *He told me he'd get out today though.*

After blinking a couple of times, dumbfounded, Tae cursed under his breath. He took a couple of steps towards the door when the realization hit me—he was going away. And that I wasn't going to handle well after hearing the full story.

I panicked.

It definitely wasn't my proudest moment, but I threw my pillow right at his back before scribbling *STAY* on top of all the other texts on the whiteboard.

He just barely glanced at me over his right shoulder. "Sorry, I have to go. I'll be right back," he said and took another step.

My chest tightened uncomfortably every step he took towards the door. While I had no idea why it affected me so hard, I didn't have time to think things through or hesitate.

"Red!" I cried as loud as my throat could handle. Then, I lowered my voice to a whisper, "Please."

Tae froze at the threshold. "What did you say?"

I froze. I had no clue why the word "red" came to my mind first, so I covered it up. "Stay? Please?"

There was a brief silence, but then Tae just told me to "Use the damn whiteboard," and crashed on the armchair over at the corner.

Feeling super guilty of making him stay, I just watched him hunt down his phone and instantly dial a number. After a couple of seconds, whoever was on the other end answered.

"Joe...can you check on Chris?" he started and tapped his fingertips against the arm of the chair, waiting for Joe's reply. "Nothing, I just think he might've slipped away during..." he continued, nodded, and then ended the call.

After wiping the now filled-to-the-brim whiteboard clean, I wrote: *I'm sorry.* I propped it up against the railing on my bed. The shame over the whole thing washed over me, and I couldn't even look at Tae's face. Hell, I had no idea why I needed him to stay with me so bad in the first place.

Instead, I tried to make myself smaller by sneaking even further under the blankets.

Thus, I didn't even notice Tae had made his way beside my bed until he touched my chin and turned my face towards him. After a while of trying to look everywhere else, I had to give up and look him straight in the eyes.

"Jag–... Joonie-ssi... Don't you dare feel guilty of making me stay. Ever," he stated with a soft look on his eyes, the immense gaze almost melting me to the spot.

The beginning sped up my heart to the point where I couldn't focus on the rest. It almost sounded like he was going to say *jagi*– a word for lovers—but then changed it at the last second. There was no way he could be...or could he? Then even my thoughts got distracted because his face was just so damn close, and I was having a hard time breathing properly. My teeth involuntarily sunk to my bottom lip again.

In that instant, Tae's eyes swept past my lips, and he retreated.

"And please stop doing that," he said with an oddly strained tone.

"Why does that bother—" My question was cut short when the door banged open and a handsome, freakishly tall, and muscular guy in a suit barged in.

"Well, you were quick," Tae stated as soon as his eyes focused on the sudden intruder. "What's up?"

"I was just around the corner. Chris isn't in his room; he was checked out. You have any idea what happened?"

I pointed at my white board.

"I see. I'll have Mr. Won to check if he's gone to his mountain hideout."

It only took a questioning glance at Tae for him to clarify for me. "This is Joe. Mr. Won is Chris' regular guard. Chris has a house on the mountains."

The brat had a house now, apparently.

The whole thing turned into a whole hassle where the said Mr. Won appeared in my room too and they made some phone calls and stuff while I totally tuned out.

At the end of it, I never got around to asking about the *jagi* thing or what was Tae's problem with my lip biting. Eventually, I gave up completely and accepted that it was my life now, to be constantly confused. Still, I couldn't wait to get out of the hospital to have an actual conversation with Tae about everything, without any distractions.

History Lesson

"Do-hyun and Minjae are coming by today," Tae said.

I offered Tae a smile as an "okay." It was too tiresome to write everything to the whiteboard, so Tae had gotten real good on reading my body language. He got it right away.

It was early morning at the hospital, and we were having breakfast in my room at the small table. Despite walking like a grandpa still, I had made my painful way across the whole room to have my cereals there. That cereal was a very exciting celebration due to the fact that (a) I could walk despite being as slow as a sloth, and (b) I got to eat solid food. Though the hospital cereals tasted bland as hell, at least I got to chew something—a privilege I took for granted until I had to be on a mash-soup diet for a few days.

"You mind if I go help Jiwoo with a press conference, meanwhile? It's practically chaos around HQ these days," Tae shook his head as the crease of worry between his eyebrows got way too deep for my liking.

Of course, you go. Who's Jiwoo? I scribbled to the corner of the whiteboard that was leaning against the plain green wall while munching down some more cereals.

There was an odd silence, so I lifted my eyes up from the bowl to Tae's face. It was pretty much blank as he stared at me, those deep eyes of his studying mine. It gave me chills, to be honest.

"What?" I mouthed, lifting my eyebrows.

He blinked a couple of times and cleared his throat. "Umm, Jiwoo's our manager. And a close friend. Sorry, I forgot you don't remember her."

My eyebrows scrunched together. *What happened to sunbae-nim Maeng?*

Tae shrugged and took a sip from his coffee. "Ugh, don't even mention his name. That scumbag scammed us. Most of the money from the first album and the first tour went straight into his own pockets. That's why we were so broke all the time, despite our music selling well."

My jaw dropped. To me, it seemed like just the other day back like last week, when he had been booking us to variety shows and what not to get us more exposure. I'd never in a million years thought he'd be a fraud. Though now that I had to give it a thought, it was weird that, despite our debut album selling gold, we were still pretty much broke. I had thought it was the way it was supposed to be. Besides, my dream never was to make lots of money; it was to sing. So, there was that. Though it would be a lie if I said it wasn't nice to suddenly wake up wealthy.

"Well, it's ancient history now. No need to wallow in it," Tae said, chuckling to my baffled expression and totally missing the point, before focusing back on his newspaper.

I turned my own attention back to the cereals. I wasn't really all that hungry anymore though and couldn't finish the whole bowl. Avoiding putting too much pressure on my sore back, I leaned back on the chair, as slowly as ever. I wasn't very successful.

I tried to stand and almost fell as my head turned light from the sudden movement. Tae grabbed my elbow like I was a one hundred-year-old senior citizen who needed assistance for everything. I pushed him away, probably ruder than I should've but it was getting pretty old to get treated like I was a piece of the finest glass that could break at any time. Tae only let out a muffled chuckle that he didn't quite manage to hide, making me snap my eyes towards his.

"I'm just wondering how you can just roll with all this," he said. When I cocked my eyebrow up at him, he added, "I'd freak out."

I didn't reply. Instead, I turned around and started to sloth my way towards the bathroom.

Because I *was* freaking out. All the time.

I wasn't even allowed to speak. There just wasn't much to do about it so why whine? By that point, it was just a relief to be able to go to the toilet without anyone's help. I had to be grateful for the smaller things in life.

It didn't take long after I got back and crashed on my bed for one fluffy-haired blond to appear at the door. He was followed closely by a black-haired man. I instantly recognized Minjae—the fluffy-haired one—so I figured the other one was Do-hyun and smiled at them.

They took it as an invitation to come inside and walked by my bed, hand in hand with a bouquet of light pink flowers of all sorts in Minjae's other. After they said their greetings, not minding my muteness, Minjae found a vase for the flowers while Do-hyun cut the stems of the flowers. Watching them work in perfect sync got me a bit taken aback of how well they worked together—you could see the years they'd been close. Kind of adorable if you ask me.

It made me wonder if I was normally like them around the other members of GRiD nowadays.

The longer I watched them, the more fit for each other they seemed. While they were both almost exactly the same height, you couldn't find two people who looked more the exact opposite of each other in every other way possible. Minjae had a lean figure, toned and fit, but not sharp on the edges like Do's. His outfit today was some light-blue skinny jeans paired with a loose white button-up—while Do sported combat boots, black jeans, studded belt, and a black t-shirt topped with a leather jacket.

As Minjae straight out sat at the other end of my bed as if he owned it, I shot a panicked glance at Tae. He had hovered around for the whole greetings ordeal, filling the silence with small-talk while I was still mute due to his own orders. He ignored my glare though and outright left me at Minjae's mercy, mouthing "good luck" towards me with a wink before disappearing to the hallway. As Do-hyun plopped down to Tae's armchair at the corner and started scrolling his phone, I had no choice but to turn my attention towards the man on my bed.

Minjae got comfortable and pulled a tablet computer from his small leather backpack.

"Hyung, you up for a history lesson?"

Of what? I scribbled to the whiteboard and laid it between us.

"Well, us, of course," Minjae replied, shrugging, and waving the tablet.

As soon as I nodded, he dove headfirst to his story. It sounded like a fairy tale to me, but he proved his points by offering facts to back everything up from the tablet, so I had no other choice than to believe him. Bewildered, I listened to him go on and on about GRiD, starting from how we got the first hardcore fans from Japan, how our first Asian tour folded out, how we started and ended our first big world tour from Gocheok Sky Dome in Seoul when we had officially made it big. He talked about our first awards—and while I saw myself speaking in award shows from the videos, it was hard to believe it was actually me.

Turns out we had done some cool stuff over the years. Our newer videos seemed like our label had actually put some serious money in them. The production value seemed off the charts. Well, that, or the new standard was way higher than before. But what freaked out the most, was the fact that I could not, for the life of me, remember doing any of it.

The whole so-called history lesson was like a slap across my face—a solid fact that forced me to realize that I had really done stuff even while my mind was telling me otherwise. I could *see* from the screen, with my own two eyes, my body doing things that I could not recall happening ever in my life. I could hear my own voice talk about things in interviews that I had never heard of.

Minjae was unfazed. And he hadn't changed one bit, it seemed. He was still a complete fluffball one second and a beast the next,

198

probably not even realizing himself how flirty he was with Do—just like I remembered he had been back in the days.

But Do-hyun, he seemed...chill. It was so out of character it freaked me out. When I asked him about it, he just glanced at Minjae with some impressive starry eyes, and even the air around them turned somehow glowy.

When Minjae was done with his story, and I was even more thoroughly screwed up in the head, we resolved to play tic-tac-toe with the whiteboard to pass the time that had started dragging. Thankfully it didn't take long for Tae to appear with a bright red-haired, gorgeous woman in tow.

She wore stunning high-heels, knee-length narrow skirt, button-up, and a pristine blazer—clearly, she was on top of her business fashion. Both Minjae and Do-hyun greeted her like she was family, so I figured she was Jiwoo and waved. She was definitely an improvement from our previous manager, at least appearance-wise. I was admittedly about as straight as a circle, but I could still appreciate her beauty.

She smiled at me and asked how I was doing with a warm voice and an apologetic smile. Tired to my bones, I just gave her a thumbs up and slumped further down on my bed.

"I'll take that as our cue to leave," Do-hyun huffed from his seat and stretched. "Let's go Min."

"Right," Minjae replied, and jumped down from my bed, before turning to face me again. "I take it you won't mind if we disappear for a week or so? The reporters are making our lives hell, and we could use an escape for a bit, to be honest..."

Quickly, I shook my head and gave them another thumbs up. Of course, I didn't want to be a burden to them, as they clearly had their own lives to live. Besides, after what I had heard about the latest scandal involving them both, it was very clear to me why they'd want some privacy. It's not like they could've done anything for me anyway.

In fact, it was a bit of a relief. Two fewer people to worry about offending because I had no idea whatsoever how to act around them. They all seemed familiar and complete strangers at the same time.

I showed them a grateful smile as they gave me their farewells. Jiwoo left with them, claiming she only wanted to see me up and about and with promises to come back soon.

As soon as the door closed behind them, I let out a long sigh of relief. It had been a long day, and I couldn't wait to have some quiet time. Tae smiled down at me before sitting halfway on the bed with his feet still on the ground and leaning back against his arms.

"I see you're tired. Want me to go too?" he asked softly.

His voice was oddly strained. Nevertheless, I shook my head and leaned back, too tired to pick up the whiteboard. For some reason, Tae's company never tired me as much as the others. I guessed it was because he had been there from the start of this nightmare and had seen me at my absolute worst.

And speaking of seeing folks in their absolute worst...I wondered what happened to Chris with a sudden bang of guilt clenching my heart. As Tae plopped down to sit on the chair in the corner and picked up a magazine, I scribbled a question to the whiteboard. *And Chris?*

"We found him," he said matter-of-factly. "He's holed up in his house in the mountains. I figured it might just be best to leave him alone for a while."

I nodded with a relieved sigh. Good thing the brat was safe.

Concept

A few days went by like that. I was just me, trying to exist without any further drama.

Physical rehab started. I got to eat more and more solid food. I needed the pain meds only now and then. The nightmares interrupted my otherwise pleasant dreams only a few more times before they ended completely.

The police tried to question me a couple of times, but as I had no clue what had happened, they quickly gave up. Instead, they harassed Tae with endless questions about Chris, for some reason. They also didn't seem very happy with Do-hyun's and Minjae's decision to flee the country either, but ultimately, they couldn't do much about it since, according to Tae and everyone else they had questioned, they weren't involved. It seemed like, although everyone was seemingly on our side, there was always the doubt as long as Min-ho—the stalker—was missing.

The stress that lingered in the air every time the topic arose was almost touchable. Everyone tried, and for the most part succeeded, to keep me in the dark—and they didn't let me out of the room very often either. "Too dangerous," they said. "Don't want to end up in the tabloids in that state," they said.

Joe made me memorize what Min-ho looked like, but other than that I had no idea what had happened with him apart from the tiny titbits I had managed to gather here and there.

I just hoped the police would find him. Soon. It was hard enough trying to piece my life back together without the added pressure of a psychotic stalker on the loose and everyone antsy about it 24-7.

Apart from all that, everything went somewhat smoothly. As far as I knew, Chris stayed at his second home up on the hills. Do and Minjae were traveling—which I could follow through the tabloids that I had developed an addiction to, ironically enough.

People visited, like...all the fucking time. Our label's officials came one by one, as well as some of my other work acquaintances. Or that's what I was told. In reality I didn't recognize any of them. Most of them hadn't even been there when we started, which made me pretty much a senior employee. Now how freaky was that? A few weeks ago, I was just a rookie.

I still couldn't quite wrap my head around the fact that I had already gone through the army, but that changed soon enough too, once a couple of guys that were from my division visited. They were supposedly my friends and my roommates, but I couldn't have recalled their faces if my life depended on it. They were quite the funny bunch and, if nothing else, I hoped we could keep in touch.

Understandably, Tae made everyone sign a confidentiality agreement, that wasn't part of our closest circle. Even if it made the visits more...awkward...a stalker was still out there looking for me. Not to mention the tabloids exploded with rumors—everything from me being dead to missing off the face of the Earth. I can't say I enjoyed seeing photos of me in the news with headlines like "GRiD lead singer dead?" I figured Tae didn't want anyone giving them more fuel for the fire if they found out about the memory loss, until it came back.

If it came back.

Jiwoo turned my hospital room into a miniature office, along with Tae who refused to leave me alone for long periods of time. I didn't dare to complain. It was nice to have company.

They mostly talked about business and how it was going with postponing the continuation of a world tour we were supposed to be on. I know they didn't mean to make me feel guilty for getting hurt, but I did.

It was an endless cycle of self-doubt. Whenever I tried to apologize, they dismissed me, saying that tours get postponed all the time for even lesser reasons like rehab. To be completely honest, I was surprised that Tae was so easy-going with having to ditch work—the Tae I remembered wasn't like that.

And Tae really stayed with me. All of the time. Even after I forced him to go sleep somewhere else, in a real bed instead of the armchair over my room's corner, he was there with me every waking hour. He came to the hospital early in the morning, most mornings even before I woke up. Then he stayed until midnight or even to the point I had to push him out the door.

Occasionally my brain got the better of me and I couldn't help but wonder...*why?*

On day seven of my new life after getting woken up from the induced coma, I was finally allowed to speak. By then, I *so* had plans for the whiteboard. Every single one of them included setting it on fire. Too bad they didn't let me do that in the hospital, so I tossed to the corner to wait for its complete destruction.

That was also the day we had an awfully awkward conversation with Jiwoo about my career.

When Tae closed the door behind him to grab us all some snacks from the cafeteria downstairs, Jiwoo scurried next to me from their makeshift office across the room. After sitting in one of the stools beside my bed, she started opening and closing her mouth nervously and fiddled with her hair. At first, I just waited for her to speak, but as she just continued the antics wordlessly...I grew anxious. It seemed bad.

"Just spit it out. I can take it," I said.

Finally, Jiwoo sighed and said, "I'm sorry Joonie-ssi. It's just that the label's pressuring me about this, and Tae won't let me speak to you about it yet... But I have to."

"I'm getting fired, aren't I?" I asked nonchalantly.

It wasn't like I hadn't guessed it already. While it had been my ultimate dream to make it as a singer, hearing it was still a harsh kick straight to my nuts. But I understood the realities. What good would a brain-damaged singer do in such an established group? Nothing.

"What? No! Of course not. Gosh, why do you guys always jump to the worst possible scenario?" Jiwoo exclaimed and flipped her hair back. A wave of immense relief wash over me. Well, up until she continued. "But uhh, the label...they still want to know..."

I rolled my eyes back at her when she hesitated. Nothing could be worse than getting the dreams you already had reached once crushed right in front of your eyes. Especially considering I didn't even remember any of it.

"Get to the point, please," I said to end the silence.

"Aish, fine," she started again. "The thing is, no one's got no clue how long it'll take for your memories to come back, right? GRiD doesn't have a lead singer without you, so they've been think-ing about shelving GRiD until your memories do get back. But the ugly truth is this: your memories might never come back. Which is why I like the second option better."

"And the second option is...?" I asked. If getting GRiD a new lead singer and kicking me out was already crossed off the list, what other solution was there?

"Would you be able to try and pull through, even if your memories don't come back right away? Can you see yourself on a stage even without your memories, like...in a few weeks? Obviously when you're otherwise physically healed?"

I didn't answer right away. At first, it seemed impossible. But I *had* gone through the training years, and those days I did remember. I remembered our debut. Plus, the choreographs from our first gigs and most of the lyrics from the first album. Now Tae said there were four full albums plus many single albums we had done during the past six years which I had no idea of other than a few clips Minjae showed me the other day. But I wouldn't have to remember all of it instantly, just the ones that we'd perform on tour. I had seen from the gig videos we had some kind of stage monitors helping with that.

204

I already knew I didn't have to have memories to know how to sing. It was like it'd been two weeks since my last vocal lesson to me. I knew the theory behind it. And, uh, singing really doesn't require much brain activity, to be honest. It was mostly breathing right and using the correct muscles to form a desired sound. Granted, I would probably need a lot of help from the guys and maybe a vocal coach since I had improved heaps from our debut year, based on the video clips I had seen.

So, maybe? It would be a stretch, I knew that much, but singing had been my number one dream for ages. I had worked towards that goal for my whole entire life. Was I really willing to let that go?

Jiwoo sat patiently waiting for me to answer for some time. I think she could see the rising anxiety with each passing thought, and she began to squirm in place. When I noticed her fidgeting, she dropped her head and said with a heavy heart, "I'm just going to put it out there, but there's always the third option too: ending GRiD."

"No!"

"Y'all have enough money to retire and live as rich men for the rest of your days. You could travel the world without having to perform. You'd always be famous, but someday you wouldn't have to worry about lunatics that much. You could even move somewhere remote and just disappear. The way I see it, it wouldn't be that bad. Though then again, I'd lose my job so forget I said anything," she explained with a ringing giggle at the end.

I stared at her like she was talking about some ridiculous nonsense. Which she was. Option three wasn't an option at all. "Do you think I could pull it off? The second option, obviously?"

"Yes."

"Then I'll try to do that." I said with both all the confidence in the world, and none of it at all. And with that decision, my life flipped upside down once again.

I got busy.

On top of physical rehab, a vocal coach visited me every other day. After Tae got over that Jiwoo had ignored his wishes to not disturb me with all the career stuff, he started going through our music with me. Over the phone, we made plans with Minjae to get me back on track with the most important choreographs as soon as he'd get back to Korea. Do-hyun promised to teach me to play the piano for a solo piece I would be required to play on tour. Chris was supposed to teach me the ways of social media. They started simplifying our world tour setlist to include more choreograph-less songs.

I was also told by Jiwoo to get myself familiarized with a concept called fanservice.

Place Called Home

On a random day of my new life, the doctor told me I was recovering well and could go home in a few days.

The only problem...where and what was home? As there was no progress whatsoever on my memory issue, I had zero ideas of how or where we lived. And let's just say researching about fanservice had made my life a hell. It seemed that I had been good at it. Now? I wasn't so sure.

It looked like we had done way more fanservice than the usual thing of acting sexy, handsome, and cute. Back where my memories were intact six years back, there were no such things as gay ships. Or if there were, I hadn't known about them. Nowadays they seemed like a common thing. Turned out we had even used them to our advantage.

Now, Do and Min... they were the ultimate ship, understandably so. But what made me anxious was the ship between Tae and me. It was a way-too-close second, popularity-wise.

I knew it was all acting and not real, alright—because let's face it, Tae was as straight as a ruler. Even if it didn't seem like it on the videos, I was convinced because he had said he was straight just... So. Many. Times. In the past.

Researching about fanservice had another consequence too...a highly uncomfortable one. Tae's presence no longer calmed me—rather, it had the complete opposite effect.

Many times, I caught myself blushing whenever he was too close, and I wasn't supposed to blush goddammit! I also found myself wanting to look good for him, which, by the way, was rather hard when half of your hair was gone and there was no make-up at hand. Tae wasn't even that handsome, but I still found my eyes lingering on his face whenever I thought he wouldn't notice.

And the damn dimple. Yeah, let's not even start on that one. It made a regular appearance in my dreams now.

Sometimes he caught me staring. While I wanted to fall off the earth whenever that happened, he usually just smirked right back at me and moved on with his life. Oh well. At least he was used to the whole flirting thing. The Tae I knew was a completely different person than this one.

Hell, the me I remembered was a completely different person compared to the Joonie in our most recent content. This new-Joonie was shameless, bold, and rocked women's clothing. Then there was the actual me, in green hospital pajamas, remembering only things like getting annoyed whenever I had been questioned about my look. Seemed like at some point I had just said "fuck it" and went for it. But I, from way back—my only true identity at this moment—oh boy, it was nothing compared to the fashion sense I was apparently supposed to have now. There was a freaking video clip on YouTube where I danced in heels on multiple occasions.

All in all, I was as confused as a teenage boy who had just had his first wet dream about hot guys. Not that I spoke from experience or anything.

Due to all that, the doctor saying I'd have to leave that room, which had become my safe haven despite the nauseating smell and green everything, got me on edge. Sure, I wanted my memories back and being trapped in a boring hospital room probably wasn't going to help. But the mere thought of leaving was terrifying, like another leap to the unknown.

As no-one else brought it up, I realized I'd have to tackle the subject of my future living arrangements myself. People forgot rather quickly that I didn't remember a thing from the past six years.

There had already been so many times when I had just stared at people dumbfounded when they had babbled on and on about something I was supposed to know, except I didn't. And it was getting old and fast.

I decided to bring the topic up over dinner.

The hospital food wasn't very pleasing to anyone's taste buds, so just like the past few days, we ordered takeout. I couldn't wait to get back to a real kitchen since I was already gaining some unwanted weight from eating only carb-filled garbage. While Tae went down to the lobby to receive our dinner, I took the chance to freshen up and to try and calm down. And maybe I might've also showered real quick and changed to some fresh hospital pajamas.

Tae got back with some containers holding bibimbap that emitted a heavenly aroma to the room. My stomach growled, and I jumped up from the bed, eager to get to my dinner and the topic I had in mind. We started eating in silence at the small table, as Tae still went over some work emails with his phone. I didn't dare to disturb him while he was working, but right as he put the phone down, I decided it was time.

"The doctor said I could get home in a few days," I started, trying to sound as indifferent as I possibly could.

"Yeah, I heard. Congrats! You made it out alive." He lifted his eyes from his bowl to meet my eyes and offered me a warm smile. Or smirk. I wasn't even sure at this point. Then he popped another piece of meat to his mouth and started chewing like it was no big deal.

Clueless. Was I seriously the only one who thought about these things?

"So... where exactly is home?" I asked and watched Tae choke on the piece of meat he was about to swallow. Served him right.

When he didn't reply anything and just kept coughing, I continued. "Do we still live in a dorm or what? Like, at least Chris has his own place, right?"

When Tae finally calmed down, he started evading my eyes and rubbed the back of his head. "We lived in a dorm—granted, in a much bigger one than you probably remember. Chris' house in the mountains is his second home."

"What do you mean 'lived'? Don't we live there anymore?"

"Well, that place is out of the question now, as it's compromised due to the crash that happened right in front of it. It was all over the news."

"Right...so, wait...we're homeless?!"

Tae let out a nervous laugh. "Not quite. Do and Min got their own place which is now being renovated when they're on their vacation. Chris has been holed up in his second home in the mountains. I bought a condo last week. We'll probably move to another dorm though sometime because it's just easier that way. Whenever we find a building big enough and secure enough, that is," he explained, then shrugged like it was all supposed to be a no-brainer and continued eating his food.

Okay so we were rich. I got it. Made sense. For them. But I still didn't fit in at any of those options.

"Do I have an apartment or...?" I asked and trailed off. What other option was there?

At first, Tae completely stopped chewing. Then he resumed and it took a long, long, long time for him to get that one mouthful swallowed. I was almost sure he wasn't going to answer me at all when he wiped his mouth with a napkin and leaned back on his chair.

"Not that I know of. We'll have to go over your finances at some point. For the time being...I kinda assumed you'd—uh—live with me."

While my face drained of all color, Tae started toying with his soda bottle's label. The silence that hung in the air felt heavier than ever. It didn't even make any sense that I was that shocked, let alone that Tae was uneasy about it. We had lived together before, right? Somehow this seemed different. No other members of GRiD there. Just the two of us. Alone.

Sure, it made sense to live with Tae for the time being. I wouldn't have to worry about finding a place with such short notice. I wouldn't have to live in a hotel room and go through the trouble of finding my own place. Especially if we'd eventually move to a dorm anyway. So, I took a long sip of soda and sighed.

"Oh. Okay then. Thanks, hyung," I replied and moved on with my dinner. No big deal, right?

Tae, however, kept on eyeing me, still fidgeting.

"What?" I asked eventually, before stuffing my mouth with more kimchi.

"There's something I really need to tell you before you agree to it," he stated, his voice hesitant and unsure. "About us."

I glanced at him. "Okay?" I said with a questioning tone between mouthfuls. "Go on."

"Weweredatingyouknowbeforethecrash."

Never, ever, had I heard Tae rush his words that much before. It was hilarious, especially paired with the flustered face he was making, so I chuckled. Unfortunately, however funny it was, I had no idea what he had just said.

"Please repeat that. Slower," I said and stuffed my face with more of the delicious food.

"We are—umm, were—dating. You and me. Before the crash and all this."

It was my turn to choke on food. While I was coughing half of my lungs out, and Tae tried to look everywhere but me, my brain started piecing the puzzle together. And I must admit, the pieces fell in place almost too well.

There was the jagi -thing the other day. The fact that he was always here, and it didn't seem to mind at all. And the way my body reacted to his closeness, and now that I thought about it, it also seemed like he was more comfortable being close to me than other people.

It made sense. Then again it didn't. It was so damn unreal; I couldn't believe it. I started to laugh. So much it made my eyes water.

"Right..." I wheezed. "You almost got me there. You aren't serious, right?"

"Quite the contrary. I'm dead serious," he replied with a steady voice, looking quite unamused.

The laughter slowly died in my throat as I studied him. Those deep brown eyes were totally blank, not one ounce of humor in them. The truth of his words hung in the air and settled my mind. Maybe there was something there after all.

Right after I had regained my ability to breathe and picked my jaw up from the floor, I realized there was at least one major problem.

"Last I checked, I'm a dude. You always said you were straight." I asked, getting sceptical again.

"Not exactly," he said and downright shrugged. "I did my research and came to a conclusion I could be something called demiromantic pansexual."

"A what?"

He shrugged again. "I don't think it matters," The corner of his mouth turned up ever so slightly. "I fell for you, and that's what does matter."

"Okay, well, suit yourself. I guess..."

He nodded and sipped some of the soda, clearly giving me time and space to let the whole thing fully sink in. And then when it did, another realization smacked me in the face…

"Wait...I'm gay?" I asked, before realizing how dumb it sounded when Tae snorted. "I mean obviously, but I'm not in the closet anymore?"

"Nope. You came out to us last fall—Minjae, Do, Chris, Jiwoo and some of the security staff. Not that it was a big deal since we kinda knew already."

"Right..." I mumbled, trailing off. "And for how long have we, err... been a thing?"

"Uhh, it was—is—pretty new. It was like a couple of months back when we were on our first date," he explained with a small smile under sad eyes.

"Do the others know about us?"

Tae hesitated for a second. "Yeah..."

"And you waited this long to tell me?"

He rubbed the back of his neck, still evading my eyes, with a cringe on his lips. "Look, I didn't plan this! It's just, uhh, I wanted to tell you myself. And at first, I hoped you'd remember it on your own, but it seems like that's not happening."

"Fair, I guess," I stated, not quite able to keep the bitterness out of my voice. It seemed like a piece of my memory puzzle that was important to my recovery.

Another heavy silence fell to the room. It was so surreal. Me and Tae, dating? I tried to wrap my head around it, but quite couldn't. Tae sounded sincere, but at the same time it was so unbelievable I had a hard time swallowing the whole thing. Then again, why would he ever lie about something like that? And what about me? The current me did not have feelings towards Tae. Or did he? Did I?

Then the third realization hit my head like a hammer. "Wait, what do you mean we *were* dating? Past tense?"

"Well, I figured it would be best for both of us if we, err, have a break..." he said, hesitating a bit at the beginning but sounding awfully convinced otherwise. "Due to the circumstances."

"Okay. That sounds..." Safe. Boring. Convenient. Was there a lump forming in my throat? "...reasonable."

Why the hell was it suddenly so hard to breathe? It wasn't like I even remembered anything of the relationship that had just ended, so there shouldn't have been any reason to feel this way. We should've been able to get back to being friends. It wasn't like we were anything more at this point anyway. And with that in mind, I filed "a relationship" under the long list of things I had lost together with my memories. Because let's face it, "a break" actually means "the end."

"I know it's…uh, weird." Tae said, probably reading the uneasiness on my face, incorrectly, I might add. "We can book you a hotel room if you feel uncomfortable—"

"No, it's fine. I can bunk at your place," I said. The last thing I wanted was to lose him for good.

"Well, it's only until we find out another option—"

I cut him off again. "Seriously, it's fine. It's not like you're gonna jump on me, right?"

"Right..." Tae said and finally looked me in the eyes. To my surprise, he tossed me a confident wink as he continued, "And I think we should worry more about you jumping on me."

Even if I wanted to smack some sense in him good, I refrained from doing so and only narrowed my eyes at him.

"Besides, the place is awesome," he added, leaning back on his chair. A cocky grin plastered on his face which seemed to brighten his eyes. And those damn dimples, now on full display.

"We'll see about that in a few days," I said and felt a smile make its way on my lips even though I tried my best to hold it back. The heavy cloud of awkwardness which had lingered around us through this whole conversation diffused.

Still, I couldn't help but wonder, what kind of weird mess had I just gotten myself into?

Under Supervision

The awkwardness around me and Tae made a comeback right the next day. A huge one. The actual realization that I had been dating him—and gods know what else—seemingly hit me with its full force with a bit of a delay.

Since then, whenever I had caught myself staring at him I was reminded of that fact. If I blushed when he caught me, there was an awkward silence and bad jokes. Very bad jokes. It was humiliating. And other times I couldn't quite believe it.

Actually, let's make that most of the time.

Then when I did believe, for the briefest second, my brain always felt the need to remind me that we weren't dating anymore. *Due to circumstances.* Not that I was bitter or anything. Nope. Not one bit.

Thankfully, three days later, it was finally time to get out of the prison called "hospital."

I was high on hope that some of the awkwardness would wear off when we weren't inside the mushy green box they had kept me in.

Basically, I spent the day chatting with Meiling, who got all excited when I promised her free tickets to our next concert in Seoul, all the while Tae shot me glances that could've frozen the room. I ignored it as best as I could, as I had no clue what I'd done wrong. He couldn't be jealous, could he? I mean...it was him who insisted that we'd not date. *Due to circumstances.* To me, it was exactly the kind of thing I had understood was good fanservice. And Meiling had said she was a fan.

The dull green walls had started to nauseate me, and the worn-out hospital pajamas weren't exactly a fashion choice I'd approve much longer. I hated the awkward cloud that had hovered above me and Tae ever since his "big reveal" of our—former—state of dating. All in all, it was good to get out.

Tae had brought me some of my own clothes from our dorm. They were just some stone-washed jeans, a plain white t-shirt, a grey hoodie, a matching beanie, and black sunglasses. Nothing special, according to Tae. I, however, nearly fainted when I saw the tags. There were at least Gucci, YSL, D&G present, along with some other probably just as expensive brands I hadn't heard of. What they all had in common was that they screamed "you can't afford me."

Lastly, Tae handed me the wallet that he had finally got back from the police station, along with my phone...or what was left of it. After glancing at the destroyed screen, I tossed it to the table and left it there. It wasn't like anything on it was going to mean much to me anyway. The wallet was from another brand I never thought I'd be able to afford. Inside was my driver's license, a few notes, some credit cards. If I was supposed to be rich, I wondered how much credit they each had on them.

We had gone through the exit strategy at least a thousand times together with Joe and some LBR Entertainment's guards. Joe had made sure I'd remember Min-ho's face everywhere, anytime, as they still hadn't caught the bastard. I was as prepared as I could be. The day's plan was just to get to Tae's place safely, and then make myself "feel at home." Whatever that meant. For the rest of the week, Tae had made me an actual schedule. To me, it seemed like a lot less than what we'd had back in the days. When I asked about it, he just said it wasn't nearly as crowded as our usual schedule was because I was still recovering. I kind of hated the fact he seemed to care so damn much.

There weren't many public appearances on that schedule, for the time being. For that, I was grateful. I wasn't even remotely ready for interviews. Most of it was me hanging out with some other GRiD members.

What got me excited was the fact that there was a visit to a beauty salon with Minjae in the near future. About time I finally got rid of the awful haircut I was still sporting. Also, there were some piano lessons with Do-hyun, as I was supposed to know how to play that thing. Tae was going to give me a more in-depth look at our music and prepare me for promoting. There even were some spots on the schedule for Chris to go over social media stuff with me.

Overwhelming? Yes. But at least it was a change to the dull, boring, and claustrophobic hospital room life. I tried my best not to complain.

In the afternoon the doctor called me into her office for a final evaluation. Tae tagged along, just like every other time I had met with the doctor. They had told me that it was because he was my "next of kin." Which to me, at this point, roughly translated as "a babysitter keeping an eye on a dangerous brain-damaged individual."

The office was large, bright, and the walls were as dull of a shade of green as my room. It was probably supposed to be a calming color—me, I was so sick of it I never wanted to see it again in my life.

Dr. Han—the exact same, older, kind-looking, brunette woman that had been with me from the start of this nightmare—was going through some papers when Meiling led us in. She glanced over her glasses and asked us to sit down. We sat down on the opposite side of her table, just like a few times before.

We stayed silent when she read through some papers and eventually piled them into two piles, one significantly thicker than the other.

"So, how are you feeling today Mr. Shin Joon-seok?" she asked.

"Fine, I guess. The pain's gone. The trainer said I could get back to dancing if I promised I'd start slowly."

"And your memories?"

"Still nothing. Even the nightmares have stopped." My face fell a bit.

"Well, if your memories are the kind that will come back only triggered, the hospital isn't the right place for you. That's why we're letting you go under supervision."

There wasn't that much to say to that, so I stayed silent. Besides, we had been through it all before.

"And you do have Mr. Gang here to help you, right?" she asked us both.

Tae nodded and I shrugged. The doctor narrowed her eyes at us, glaring over her glasses. She probably sensed something had changed between us, but eventually shifted her gaze back to the pile of papers. When she had gone through them one more time, she lifted her eyes back to me.

"Well, here's the diagnosis, the prognosis, some guidelines and a few leaflets about memory loss and coping with it." She handed me the larger pile of papers. "Now that your brain has recovered for the most parts physically, it would be wise to give it something to do. That means you'll have to put yourself into situations that are both new and to situations that might trigger your memories.

"Don't be afraid to ask questions. If you have no luck with that in the next month or so, I'd suggest you prepare mentally for the possibility of not regaining those memories. Maybe even consider seeing a therapist." She smiled at Tae. "I've said this before, but I'll say this one more time. It's a good thing he has you by his side."

Tae nodded. "Of course."

I rolled my eyes. Yeah, right. Weren't we supposed to be on a break now, *due to circumstances*?

"And you won't need to worry about overwhelming him anymore—in fact, I'd highly recommend you try and do that," the doctor continued to Tae.

I gulped and glanced at Tae. He still sported a very blank expression. It seemed like weeks since I'd last seen the dimple, despite only being a few days.

"There's a check-up schedule somewhere in that pile," Dr. Han said, to me this time. "I'd highly recommend that you go through the papers as soon as you feel comfortable. Any questions?"

I ogled the thinner paper pile on the table. It was hard to read it upside down, but I was certain I had seen my name on the top right corner of the document. "What are those?"

"Oh, these?" she asked, almost like she'd only just remembered their existence. "They're just some results from some tests from before the car crash. Let's see..." She split the smaller pile into two. One part she handed to Tae and the other she tried to hand out to me, while saying, "Congrats, you're both clean. And before you ask, it's totally okay to have—"

Tae cut her off by snatching the papers out of my reach. "Thanks! We'll go through those later."

The doctor had a hard time holding in a chuckle. I just stared back and forth between him and at the doctor with my mouth hanging open.

"You haven't told him yet?" Dr. Han asked Tae when she swallowed the laughter she clearly didn't want to let out.

"Uhh, it hasn't come up yet." Tae attempted to hide his blush, unsuccessfully.

Dr. Han *actually* laughed that time. "Well, good luck to you both, then...now shoo." She waved at us off in a dismissive manner.

The immense sense of freedom hit me as we stood up and headed to the door side by side. Whatever Tae tried to hide from me, could wait for another day. Now, it was time to get out of the hospital and get an actual life.

Crib

One final glance around the room that had been my home for the past few weeks—one of them unconscious—and we were off.

Even though I was supposed to be mentally prepared for the whole event, the army of guards accompanied by police that had gathered in my room and the hallway just to take me to a car safely wasn't something I thought I'd ever get used to. The guards I saw in the hallway were all stern-looking men wearing pristine suits. To top it off, I knew there were some police dressed as civilians in the crowd outside, based on what Joe had told me before. It was…hopefully an overkill.

I shot an apprehensive glance at Tae. He shot me back with another one of his dull apologetic smiles that certainly didn't show the dimple I'd been obsessing over the past days.

"I know it's a lot, but it's as much for LBR Entertainment's and the police's sake as it is for you," Tae explained. "It already looked bad they let the 'accident' happen in the first place."

One deep breath and I once again pulled my shit together. I hopped down the stairs together with the guards and Tae, floor after floor. I wasn't even allowed to carry my own bag—one of the guards did. The reason Joe provided me with was ridiculous, "…for faster escape if something went south." While I'd laughed my ass off at first, everyone else's dead serious faces had made me stop.

As soon as we got downstairs, we headed for the main entrance of the hospital. Apparently, it would be crucial for the reporters to get a few photos of me when getting out of the hospital, just for the sole purpose of the fans getting a glimpse of me alive to stop the stupid rumors that had been circling around. The ones that assumed I was dead.

It would've been super cliched to get myself killed at the age of 27—the rockstar life expectancy.

I had agreed to the whole thing with no further complaints, but when I saw the crowd waiting outside through the glass doors, I wanted to scream, hide, and disappear. Maybe fall off the earth entirely. I froze to the spot, waiting for the floor to swallow me as a whole.

Sadly, it didn't happen. I was terrified. The crowd outside...they were waiting for someone, who wasn't even me, to walk through the door.

Despite my disgust with the stage name LBR had forced on me, these people wanted to have a glimpse of that person. They wanted Sweet. They waited for Sweet. They wanted to know if Sweet was alive. That was the cheerful, bright person I had seen a glimpse from the videos I had watched during my hospital days. I was nothing like that overconfident person.

Half of my hair was shaved off. I didn't have an ounce of make-up on my face. The clothes I wore were boring and grey. I was an imposter.

Gathering all the confidence I could possibly muster up at that moment, and hoping to hide the copycat in me, I pulled the hood over my head. After confirming that the beanie was still effectively hiding the disaster that was my hair and showing the sunglasses on my face, I took a deep breath. Tae touched my lower back and offered me another smile, for encouragement I suppose. I took a hesitant step forward. Then another slightly more confident.

Fake it till I make it, right?

But the closer I got to the door, the louder my heart pounded inside my chest. Fortunately, that meant the adrenaline was kicking in. There was an aisle of sorts cleared through the crowd and security staff lined up each side. It led straight to the open door of the SUV that was waiting at the end. Roughly twenty steps, and I'd be out of there—I counted.

By the time I reached the glass doors of the hospital, I had channeled all the rockstar energy I possibly could and was able to plaster a fake grin on my lips. The double doors opened. Trying not to look around too much, I started walking the few steps with just a quick wave and a glance to the crowd. Some of them even cheered.

The paparazzi started shooting photos, and it felt like each and every click and flashing light pierced right through me like bullets. I was blinded by the brightness of the flashes and nailed my eyes back to my goal: the open door of the black SUV at the end of the narrow clearing surrounded by a seemingly endless sea of people.

Nodding to Joe, who watched me enter the car through the rear-view mirror, I plopped down to sit in the furthest possible seat in the back. Shortly thereafter, Tae climbed in too with another guard in tow, and the door slid shut from the outside. Joe started driving.

Some of the photographers tried to take photos even through the windows of the car, jogging beside us as we left. They followed until we turned around the corner and Joe hit the gas. Me being famous...it started to feel real, alright. Absurd, but real for the first time since I woke up.

Soon enough, the car blended into a crowd of millions of similar cars, and I could breathe. The rush hour was at its worst, so it took us a while to get to Tae's apartment. I leaned back at the seat, my hands starting to shake as the adrenaline worked its way out of my system. My heartbeat started slowing down to a much more reasonable speed.

I closed my eyes and took in deep breaths before I started looking outside at the slowly passing buildings. The outside world hadn't changed that much at all in the six years, at least in that part of the city. I wondered if we'd cross the Han river on our way.

Tae took my hand in his and distracted me from the outside world and to his eyes. He just smiled back at me before starting to trail those familiar soothing circles to the back of my hand. I was

222

both a little sad of the fact it was just a friendly gesture, and glad of the fact that it worked wonders for my nerves.

"You're doing so great," he said. "I thought you'd be afraid of riding in a car again."

I blinked at him and his weird statement. "Why?"

"Well, you know...because of the two crashes."

"Oh..." I hadn't really thought about it, but it was kind of weird to have happened twice, but I just shrugged. "I hardly even remember the first one and the last...I don't remember at all."

"Right," Tae simply said, turning his gaze to the window. "Anyway, we're getting close."

"We are?" I asked and looked outside myself.

We were in an area surrounded by glass-covered buildings that reached the clouds. Or so it seemed. Everywhere I looked, everything was pristine, clean, and overwhelming. New. Bright. There were malls. Office buildings. A park. And one particularly beautiful, tall, and enormous building right beside said park.

Sure enough, we circled to the back of that very building and drove through a maze of a parking hall below. After Joe pointed to what at first seemed like a metal wall, with some kind of a remote, the wall swiftly disappeared to the structures. We drove right through the opening and entered a smaller, secluded area of the parking hall. The room had five parking spots, though only two of them were taken. There was one big-ass black statement car, and besides that was a low-key black sedan with heavily tinted windows.

I pointed at the two cars with my thumb as soon as we climbed out of the SUV. "Those yours?"

"The Maserati's mine. Kind of a collectible which makes it an investment. The other's Joe's," Tae explained, smiling to my amusement. "The SUV's technically mine too We use it the most because it blends well."

Just then Joe hopped out from the driver's seat of the SUV, then plopped down to the driver's seat of the sedan. The other guard followed his lead and sat in the passenger seat. With just a curt nod towards us, they were out of the garage in a flash. The metal door dropped down ominously behind them, with a loud bang.

"Don't worry, we won't need them here. This place is more guarded than LBR HQ and our previous dorm combined. It's practically a bunker," Tae explained.

I rolled my eyes at him. "I'm not afraid or anything. It's just the sole amount of money around me that's a lot to take in."

Tae gave a look, looking a bit weirded out, but ultimately let it drop. He took my bag from the ground where the guard had left it, and we started walking towards the elevator that was at the other end of the private parking hall.

My brain was trying to keep up, but it was failing miserably. To me, it was like yesterday when I had done extra shifts as a waiter to make ends meet. And now, I was suddenly entering this luxury lifestyle that involved actual safety guards, shiny Maseratis, private garages under skyscrapers, and clothes from exclusive brands. And apparently a filthy rich ex-boyfriend willing to take me to live under his roof.

It was a lot to take in. To be honest, half the time I was convinced I was still in a coma and dreaming or something. It was just so surreal. And it felt like I had gotten it for free, even though I knew we had worked towards this for years.

My thoughts were interrupted when we reached the elevator. There were no buttons whatsoever, so I turned to look at Tae. He handed me a small, black, plastic disk. Its diameter was maybe an inch or so, and there was a key chain attached to it. The other end of that key chain had a cute, light-pink crystal heart-shaped jewel, that sparkled brightly under the dim lights.

"It's your key," he explained.

"It doesn't look like a key," I said, with my eyebrows scrunching together, still mesmerized by the sparkling jewel that was attached to it.

"It's an electronic key that has your details encoded in the chip inside. Here, just show it to the scanner." He pointed at the small circle that was at the right side of the lift, where the call buttons normally were.

I did what I was told. The scanner flashed a green light and the lift's doors opened. Cool.

"You only have to scan the key again, and the lift will take you to the correct floor," Tae said, stepping into the elevator. "You just have to confirm the choice by tapping the touch screen."

In awe, I held the key-disk in front of another circle that was where the floor buttons should've been and tapped the touch screen to confirm the floor according to Tae's instructions. The doors closed behind us.

I let out a small giggle like an excited child and turned on my heels to face Tae. But I was stopped in my tracks when my eyes met his, and the look on his face made a shiver run down my spine. His darkened eyes that seemingly pierced straight through mine, made my heartbeat double the speed. Some kind of electricity started sizzling around us when he took a step closer. There was even a weird pull that tried to drag me closer to him.

Out of habit, I bit my lower lip.

Something even darker flashed in Tae's eyes right before they cleared up and he stepped back, his Adam's apple moving visibly as he gulped. He snapped his eyes away precisely at the same time I turned my gaze to the floor. That damn blush, which had been a constant, annoying, companion to me since waking up from the coma, sneaked up on my neck.

The moment was over.

If my mind had been a mess before, it was now in complete chaos. However, brief the moment had been, my body had already reacted to the closeness of Tae's. Without my brain's consent, I had wanted Tae to kiss me with my whole damn body. It was almost scary to admit, I had wanted to throw myself at him like a lovesick puppy. Not to even mention the weight that had dropped to the bottom of my stomach, before eventually reaching my crotch—

With shame, I admitted that Tae might've been onto something when he said we should worry about me jumping on him.

The elevator stopped with a bling sound, ripping me violently back to reality. The elevator doors opened, and Tae stepped out, seemingly more relaxed than I was. I dared to sneak a glance at his face. He grinned, and my favorite dimple made an appearance for the first time in days.

"Welcome to my crib," he said, his eyes sparkling.

Master Bedroom

We stepped straight into an entrance area of some sort. There was no hallway or front door like there normally was in an apartment building—we were in the apartment right out of the lift, it seemed. To make sure it wasn't another product of head trauma, I glanced back. Sure enough, the lift was still there.

Tae chuckled at my expression and dropped his keys to a bowl on top of a drawer then proceeded to shrugging off his jacket. He hung it in the closet on the right before kicking his shoes to the corner. I did the same.

After a short hallway, we walked into a room that was larger than life. Open, spacious and minimalist would all be great words too. But I couldn't focus on the interior when the back wall was all glass, revealing an amazing view of the city. And we were super high. Like high-high. On top of the building high.

"This is a penthouse?" I walked straight to the back wall and touched the glass to confirm it was, indeed, there.

"Nothing less for my jag—err, yeah, got it cheap from Dad."

There it was again. The jagi -thing. Despite the fact that I was not his lover in any way. We were on a break. Which he had insisted on. *Due to circumstances*. But there was something else that bothered me even more.

"You're back in touch with your father?"

"Somewhat," he said, shrugging and averting my gaze.

Really? Back where my memories were intact, they most definitely had not been in any kind of relationship, let alone on good terms. "How come?"

"Long story. It involved Gran passing away, and all this shit that has happened lately." If I wasn't mistaken, there was a little pain on his face as he said it.

For good reason. Mrs. Gang Eon-ju was gone. I couldn't believe it. I hadn't seen her much except for one time from a distance at a concert, but I had heard a lot about her. To my knowledge, she was supposed to be the strongest woman alive...and the closest thing Tae had had to a family. I wanted to know more, but as it seemed like a difficult topic for Tae, so I dropped it after a quick, "I'm sorry."

As the awkward silence grew around us, I let my eyes wander, desperate to find something else to talk about. Trying to not get distracted by the view again, I forced my eyes to focus on just about anything else.

The condo was beautiful in its own way but also very plain. If I'd had to describe it in one word, it would've been "masculine." It was almost like there was only absolute basic stuff around, but no personal belongings, which seemed a bit odd. Then again, maybe Tae hadn't had the chance to decorate yet.

Otherwise, the apartment was stunning. We were practically surrounded by dark, quality materials. The gigantic couch that dominated the lounge kind of thing in the middle, was all black leather. In front of it was a glass table, on a black and grey rug. The stained, wooden floor was paired with simple dark grey walls. If it would've been my apartment, I would've put up maybe a painting or two, to add some color here and there. To balance it out.

A black iron staircase circled upstairs on my left, and a simple yet elegant open kitchen was on my right. It was equipped to satisfy a professional chef, and most importantly: there was an expensive-looking coffee maker.

Somehow the apartment still wasn't dark. Maybe it was the fact that the whole of the back wall was literally just a window, or that the lighting was designed to brighten up the place. All things considered; I had never seen such an over-the-top place with my own two eyes in my life. I thought these kinds of condos only existed in futuristic movies, not in real life.

I didn't even notice Tae had already made his way to the staircase before he cleared his throat.

"You done ogling downstairs and do you wanna see your room or...?"

"I have a room?" I asked, still marveling at the beauty of the place.

Tae sort of hummed in an amused manner under his breath and started hopping up the stairs two at a time, "You didn't think you'd sleep on the couch, right?"

To be honest, that was exactly what I had thought. In retrospect, the leather couch probably wasn't that comfortable to sleep on, so I followed him up. The stairs led to a loft where you could still admire the view, as the window-wall was two floors high. There was another leather couch in the middle that overlooked the view as well. Behind that were three doors—one in the middle and two on each side.

Tae took me to the one on the left.

"You can have the master," he explained and opened the door.

I started to protest, but all possible arguments died to my throat as I saw the actual room.

The bed was king size, possibly even a bit wider than that. Its interior design was also dark, but the giant window—or at this point just a wall made of glass—continued to this room too. Otherwise, the layout was super spacious but simple. On the right, there were two doors. My bag that Tae tossed in looked lonely all by itself on the floor, thankfully not for long as I'd get more clothes the next day when we went to visit the old dorms to get some of my personal things.

On the left side of the bed, next to the glass wall that seemed to continue even further, was an opening that led to another room. Getting curious, I walked over, only to find the most extravagant bathroom I had ever seen. It was practically all dark tiles and marble.

Directly in front of the window was a huge jacuzzi, and behind that a shower that could've easily fit two persons at the same time. Over at the right were a couple of sinks with drawers below them and a huge vanity mirror on the wall with mounted lights.

I turned on my heels to face Tae who was leaning on the doorway to the bathroom with arms crossed over his chest and a lopsided grin on his face.

"I—I can't possibly take this. Take me to a dark and tiny guest room, please, and have this thing to yourself as you're the one that has paid for it," I stated. "I can't possibly afford this."

"Joonie, there is no 'dark and tiny' guest room. And you'll have to grasp this: you most certainly *can* afford this."

"Really? Then I guess I'll pay rent for it. How much?"

Tae just laughed. "No rent. But if it makes you feel better, I can show you the second bedroom where I'm staying, so you'll see it isn't really that different from this."

I followed him out, although a bit sad I had to leave the beautiful bathroom behind without taking a dip in the jacuzzi. We headed straight across the upstairs lobby to another bedroom that was, as he promised, much like the other one. Only this one didn't have a bathroom with a view—instead, it was just a tiny bit smaller one on the back beside his walk-in closet. It didn't matter though; I could've taken that too anytime. But Tae claimed he had already settled in that room so it would be an unnecessary hassle to move now. Reluctantly, I accepted my torturous fate of taking over the gorgeous master bedroom.

As we exited Tae's room, he headed straight back downstairs to show me the rest of the condo I stopped at the middle door we hadn't touched and called after Tae, "What's in this one?"

"Uhh, I'm not sure yet. It's kind of a work in progress. It's supposed to be another bedroom, but I don't know what to do with it so...it just is."

Fair enough. With no further questions I followed Tae downstairs. It seemed that he was so rich he could have a completely empty room which he had no use for, whatsoever. To me, a mere waiter, it was weird to even think like that. And it was a total waste in my books.

There were only two extra rooms downstairs, as the open living room and kitchen took most of the space. One was a gym with a stunning view, and the one beside that was an office of some sort, where Tae had set up his home recording things. Oh yeah, and there was a bathroom near the entrance area that I had totally missed when we first came in. And a room for laundry and other housekeeping stuff.

We were both hungry when the tour was over. I would've liked to cook, but as Tae had not spent much time there, he hadn't asked his housekeeper to fill up the groceries. Thus, he ordered some takeout, and a bellboy brought it straight up to his condo. That, too, had me overwhelmed—who has a freaking housekeeper? Who lived in a place that had a bellboy deliver the take-out straight to your apartment? Then I remembered what a hassle leaving the hospital had been, it somewhat made sense to have people handling all the public affairs...maybe.

Still, it all was way too much. The relief that filled me after dinner, when Tae asked if I was up for a movie night, was immense. I happily agreed as it would be a nice escape from my life that had become even weirder than it already had been overnight. The only problem was that I hadn't seen a TV in the whole apartment. I didn't dare to ask, because maybe I was just stuck in the past again. Maybe the whole damn window-wall was a television.

I followed Tae upstairs. He went to the couch in the middle of the upstairs lounge. Not knowing what else I'd do, I sat down next to him.

"So uh, you know, the view's nice and all...but it doesn't really pass as a movie," I said while Tae just played with his phone. Or that's what it seemed like, until he chuckled, clicked something on his phone, and a giant screen rolled down from the ceiling, right in front of us.

Some movie posters appeared on the screen as Tae threw his phone to me.

"This reminds me, we need to get you your own phone asap."

I nodded and stared at Tae's phone.

"Your pick," Tae clarified.

Right. The phone's screen was somehow cast to the big screen. I took a more comfortable position and started browsing, but there was just so much content. I couldn't decide, until I found the classics and spotted "Moulin Rouge." Now that's a favorite I couldn't pass, so I hit play.

"I can't believe you're still obsessed with this..." Tae muttered but nevertheless turned his gaze towards the screen when I put his phone down on the table in front of us. He tapped something on the screen and all the lights of the whole penthouse dimmed down. I have no idea where the sounds came from, but they had me immersed in a nanosecond.

It didn't take long for my eyelids starting to droop, as the day had lasted for what felt like centuries. I tried to fight it but lost the battle, somewhere around the Elephant love medley. Even though it was my favorite part of the movie, my eyes fluttered shut.

The next thing I knew, I was in Tae's arms, clinging to his neck. The longing from the elevator came rushing back, so fast it caught me completely by surprise. Because of my half-asleep state, I didn't have the energy to resist the urge to cling to him even tighter. Tae didn't seem to mind when I nuzzled my face against the nook of his neck, inhaling the intoxicating scent of a faint trace of his cologne. He laid me gently down on the gigantic bed that was now mine.

All I wanted to do was to hold tight on him so he wouldn't go, but as I was tired as fuck, I couldn't really put up a good fight. The last thing my mind registered was the warmness of the thick blanket that was laid on top of me. And maybe, a warm touch that brushed my cheek softly, but at that point, I couldn't be sure.

Grey Sweatpants

It was the best sleep I had managed to get in a long, long time.

But when I did wake up, I didn't recognize my surroundings at first. I jumped up to sit on the bed, panicked. Quickly though, it set in that I was at Tae's apartment, and let my head hit the pillow for a little while longer.

I tried my best, tossing and turning in the super-soft satin sheets, but couldn't fall back asleep. After a while, I gave up and heaved myself off the bed. It was so damn dark, and I had to fiddled with the odd-looking control panel near the bed for a while before I could see anything. I must've flicked the lights on and off, one by one, maybe a thousand times trying to figure out how the hell the blinds worked. Giving up, I smashed them all at once, and the black sheet finally rolled up, revealing the almost unreal view.

Natural light poured in. It was semi-cloudy, but the sun still managed to peek through here and there, casting light over the cherry trees that were about to bloom in the park below. I was so high up that the trees were tiny and cars that slugged forward in the morning rush looked like toy cars.

I caught a glimpse of my reflection in the window, still wearing the t-shirt and jeans from the day before. Gross. I threw them off and entered the amazing mini-spa that was my bathroom. There were some clean towels laid on top of the drawer on my right. I was almost touched by Tae's consideration towards me before I realized it was probably his housekeeper that had filled up the room.

The hot tub looked so inviting I almost gave in and filled it up. But I resisted the urge and headed to the shower instead. Which, in all fairness, was an awesome experience too. At first, it was a bit…awkward… to shower in front of the huge window, but I got over it as soon as I realized the glass was probably a mirror from the outside. At least that's what the building had looked like when we drove past. The shower itself was way easier to operate than the blinds had been, so I set it to a rain mode with ease and stood below the warm stream for a small eternity.

I took the time to do a close shave, when I found a good razor that was still in its sealed package. It was most definitely a way more comfortable experience than the cheap single blades they had had at the hospital. Even after that, I stayed for a few minutes, just letting the warm water erase all the anxiety, tension and stress from my body.

A bit reluctantly, I eventually stepped out and dried myself with an incredibly soft towel while going through all the drawers. Luckily, I found a blow dryer in one of the boxes and hurried to dry my hair.

Honestly, I was already getting a bit eager to go and see the dorms we had lived in. Naturally, I wanted more clothes that weren't picked by Tae, but I was also curious to find out what our dorm had been like. If I was lucky, maybe I'd even get a memory or two back while going through my personal shit.

Deciding what to wear was easy, as I only had one clean outfit left. And I had saved the cutest for last: a cream-colored, oversized cardigan and some light blue jeans. It was still boring and clearly Tae didn't understand the importance of accessories because there were none. That was for sure going to change after our visit to the dorms. I planned to pack as many outfits as I possibly could I finished up and tiptoed downstairs. Music and strange noises came through the cracked door to the gym. I peeked inside.

Huge mistake.

I froze on the threshold. Tae. Shirtless. Doing pull-ups with his back towards me. And what a hot back that was indeed.

I transfixed on his muscles which flexed and relaxed in tune with the movement, then moved on to a bead of sweat that formed on his neck and traveled down by the prominent spinal dip between his shoulder blades...and all the way down to his waist and then hip where his grey sweatpants were hanging low, just barely high enough to conceal the crack of his perfectly round but firm looking behind.

What. A. Sight.

Before I got too caught up, Tae hopped down, ripping me out from my daydreams. Quickly, I wiped my face off all possible expressions to try and not look like I had been staring. Only then when I had—thankfully—gathered my spare sane thoughts back to my messed up brain, Tae turned around. A grin spread to his lips as soon as he saw me. Suddenly that little expression seemed to light up the whole room. I couldn't help but smile back at him.

"Good morning," I said, barely keeping my voice indifferent.

It was torture trying to keep my eyes away from his tanned chest, chiseled abs that practically screamed to my eyes to at least glance at them. Not to even mention the thin trail of dark brown hair that started from his navel and disappeared somewhere behind the damn sweatpants that were, again, in the way of my view—

"Morning," he said, making me snap my eyes back to his. Again. He glanced at the wall behind him, which I now noticed had a digital clock. The bright red letters said 06:04. He grabbed a towel. "You're up early."

"Yeah, I guess I fell asleep too early last night," I managed to choke out.

"You sure did pass out good." He wiped the sweat off his neck.

Determined to not get distracted by his shirtless body all over again, I leaned to the door frame and turned my gaze to the window and the view behind it instead. I only blinked at his statement, as my brain couldn't come up with anything to say at that moment.

Tae seemed hell-bent on making my life so very difficult though. His naked body appeared uncomfortably close, right in front of me. Stubbornly, I still looked past him, trying to focus on the outside world. He stared at me, bothering me with his gaze, for as long as it took for my eyes to finally take a glance at his.

Only then, he spoke again. "I'm gonna hit the shower. Can you manage the coffee meanwhile?"

"I think I'll be able to handle that," I said with a snort. I might've been brain damaged and distracted, but surely, I could handle one fancy-looking coffee maker.

He nodded before walking across the living room and hopping up the stairs, two at a time.

As soon as he disappeared from my sight, I stood there for a minute, trying to calm down my wildly racing heart. Then I shook my head to try and focus on the moment before walking over to the kitchen.

Turns out, the coffee maker wasn't as easy to handle as I had thought, but somehow, I managed to get it going, hopefully not messing up too badly. At that point, I was craving caffeine so badly it almost didn't even matter. As long as it was even somewhat drinkable, I'd chug it down eagerly.

Tae didn't take long to shower. As the coffee maker beeped to let me know the beverage was ready, right as he walked down the stairs. And damn he looked hot in some simple dark blue jeans and a plain white t-shirt, now that I had seen what was underneath.

While I was still in the daydream-lands, Tae hunted down some mugs from his cupboards and topped them up. Again, he handed me a mug that seemed like it was exactly how I liked my coffee. To test the theory, I took a little sip, and yes, it was heavenly. Way better than the shit they made me drink in the hospital that made my insides burn after one cup.

"What do you want for breakfast? I have cereal...and cereal," he said, chuckling.

"Cereal it is, then," I replied, smiling right back at him while I made my way to the dining table. It was good to notice the awkwardness had eased up a bit.

"I'm sorry. The kitchen was supposed to get restocked. My housekeeper's an airhead," he said, filling up two bowls and bringing them both over.

"Tae, stop it...I've already used up your hospitality enough. I can manage with cereal."

There was a brief silence as Tae laid down the bowls and fished out some spoons before plopping down to sit right in front of me. Then he started moving the cereals around in his bowl absentmindedly.

"What's wrong?" I asked, "Look, you need to relax. There's no way you could ever bother me. Actually, we should talk about something—" he finally started, only to get cut off abruptly by the sound of the lift.

We both turned our eyes towards the entrance. A middle-aged woman, definitely not Korean, walked inside with a few filled up to the brim shopping bags. Tae let out a relieved sigh, before mouthing me that it was his housekeeper. Then he instantly shot up to help the lady put the bags down.

I couldn't decide if I was relieved or annoyed by the interruption.

Dorm Tour

On the way to the dorms, Joe and Tae talked about the changes the security staff was going through due to the incident. I listened, but as I couldn't really contribute to the subject, so I stayed silent. Apparently, Joe was planning to step down from the lead, as he felt like he wasn't suitable for the job. Tae tried to argue, but Joe insisted he was more action type of guy and meddling with papers wasn't his thing. He even claimed it was like doing two jobs badly, instead of doing one job properly.

He was going to promote one of his senior employees to be the next managing director. I zoned out when they started going over the possibilities, as I had practically no clue about the persons behind the names. The only one I had a face to the name was Chris' previous regular Mr. Won, who had been holed up at Chris' mountain house for the past couple of weeks. As far as I understood, it was logistically speaking the easiest option; he wanted a desk job because his family was getting a newcomer soon.

All the things that happened around me made me all the more aware how much I didn't remember. It was like my head had this hole inside, or a room that someone locked and then threw away the key. Now I couldn't find the damn key. Most of the time I managed to forget the room existed, but these kinds of conversations made me painfully aware.

Every time I realized that hole in my memory existed, it started a cycle of endless questions. At first, I usually wondered about things like: what was it like being famous? How much money did I have? Trivial things like that.

It was almost fun to some extent, as it was somewhat like daydreaming. But then it shifted and moved on to deeper things, like the people in my life.

What was the deal between Tae and I? Was I missing something or someone even more important? Who I was friendly with? Who I didn't like? Then those questions would lead to even deeper self-doubt...

Who am I? What is my favorite color nowadays? What do I really feel for Tae?

When we finally reached our former dorms, the sight took me by a surprise.

The building towered over the surrounding houses. A large section of the road beside it, was still separated with some bright yellow crime scene tapes and traffic cones. Even a couple of officers loitered around. Tae seemed unfazed though, like he had seen the scene one too many times before.

Joe talked with the officers for a bit, and they let us go through. We drove straight to an underground garage. It seemed like the parking hall took most of the underground floor. Though there were only three cars around. My eyes got caught up on a bright red sports car and a silver one next to it. I only had to glance questioningly at Tae for him to simply say, "Do," and the rest I could figure out from there.

The last car was a white van that didn't seem to belong. Joe parked next to it and talked with the guys that hopped out. Turned out they were from the moving company Tae had hired to take care of delivering my stuff to his place. We headed over to the elevators with Joe and another guard, while the other security staff talked more with the guys from the moving company and started checking the van.

The lift seemed ancient compared to Tae's fancy, futuristic one. It had regular buttons instead of some fancy touch screen thing. Still, it felt more luxurious than I had seen in my life…you know, besides the one at Tae's place. Every centimeter closer we got to finally seeing the dorms, my heart beat a tick faster. Meanwhile, Tae smashed the top button nonchalantly, probably just like he had done a million times before.

When we reached our floor, Joe went ahead, checking the place as if someone could jump from around the corner at any moment. Tae and I stepped in a way far more relaxed. We entered some kind of a lobby, which continued straight ahead to a long hallway with doors on each side. Tae opened the first one on the right.

"This is...was...my room," he said.

I peeked in. It was simple but super spacious. Cardboard boxes were laid out, and he had emptied his table at the corner already. I guessed it had once held a similar recording setup to the one he had at his new place. Perhaps the very same one.

We went past the other rooms. They were all the same layout, just the colors and decorations inside changed. I could connect each room to their owners' personalities right away, which made me smile. Like Minjae's was filled to the brim with decorations, books, sheet music. It was messy as hell but at the same time so very cozy. Took me by a surprise too, I guessed people don't change that much in six years…at least on the inside.

Then we finally reached my room, the last one on the right. Hesitantly, I turned the handle and stepped in. Glancing around, I waited for a memory, or even a feeling, a hunch, to emerge. Nothing did. I couldn't recall this room in the slightest.

But it was nice, at least. My walls were light. I had a red couch with a matching bed cover and curtains. There was art on the walls. On one shelf, was the first familiar thing I spotted—an age-old photo of me, mom, and dad. I grabbed it and brushed the smooth glass with my thumb, just to confirm it was real. Quite literally, it was the first thing that grounded me to this new life.

Tae cleared his throat behind me, ripping me back from the memories I actually could access of this futuristic life I was supposed to have.

"Do you want to start packing right away or would you like to have a tour?" he asked.

"Tour."

Tae led me to a huge living suite, which had an open kitchen, a dining area and humongous couch and a large tv that was easily 60 inches wide. It also seemed that we were alcoholics, based on the fact that there was literally a full wall of shelves filled with all kinds of wine and soju-bottles. I wondered for an instant if I could sneak one with me, before remembering alcohol was pretty much banned.

Downstairs was boring—just practice rooms, a small recording studio, and some housekeeping stuff. Tae told me we'd had a housekeeper there too, whom Do-hyun and Minjae had hired to their new place. The two floors below our two-story apartment were for the security staff and had Joe's company's office. Now they had it temporarily at LBR Entertainment's premises.

In some sick way, I was kind of relieved to realize that everyone else was going through some major shit too. It wasn't just me being lost all the time. Maybe it was a bit mean to think like that, but I couldn't help it.

At least I wasn't the only one who got fucked in the ass without lube by this senseless car crash caused by a lunatic.

Savage

I never lost hope for some memories to appear out of thin air. But as hard as I tried, the door to the room locked inside my head stayed firmly shut, and the key was still missing. The dorm tour ended, and I returned to my room where I saw an actual door that looked like it could've led to a wardrobe of some sort. Me and my brain damage didn't change the fact that I would have to get some clothes over at Tae's new place, so I yanked it open.

My jaw dropped. I had a hard time not fainting. There was no way the gigantic room filled with high-end clothing and accessories belonged to me. It wasn't even crowded, which was amazing considering the size of at least half the main room. There was a mirror at the back end, reaching from the floor all the way to the ceiling. Rows after rows and hangers after hangers were filled with all kinds of styles, colors, and materials.

I spotted a small collection of high heels…for some reason? There were five pairs, carefully arranged on one shelf in the middle—almost like they were on display. With no apparent reason, I started gravitating towards them like I was drugged.

The room looked like a miniature clothes store, though not as organized. I couldn't help but reach out with my fingertips and touch everything as I walked by. The clothes and accessories felt high quality to the touch, and for a moment I was sure I was hallucinating as I only spotted luxury brands.

"Is this real?" I couldn't help but ask, muttering the words mostly to myself.

Tae chuckled and offered me an amused half-smile while leaning on the doorpost with arms crossed over his chest. "Yes. And that's only your day-to-day wear. We have stored the stage outfits elsewhere."

"Wait, what? This is all just...mine?"

"Well, yeah," he stated, cocking one of his eyebrows up questioningly.

I was left completely and utterly speechless. When the hell ever had I even had time to wear all those outfits?

To my dismay, the guys from the moving company appeared with a pile of boxes, and I was forced to get to work.

At random, I grabbed one of the heels I had admired from afar and took a closer look. The heel of the shoe was made of metal while the rest of it was high-quality leather. I assumed it was supposed to somehow be strapped to one's foot with the long straps. I had no clue how anyone could possibly walk in them.

I didn't even notice Tae had made his way inside the room too and was standing right behind me, until he spoke.

"I think these were your favorites," he said, reaching for a very high, block-heeled pair that was all black suede leather. "At least you wore them most often."

I put the pair I was holding back and took the black one from Tae. In awe, I studied the gorgeous pair. Indeed, they had some signs of wear in them. I had kept good care of them, though.

"I—I actually wear these? On a daily basis?" I asked. Sure, back in the day, I had secretly drooled upon encountering some beautiful heels and dreamed of owning a pair someday, but to actually wear them? In this society? Not on stage?

"Well, not always. Mostly on special occasions. I think those are your daily wear," he said, pointing to the corner with his thumb where I had a pile of worn-out, boring, regular shoes. There were some Converses and Timberlands in there somewhere. I made a mental note to remember to take at least one black pair of sneakers with me.

"...but why?" I asked, holding the heels delicately in my hands as if they'd disappear if I made one wrong move.

Tae chuckled. "I asked you the same thing once. You explained it to me then, and I quote: 'Clothes don't have a gender. I do like to own a dick but there's nothing wrong with rocking some beautiful pumps every once in a while', and then you made me wear a hideous pair of pink heart-shaped sunglasses in public for a couple of days for asking such stupid questions. The tabloids had fun with it for weeks."

Tae looked to the distance with a glassed up gaze, a small smile lighting up his face like he was caught up in a wonderful memory. I, however, still got nothing. Not even a fragment of a hunch I had said something like that, out loud, ever in my life. It sounded like something I would totally think. But to say it out loud? Not in a million years.

Well, apparently within six years, but you know, not the point.

"Was this when we were dating?" I asked, trying to pin a timeline together, if nothing else.

"Way before," Tae said. "Even before the army. It was kind of this phase of yours. You've worn them less recently."

So, I had been bold for a long time.

"Try them on," Tae said and nudged me with his elbow.

"Nah, we should get to work." I tried to put the pumps back to their designated place on the shelf.

Tae, however, didn't let me. "Oh, come on, it's not like we're in that much of a hurry." He dropped to his knees and downright yanked my sneaker off, making me stagger and throw a giggling fit—it tingled.

"Aish, fine!" I shoved him off with my foot. He laughed at me, falling to his ass. "I can take off my own shoes."

I tossed the pumps to the floor while kicking off the other sneaker and wiggled my feet in the high heeled pair. The shoes had been worn so much they fit my feet perfectly. While Tae made his way up from the floor, I tied up the laces and stood up, now standing as tall as him. It was weird looking at him at the same level. I took a few hesitant steps and realized they weren't that hard to walk in, at least on a smooth and straight surface.

"See, you're made for this," Tae said, his arms open and ready to catch me if I fell. I managed to keep myself in check. Barely.

"Yeah, yeah...now get to work," I said, grabbed two cardboard boxes and tossed one of them to him.

He sighed, but eventually made his way to the main room with the box and asked me to toss him anything I'd want to take with.

After a while of just going through all the clothes in plain sight, I proceeded to go through the drawers, opening and closing them to get a glance inside. It didn't surprise me that they were filled with underwear, socks, and some accessories. Nothing out of the ordinary. Except for the fact that even the socks and underwear were from exclusive brands. And that there were a few highly provocative pieces of women's underwear. Panties. Yikes.

Honestly though, the rest of it became boring quite quickly. Until I reached the furthest and lowest drawer on the right. It seemed oddly empty compared to all the other ones, barely a couple of scarfs on top. They didn't seem all that important at glance. I reached inside to take one out...but my fingertips met the bottom way too early, considering how big the box appeared from outside.

Curiosity peaking, I started feeling around the bottom with my eyebrows scrunched together. I found a small hole on the side, slid my finger through it, and managed to loosen a fake base.

A loud noise startled me. Tae dropped a full, heavy box to the floor with a loud thump and sent me reeling back. I turned to look at him over my shoulder, trying my hardest to not look like I had been doing something forbidden. Which I probably wasn't; it *was* my stuff. But it felt like I was. In any case, Tae stared at his phone with his eyebrows knitted together, clearly bothered by what he saw.

"What's up?" I asked, baffled by his expression.

"Nothing, uhh, I'm gonna grab some things from my room. I'll be right back," he said with a bit of a plain tone. He turned on his heels and headed out.

For a second, I considered going after him, but as I remembered a little bit of privacy wouldn't hurt with trying to figure out what the drawer held inside. I returned to the drawer, moved some of the scarfs aside, and lifted the panel.

It was filled with notebooks, of all possible kinds. Obviously none of them rang any bells in my head, and I had no idea why they were hidden in a scarf-drawer. I picked up a small one and opened it.

The pages were filled to the brim with tiny handwriting. At first, it didn't seem like it was anything sensical, because there were words everywhere, even on top of each other. A part of something here, part of something different there. Some of it was lyrical, like poems. One of those easily caught my attention with just one word: "heels"—naturally because I was wearing a pair, oddly enough.

Eavesdropping, rumors, even interceptions
Keep talking, I'm busy spending my riches
Slaying in heels like it's none of your business
You think I'm Sweet, well my real name is savage

And guess what, you're in luck, I'll spill all my secrets
The fact that I'm trouble don't mean I'm no Mister
High fashion, make-up, and some diamond rings
Me being pretty don't mean I'm a "Mrs."

I had never heard such lyrics. And we had gone over our music from the past years with Tae, so I guessed this one was more personal. The only tune that came to mind was the melody that Meiling had sung back at the hospital, so I started humming it. Oddly enough, the lyrics sort of matched.

It wasn't exactly a memory rather than just a feeling, but finding the song made me believe in this new reality much more than I had before. Somehow, it connected the past me with the new one I had supposed to be. I made a mental note to ask Tae if this song existed and grabbed another notebook.

That one had a part that seemed like it was a five-page story of some sort, but then I had used the margins for totally unrelated texts. Other than that, it was just like the other before—random texts, poems, and partial lyrics.

My time alone was probably going to be up soon, so I grabbed a box and filled the bottom with as many notebooks as I could fit without the ripping the box. Then I tossed in some totally random clothes, quickly sealed the box with tape, and marked it with a tiny x in one corner. I put the box in the pile with others and went right back to packing.

Risk-Free

It didn't take more than a few minutes for Tae to get back after that. The best part? He brought lunch.

"Do and Min are safely back in Korea," he said and handed me a container.

I went to the red couch, my stomach growling. Popping the pair of chopsticks apart, I mumbled my reply rather absentmindedly while sitting, "and?"

Tae shrugged before sitting down beside me. "You used to care, that's all."

Ouch? I turned my narrowed eyes to Tae and cocked my eyebrow up. Was he implying I didn't care now?

"I didn't mean it like that," he laughed, nudging my elbow with his as if to cheer me up. "We, err, you and me—uh—over the years, we became a pack of some sort. You kept the schedule in check and practically fed us, while I handled the business. It became a habit to tell you everyone's whereabouts. Did you really think I could've kept those two lovebirds and Chris in line all by myself? Surely you know they're too hazardous to function."

I snorted and started to munch down the chicken noodle soup. So that's where the "eomma and appa of GRiD" concept came from. Suddenly the jokes I had seen on the internet while researching fanservice made much more sense. I guess it wasn't that far from the truth considering we had eventually started dating.

After lunch, Tae helped me with the rest of stuff I wanted to have over at his place. The work quickly got mundane, but hey, at least I did something useful for a change.

Some clothes I left behind, gladly. Let's be real, I was more than content to forget that bright purple suit, the neon green jeans, some super weird sunglasses, and countless other odd things. When I asked why I'd ever even bought such monstrosities, Tae shrugged it off explaining that the brands wanted us to wear their collections and sent us the weirdest things. Why on earth had I ever kept these things that couldn't even be described as proper clothes?

Honestly though, I wanted to try them all on, apart from the weirdest ones. But as it would've probably been too time consuming, I held down the urge. The awe over the designer clothes toned down a bit after an hour or so of sorting out what I wanted to keep and what I wanted to leave behind.

After I picked up some other things—like the picture of me and my parents, some hygiene products, and make-up—the guys from the moving company and Joe appeared at my room's threshold.

"We're done?" one of the guys asked.

"I guess..." I replied. Somehow, I still wanted to stay and try to figure out more of my life, as that room was the first place that had felt at least somewhat familiar so far.

To my relief, I didn't have to say it all out loud, as Tae practically read my mind once again. "Yeah, we're mostly done, but I think we'd like to stay for a bit," he said. "You can get to my place though, there'll be staff to meet you and help with the entrance and stuff. My housekeeper, Mrs. Phan, will show you where to put the boxes."

The guy left a few boxes for us and walked out the door.

"We'll wait downstairs. Hit me with a text when you're done, will you?" Joe asked Tae, who nodded, and then he was out too.

As soon as everyone else was gone besides Tae and me, I sighed and plopped down on the red couch again. The exhaustion started to weigh on me—apart from the quick lunch break earlier, we had been packing the whole day.

Crossing my legs, I leaned back and took the camera from the side table to give my hands something to do. Tae sat next to me as I turned it on. The controls were pretty much the same as in the ancient one I had had back in the day, same brand and all. My curiosity peaked, and I checked if there were any pictures in it.

There was...a lot. Looked like they were all from this one place that was very beautiful but also had this sad, almost creepy feeling to it. The dead leaves growing over a carousel and old ride cart hinted to me that it had been an amusement park of some sort, an abandoned one by the looks of it.

There were photos of the decaying rides, some ruined buildings, and then of Tae and me as I scrolled further in.

"What are you looking at?" Tae asked softly.

I turned the LCD towards him.

"Oh, those."

Something about his tone of voice told me those photos were more than just a casual trip to your local ghost-town theme park. "What are these?"

"Uhh—" He hesitated. "Those pics are from our first—and only—actual date."

"Hmm..." I turned my gaze back to the screen, and scrolled all the way back to the beginning, and a new viewpoint. Leaning forward, I tried to focus. The photos were suddenly so much more interesting.

The absolute first one was from the gate. "Yongma Land," the sign stated with bold, red, rusty letters.

A weird place for a date, but somehow it seemed so right for us at the same time. It was clear to me only by looking at the photos, that I'd had a lot of fun. I had taken some good photos— and a lot of bad ones. There were some I guessed Tae had taken of me too, and I looked...happy.

If it was possible to be jealous of oneself, I certainly was. Who gave this Joonie— who I had no memory of—the right to have so much fun while I had to be brain damaged and useless? Why did he get to be on dates, all head over heels in love, while I had to be on a break *due to some bullshit circumstances*? What did the Joonie in the photos have over me? Why had Tae had taken him to as awesome dates like this one in the photos?

"Joon, talk to me. You look upset," Tae whispered almost inaudibly from my side, dragging me back to reality with that statement. "What are you thinking?"

"You want an honest answer?" I asked, almost as quietly.

"Honest. Always honest." He curled his hand behind my back and let it rest on the side of my waist. I tried to ignore the jolt of heat that his touch spread to my whole body in a split second and focus.

"I'm thinking that you have to be the shittiest boyfriend ever," I said and shrugged.

After two second's silence, Tae exploded, into manic laughter.

"What?" I asked, only slightly amused by his sudden outburst.

"Oh, nothing important. It's just that I'm glad to see you're still as blunt as you were before," he explained, shaking his head. "But you've made me curious. How come I'm the shittiest boyfriend of all time?"

"Shouldn't you be like...sweeping me off my feet by now? Instead of breaking up with me and then giving me some clues here and there. It's driving me nuts."

"First of all, a break is different from a break-up," he started, to which I rolled my eyes. "And secondly, was the 21-year-old you in love with me?"

"Well, no, but—" I started, but got cut off.

"Then there you have it. I have no clue how to 'sweep you off your feet.' No buts."

"Hmph, but there is," I said and searched the pic of me looking at him with some impressive lovestruck eyes. "You clearly knew how to charm the 27-year-old Joonie."

"I have no idea how I managed that the first time over. I ain't taking risks here. Besides, it's different."

"No, it isn't. This—" I said and pointed at the photo on the LCD again, "—is the more recent me. And I want it back."

Tae sighed. "Do you really think I don't want that too? It's a bit more complicated than that, don't you think?"

"Only if you make it more complicated!" I exclaimed. How could he not get it through his stubborn head? I wanted my old life back, not to avoid it. I knew he did what he did for me, but maybe that wasn't what I needed. I drew in a deep breath to calm myself and asked the question I feared the answer to, in a softer tone, "I mean... Do you still have feelings for me?"

"Of course, I do!" He watched me with eyes blazing with fire. He answered so quick. So sure. The rough tone in his voice and the passion made me pretty much speechless, and I couldn't do much else than look at him with my jaw hanging open. He hung his head low, "I'm just worried about you. I don't want to chase you away..."

"Still, I don't think it's that different," I added after a short silence.

"What exactly do you want me to do?" he asked. "I can't magically bring back your memories or anything."

Sadly true. I slumped further down on the couch and scrolled through some more pictures, getting more depressed every damn happy photo I passed. If only I could—

An idea struck my brain like lightning. I hastily put the camera to the side table and turned my attention back to Tae.

"You heard the doctor. Put me in situations that might trigger some memories."

"Knowing you, I'm not sure if wherever this is heading, is a good idea," he said hesitantly, while I sat on his lap, facing him. He didn't stop me though, which gave me some more courage.

"Stop overanalyzing everything," I said, and wrapped my hands around behind his neck, "and kiss me."

"Joon, what? I don't think we should—"

"No. Just shut up and kiss me!"

"You sure?" His worried eyes studying mine.

I leaned closer. "One thousand percent yes."

Tae's eyes darkened as they pierced through mine, sending similar warmth through my whole body as he had at the elevator when we first got to his place, and I nearly threw myself at him. But this time, I let myself lean against his broad, warm chest. I could feel his breath tingle my lips, as his own only an inch from mine. He laid his hands on the sides of my thighs. Then he slid them upwards before circling them to rest on the small of my back. Agonizingly slow, he started to stroke my spinal dip through the thin fabric...teasing me, testing me.

I scrunched my eyebrows together and tried to tell him wordlessly to hurry up before I lost my confidence. Involuntarily, my teeth sunk into my bottom lip.

With a groan, Tae gave up. One sudden pull, and I was held even more tightly against his chest. The surprise made me gasp and release my lower lip from the hold of my teeth. His hot and soft lips finally, *finally*, landed on my equally feverish ones.

And I was more alive than ever.

A slight shudder, that I couldn't stop, went down my spine. A whole lot of other sensations exploded inside me as our lips started their slow but passionate dance. My heart tried to hammer its way out of my chest. My lungs were quickly out of breath.

Still, I wanted more. Yearned more. And went for more. Until we both were a hot, panting mess, disconnecting our lips only to push our foreheads together. Like that, we tried to catch our breaths, eyes shut.

"Well, did it work?" Tae asked, collecting himself way faster than I ever could.

I took a few seconds to even decipher what he had asked. Then I took a few more to process if I had recollected any memories. Which, sadly, was still a sound no. I sighed, leaned slightly back on his embrace, and opened my eyes. "No."

Tae's face fell, clearly defeated.

While I was also sad, I couldn't help but add, "but it was still a nice experiment," with a slight smile.

To my complete disappointment, the smile that stretched his lips after my statement wasn't the one I wanted to see. This one didn't show the dimple I had already grown to love.

When he still didn't reply anything and started evading my line of sight, I said, "We can experiment some more if you want."

That finally coaxed out the actual, wide smile of Tae's. Dimple and all.

"I think we've done enough experimenting for one day" He let go of my waist.

My body instantly longed for his touch again. Nevertheless, I unwrapped myself from him and stood up.

"I guess so," I said, admittedly a bit disappointed. But he had left some room for experimenting some other day, so I didn't totally lose hope.

After an awkward silence it seemed like it was time to head back to Tae's. I gave the room a final glance around.

Sadly, it still felt just as foreign to me as it had felt that morning. Absolutely no progress was made on my memory, if getting my hopes up didn't count.

At least I had some clothes now. And I learned some things about myself.

I was still very much into fashion—although some of the outfits went way too far. Apparently, I had also developed a habit of writing in notebooks? Maybe I could learn more about myself if I took a look. That one cardboard box, with a tiny x in one corner, was waiting for me to explore it and I couldn't wait.

But most importantly, I had learned that I still—or all over again—had some romantic feelings for Tae. Or at least my body had, based on the sensations that had taken a hold of my every damn sense, intensely.

And I realized I wanted more than just one kiss. So much more.

Loss of Pink

"Hello? Are you here or somewhere else?" Minjae asked, reaching out to wave his hand in front of my face from the barber's chair next to mine. It was early in the morning, and already it had become very clear to me that Minjae still wasn't a morning person. In the least bit. And that tone of voice proved it.

I blinked a couple of times to let my eyes focus before turning my attention to him. "Uhh, yeah?"

"What's with you hyungs lately, always spacing out?" He shook his head. "Noona over here is asking what you want to do with the hair," He nodded toward the thirty-something, brown-haired woman behind me, who held up a hair color chart.

I glanced at my hairdresser through the mirror and said, "Mianhae." Had I lost all my manners overnight? In my defence, I hadn't slept very well for a couple of days, due to...well, obvious reasons. And these ladies were supposed to be familiar, as we'd been using the same salon for a while, so Minjae asked me to be a bit informal. I tried to focus; here was the last place I wanted to space out.

"It's ok. I was just asking if you want to keep the pink?" the woman asked, clearly having a bit of trouble keeping a straight face. I could see her lips twitch upwards.

"We have bigger problems than the color right now," I admitted a bit reluctantly, and yanked off the beanie that was covering the worst part.

While Minjae snickered, the hairdresser gasped. Audibly. She even dropped the hair color chart to the floor with a loud clank that made me jump. And people called me over-dramatic.

"What have you done?" she breathed, not even bothering to pick up the chart before reaching towards my hair...or what was left of it.

"I'm innocent. Surely, you've seen the news," I said, suppressing some chuckles that were about to escape. "They're totally mental at the hospital, shaving unconscious people's hair off without their consent."

"So it would seem," she said, still examining my hair, flipping it over and trying to search if I had any other bald spots, I assumed. "And here I thought I'd just have to deal with overgrown roots."

"Can't you make it an undercut or something?" I asked.

"Definitely. Want it on just this side or both sides?"

"I think both?"

"Good, I thought so too." She started to gather the equipment. "Okay, here's the deal. We're gonna draft out the undercuts first. Then you're both getting dyed. And after I've dealt with his maintenance cut, we can get back to this...disaster."

I nodded. The lady finally picked up the color chart and turned the page to darker shades, before handing it to Minjae who picked out a dark brown color that pretty much matched his roots.

I was shocked. The blond suited him.

"You're going brunet?"

"Yeah, this mop's not handling another bleach," He ran his fingers through his hair. "You, though, would look great in blond."

"Is it possible?" I asked the stylist, slightly worried about applying bleach over the fainted pink.

"Sure, why not," she said. "One bleach to get the roots to match, and then tone the pink away...I can pull that off."

"In that case, let's go blond," I said, finally letting my shoulders roll down as I relaxed.

Blond sounded great. Blond was pretty much blank, just like my damaged mind. Not that I was getting bitter or anything.

The stylist started to work. Thankfully she wasn't the kind that would blabber some boring small-talk all the way through the whole ordeal, as I wasn't exactly in a mood for that. A few strands of pink hair dropped to the floor while I tried not to weep for the loss. After that, it didn't take long for the stylist to get both mine and Minjae's hair covered with the hair-dye goo.

The stylist excused herself for the time the hair dyes did their job and disappeared to the back room. Minjae was probably texting with Do, based on the dreamy look on his face and the smile that tugged at the corners of his mouth. While I was glad for them and their seemingly well-going relationship, I couldn't help but get a little jealous. And annoyed, as it had been a pain in the ass to drag Minjae away from Do and out of their new home that morning, although it was supposed to be him babysitting me. Even if they didn't want to admit to me that's what they were doing.

Yes, I had seen a pattern in the schedule they had made for me—every time Tae couldn't be with me, there would be someone else. Today was Minjae's turn, as Tae was in a meeting. As far as I knew, he was dealing with some official LBR Entertainment stuff as a shareholder, or that's what he told me. Another mind-fuck thing right there—Tae being a shareholder of our freaking record label.

Just past the window, Seong-gi lit up another smoke on the street, chatting with Joe who leaned against his BMW's side. Apart from the light tapping sound from Minjae's texting, it was silent.

Enjoying the eerie atmosphere, I picked up the phone Tae had given me after dinner the night before. Mrs. Tien had already gotten it all set up, so I could control everything back at Tae's place. Even the lights in my room could be adjusted with it, which had blew my brains. It was like living in the future.

Unfortunately, the phone couldn't distract me enough from the same thoughts that had kept me up all night. No, not even social media could keep me from wondering these things. Things like...how was I supposed to act around Tae, considering he was potentially my lover? Just a past date? Ex? Or...just a friend? A *co-*

worker? I winced at the last one now that I had figured out my own feelings towards him.

"You're unusually quiet. What's up?" Minjae asked, thankfully ripping my mind off the endless cycle of doubting everything.

I sighed. "It's just Tae. He's been a bit impossible, lately."

"What do you mean?"

"Well first, he told me we were in a relationship—"

Minjae reached over and downright slapped his hand over my mouth, hissing, "Are you insane?! Do you want to end up in the tabloids?"

"You asked," I mumbled through his hand.

He avoided my eyes after he realized what he'd done. "Sorry hyung, uhh... Let's talk about this later, alright? In private?"

Right. I cringed and snapped my mouth shut.

"And yes, you are together. Cost me a car too," he mumbled.

The stylist came back, stopping me from questioning what the hell that meant.

An hour later, I was totally blond. The length was way shorter than I was used to, with undercuts on both sides. The weird thing was, that the shorter haircut made the slight waves in my hair a tiny bit curlier, so I bought a straightener. Overall, I liked my new haircut—at least it looked neat and styled. And most importantly, not a complete disaster.

Minjae looked great with dark hair too. He was hopeful he could now go with not dyeing it regularly. Which seemed like a good idea, to be honest.

We paid and thanked the stylist, and off we were. There was nothing else on my schedule for today, according to the app Tae had installed on my new phone that held our synced calendar, but Minjae had promised me a tour at the current LBR headquarters so that's where we headed with Joe and Seong-gi. Besides, there would've been no-one at Tae's condo anyway at this hour, since Tae was still at his meetings and then supposed to work on arranging the new setlist for the world tour with Do-hyun at the HQ.

We were supposed to meet Tae and Do-hyun there. Tae had also tried to reach Chris but had given up when didn't answer his phone, and he didn't feel like bothering Mr. Won with only that.

The new HQ was gigantic compared to the small recording studio I remembered. We started the tour from the bottom floor, which was mostly a giant hall. Minjae said it was a space where we and other LBR groups could rehearse on actual mockup stages. We could build them from parts however we wanted. At the time, it was supposed to be the setup of this new group's first tour, as we were supposed to be on tour by then. Minjae greeted the guys that were rehearsing on the stage, while I tried to look like I knew them—I didn't.

We continued to the ground floor that had a lobby, a big cafeteria that was empty in the morning. Then we moved on to some recording studios, meeting rooms, practice studios, a freaking gym, break rooms, offices, and ended on floor number four which Minjae referred to as "our floor."

It was nice and cozy. Kind of. The middle was almost like a living room, with tv and couches and everything. We had a kitchen. There were rooms on the right side of the open space and glass-walled meeting rooms in varying sizes on the left. We headed straight to one that had a giant number four on its frosted glass door.

Minjae plopped down on one of the chairs and sighed. I followed his lead and sat down, looking around. There was a huge tv on the black wall and a nice view behind the window. But most importantly, it seemed like a private enough space to continue the conversation from the salon, and my source of information was right there, playing with his phone.

"Is this private enough?" I asked.

"I guess. What do you want to know?"

"Well first of all, what did the car -thing mean?" I asked, cocking my eyebrow up.

Minjae scratched the back of his neck. "Err, just a stupid bet I had with Do about you and Tae. Nothing important. I lost and had to buy a car for Do-hyun. End of story."

I tried not to think about the fact that they were so filthy rich they could have a bet over a car. I wasn't successful. "That's absurd."

"Tell me about it," he muttered and started playing with a pen he took from the stand in the middle of the table. "Anyway, did you have something else in mind? I know Tae and Do are still busy for like half an hour, so I'm all yours."

"Yes, I guess I do. It's just that I don't know where to even start. I found out about us myself a few days ago, back at the hospital. And then he broke up with me when I did, so I don't know what to think—"

"Whoa wait, hold up. He broke up with you?" he asked, the surprise very evident on his face, as he effectively cut off my blabbering. "No way!"

"Well yeah, at least that's what it sounded like to me," I leaned against the table and rubbed my temple. I was getting a serious headache.

"Okay let's back up for a moment. What did he say to you, *exactly*?" Minjae asked, his eyes completely focused on mine, as if this was the most concerning thing in his whole life.

With my best Tae impression, I said, "*'it would be best for both of us if we don't, due to the circumstances.'*"

Minjae rolled his eyes. "As an expert of misunderstandings, I can assure you this is probably one."

"How can you be so sure?"

"First of all, I think you should talk this through with Tae, not me. And secondly, you have no idea how broken he was after the crash, but I do..." Minjae's eyes glassing up and a shudder shook his body. "He was…a wreck. I guarantee you, that man loves you and there's no way he'd ever break-up with you."

So I was right then, he is just a shitty boyfriend. I thought to myself. Out loud I said, "How am I supposed to know? He doesn't talk to me about these things." *And, he has been avoiding me ever since the kiss.* But I wasn't going to tell *that* to Minjae.

"Are you delusional? Can't you for one second put yourself in his shoes?" Minjae asked.

"What do you mean?"

"Look, you weren't together six years ago. Hell, you weren't together six months ago. You lost your memories from a very long period. He probably thinks *you* don't love *him*. At least I'd think you weren't in love with him six years back?"

"I wasn't," I confirmed. "But I think I might be now," I added with the smallest voice.

"See! It's just a misunderstanding. I think it's kinda sweet that he's giving you some space."

"Doesn't feel like it."

"Oh, just talk to him," Minjae said and threw his arms up as if he was giving up.

"Couldn't agree more," another voice—Do's voice—said behind me, and I jumped up.

I panicked and spun around. When I realized it was only Do, I slumped back on the chair with a huff. A relieved one. I don't know what I would have done if it had been Tae.

Still in Love

"That's it. We need food," Tae exclaimed with a huff when my stomach grumbled loudly for the second time that evening.

We had gotten back to Tae's place, where I decided the stuff we'd picked up from our old dorms needed unpacking so I could wear something nice for a change.

"Calm down. I want to get this done," I replied, digging up another shirt from a cardboard box and setting it on the shelf.

"How about this: I make us dinner, you unpack?" Tae asked, throwing me another shirt from the box in front of him.

"No thanks, hyung. I've eaten enough take-out for the rest of my life," I replied and headed to the door. "I'll whip us something quick—"

Tae grabbed my wrist. "I can cook now, Joon."

I only cocked my eyebrow up as a reply.

"More than just breakfast and take-out," he continued with a smirk.

It was the appearance of the dimple that convinced me. "Fine."

"And stop with the 'hyung,' it creeps me out," Tae said before disappearing downstairs.

I sat on the floor, suddenly hyper-aware of my aching feet from spending all day in the black heels *Aish* those things weren't the most comfortable footwear ever created. I forgot I had tried them on.

I yanked the zippers open and kicked the shoes off my swollen feet. For a moment, I didn't care that the expensive shoes flew across the floor and slammed to the side of a box with a loud thud. But as soon as the blood started properly circulating through every part of my feet and the tingling stopped, I felt bad for the beautiful shoes and reached for them. The box they'd hit was the one with a tiny x, right beside a dent the heel had made on impact. At once, my focus shifted—how the hell had I already managed to forget the notebooks?

I laid the shoes on a random shelf, then reached for the knife laying on the floor. It didn't take me long to rip it open and reach for a random notebook. It was brown, leather-covered, but otherwise tiny. It was worn out and some pages didn't even feel like staying in their rightful places anymore.

The pages were filled with text, just like in the one I had browsed back at the old dorms. It didn't take much of a glance to figure out it was from my military years, since most of the names I saw were the same ones I had been introduced to at the hospital. No longer interested, I tossed the thing over my shoulder and reached for the next one.

Most of it was just random scribbles. Some were like diary entries, only without a date so I had no idea when the things had happened. The others were poetry? More lyrics? Some were just random rants.

Damn.

I should probably be more organised in the future in case I lose six years of memory again. I browsed through a few. I was almost giving up on them before I stumbled upon one that seemed kind of new. It was pink and not even remotely as worn as the others. There were some empty pages left at the end, so I figured it was the most recent one that was still a work in progress. Getting my hopes up, I turned the pages more slowly...until my eyes transfixed on one series of numbers.

It was a date. Last fall. It was the first date I saw in any of the notebooks, so it must've been important. The note below the date was a plain "I'm saying it today," and nothing more.

Saying what? To whom? I browsed further in, skimming for texts with dates, hoping I'd see the outcome. Unfortunately, there weren't any more dates. I circled back to the beginning to shift through slower.

There were a lot of poems, lyrics, most of them themed with jealousy in the beginning. Others were angst, about unrequited love of some sort—about always having to be the second-best. Jeez, I wasn't very fun back then, was I? I read through it all up until the page with the date; it was a miserable read.

After the page with the date, the tone of notes took a slight turn. It seemed like I became happier, or relieved. There were some parts where I had referred to hiding, putting on a brave face, making me wonder if it had something to do with the fact I had come out of the closet around that time, according to Tae. Speaking of which, coming out still seemed slightly odd to me, since the me from six years back was so deep in the closet he was living in Narnia.

I didn't even have to, in my memory, come out of the closet, and now everyone knew, and nobody seemed to have a problem with it. They dealt with it like it was something normal. And I guess it sort of was?

I mean, my hair had been pink. The videos and promotional material I had seen showed me a very confident, gay Joonie, which was why that personality seemed so alien to me. And I knew clothes had nothing to do with sexuality, but I couldn't ignore the fact that I had collection heels and a huge pile of women's clothing. Not that I hadn't wanted to rock that kind of style, I had never thought I'd really do it. Then again, to Tae, it had seemed like a normal thing, so I guess...maybe?

But something else bothered me in those notes too. Tae had avoided me for a while after that dated page—for a long while, based on the rants I had scribbled upside down—for some reason— on top of other texts. They were hard to decipher, but I managed. I wondered if it had something to do with our history.

Then there was another change in the tone, a questioning one. Then a few pages after, a happy one. It all boiled down to one page—a short letter of some sort—that made my heart stop.

Mom...

Today was special.

He took me to date, and it was one of the best days of my life. Right up there with our debut. I still wish I could've told the story of today to you myself, but I'm counting on the winds to carry the message from Han-river to you... So, I won't repeat it.

I guess the main point that I wanted to tell you, is that after all, I did fall in love with him.

- Joon

The realization hit me like a truck: I had been writing these notes to Mom. That's why I didn't remember having such a habit; I had started writing them only after the first car crash. And they were so personal. No wonder I'd hidden them.

The missing puzzle pieces that had been keeping me up at night started falling into their rightful places. I still didn't have the whole story, by any means, but I started to see some clarity in it—the fact that Tae was there when I woke up from the coma. The way he was annoyed when I called him hyung. The way he kept talking to me like I was more than a friend.

And there was the undeniable chemistry between us that had caught me off guard back at the hospital. All the moments his eyes had darkened when I bit my lips. The moment in the elevator, when he first brought me here, when I had almost lost it and thrown myself at him. And last but not least...the kiss at the old dorm that had made my feelings towards Tae explode so powerfully that I had to admit they existed.

It was all real. Sure, I had heard from Tae that we had been dating. And I had talked about it with Minjae too and had been thinking about it for days. But seeing all that written with my handwriting, and thinking this through myself, it seemed even more real. And I realized...no, I admitted to myself fully…that I was in love with him. Even while having no recollection of falling in love with him in the first place.

I was ripped out of my thoughts almost violently when I heard footsteps approach the room. I slammed the notebook shut, gathered the others around me and hastily tossed them all to the box where I had taken them, right before there was a knock on my door and the handle turned.

"The dinner's ready," Tae said as he entered and eyed the unpacked pile of boxes that I had forgotten even existed in the first place. "I thought you were supposed to unpack?"

"Yeah, I just got caught up on something," I started, feverishly trying to figure out a plausible excuse.

Thankfully Tae's focus was shifted elsewhere when my stomach grumbled loudly again.

"Alright..." he said with his forehead still crinkled downward. "Let's eat before you collapse." I glanced at the box with the x one more time before following him downstairs.

Big News

One restless night, a day full of going over our most important choreographs with Minjae, spending the evening going over the songs on our world tour setlist with Do, and then one more sleepless night later, it was finally Friday.

One more day and I'd have a whole weekend off. But first, I was supposed to go over social media, and other stuff our fans would be expecting me to do on tour, with Chris. Because I was clueless.

But noon rolled around, and I hadn't heard a thing from Chris. He didn't answer his phone. I checked the schedule for the millionth time to make sure I hadn't missed something. Nope. Plain as day. It had Tae's address written on the time slot.

I paced back and forth in front of the glass wall in Tae's living room and tried to call Chris again. As he still didn't answer. A ball of worry settled in my stomach. I hovered my finger on top of Mr. Won's phone number, contemplating if I should call him or not.

That's when Tae emerged from his study where he had been checking the new world tour setlist's tracks the whole morning. Yawning, he asked, "Chris still not here?" and headed towards the kitchen.

"No. He isn't answering my calls either."

"Have you tried Mr. Won yet?" He scrunched his eyebrows together and turned the coffee maker on.

"No. Should I?"

"I think you should," he replied.

I turned to face the glass-wall and tapped the green icon on the screen.

He answered only after a couple of beeps in a relaxed manner. "Hey Joon, what's up?"

"Annyeong haseyo," I started politely. "I was wondering what's up with Chris. He hasn't shown up. According to the schedule, we were supposed to meet up at eleven."

"Oh, right. Sorry, I forgot. And Chris...I don't think he has picked up his phone in days. Maybe it's best if you'll clear up his calendar for now if there's not anything super important."

My eyebrows scrunched together. "Why?"

"Err...it's been rough few days up here—" he started but got cut off by a loud bang followed by a sound that reminded me of glass shattering and a yell that remotely sounded like Chris cursing.

I gasped.

There was a sigh on the other end of the call.

"Looks like this is one of the bad days too. Look, I have to go. Let's talk later," Mr. Won said and hung up.

Baffled, I locked the screen and walked to the kitchen. Tae handed me a cup of coffee, and I sat by the kitchen island, slumping onto the counter with my phone still in hand.

"What's wrong?" Tae asked, sitting next to me with his coffee cup in tow.

"I don't know. Mr. Won said something about this being one of the bad days and hung up," I explained, taking a sip.

"Oh, right, yes. They warned us at the hospital that something like this might happen. You know, as he remembers the crash and all. Mr. Won did say there have been some bad days lately, but that Chris is refusing to get any help."

"Great. Now I feel bad about how I treated him in the hospital," I huffed, casting my eyes down. "Like a stranger. I must've made it worse."

"Hey, it's not your fault any of this happened," Tae said and touched my lower back reassuringly. "And we'll have to deal with Chris later 'cause I've got some news."

"News?" I asked with narrow eyes. Tae sure sounded far too giddy and enthusiastic for the topic at hand.

"Big news." He pulled his phone from his pocket, unlocked it, and handed it to me. "Jiwoo just sent this to the group chat."

It was a selfie of Jiwoo, grinning like a maniac and holding up five fancy-looking envelopes. Below was a caption that was a long keyboard smash followed by this: 'Buckle up your seatbelts, 'cause we're going BILLBOARDS!'

I stumbled off the chair and a couple of steps back, almost choking. "She's joking right?"

"Nope," Tae said, also hopping down from his chair. "I checked the official briefing she forwarded to my email. Seems legit. We've been nominated 'Top Social Artist' and 'Top Duo/Group.'"

"What?! *How*?" I yelled, almost bouncing from the bubbly sensation that had already turned my stomach upside down.

"That's not even the extent of it. We're going to perform at the show too!" he exclaimed.

"No way! I mean yes way! I mean what?" I wasn't even sure what to ask or expect. Or even think.

But before I got my scattered thoughts even remotely together, Tae grabbed me into a tight hug and started spinning me around. I couldn't help but giggle uncontrollably like a schoolgirl; it all was that surreal.

The afternoon had turned from depressing to unbelievably fantastic in a minute. And I had a hard time wrapping my head around it. But all that didn't even matter as we collapsed on Tae's couch, both still giddy and panting from the sudden outburst of absolute happiness that was only hindered by whatever was going on with Chris.

Unfortunately, I came crashing down from the hype soon enough. First, the doubts started lingering on the edges of my consciousness. Then the shadows gathered more space in my head. It didn't take long for them to be all that I thought of.

Yes, Billboards had been our ultimate goal—or more like a distant dream— since our debut. And as far as I knew, we hadn't been there ever before. To my recently gained knowledge, kpop had only gained popularity in the west while we had been serving in the military. To think we had been presented the opportunity to not only attend but to perform…that was something huge.

And here I was, still lacking the past six years of experience in performing. And that Billboard performance…it would have to be perfect. I certainly wasn't ready for it and wouldn't be on such a short notice. Not when I wasn't myself. The exposure we'd get would land us many interviews, not to even mention the ones we'd have to have on the red carpet.

"I can see you're thinking too hard," Tae said and poked the spot between my eyebrows with his index finger softly. "What is it this time?"

"It's just... I don't think I'm ready for that yet. What do I even say in the interviews? And that kind of performance has to be perfect..." I trailed off, admittedly with a smaller voice than I thought possible from my big mouth.

"Relax. There are four of us to handle the interviews. All you have to do is stand there and look pretty," he said and lifted my chin with his index finger.

I smacked his shoulder. "Oh yeah? How about the performance?"

"You'll have to learn the choreography anyway for the world tour. I see no problem."

"I don't know..." I rubbed my neck, not even slightly convinced by his reasoning. I hadn't even done one public appearance since the incident.

"Look, we don't have to worry about that now. And I assure you, you'll be fine." His tone pulled more serious, but he held a reassuring smile on his face.

If he was convinced I could pull it off in my state, who was I to disagree? I had lost control of my own life once and for all, and I accepted that. I slouched on the couch. This rollercoaster of opposite emotions fighting within me only got more exhausting each day.

"Anyway, they're announcing the nominees' list at midnight their time," Tae said, ending the silence. He glanced at the clock on his phone's screen. "Like, in less than an hour on our time. If you want, we could have a vlive chat about it with the fans after?"

"You sure?" I asked, the wrinkle of worry already making its way between my eyebrows. "What if I say something stupid?

"Yeah. It's going to be fine. Just wear something the—uhh—current you would wear, and let's meet back here in an hour."

I glanced down. I was wearing some stonewashed skinny jeans and Tae's hoodie I had stolen because I had grown slightly too terrified to wear most of the clothes we had rescued from our old dorms. "These won't do then I guess?"

Tae laughed. "No. Go crazy. Wear make-up. I know you want to," he said and winked, before hopping up from the couch.

Well, he isn't wrong, I admitted and stood up, heading to the stairs. "Alright."

"I'll go change to something a bit more presentable too," he said and followed me upstairs.

After glancing at his outfit that was simple grey sweatpants and a black t-shirt, I approved of his decision to change with a nod. It was, after all, even worse than what I wore. We both dashed to our rooms, and I was left with an hour to get myself to look like the Joonie I was supposed to be.

The good thing about limited time was that there was no time for doubts. So instead of starting to panic, my need to get myself to look better overpowered the fears. I walked briskly inside my closet and started going through the clothes.

It was springtime, so some light or bright colored would make sense. Some coral colored jeans caught my eyes, and I took them out. I eyed them for a short while, still doubting if I'd be able to pull off such a bold color.

"Fuck it," I muttered and proceeded to wiggle my way out of the boring jeans and into the coral-colored ones. They snug even closer than I anticipated, probably because of all the junk food I had consumed lately. Thankfully I got them on and even got the top button closed without too much trouble. Not daring to even glance at the mirror just yet, I took out a black tank top and paired it with a loose, very short white jersey.

With only half an hour left, I only glanced at the mirror before pulling out the accessories. Almost at random, I pulled out a bunch of black and silver bracelets that would match the simple earrings I had on, because I didn't have time to change them. Then I dashed to the bathroom where I had the make-up I had brought from our old dorms stored in one of the drawers I hadn't even opened after the day I had unpacked.

After dumbfoundedly staring at the sole number of products, I pulled out my phone in hopes of finding something even remotely duplicable. I scrolled through the most recent selfies I had posted on our Twitter page before the whole memory-loss thing. I did find one that looked simple enough—just some peach-colored eyeshadow in the outer corners of my eyes and black kajal on the lash lines.

It was simple enough to recreate. After fifteen minutes of slapping on some tinted day cream that would hopefully hide the small imperfections on my face, brushing on a small amount of the eyeshadow and smudging the black eyeliner, I was done.

Both Tae and I exited our respective rooms at the same time. He was wearing some dark blue jeans and a loose button-up, paired with a simple chain acting as a necklace. Not half bad.

Tae checked me out too, blowing a low whistle under his breath. Almost made me blush all over again.

"Do I look like myself?" I asked.

"Totally," he said and smiled. "Let's get this going, shall we?"

We both headed downstairs. Once I was comfortable on the couch, I pulled out my phone once again. It was already past the time they should've announced the nominees, so I entered the Billboards site. My heart beating like crazy, I scrolled down the nominees' list...

Sure enough, there was us listed in the two categories, paired with a group photo.

Holy shit. It was happening. We were going to the Billboards. As absurd as it sounded, there it was for the whole world to see.

Tae had already propped a large tablet computer on top of the side table with a tripod when I was done scrolling. I put the phone down and tried to take a more comfortable position—but Tae had other ideas. Circling his hand around my waist, he pulled me right beside him, so close that my whole body was technically leaning on his. My heart pounded even faster. I glanced at him dumbfounded; it was so freaking sudden after days of barely even seeing him.

He smirked back. "No need to be strangers here," he said and leaned closer. "Fanservice, remember?" he breathed to my ear, effectively making my heart stop and a shiver run down my spine. Flustered, I turned my face the opposite way.

Well, this should be interesting.

Glowing Lights

Surprisingly enough, our vlive broadcast went great. Well, after I got used to the Tae's closeness and relaxed. It was kind of hilarious reading the comments, because apart from the positive fuss around our nominations on the Billboard awards, the GRiD Crew was thrilled to see me up and about. Alive. And according to them, I was looking way better than in the photos they had seen of me exiting the hospital.

The rest of the day went by in a blurry haze, the reality of it all not quite settling in until late at night. That's when the doubts made a comeback, and the endless circle of negative thoughts once again flooded my mind. It was another restless night to add to my exhausting list.

For the life of me, I couldn't fall asleep the next night either. Even though the pure exhaustion weighed my whole body down because Minjae had worked me to my limits with the choreographs. Yeah, the free weekend had been cancelled right after Minjae got the news about Billboards and panicked about getting me whipped into shape. No surprises there.

Instead of sleeping, my brain decided to obsess over everything. Mostly the Billboards and the damn notebooks, as if I hadn't already read them all from start to end and all the way back again.

I may've been *a little* obsessing over the story behind Tae and me thanks to the notebooks. I knew why he hadn't talked to me about it—I wanted to remember it on my own too. Especially after that damn explosive kiss back at the old dorm. Those kinds of feelings couldn't just appear out of thin air, right? It was almost like Tae had left a lingering imprint on my skin that my mind couldn't handle yet, but my body certainly remembered.

What made it worse was that there had been no more experimenting with Tae after that one kiss. I was positive he had kept even more distance from me after that day, apart from vlive with the Billboards invite and all. Not that I was salty or anything.

And when I had managed to sleep some...let's just say waking up had been a bit uncomfortable. In the few dreams I had, there was *a lot* of experimenting with Tae. I was like I was fifteen all over again, and that's a bit confusing when you're supposed to be twenty-fucking-seven. Wasn't I supposed to be an adult now and handle myself? Weren't the hormones supposed to have settled?

I sighed and rolled over once more, staring at the blank white ceiling. I tried to adjust the larger than life pillow I had grown attached to, but it didn't want to cooperate with me. And it was too dark. I opened the blinds, but then it was too bright, the glowing lights of Seoul pouring in. I closed the blinds again.

My throat was as dry as a desert, and swallowing felt like inhaling sand. With no other choice, I heaved my tired body off the bed, yanked on some random underwear and wrapped the duvet around me. Not bothering to put on any lights, I dragged myself through the upstairs loft and to the iron staircase.

Of course, my eyes nailed to the nightly cityscape, as I walked to the glass wall and stared ahead, wondering how many people were up in the city as sleepless as I was.

I felt so small. My worries started to seem so very tiny. I was almost ashamed of myself.

Who was I to agonize over minor inconveniences this memory-loss had caused? Living in a penthouse that 99% of people down below could never even dream to afford? Going to Billboard awards in a few weeks?

There were probably many people that had it worse than me. Maybe there was a businessman somewhere, stressed about tomorrow's workday. Perhaps a bullied kid, terrified to go to school tomorrow. Or a single mother, wondering how to make ends meet for one more week.

Even Do-hyun and Minjae were in there somewhere, and they had had to go through a huge scandal only a hot minute ago. They had one of their most intimate moments forever on the internet. The paparazzi were following them more than the rest of us combined.

And Chris. Hiding somewhere in the mountains on my right, as far as I knew, most likely dealing with much worse shit than I was. As he had to remember the whole incident. He had to remember Min-ho and what he had done. Not to even mention the fact that it was his face that got mutilated by the whole incident, not mine.

Maybe it was, after all, me, who got the easiest part in this shitshow.

I closed my eyes for a brief second before taking a deep breath and heading to the kitchen to get the drink I'd come for. I passed Tae's office, where the door was left cracked open, and some light poured through the opening. Of course, I was curious and pushed the door more open as silent as I could to peek inside.

Tae was sitting cross-legged in his chair, only wearing some sweatpants but no shirt whatsoever. Looked like he couldn't sleep either. He stared at the computer screen with headphones on and tapped his fingers against the table. I couldn't decipher what was going on in his screen but since he had his keyboard set up on his side and plugged in, I figured he was working on some music.

As I watched, he reached for the keyboard and played something. The keyboard didn't produce any sound when he tapped the keys. I guess he had set it up so that only he could hear it through his headphones. That explained why I couldn't hear anything upstairs.

I stalked him for a short while, not being able to pry my eyes away. It seemed private though, so as I got over the sight, I pulled the door back to its original position and finally made my way to the kitchen.

The kitchen had become familiar, so I didn't bother putting the lights on. I hunted down a glass and filled it up with juice from the fridge. As I turned I somehow managed to trip to the duvet I was using to cover myself. I faceplanted on the hard as fuck tiled floor, sending the glass flying in the air. Apparently my mind was filled with too much shit to even handle a thing like basic walking.

The glass crashed to the floor and shattered to a million tiny pieces in front of me. *Ugh.* With a grunt, I heaved myself to sit cross-legged on the floor and tightened the duvet around me before starting to gather the bigger pieces of the glass together to try and clean the mess I'd caused.

Sharp pain in my middle finger made me flinch.

"Aish, fuck—" I hissed as warm blood started oozing from my fingertip. *Great.* That just fit right into my luck, didn't it?

Just then the lights flickered on, blinding me. I covered my eyes with my hand like a visor and I lifted them to Tae, who was already rushing towards me wearing only sweatpants…and nothing on his feet…in a room filled with broken glass.

"Stop!" I shouted and threw up my hands.

He obeyed, thank the gods. Tae had a hard enough time learning choreography without glass stuck to his foot. I pointed to the floor and the shimmering bits of sharp glass.

"What happened?" he asked with a calm voice, but forehead scrunched as he eyed the mess.

"Just me being clumsy as usual. Go back to work, I'll clean it up," I mumbled, trying to hide the bleeding finger.

I didn't succeed.

"Don't be stubborn Joon, you're bleeding," Tae said with an unimpressed tone and straight-up tip-toed through the whole mess to me.

With what looked like hardly any effort, Tae collected the duvet and me as one big-ass burrito and proceeded to carry me across the whole floor. I ended up sitting on the leather couch, still clutching on the duvet and eyeing Tae like he'd lost his mind.

"You know I can walk by myself, right?"

I caught a glimpse of a small, sad smile on Tae's face before he turned around.

"You used to love getting carried everywhere, even demanded it," he muttered, before clearing his throat. "Stay put, I'll go get some disinfectant and bandages."

The guilt trip hit me like a bullet, tiny but fast and destructive. Of course, he'd want to have a break from me, I wasn't the Joonie he had fallen in love with. Hell, I still didn't even know what that person was like, or how I was supposed to act. On top of that, I was useless. I had to have a babysitter all the time, chaos and destruction quickly becoming my new middle names.

The exhaustion and confusion took an even tighter grip on me. My heart clenched almost painfully as I tried to hold back the tears that formed. I was too tired to muster up enough willpower to focus before Tae came back with the supplies.

Through a blurry haze of tears, I watched him kneel on the floor in front of me and soak a cotton ball with the disinfectant. I sniffed silently, trying to push back more tears as they started to burn. Thankfully Tae was so absorbed in his task he didn't seem to notice. He grabbed my hand and pressed the soaked cotton ball against the wound. The disinfectant stung, to which I flinched, but at least the burning sensation took my focus momentarily away from the storm that was forming inside me.

With extremely careful motions, Tae wiped the finger clean. The cut was surprisingly tiny after the blood was wiped off, and I nearly died from humiliation. That shame, in turn, broke the waterworks despite my best efforts.

Oh great, now I'm a cry-baby too.

I dried the first teardrop off with my other hand when it reached my chin, but I wasn't quick enough Tae lifted his eyes to my face, and I looked away.

"I'm sorry if it hurts, it'll only sting for a moment," he said with such a soft tone it could've melted me from the inside. Why was he so damn nice to me while at the same time wanting a break from me and keeping his distance after the kiss?

I couldn't hold back any longer. I completely broke down.

Sobbing. Exhausted. A whole freaking mess. Not one of my proudest moments, I admit.

Through the sobs, I muttered, "No, it doesn't h-hurt, I'm just s-so tired—" but got cut off by Tae who finished putting the bandage on and grabbed me to a tight hug.

"Shh, it's okay." He rocked us back and forth.

It made everything even worse. I went full-on ugly cry mode against Tae's chest. Every mixed feeling, all the irritation over everything, the saltiness, the whole fucked-up situation I was in, and the complete exhaustion crashed on me all at once.

Even though my face was soon covered in snot and tears, Tae didn't care one bit. And he didn't even try to talk anymore. Instead, he let me get it all out of my system, holding me tightly against him.

An eternity later, the tears stopped. The sobs died down. I could breathe again, somewhat. Though my whole face hurt, especially my eyes, somehow I felt so much better. Sniffing, I leaned back. "I'm sorry. I didn't mean to break down on you."

Tae gently let me go. "It's okay. I was wondering when this would happen anyway."

"Yeah..." I admitted, trying to clean up the mess on my face with the palms of my hands.

Tae took my hands in his and stopped me. "Tell you what, how about you go rinse your face, and I'll make us some tea, hmm? Or do you want to go to sleep?"

"Can't sleep. Tea sounds great," I replied. "And speaking of tea, can we, uh, talk about us?"

He sighed, suddenly looking just as exhausted as I felt. "Yeah, I think we should at this point..."

I got up to my wobbly feet. Tae smiled and swept me off the ground, again with the duvet and all. He carried me straight to the downstairs bathroom like I weighed nothing at all.

This time I knew not to complain.

All Mine

The lukewarm water I splashed on my face felt heavenly, but to ease up the swelling around my aching eyes, I had to turn it to ice cold.

Still didn't really help much.

I leaned against the sink and lifted my gaze to the mirror. What a mistake. To put it bluntly, I looked like shit. The bags under my eyes were more prominent than ever. There was a breakout starting on my left cheek, while otherwise my skin was as dry as a desert.

It was more than likely the worst time for the conversation I had in mind. But let's face it, was there ever going to be a good time? Does such a concept as "a good time" even exist? I had already lost six years from my twenties, and I wasn't too keen on wasting more. I was in love with Tae, and that was what mattered. I'd just have to convince him to stop overthinking this memory-loss thing—after all he had already said he still had feelings for me.

So technically, it was a done deal already.

Then why was my stomach turning upside down and my palms sweating? Why did I freeze from the pure tension that took over my body? All for the sole fact that I needed to talk things through with Tae, come what may.

But then again, it had already been almost a month and not even a single memory from the past six years had popped back in my head. It started to seem like I couldn't count on them appearing anytime soon. And I was positive I wouldn't be able to sleep properly until at least one aspect of my freaking life was sorted out.

So... why not start with Tae? He was like, *right there,* after all. Waiting for me to emerge from the bathroom. Might as well start to try and get my life together so I could live in the present and not get stuck on the past all of the time.

I toweled my face, took a deep breath, wrapped the duvet back around myself, and walked to the kitchen with my head held high. If I had to, I'd stay up all night trying to convince him this—us— was a good idea. Even considering the *circumstances.*

As predicted, Tae was already waiting for me with two steaming hot cups of tea laid out on the dining table—one cup for him to toy with, and another across the table for me. While yanking the duvet a bit tighter around me, I tiptoed past the kitchen. He had already cleaned the mess of glass and juice I'd left behind.

After hesitating for only a second or two, I sat across Tae.

He didn't utter a single word and neither did I. The silence was so thick I could've cut it with a knife. We both evaded each other's eyes. It was awkward as hell, but I think I can talk for both of us when I say it was the time to get this conversation over and done with. In fact, it was already long overdue.

I guess Tae's chain of thought went pretty much in line with mine since we started speaking precisely at the same time.

"Tae..."

"Joonie..."

Another awkward silence ensued, until I chuckled, and Tae smirked.

"You go first—" we both said in unison.

After I was done facepalming, a silent argument started about who would go first. We waved our hands like idiots, both trying to get the other to speak first. Eventually, I gave up.

"For fuck's sake, I don't care what you're about to say! Only don't you dare to break-up with me, or we're gonna have a problem—" I shouted on top of Tae, who at the same time said something I couldn't hear over my own damn voice. "Can you just listen to me this one time?" was all I picked up from Tae after I finished my blabbering.

This was getting old. I slumped back on my chair and took a sip of tea before gesturing for Tae to continue. He opened his mouth twice to speak, probably to make sure I wasn't going to chime in, before finally saying out loud, "Now, here's the deal..." He gripped the mug in front of him so tightly his knuckles turned white. "At this point, I don't give a crap if you remember us or not. I want you. All of you. And if you reject me, I'll just annoy you as long as it'll take for you to fall back in love with me."

When he didn't continue, I raised my eyebrows. Well, this went better than I imagined. Why did I feel a "but" coming, though?

"...but?"

"No buts. That's it. That's the tea." He literally sipped some tea at the same time.

"So, if I say I feel the same way about you...we're back together?"

"I'd say so." The corners of his mouth turned up gently into a half-smile.

Um. What? This turn of events wasn't at all what I had anticipated. I was prepared to fight, goddammit!

"Just like that?" I crossed my arms over my chest.

"Just like that," Tae confirmed, taking another sip.

I threw my hands up in the air in a sign of surrender. "Fine."

We both tried to read the other's mind, unsuccessfully, as we silently stared each other down. But the weight that had been a constant resident in the pit of my stomach for days now, lifted. It turned to something almost bubbly. I couldn't resist it for long and started laughing; At the same time, Tae lost it too.

Who in their right mind argues when they both agree? To be fair, I wasn't in the right mind, so there was that.

But for once, I couldn't care less. About anything unimportant. I was convinced that as long as Tae and I stayed together, everything else wouldn't even matter. At that second, laughing so hard my eyes started to water, I felt like everything else around me would fall in their places soon enough without me stressing about it.

It did take a while, but we somehow managed to calm down. After drying up the corners of my eyes and taking a sip of the tea, I glanced at Tae who was leaning his chin on his hand and staring at me. He was smiling, that full-smile I had grown to love, with the dimple on display and all.

"What happens now?" I asked, toying with the mug.

"I don't know, and frankly, I don't even care. But I gotta say you look super cute buried in that duvet."

"Oh, shut up," I said and buried myself deeper, getting self-conscious all over again. Why the hell was it so easy for Tae to make me blush? No-one else had managed to do that before.

Tae stood up, circled the table, walked right by me, offering me his hand on his way. "Come here. I'll show you something."

It wasn't a question, but rather an order. I didn't even bother to argue. I simply gathered the blanket in one hand and took his hand with the other. He pulled me up and walked me past the couch, all the way to the glass wall—the giant window that overlooked the city.

After a quick smile, Tae turned his gaze towards the magnificent view, so I did the same. The night-mode Seoul spread as far as the eye could see, endless lights twinkling throughout the city, the Han River lazily flowing in the middle. I still couldn't get past how beautiful the view was.

"Do you like the view?" Tae asked, softly squeezing my hand that was still holding his.

"I love it." And I really meant it. Truth to be told, I never wanted to give up the view;, it reminded me of Mom and Dad every time I saw the river and the city around it. They loved Seoul so much. I missed them. "I can see the Han River."

"Good to hear," Tae said. "'Cause it's half yours."

That statement ripped me right back to reality. "What do you mean?"

"The condo...I bought it for you. The papers have your name on them too.".

"That's insane!" I exclaimed, snapping my eyes to his. "This must've cost a fortune!"

Tae smiled down at me and nodded. "As I've said before, nothing less for my jagi."

"Hmph, now I feel like a prostitute."

"Nonsense. Besides, you could've bought this yourself I think," he stated. "But it's not only about the money, Joon. Apartments with these kinds of views go on sale only once in a decade. Dad showed it to me when they were finishing the construction of this building, and the view reminded me of you. So, I bought it. It's yours. Get used to it."

"Wow. I—I don't know what to say," I said, so moved. My chest swell from the inside out, as if my heart grew twice the size.

Tae pulled me against him and laid a soft kiss on my forehead. It sent shivers down my spine, but I loved everything about it.

"Don't say anything, just start designing the interior. I did nothing so it's practically a blank canvas for you to fill up. We both know you've got a better taste anyway."

Eyes wide, I stared at him completely speechless. It was hard to wrap my head around it. No, scratch that...it was hard to wrap my head around the whole night. I had already gone from depressed to the top of the world, and now this?

"Well, thank you, I guess," I said and glanced outside once again. The view, it was all mine. No. He had said *half* mine. Which meant..."You're gonna stay, right?"

"As long as you'll have me," he said and leaned in for a kiss.

Good Idea

Like the first time back at our dorms, all my feelings for Tae exploded as soon as our lips touched. Only this time, it didn't feel as foreign as the first time. And instead of getting scared, I embraced it.

The world around us stopped—or at least it felt like we were the only ones moving. Nothing else mattered other than the moment. Not my memory loss. Not the past six year. Not the Billboards. There was no past or future, only present.

What did matter was the feeling of his hand sneaking behind my neck, and then the way he pulled me closer. The way I gave up on hiding myself and dropped the duvet to freely touch him. Hastily, I curled my hands around his waist, already planning on never letting go. The way he let out a small groan against my lips before wrapping his other hand around my waist and yanking me against him made my heart race.

We formed our own little bubble, so strong that nothing could've burst it from the outside.

Unfortunately, the threat came from inside said bubble.

That threat was me—my inability to control my body after endless nights of experimenting in my dreams. And how did I know I was the problem? Because it was the exact second of my hardening dick touched his thigh, when he decided to stop and break the kiss.

Panting, I asked, "Why did you stop?" refusing to let go of his waist even though he dropped his hands and tried to step back.

"Because speaking from experience you lack, I know...if we don't stop now, we won't be able to later," he said, almost as breathless as I was.

"I'd guess we've had sex before, then?"

He nodded and leaned his forehead against mine, closing his eyes.

I continued, "what's it like?"

"You have no idea." He straightened himself to his full height, his piercing eyes promising things I probably couldn't even begin to imagine.

But I could see the same lust smoulder inside me burning in his eyes too. He wanted this as badly as I did.

I cocked my eyebrow up, dropping my arms from around him and crossing them against my chest. "Then show me."

"Err...I'm not sure if that's a good idea," he said, scratching the back of his neck.

"Stop thinking too much."

I could practically see the gears turn in his head while he thought it out, waiting for me to take my words back with an intense stare. But I didn't give up an inch. I had been dreaming about it for long enough, and I could see he wanted it too.

"Then..." he started, hesitantly, about an eternity later. "Do you trust me?"

"No," I said, half-joking.

"Forget it, then." He turned to walk away, but not before I saw a small glimpse of sparkle in his eyes.

"Oh, come on! Of course, I do," I said. "Only...are you implying we used to have some of the more...wicked...sex?"

He glanced at me over his shoulder, "...maybe?"

"Interesting. Did we have a safe word?" I smirked. Was the Fifty Shades stuff still in, or what?

Tae turned to face me. "Actually, we did. But you're not going to need it tonight even if something happens."

If something happens? So, there was still hope? "How would you know that I won't need it?"

"Because we're not going down that path tonight."

I raised my chin, strong and bold. I was arrogantly positive that he wouldn't be able to follow through his implications. "Now that's a bummer."

"Besides, you already used that word on me once," Tae continued. "*After* waking up in the hospital. I'm confident you will use it again if anything becomes too much."

Wait, what? "When?"

"Doesn't matter. I'm still not convinced this is a good idea in the first place," he said, but at the same time stared me down with an intense glare, one that set me on fire.

"I agree, it's not a good idea. It's a *very good* idea."

"Okay, then, but just remember you asked for this," Tae muttered, and like a flip of a switch, he turned into a whole different person. One with *authority*. A little bit of a scary amount of it. The stiff smirk that was still on his lips sent wicked tingles to the pit of my stomach. Forcing my feet to move, one at a time, I managed to back off one step.

I was already chewing my lip out of pure habit. Tae reached his hand out to cup my chin. With a gentle yet demanding gesture, he released my bottom lip from the hold of my teeth with his thumb.

"I really wouldn't do that if I were you," he stated with such a low and harsh voice that it gave me actual fucking chills. The pleasurable ones. His voice, or more like the tone of it, vibrated through my whole body. "It drives me mad."

And I, a person who took pride in having a response to everything, couldn't mutter out a single word. My eyes widened as I wondered what kind of witchcraft he was practicing to have this kind of effect on me. My breath hitched, and my heart pounded so hard I was sure it was going to blow up at this rate.

I still couldn't get my voice to work as he took another step towards me, which I immediately countered by taking another step back. My back hit the glass, making me gasp and glance to the side. A huge mistake. As if I was standing right on the edge of a cliff, hundreds of feet above the ground. The survival instinct made me step away, but then when I did, I collided with Tae. My eyes snapped to his, which again nailed me to the spot.

"Give me your hands," he said, his tone dripping with authority.

Gulping, I let go of the last bits of control I had over the whole situation. As soon as I lifted them, Tae took both of my wrists in a tight grip, pulling me against his chest. I gasped when he lifted my hands above my head...so far up I almost had to stand on my toes. Before I could even react, he had me pushed against the cold glass. My eyes fluttered close.

Tae leaned against me with his full body, pinning me between him and the glass. The contrast of the two temperatures—his burning body and the freezing cold glass—drove me insane. The sensation woke up the surface of my skin, throughout my body, making the sensitivity of it heighten tenfold.

Tae crossed my wrists and pinned them against the glass, tight, leaving his other hand free. It slowly dropped down, as he slid his fingertips down my arm, over my armpit, eventually reaching the extremely sensitive skin on the side of my stomach.

An involuntary moan escaped my lips, which he quickly shushed by pushing his index finger across them.

"Shh, love, save your voice for later," he said, making me snap my eyes half-way open to meet his almost pitch black gaze. "You've made me wait for this so long we're taking this slow."

I struggled against his hold to protest the slow pace. I wanted everything, and I wanted it now. But as he was way stronger than me, my struggling didn't have any effect whatsoever. And instead of letting me have my way, he forced his leg between mine and pressed it against my already aching cock.

Another moan escaped my lips as I threw my head back. Tae took the opportunity and started roaming on my neck with his lips. His touch was rough as he circled his hand behind my back and made me arch against him.

Everything Tae could reach with only his lips, he touched, nibbled, and sucked. I lost count in no time, but it didn't matter— all his actions promised me none of it was going to be the last time.

And I was more than fine with that.

Just as I was about to lose my balance, Tae finally let my wrists from his tight grip. I slumped against him, my legs almost shaking from the tension. He held me up, the whole weight of my body in his arms.

"Too much?" he asked, smirking.

In response I threw my arms around his neck and clashed my lips against his. Because even though I was exhausted and his touch was intense, I wanted more. He smiled against my lips before starting to move them in unison with mine. I knew I had given up way too easy and was most likely going to beg for him to fuck me into oblivion sooner rather than later. But as I rolled my crotch against him, feeling up his rather impressive sized boner, I knew he was as into it as I was.

And I was very much fine with that, too.

It was like my body knew how to react, and I merely followed the instincts.

After wallowing in negative thoughts and doubting everything, it felt unbelievably good to let my body take control over my mind. As soon as Tae's hold loosened for a fraction of a second, I took my chances; I jumped up to cling to him, wrapped my legs around his waist, and held myself up with my arms still wrapped around his neck and shoulders.

I breathed into his ear. "Take me to bed, now."

Great Distraction

Tae groaned in response, grabbing a tight hold of me. That's when I knew I'd really get what I wanted. For once, I had the upper hand. I giggled the whole way, clinging to his body, feeling his muscles work...only slightly worried about making us both fall down the stairs as Tae didn't let my feet touch the ground once.

Tae's door wasn't properly closed, and it only took a kick from him to get us through. A small giggle escaped my lips again when he sucked the delicate skin right above my collarbone, but that giggle turned into a gasp when I was flying through the air the next second. My back hit the sheets before I even managed to grasp the fact that he had downright thrown me on the bed.

I didn't even have the chance to get self-conscious about my almost naked body on full display before he yanked me by my ankle, making me slide towards the edge of the bed. My eyes widened when he pressed his lips against my calf and pulled his pants down, totally distracting me with the view that was getting revealed. He moved further up, to kiss the side of my knee, then inner thigh...at the same time curling his fingers under the elastic of my boxers and then proceeded to pull them right off.

Completely ignoring my erection, he continued his journey up and kissed the skin right below my navel. Then above it. Then took one of my hardened nipples in between his sharp teeth, but only for a second before he nibbled the skin on my collarbone...then the neck, then jawline.

In between the kisses, he always took a glance at me—there was something special in the way his eyes me made me feel—like *I* was something special. It was more than enough to take my breath away. Thankfully we weren't upright anymore, since surely my legs would have given up.

Finally, his lips landed on mine. And I was gone. Somewhere past this world.

I kissed him back with all I had in me, making him groan again as I sucked his lower lip between mine and sunk my teeth in it.

With expert motions, he propped himself up. As if he'd done it a hundred times before, he pulled the drawer of his nightstand open, not even letting our kiss break once. He fished out a bottle of some clear liquid. Lube, I realized with a bit of delay, when he had already poured some to his hand and bent my knee before letting our lips part.

If his stare had been intense before, it was even more overwhelming being at his mercy. His lube coated hand slid down past my balls until his fingers reached my entrance. Blood rushed on my face, and my eyes fluttered close as the sensation made my stomach clench. A sudden shame rushed over me, and I threw my hand across my face.

All movement stopped until I felt Tae's hand prying mine away from my face.

"Don't hide, I want to see you," he whispered with that same powerful tone that had made me melt downstairs.

As Tae managed to pry my hand away from my face, he also slid one finger inside me, so slowly I had plenty of time to get used to the feeling of filling up. But as he curled his finger that was inside me, something made me clench against it and arch my back. A surprised cry escaped me at the same time every ashamed feeling evaporated—Tae's finger that massaged the magic spot inside me was more than enough for me to handle.

It drove me absolutely wild. Out of control, I started to whine and moan and writhe below Tae, who quickly pinned me down. Possibly making it even worse—or better—he inserted another finger which slid in just as easily as the first one. My brain couldn't register anything other than absolute bliss.

But he didn't go any further than teasing. No matter how much I whined, how much I struggled against him or moaned, nothing had any effect. He just kept working my hole and dick, so long that pre-cum started to leak from the slit on my aching cock.

I was on the verge of losing my mind in only a few minutes, and Tae hadn't even used his dick yet. I wanted him to become one with me, fill me up and make me a whole mess. I didn't care if he'd be rough or gentle, fast or slow—as long as he'd be inside me as soon as possible.

"Please," I begged, becoming needy, even one tear escaping the corner of my eye. "I can't take it much longer."

With an animalistic grunt escaping his throat, he instantly pulled his fingers off and lubed up his cock.

That's when one sane thought passed the lustful haze in my brain and my eyes opened halfway. "Tae..." I breathed. "Condom..."

"We don't need one," he said, smirking. "We're both clean and tested."

A flash from the doctor's office crossed my mind, where Mrs. Han had held up the smaller paper bundle. *So that's what they had meant back then.* But that thought was all but a passing memory a second later when Tae's whole weight slowly fell on top of me as his thick cock slid inside me, inch by inch.

My eyes squeezed back shut again as I took a long, shaky breath and dug my nails on Tae's back.

"Breathe," Tae said with a strained tone, before pressing his lips on mine.

But I couldn't focus on the kiss at all. Tae's cock filled way more of me than his fingers had, making me a bit uncomfortable and all stretched out. It didn't hurt, as I had anticipated; it was just...intense. Like everything else that night but times ten.

My entire being plunged into pure ecstasy. The pleasure was so great I had a hard time enduring all of it, so I became totally silent and unmoving for a few seconds.

"Breathe, love," Tae reminded me again, breaking the kiss. "Do you want me to pull out?"

"No," I said and took a shaky breath.

Prying my eyes half-way open, I met his concerned gaze. He was breathing heavily, a small bead of sweat forming in his temple. Slowly, my grasp on his back loosened, and I slid my hands down, my fingertips brushing the skin on his spinal dip. One by one, my clenched muscles started to ease up as I relaxed. And whole new sensations took the place of the discomfort.

"It feels amazing," I whispered.

I ran my hands slowly back up, just as he put his hand beside my face and caressed my jawline with his thumb.

"*You* are amazing," he breathed. "Can I move now?"

The look in his eyes made it impossible to look away or speak, so I only nodded. Ever so gently, he started moving inside me, rocking us towards the edge. His skin started to glow from the sweat, his muscles flexed by the movements. We didn't break eye contact once.

That first time after all the drama was gentle, slow and extraordinarily passionate.

And there was one more lesson learned that night. While sex might've not "cured" me in any way...nor brought any memories back...

It would've been a big fat lie if I had said it wasn't a damn good distraction.

Actual Clothes

"Joon, wake up. I'm bored," Tae whined, the voice coming from somewhere on my right.

To be honest, I was already awake, but I didn't want to open my eyes. Or get up from under the warm blanket. Especially after having to fight for it a few times during the night, until Tae had sunk in deep enough slumber for me to steal a corner. It had escalated to the point I had considered moving to my bedroom across the loft...but I had left my duvet downstairs and didn't feel like fetching it.

"Please," he continued as I refused to acknowledge him even though he had sneaked his hand under the sheets and started stroking my side. "I made breakfast."

"Five more minutes," I mumbled, pulling the duvet tighter around me.

"Well, your loss, and your cold coffee," Tae said and his hand vanished. *Ugh.*

I groaned. "What time is it anyway?"

"Eleven thirty."

My eyes popped open, and I sat upright. "Fuck!"

I tried to stand, but Tae yanked me back. "Where are you going? What's wrong?"

"I'm supposed to meet Minjae at the HQ at twelve for the choreography! Why didn't you wake me up?!"

"First of all, I tried. And secondly, it's canceled. Everything's canceled."

I flopped down with a relieved huff and wrapped the blanket back around me. "Alright, great. But why?"

Tae shrugged. "Look, I just got you back. I am not gonna let you go, and the rest of the world can survive without you for a couple of days."

"You…canceled everything?" I asked, raising an eyebrow. It was another thing the Tae from back in the days did not do. Ever. "I wonder how Minjae took it..."

He smiled at me and plopped a tray full of food on my lap. "Don't care. Perks of being the boss—well, apart from bossing everyone around. Like you, right now. Here, drink your coffee."

Snorting, I glugged down the first heavenly tasting sip of coffee that most likely had exactly one sweetener and lots of milk. Precisely how I liked it. Apart from that, there was practically everything from fried eggs to fruits of several kinds present.

"I can't possibly eat all this," I huffed. Was present-day Joonie okay with wasting this much food?

Tae popped a grape to his mouth, sneaking under the blanket too. "Half of it is for me of course."

"Hmph," I mumbled, but deep down I was happier than ever.

No work. No outside world. For a day or two, I could only be and live and breathe. I was more than content with that.

I let myself relax and started munching down some apple slices. Tae snatched half of every slice, but I didn't mind. I continued with everything else on the tray. Only fifteen minutes later, I was positively stuffed.

And bored.

"Anything you'd want to do today?" I asked after swallowing the last drops of the delicious coffee.

When I heard no reply, I turned my gaze down to Tae who had his head on my lap, the food tray already put to the side table. He had his eyes closed and a small smile lingering on his lips. His hair was all messy due to last night, which caused me to have this overpowering urge to run my hand through it.

He opened his eyes when I did.

"We could spend the whole day in bed," he said with a twinkle in his eyes.

My reply was a gentle slap on the back of his head which caused him to chuckle. As much as I'd liked the previous night...I wasn't sure if my ass could handle another round, to put it bluntly.

"Okay-okay, no bed then. How about a bath? I know you haven't gotten around to test the jacuzzi yet."

"Do you have anything in mind that involves putting on some actual clothes?"

"No," he said with a completely blank deadpan on his face.

"Then, a bath sounds nice," I said and smiled. "But only if you carry me there and join me."

"Deal," he said and hopped up.

I put the coffee mug down on the tray that we moved to the nightstand before Tae downright rolled me inside the duvet and proceeded to carry me right across the upstairs loft and to my bedroom. After laying me on the other bed ever so gently, he kissed my forehead and scurried to my bathroom to fill up the hot tub. I used my legs for the first time that day to go to the toilet.

The reflection on the mirror as I washed my hands made me pleasantly surprised. The dark circles around my eyes had all but evaporated, and I had this certain glow on my skin. I almost looked as happy as in the photos from the amusement park.

I toweled my hands dry before grabbing the camera from the drawer where I had left it after unpacking all my stuff. I sat cross-legged on my bed, pulled up the duvet to cover my legs and rested my back against the headboard.

With my heartbeat accelerating for no apparent reason, I turned the camera on. I didn't know what I was looking for in the photos, but I nevertheless started scrolling through them all over again. The Joonie in the photos...he didn't seem as unfamiliar as before. He had gone from a total stranger to an acquaintance of some sort— maybe a person I'd want to aspire to become someday.

I was ripped out of my thoughts by Tae who hopped down to sit beside me.

"It was a nice day," he mumbled after glancing at the LCD.

The tone he used, a somewhat sad one, took me off guard. The jealousy I had for my past self, washed over me once again. It clenched my heart so badly it physically hurt, and the air around us became thicker, making it hard to breathe.

I wanted to have the memory of that day back, so much it became hard to concentrate on the present. The mushy, dark thoughts started to gain some space in my head again. Even seeing the photos settled a weird feeling in the pit of my stomach, almost like the place had some significant meaning, or held an answer to all this mess.

"Can we go there?" I asked. I hadn't really meant to. It just came out, and yet, once I said it, I knew it was what I needed.

"Yeah, maybe someday."

"No, I meant like...today?"

"Err, I don't think that's a good idea," Tae stated, leaning back. "You know, with certain things the way they are."

"Nothing's ever a good idea in your books." A strong bitterness rang through my tone. *Certain things*? The implications in those words had me fuming. "Why? Why not? Because I'm not *that* Joonie yet?" I tilted my head towards the camera screen displaying a photo of old-me smiling beside a very vintage and decaying carousel.

"No. Joon, It's not like that," Tae said. He took the camera out of my hands, clicked it shut and placed it to my nightstand. "It's just that—uhh—it would be dangerous until they get Min-ho caught."

Right. Somehow, I had forgotten there was an actual person out there who had gotten me into this mess in the first place. It was his fault. He'd taken this experience away from me. I couldn't let someone I'd never even met in my memories keep taking things from me. Not when I needed it so badly.

"I still want to go. It's...it's this feeling," I started, leaning against Tae's side, and turning my eyes to his. "Please... I—I can't explain why but I really need to go."

Tae searched my eyes for a long while and I stared right back. At some point, he narrowed his eyes, but I didn't back off. Wanting to go to Yongma Land was all I could focus on, and I wasn't giving up.

Tae sighed and shook his head, and I knew instantly that I had won.

"Aish, it seems like I can't deny you anything these days..."

"We will go? Now?" I asked, the bubbling anticipation already making me almost jump off the bed.

"Well, not today..." he started, hesitantly. Almost making me fall right back to depression real fast. That is until he continued with a stern voice. "However, I could, maybe, try to arrange that for tomorrow. And for the record, we'll have to get Joe on board too; we're not leaving anything, and I mean *anything*, to chance."

A full smile crept on my lips. "Deal."

Finally smiling again, Tae hopped out of the bed and offered his hand to me. "But for today, you're mine. Come on, let's have that bath."

As I took his hand, he yanked me up and led me to the bathroom. Hesitantly, I dipped my toes in first—the perfect temperature. Not too hot, but not too cold either. Tae had filled it way too full, and the water splashed everywhere when I stepped in. Even more so when Tae threw his sweatpants and boxer briefs off before stepping in after me.

The tub was so big it easily fit two people without us having to even touch each other. Nevertheless, I made my way between Tae's legs, turned around and leaned my back against his chest as he made room for me.

He laid a gentle kiss on the side of my neck as I leaned my head back against his shoulder.

I closed my eyes.

"Thank you, for everything."

Triggered

There was something inexplicably beautiful in the way that nature had taken over the abandoned amusement park. The old asphalt was cracked, and most of the rides collapsed. The cherry trees were overgrown from the lack of grooming, but still attractive in full bloom.

My hands were itching to take some photos, but Tae had made me leave the camera behind—claiming I had already photographed everything here, twice. I had tried to counter by claiming it had been a different season, but I hadn't had much luck with that.

Thus, we only fooled around the park, me discovering everything seemingly for the first time, Tae sharing my enthusiasm despite having memories from two times before. I tried not to think about it too much, enjoying the warm spring morning. Sun was shining, the wind wasn't too strong, the air was easy to breathe. It was perfect.

We were always surrounded by our security staff, much to my dismay. They were on full alert, always getting in my line of sight. It wasn't nearly as private as I had wanted it to be.

But then again, it was necessary, or so they had told me. Joe had only agreed to bring us after he had gotten nearly all of his staff to attend, apart from Mr. Won who was still trapped in the mountains with Chris. Even Minjae and Do-hyun had had to agree to stay indoors the whole day because Seong-gi was here too, and Joe wasn't letting any new recruits of his spend any alone time with any of us.

A pang of guilt hit me for the hundredth time that day. None of them were having a day off and Min and Do had to stay at their barely finished home for the whole freaking day. Then again, those two wouldn't probably be too upset about it, if it was anything like the day before had been for Tae and me.

By late morning, everything relaxed. Most of the guards gathered at the picnic tables at the main square. Some of them started playing cards, others entertained themselves with their phones. There was literally no-one else at the whole park other than our party, as Tae had bribed the owner—a grumpy looking old man—again.

We ended up loitering around a half-way collapsed castle-like building that was the furthest thing from the main square to try and have some privacy. It was hard to fully relax though, as I knew Joe was hovering around somewhere—that guy never rests, I swear. But I tried my best to ignore him.

It wasn't until Tae sat me down beside him at one of the still intact benches near the half-collapsed entrance to the castle and circled his hand around my waist when the tension finally fully melted away. The silence around us wasn't awkward at all, as I lifted my eyes from the ground to Tae's. He smiled at me before we shared a short but sweet kiss.

It had truly been a very nice morning. No, I still hadn't gotten any of my memories back, but with each passing hour it mattered less and less. Because I had Tae by my side.

He had been there through the worst. He had seen me at my worst. He had given me space. Were there any more I could ask from him?

With him next to me, I accepted the possibility that I might never get my memories back. I could focus on making new ones. With Tae, and even the other members of GRiD. We were, after all, heading to the Billboard awards, despite all the shit we had gone through.

With a sudden need to say it all out loud to start a new leaf in my life, I unwrapped Tae's hand from around my waist and took it in mine instead, interlacing our fingers.

"Tae..." I started. At once, I had Tae's full attention. He only looked at me questioningly, wordlessly encouraging me to continue. Smiling the full smile, dimple and all. And I had a hunch he already knew what I was going to say. I decided to say it out loud anyway. "I want you to know that I'm in love with you...with or without the memories."

Without a word, Tae squeezed my hand before lifting it and pressing his lips against the back. For maybe two seconds, he let the moment linger, closing his eyes. It almost looked like he wanted to stop the moment to fully appreciate it before he opened his eyes again and laid our interlaced hands on his thigh.

"Joon, you won't even believe how long I've wanted to say this..." His eyes pierced mine with intensity I didn't know was possible. "But same. I'm in love with you too."

I let out a breath I didn't even know I had been holding and rested my head on his shoulder. "Good thing, because I'm not letting you go ever again."

And just like that, we marveled in the beauty of the park silently for a long, long while. It only ended when my lower back started aching due to the not-so-ideal position. Reluctantly letting go of Tae's hand, I stood and stretched the stiffness away.

Tae rose too and wrapped his arms around me from behind, before laying his chin on my shoulder. "Should we head home?"

"Yeah, I guess..." I said, taking once last glance at the beautiful park. "Just a couple of photos first, please?" I held up my phone.

Tae hung his head and let go of my waist. "Ugh, fine."

I only smiled back at him before tapping the small camera icon on my phone's screen.

"You have five minutes. I think I saw a toilet sign in the castle. Maybe it'll work, and I can take a leak," he said, but I was already immersed in trying to capture the beauty of the park through the lens.

There was an old space-themed ride nearby, to which I gravitated. The photos in my real camera back at Tae's—no, *our*—place, had all been from the overall atmosphere, so I decided to capture the smaller details this time. Like the baby cherry tree that had started to grow through a crack in the middle of a former pathway. And the rusty, broken seat on the space-themed ride. A broken lamp.

I was so immersed in my phone's screen that I didn't pay attention to my feet. Naturally, on the uneven and broken paths, I tripped, and the phone flew from my grip almost like it was in slow motion. I watched it drop straight to the gap between the stairs to the ride and the ride's floor.

Cursing under my breath, I dropped down on my knees and tried to fish it up. Even with my arm shoulder-deep in the gap, I could only touch the screen with my fingertips, not curl them around it to have a proper grip. I straightened up and turned to look back, hoping Tae's arm would be long enough to reach the damn phone.

He was nowhere in sight.

"Tae?" I hollered but got no answer.

I walked back to the castle's entrance where the toilet sign that he had been talking about hung. I leaned against the wall, crossing my arms across my chest, waiting.

A minute passed. Then another. How long could one guy take in the toilet? I peeked inside, taking a hesitant step. Then another, slightly further in.

"Tae! Where are you?" I shouted, expecting him to jump behind a corner at any given time. But he didn't.

The floorboards creaked under every footstep, but other than that, it was deadly silent and semi-dark—only some daylight made its way inside through the gaps of the windows that had been nailed shut ages ago. Every hair on the back of my neck stood up. A light source of some sort would've been helpful, but my phone was still outside, and out of my reach.

"This isn't funny anymore!" I hollered again to the void.

"Let's go home—" A hand shot out of the shadows and slapped across my mouth. Before I could even attempt to scream, another hand pulled me to the shadows.

"Shh," said someone in my ear and released the hold on my mouth. Even through the dark, I recognised Joe, holding his index finger over his lips. He tilted his head downward, pulling my gaze to his foot which had gone through the rotten floor. Blood dripped slowly from the part where a large splinter had pierced through the skin on his calf. I cringed—it didn't look good.

"You're walking into a trap," Joe whispered, so quietly I had a hard time hearing. "Min-ho is waiting for you at the end of the aisle. He has Tae and a gun."

My heart stopped. When it kicked up again, it beat my chest like a hammer. I opened my mouth to release a horrified holler, but Joe slapped his hand across my mouth again.

"Shh, there's no time for panicking, Joonie," he hissed. "Focus!"

He glared me straight in the eyes, and I nodded while taking a silent deep breath.

Joe released my mouth again and reached for his back. He put something hard and metal into my palm and made me grip it.

A gun.

"Take this," he said

"I don't know how to use it!" I whisper-shouted, resisting the urge to drop the thing on the ground and out of my possession.

"Nonsense. I've seen your army records. Now cut the little miss innocent act and snap out of it."

As if that would comfort me in any way. I had no recollection of those days for fuck's sake!

"Listen closely. He's somewhere on the right when you reach the end of this aisle. I'd go there myself, but I can't move enough without making too much noise. There's no time to fetch the others. So, you take the shot, I'll take the blame. Now go," he whispered and downright pushed me back to the corridor.

The gun was heavy in my hand, but the weight of it was oddly familiar. Halfway expecting my hands to start to shake, I lifted it to take a closer look. It was already loaded with a full magazine. I grabbed the handle with both hands, my finger finding the other safety pin on the side so easily as if I knew what I was doing. Which I didn't. It just happened.

With the gun in my surprisingly non-shaking hands, I studied the scene from the dark shadows. Tae was on his knees against the left wall, his back against Min-ho who held him at gunpoint. My heart started pumping the adrenaline through my body, the sensation drowned by the concentration high I was already on. And time...it lost its meaning. I had all the time in the world to focus on details.

Min-ho looked...not at all what he had looked like in the photos. The thing that at some point must've been his nose was crooked beyond recognition, and the cuts on his face were clearly infected. But I still recognized.

"I knew you'd come back here at some point," Min-ho muttered to Tae, waving the gun in front of his face. There was a wild look on Min-ho's eyes—a very creepy one.

A burning rage started rushing in my veins, turning my whole being into a focused machine. This bitch was pointing a gun on the love of my life, and I wasn't having it. But what I was even more aware of, was that the outline of Min-ho's body somewhat resembled a human-shaped target board from my viewpoint.

Upon that realization, a strong pair of hands wrap around my waist and a stubble scratched my shoulder. It was a well-known feeling, but even I knew it wasn't real., There wasn't anyone behind me. A familiar scent of strong cologne hung in the air when I heard a deep voice inside my mind.

"If you want to kill a man, you aim lower. The chance of getting a headshot is very slim with an unfamiliar weapon and a moving target."

Wait. A memory? An actual honest to gods memory? And I trusted it. I trusted the voice and obeyed.

In one swift motion, I slide the gun to eye level and point at Min-ho's chest, my index finger resting gently on the side of the weapon.

The voice in my head stopped me again. *"But you don't always have to kill a man to survive. By aiming lower, you can incapacitate the opponent."*

I aimed at his crotch.

"Now that's just cruel..." the voice in my head said.

"Well, maybe this fucker deserves his dick shot off," I heard myself reply inside my own memory.

Nevertheless, I aimed at the target's upper thigh.

"Good. Now finger on the trigger. Prepare for the kickback and go for it."

Without a moment of hesitation, I pulled the trigger.

Everything Lost

The bang of the gun going off rattled my eardrums so hard they almost exploded. Sound disappeared, replaced by nothing but a high pitched ring. My arms took the blow of the recoil, and I retained my aim. I didn't even blink.

Pure chaos erupted around me while I stayed at the center, unaffected. Totally separated from reality. So high on adrenaline, I could easily grasp even the tiniest details.

My aim was off—the bullet made a hole in Min-ho's stomach and the impact made him stagger and then fall with a gut-wrenching screech emerging from his lungs. He dropped the gun which slid far from his reach as he writhed in agony. Strangely enough, seeing the blood gush out of the small wound didn't make me sick. In fact, my mind was serene—calm.

Before either Tae or Min-ho had the slightest chance grasping what'd happened, Joe limped beside me and pried the gun out of my hands that were clasped around the thing so tightly that my knuckles were white. I breathed, released my fingers, and took a step back. Then another.

"Good job," the voice in my head said. Sergeant Gwon. I knew his name. That memory was from a late-night one-on-one training session back at the military. The guy... he had been my first.

I guess it was true what they say that one can never forget their first.

The longer I held onto the memory, the less vivid it became but stayed in the back of my mind like it was supposed to, making room for other thoughts.

And another memory appeared. Actually, let's make that a thousand. In fact, it all rushed back to me like a tsunami, overwhelming me so much I almost fainted to the spot.

Every kiss I had shared with Tae came back to me. How I had realized I was in love with him during the time we were rooting for Minjae and Do-hyun. Our first night, only sleeping together...the first date, right here in this same amusement park—how there was a slow, beautiful snowfall, one you could only see in movies and once in real life. The first time we had sex, Tae being all awkward and adorable. Then the dozen times after that when he had not been adorable at all, but rather a beast in bed.

Not every memory was a good one. I'd been devastated for months after Mom and Dad passed away. I remembered the day I let their ashes fly on the wind of the riverbank of river Han and how I couldn't stop my tears from flowing.

Even the scary ones came back. The first time I received a weird phone call. All the times I had listened to the creepy messages Min-ho had left me. I remembered my old guard, Mr. Choi, who had been in the car with me that awful day. I hadn't seen him since.

Joe stepped in the room to the light that poured in from the busted window behind Tae and Min-ho. I forced myself to focus on the present, cursing the timing my memories finally decided to make a comeback.

Tae's whole body was shaking as he tried to adjust to what was happening around him. With the gun pointed at the guy on the floor, who had started to swear profusely, Joe made it across the room and kicked the gun even further away from him.

"Get out of here, now. Call 112," he spat to Tae through his clenched teeth. "I'll deal with this motherfucker."

I forced my feet to move too.

I ran outside, as fast as my shaking feet could carry me, not even caring that the sunlight burned my eyes. I staggered to the edge of the main square. Seong-gi was smoking a cigarette in one of the picnic tables, playing cards with some of the newer guards, but snapped his gaze to me as soon as he spotted me.

Had they not heard the gun go off?!

My legs failed me. I crashed on my knees to the asphalt, hard, my head spinning. Seong-gi threw his cigarette away and dashed beside me. He grabbed my shoulder.

"What happened?" He shook me slightly. For a while, I just stared at him in his eyes.

Yes, what did happen? I wondered. Funny how I could remember everything clearly but not what happened a minute ago. It was so...Grey. Mushy. Hazy.

"Min-ho," I breathed, out of breath and seeing stars. "Uhh— Joe... Err... Tae... Fuck it, call 112. They're inside the castle."

He yelled something to the other guards that I could no longer hear through the ringing in my ears. Some of them jogged past us, others gathered around me. Seong-gi cursed under his breath and picked up his phone, starting to explain the situation almost instantly to the other end.

Another hand landed on my shoulder, as Tae crashed beside me, out of breath.

I couldn't focus on him. Or anything, for that matter. My mind was filled with more and more memories coming back to me, a flash here and there. None of it in any sensical order. It was as if the room that had been locked before was not only opened, but like my notebooks, everything was a big old pile of mess.

My stomach turned upside down. My head spun. The ringing in my ears got louder and louder until it was all I could hear.

I dropped on all fours, the small rocks on the asphalt sinking in my palms. It hurt like hell. But nothing, not even the pain, could take me back to the present.

The churning of my stomach won, and the lunch salad we'd had earlier forced its way out of my system in one go. The soda too. Lastly, the gastric acid, burning my throat on its way out.

My eyes watered, and I could hardly keep myself from falling. Every single muscle in my stomach clenched as it forced everything out.

It wasn't until Tae's hand landed on my lower back and starting to make those familiar soothing circles when the ringing in my ears started to subside.

Soon enough, I could hear some bits and pieces of things that happened around me. There was a lot of yelling. A siren going off in the distance. But I focused on one voice that came beside me: Tae's.

"It's okay, it's over, everything's alright," he said.

After one last cough, there wasn't anything more left in my stomach to vomit. I tried to stand up, but my head started spinning again.

I was able to meet Tae's worried gaze. It looked funny to me, somehow, and I started laughing like a maniac.

"I can remember," I managed to cough out when Tae grabbed my waist and forced me to sit on the asphalt.

"Umm, what?" he asked, his face telling me he thought I had gone totally insane.

I laughed some more. "I can remember!" I yelled at him, grabbing his shoulders, and shaking him.

He scrunched his eyebrows together. "What do you remember?"

Only one word came to mind: "Everything."

But before I could get my mind to wrap around it, the edges of my vision started to get blurry.

Slowly but surely, the world around me blackened.

Safe Word

The next thing I noticed was the all too familiar mushy-green walls as I fluttered my eyes open. The stench of disinfectant and latex gloves filled my nose when I took a deep breath. Someone grabbed my right shoulder to ground me to reality.

For fuck's sake, not again.

Gasping for air, I heaved myself to a sitting position. It was hard to breathe but at least I didn't have a breathing tube jammed down my throat. There were no drips attached to the backs of my hands either. And I wasn't in any pain, whatsoever. My head still spun, but not as bad as last time I woke up in this green prison.

Wait...how did I end up here?

And more importantly, what happened to Tae? He had gone to take a leak back at Yongma Land, but my phone...it had dropped...then I woke up here, huh? No that wasn't it. Something else had to have happened for me to end up here again. But what?

Grasping my hair, I tried to remember. It was all sort of grey in my mind. Had I gone inside the castle to look? I knew I had thought about it. But I couldn't recall anything that had happened after my phone had dropped and I had realized Tae wasn't behind me.

"Tae!" I gasped, getting frustrated. "Where's Tae? Is he okay?"

"Shh, I'm right here," he said grabbing my hand in his, making me snap my eyes to my left.

And there he was indeed, looking as good as ever. As soon as our eyes met, he circled his hand around my waist and held me tight against his chest. Suddenly air flowed in and out of my lungs effortlessly and my eyes finally focused.

I couldn't help myself. The relief that washed over me was so powerful that my arms threw themselves around Tae involuntarily, and I all but squeezed the living shit out of him, all the while he continued whispering some calm and soothing things in my ear. At some point, but I had no idea if it took minutes or hours, I was able to remove myself from plastering my whole being against Tae's warm chest.

It took some effort, but my arms that clenched his waist loosened a bit, and I could take a good look at his face. Just to confirm, once again, that he was real, and not hurt in any way, I lifted my hand and touched the side of his face. He closed his eyes, leaned against it, and laid his hand on top of mine as my thumb caressed his cheek.

I sneaked my other hand behind his neck and yanked him into a passionate kiss. Screw gentle and soft, I wanted to feel it all—so I went for it. He smirked against my lips, to which I responded by sinking my teeth into his bottom lip.

Someone cleared their throat behind me, ripping me back to reality. Instantly, we snapped away from each other, the world around us making its presence a tad too clear for my tastes.

Reluctantly, I turned myself towards the voice.

"Meiling!" I yelped. Boy was I glad to see her. To be completely honest, I was glad I could remember her, too.

"Yes, now can you stop sucking each other's faces off so I can do the check-up?" She pouted, but I didn't miss the smile that flashed on her face for a nanosecond.

I grinned and leaned back on the bed, after fully unwrapping myself from around Tae. He chuckled and didn't let go of me completely, only sat back down on his chair instead and took my hand in his.

"Alright, do your thing," I said to Meiling. "Then let me out of here as soon as possible. I'm sick and tired of this place."

"Not so fast. You fainted, so we'll have to monitor your health for a while considering your recent medical history. How long, is for the doctor to decide. I see at least some of your memories are still intact?" she asked, already writing something to her chart.

I didn't know what to say to that, so I only nodded. Although the flashes were still pretty much a tangled mess in my head, I definitely had more memories than I had the first time around. I wasn't really sure if any of it was real or just some sort of hallucination.

"You hungry?" Meiling asked, bringing me back to the present once again.

"Definitely. Though I'm not sure if I can keep anything down..." I placed my hands on my growling but nauseous stomach. "Any pain?"

I performed a quick check on my entire body. "None. I'm as peachy as I can get at this point."

"Good, now look this way." She took a firm grip on my chin and pointed a bright light at my eyes. When she was satisfied with the results, she stepped back.

"Looking good, Joonie. Welcome back to the land of the living," she exclaimed, and for the first time flashed me a wide smile. "I'll bring you some food. Let's see if we can get your blood sugar up a bit."

After the door closed behind Meiling, I turned to Tae and yanked him closer. After all the mess, I couldn't keep my hands off him, and even more importantly, my lips apart from his.

Tae cut our kiss short this time though. "Err...Joon, you mentioned something about, uhh, remembering things...back at the park?" he asked, a deep wrinkle of worry set between his eyebrows. "Though I'm not sure if that counts since you pretty much lost it..."

For the first time since waking up, I searched through the memories I'd gotten back. They were still there. They felt real enough. "Umm, yeah. I think I can remember most, if not all, of the past six years now. Though I'm not sure about the order and stuff. It's a bit messy around here," I tapped my temple.

Tae stayed silent for a long while before opening his mouth. "Prove it."

I sorted through everything once more. Clearly, I needed to give him something major, something tangible. Nothing that my imagination would be able to produce on its own. Something that would convince him enough.

"The safe word is red."

Tae grinned and said, "I'm glad you're back."

My own smile was smothered by mages of Tae banging me against his office desk. He had pulled my hair, not giving a single fuck about being tender or going slow. "You've been holding back on me the past couple of nights."

He laughed. "Yes, I've held back...for a good reason. Our usual style isn't for the fainthearted. Or for recovering amnesia patients."

"Hmph," I mumbled, as the door opened and Meiling walked back in with a tray.

"But just wait until we get back home," Tae whispered to my ear, sending shivers down my spine and a blush creeping up my neck at an alarming speed. And I remembered blushing around Tae hadn't been my problem only during recovery...rather it had started way before.

Okay, so some things I would've gladly forgotten. *Ugh.*

Meiling deadpanned. "Did I interrupt something?"

"Nah, Joon here just got his memories back. The lost ones," Tae said, straightening up with a full grin on his face. Yes, the dimple appeared too.

Meiling, however, nearly dropped her tray but was able to collect herself right on time. "Oh, uh. Well. That's...interesting. I guess we'll need to call Dr. Han in. She'll want to hear it all."

I smacked Tae's stomach with my fist, lightly. He and his big mouth. But Tae only chuckled at me, not affected.

So much for getting home anytime soon.

Bubble

Endless questions, having to tell my freaking life story about eight times, then staying in the hospital for the night, a lot of tests, and a brain scan of some sort later...I finally got to Dr. Han's office for another final evaluation.

"Well, I didn't mean you'd have to get yourself involved with actual guns when I said the memories might appear when triggered..." Dr. Han stared at me over the glasses that barely hung on the tip of her nose.

We had told her the whole story, twice. We had told the same story to the police at least three times when they had appeared to question Tae and me at the hospital sometime during the day. Tae had filled me in for the part I had no recollection of, which apparently was that Joe had shot Min-ho and that was the end of the most dramatic part. After that, I had gone into shock as my memories had decided to make a comeback upon hearing the gunshot. Then I vomited and passed out. Not a very interesting story if you ask me. Rather, it made me sick.

"Yes, irony is usually strong within a kilometer from me," I said, glaring back at her.

"Well, I think we both agree it's good to have you back, right?" she eventually continued.

"Yes, it's nice to know people. Especially myself."

"Can't even imagine," she said, pushing her glasses back in place with her index finger. "And the fact that you still can't remember the latest car crash or all of yesterday's events, doesn't bother you?"

"Not one bit." Honestly, why would it?

"All right then. You're good to go home. Keep in mind memories are never one hundred percent accurate, and you might notice some of them are faded. It's totally normal, that's how memories work. And it'll take a while for them to fall into the right timeline, so to speak. But if you keep that in mind you'll be fine. Quite frankly, I don't see a reason why we couldn't declare that your amnesia has officially passed."

I'd know that was true for the past few days but hearing it from the doctor made it so much more really. *Officially passed.* I was free.

I almost let out a relieved sigh, but I wasn't fast enough before Tae ruined the moment. Again.

"How about yesterday? I mean, he fainted, right? Shouldn't he stay in the hospital for a couple of days for monitoring?" Tae asked the doctor at a million words a second.

Couldn't he shut up already? After that juicy hint of a promise about what would happen after we'd get back home, the fact that Tae kept opening that big mouth of his at the worst possible times started to get on my nerves. Sure, he was worried about me and all that, but the endless questions tended to lengthen our stay at the hospital at least by half an hour, each.

Luckily, the doctor was with me on this one. "Mr. Gang, I know you're worried, but I think the fainting yesterday was only because so much happened at once. It's a normal shock reaction. Just don't leave him alone tonight."

Oh, I'm counting on that last part.

"Now get out and please don't come back for a while," the doctor said and waved us off, much like the last time we left this place. And I couldn't even begin to describe how goddamn good it felt to remember such trivial details.

When we stood up and headed to the door, the doctor continued, making us stop on our tracks. "Except we'll have a check-up in about two months from now, I'll send more info at a later date to both of your emails."

"Noted. Can we go now?" I asked.

"Yes, get out of my hair already," she let out a chuckle and waved the back of her hand at the door.

We didn't need another word to get out of the office, gather our things at the all too familiar mushy green room, and set off. I could almost taste the freedom...until we hit the lobby, and I saw the sea of reporters outside.

Tae halted in the middle of the lobby. "How are they already here?" He turned to Joe, who had been tailing us the whole day with Seong-gi keeping him company. "Who leaked this?"

"I did," Jiwoo's voice ringed from the other end of the room. "Come on, just a couple of words for the press and you'll be done."

Oh, come on! What does a man need to do to get home for some dick in the ass around here?

She must've seen the horrified looks on our faces, because she threw her hands on her hips and said, "What? Some publicity never hurt anyone."

Tae sighed. "Okay. We'll have to push through. Joe?"

Joe shrugged. "Min-ho's caught. That isn't a super large crowd. Let's get outta here."

Tae rubbed his temples. "Fine. To get our stories straight: this was a routine check-up, nothing more. Other than that, it's 'no comments' policy. Do we have a deal?"

Jiwoo threw her arms up defensively. "Hey, I'm good if you only get your faces to the papers. It's the least you can do after leaving me to handle all this drama."

I nodded. "Deal."

"Let's go then," Tae said and laid his hand on the small of my back, starting to push me towards the main doors of the hospital.

As we forced our way through the crowd with Joe and Seong-gi, I couldn't care less about the hyenas around us. I let Tae do the talking. My goal was the familiar SUV that appeared behind the crowd.

I could only properly breathe when we had forced our way all the way through to the SUV and sat on the backseat. Joe climbed to the driver's seat as the new guy switched to the front passenger's seat. After Seong-gi slammed the sliding door shut behind us, we were—finally—on our way towards home.

It was already past rush hour, and there was little to no traffic on the streets. Which meant we were at Tae's place—no, scratch that...at *our* place in no time. When we passed the metal gate to the private garage, Tae laid his hand on my leg. I hadn't even realize I had been shaking it the whole ride. With a smirk, he whispered, "getting restless around here are we?"

I knew all his weaknesses now. My only reply to him was a "Maybe," followed by my tongue flicking across my bottom lip before I sucked it in. Then, I released the lip from the hold of my teeth so slowly my poker face almost betrayed me. The familiar dark, burning fire ignited in Tae's eyes.

I'm so *in for a treat...*

Seong-gi opening the sliding door of the SUV.

"Please don't leave this place for a day or two. My men need a day-off," Joe pleaded as he hopped off from the driver's seat and we emerged from the back seats. "And no drama."

"Deal," Tae called to Joe, who had already turned his back on us and was walking briskly towards his BMW with the other guards following right after.

In a strange silence, we watched them go. We'd been so busy for the past two days that I hadn't had time to stop to think. At all. Right then everything seemed to stop as soon as the metal door clanked down after Joe and the others.

The tension that had built up to my shoulders all but melted away. My breath flowed freely after what seemed like months now that I remembered almost everything. The relief damn nearly knocked me out; that was how powerful it was.

All the drama was, in fact, over. Behind us. Dealt with.

I wouldn't have to be anxious every time when glancing at my phone anymore, fearing whatever sick, creepy message would wait for me there. I could stop glancing over my shoulder every time I thought someone was watching me. At least for now.

Most importantly of all, I would finally be able to spend some actual quality time with the love of my life, without having to worry about everything at the same time. I could bathe in the glow of newfound love, with the same man that glanced down at me right then, with a smile on his lips.

"Let's go home?"

I turned around and all but smashed the plastic disk on the scanner circle to call the lift.

As soon as the doors opened, we stepped inside in a total silence. Then we both turned around to watch the doors close, taking a deep breath almost precisely at the same time. As what was about to happen once we reached the penthouse sunk in, my hands became clammy and that bubbly feeling, that I always had in the pit of my stomach whenever Tae was around, got stronger. A hint: none of it involved clothes.

But something snapped as soon as the doors closed.

It only took one shared look in each other's eyes, and our bags dropped to the floor with a thud. I threw my whole body against Tae, who countered by circling his hands behind my butt and lifting me up against the wall. While I was wrapping my legs around him, he found my neck with his feverish lips, and I couldn't help but throw my head back, bathing in the familiar but all too distracting feeling of his lips on my skin.

The lift ride was over all too soon. But for once, our moment was far from over, as Tae kicked our bags to the entrance room of the condo. He followed them, still carrying me as if I was as light as a feather. Once again I thanked all the gods there are, that this man's muscles weren't only for visual pleasure. Not that I minded the visual pleasure either.

My back hit the wall when Tae pushed me against it harshly, almost knocking the air out of my lungs. But I couldn't care less about the pain once Tae's lips finally found mine. It was all I could focus on…other than yanking his jacket off, without being very successful. The denim was way too stubborn of a material for my taste.

With a groan, Tae let go of me as soon as he caught on what I was trying to do. I hopped down, at the same time pulling the jacket off. It ended up on the floor, somewhere, when we made our way across the room to the door that led further in the condo. My jacket found its way to the floor too, along with both of our shoes which we kicked off right before entering the short hallway.

I didn't get to take any more steps on my own. Instead of letting me walk, Tae spun me around, and I was back in his arms, moving forward. I couldn't help but let out a small giggle at his impatience, which ended shortly as he dropped me down on the kitchen counter before attacking my neck with his lips all over again.

It was only when my hands had finally made their way under the annoying amount of clothes to touch his naked back, and Tae's hands had found their way to my back pockets, when the sound of someone clearing their throat pierced through our lust-filled bubble.

We both jumped and snapped away from each other.

I had to shake my head a bit to clear it up, before turning to face the direction where the sound came…and where my eyes met with a middle-aged, brown-haired, familiar-looking man in a pristine suit, sitting at the dinner table. He was eyeing us with a deep frown between his eyebrows, that reminded me of Tae when he was being overly serious about something.

Tae gulped, standing still as a statue. "Dad?"

Shit.

Spare Key

"Dad?"

"The one and only," the older Mr. Gang Jae-sung said, raising one of his eyebrows—a gesture Tae had totally picked up from him. The similarity was striking.

It took me a while to realign my thoughts from the heated moment to the embarrassing present. But when it did hit me, my heart stopped, and my breath hitched. Not in a pleasurable way. Rather, it made me wonder if my body was shutting down on me.

Aish-shit-fuck-no-this-isn't-happening. Hell. To. The. No.

While my brain went over every curse word I could think of, Tae took a step back. I slid down from the top of the counter as gracefully as possible while deeply ashamed and trying to discreetly straighten my shirt. Somehow, miraculously, my feet didn't fail me, and I was able to keep myself standing upright and even take one more step away from Tae, who was staring at his father, pure horror still displaying on his face.

Not only was I facing my boyfriend's father face to face for the first time after the drama, but I had also been caught red-handed, with my hands under said boyfriend's shirt. Not to even mention that said boyfriends' lips had been roaming my neck. Let's not even start with the fact that the said boyfriend's father was homophobic as fuck.

Tae managed to speak before I even started to get my shit together.

"How did—?"

"Spare key card. The one you left me, remember?"

"Why—?"

"Papers..." He held up a bundle of papers. "The ones you asked me to bring?"

Tae almost facepalmed—I could see his hand twitch. It was almost like he stopped himself at the last minute. "Right..."

Dammit Tae. You were supposed to know he was going to be here? Way to drop the ball on that one. In his defence, after the event at the park and all the teasing at the hospital, I would've forgotten it too.

"You're an hour late," Jae-sung said with a disapproving tone that downright pissed me off, even over the raging embarrassment.

"There were some unpredictable events. Our apologies," Tae said, with a tone I couldn't decipher. It was way more formal than how he spoke with me.

No-one knew what to say or do, so we all stared at each other in looming silence. Or rather, Tae and his dad had some kind of a staring contest while my eyes darted between the two.

No. After everything I'd been through, I was done with this game. This was our home. We could do whatever the hell we wanted at our own freaking home. And if he was the one who sold this to Tae, surely he knew it was half-mine? It couldn't be that hard to do the math and figure out we were more than friends.

I could handle one or two of those stubborn Mr. Gangs any given day. I knew how these men worked. I had absolutely nothing to be ashamed or afraid of.

I stood straight and cleared my throat. "Good evening, Jaesung-nim. Would you like to have some coffee?" I could tell he was the kind of guy who used honorifics and actual names, not nicknames.

It broke the almost visible string of tension between the two men. Tae's father was the one that recovered first, nodding slightly to my direction. "That would be nice Joonseok-ssi, thank you."

I escaped to the kitchen, staring at the coffee maker for a second or two while I gathered my thoughts. I took another deep breath.

It took sheer willpower to stop my hands from shaking, to get the coffee brewing, and arrange all the cups and saucers to a tray. Tae's footsteps headed towards the dining table and some small-talk exchanged between the two. I couldn't focus on what they were saying, I had my hands full with the coffee-task.

All too soon, the coffee was brewed, the dishes arranged, and snacks prepared. I had no other choice than to face the music and walk my way over to the dining table with the tray in tow. Thankfully, serving was still something that came straight from my spine, so I didn't mess up while laying the things to the table—one cup for Tae's dad, one for Tae who sat directly opposite of him, and one for me.

One more task completed, and the silence started to weigh on me again as I sat down next to Tae. My heart tried to beat its way out of my chest. I wasn't sure if Jae-sung did it on purpose, but it took him an uncommon amount of time to get the coffee poured into our mugs. That was his duty as the eldest. Maybe the bastard wanted to mess with us. I wouldn't have been surprised.

When he was finally done, both Tae and I nodded simultaneously. "Gamsahamnida."

He didn't mutter out another word while topping up his own mug. None of us did. As soon as he laid the carafe back to the table, the whole deadly silence thing made a comeback.

Eventually, after taking a couple of sips of his beverage, Jae-sung slid the papers across the table to Tae.

"Well, here you go," Jae-sung said, the tone of his voice giving nothing away. "My signature is on them already; you can go through them with your lawyer before signing. There's a copy for each of us."

So, this is basically a business meeting?

"Thank you," Tae said, with the exact same tone as his father had used. Not even touching the papers. Then he turned towards me. "They're the official papers of this apartment." Tae turned his eyes back to Jae-sung. "We'll go through them and return your copy at the soonest possible date."

Jae-sung nodded and took another sip.

"Thank you again, Joonseok-ssi, for filling in when we were in need. The ad got tremendously great response within the target audience," he said, but this time I didn't miss a hint of disappointment in his tone.

But truth to be told, I had forgotten all about the advertorial thing I did for his company some time ago. And for once, it wasn't because of amnesia—instead, I had shoved the memory to the furthest corner of my mind and left it there. Like normal people did. That lifted my mood so much that instead of bitching, I replied as politely as I possibly could. "No, it's all thanks to you. It was an honor to work with you."

I could tell that wasn't the response he anticipated by the "Hmph," he released from his chest as his eyes lowered for a split second to his coffee. "I see you've recovered."

Changing the topic to something still raw and painful so quickly? He was messing with me, wasn't he? Trying to get me to make a mistake—any reason to hate me. He knew what he was doing, and it made my blood boil. I didn't quite manage to keep all the venom from slipping to my voice when I replied. "Yes, in full. Thank you very much for your concern."

"How's Ye-rin?" Tae asked after clearing his throat, probably sensing the atmosphere turning sour.

The mention of his wife seemed to loosen Jae-sung's stiffness a bit—even the slightest of smiles managed to slip on his stoic face. "She's good, thank you for asking." He glanced at his wristwatch. "Which reminds me, I should head home. I'm already late for dinner."

I almost managed to relax my shoulders in relief. But in perfect Tae-fashion, he had to open his big-mouth and stall out my misery

"Before you go, there's something else we need to discuss," Tae said, getting visibly uneasy shifting in his chair.

Oh. Gods no. Please not now, Tae. The older Mr. Gang had majorly pissed me off already, and I couldn't even imagine what would be the outcome if Tae was going to say what I sensed he was going to say.

"Alright. What do you have in mind?" Jae-sung asked calmly, as if he didn't at all feel the tense atmosphere..

In my stiff, pissed off state, I completely ignored Tae's hand which landed on my thigh under the table. And this time, the soothing circles he started to trail with his thumb didn't manage to calm me down.

"Look, I know your views on these matters, but quite frankly, I no longer care." Tae stared at his own father with an amazing determination, his voice steadier than ever. He took one more deep breath. "I know you two have met before. But as your son, I'd like to officially introduce Shin Joonseok-ssi to you again...as my boyfriend."

I was right. I was always fucking right. For once, I would have been perfectly content being wrong.

I glanced at Tae, who still stared his father straight in the eyes. Even though I was beyond infuriated that he brought it up discussing it with me first, I couldn't help but feel a little proud of him. He had managed to say it in such a perfect way, that it was both polite but at the same time final. There wasn't any room for doubts. That took some balls.

"I've figured as much," was Jae-sung's simple reply. "However, I do appreciate that you told me yourself."

While I doubted every word this sneaky bastard said, looked like the statement managed to take Tae by a surprise. "So, you accept it? Just like that?"

Narrowing his eyes, Jae-sun studied us both for a long while, carefully choosing his words. "Well, I wouldn't say I accept it...but I think I can tolerate it as long as you two don't make it unnecessarily public, ruining both of our businesses."

I knew it.

My blood not only boiled but burst in flames inside me. "Tolerate—" My fists dug into the table.

But again, Tae cut me off by clenching my thigh under the table. "Thank you, we really appreciate—" Tae started to say to his father.

"Tae, shut up," I spat.

I wasn't having it at this point. All the tension, the bent up anger, and trying to hold myself back in front of this excuse of a man called Gang Jae-sung, had already taken its toll. And Tae was agreeing with this? Hell no.

A complete silence fell as both men turned their eyes on me.

"With all due respect, Jaesung-nim..." I nearly shook from rage. Meanwhile, Tae's fingers sunk so deep in my thigh, it almost started to hurt. Still, I ignored it and continued.

"But let me tell you this: if we decide to go public, it has nothing to do with business. Even less with your business. In fact, if your company can't handle your son living the way he wants to, it's weak and you might want to re-evaluate its worth."

Completely out of breath, spent and having spilled all my thoughts on the matter, I slumped down on my seat. After taking a sip of my coffee, I added, "I'm done, you may breathe."

While Tae was scared stiff beside me, Jae-sung's face twitched...right before he completely lost his shit and started—believe it or not—laughing. Loudly. So hard he doubled over, and his eyes watered.

Bewildered, I watched the man lose every single bit of the sternness and stiffness he had held up to this point. One by one, Tae's fingers unclenched themselves on my thigh as his focus shifted from trying to stop me to watching his wheezing father with wide eyes. Done with the whole conversation—no, with the whole day—I proceeded to focus on my coffee, no longer giving a single fuck.

Eventually, both of them calmed down. Tae visibly relaxed as Jae-sung resorted to his calmer self, still chuckling from time to time while wiping the corners of his eyes.

"I give up. You two do whatever the hell you want," Jae-sung finally stated, sitting upright. "I must say, Joonseok-ssi, that you remind me of my mother. She, too, had her fairly blunt way with words."

I nodded politely. "Thank you," I said, for the first time sincerely during the whole evening. "Mrs. Gang Eun-ju was one fine lady. I'm honored I got to meet her."

"Right," Jae-sung said, standing up. "I think it's my time to go. Thank you again for entertaining me tonight. I don't think I've had this much amusement in a while."

Hastily, both me and Tae stood up too and bowed.

"No need, you can stay," I said, not wanting to appear even ruder after spilling my guts to this man…who was also my lover's father, despite how douche-y he had acted.

"It's alright," he said and laid his hand on my shoulder while passing by. "Just take care of my son, will you?"

I was positive I had never been so beet red in my life. Awkwardly, I muttered, "I'll try," to which he chuckled almost inaudibly.

After slightly squeezing my shoulder, he let his hand drop. "See you around"

"Wait!" I exclaimed suddenly, making the old man turn from the door with that same eyebrow arched up.

"What more can there be at this point?" he asked.

Amused, I held out my hand. "The spare key. I want it back."

The older Mr. Gang's lips twitched before he let out a faint chuckle while going through his pockets. Eventually, he tossed it to me and proceeded to walk towards the entrance hall. I caught the small black plastic disk easily and laid it on the dining table as he disappeared out the door.

Senseless

The cups and plates tinkled together when I threw them in the dishwasher and slammed the door shut. Our dinner had been awfully quiet, to say the least, and left a sour taste in my mouth. Yeah, I was still mad. Mostly at Tae but also at myself. How could I have let it get to that point? Leaning my palms against the counter, I tried to calm down, but even counting to ten didn't help. I was still so pissed that my whole body was shaking and having Tae hover behind my back irritated me even more. If possible.

"Joon, talk to me."

I took a deep breath and closed my eyes. "I don't want to right now You threw me under a fucking bus."

"Err, you let Dad get under your skin all by yourself," he replied, calm as ever. He grabbed my hips and spun me around to face him. "Look, I know you, and I know my father. That was bound to happen sooner or later, so I chose sooner. He literally caught us. It wasn't like he didn't know. And everything went fine. Better that I could've imagined, even. So, what's the problem?"

It became nearly impossible to not melt under his warm gaze. "A warning would've been nice."

"I know, and I am sorry. For the record."

My defences were crumbling down at an alarming speed when I sighed and leaned my forehead against his chest. "Aish, that was so embarrassing."

Tae chuckled and stroked the back of my head softly with his fingers. "I know."

We stayed silent for a moment while Tae played with my hair. Other sensations filled the void that the lack of irritation left behind, especially when Tae ran his hand through my hair and proceeded to brush my neck with just the very tip of his finger, leaving behind an almost ticklish trail.

"Now...should we continue where we left off?" Tae murmured with that rough, deep voice of his that sent a whole bunch of familiar shivers down my back.

I surrendered and lifted my eyes to meet his. They were already burning, and soon the same fire ignited in the pit of my stomach. He cupped the side of my face and pushed me against the counter with his body, his other hand landing on my waist. As I didn't reply, he sneaked his hand under my shirt and leaned in, his lips landing softly on mine.

And I was gone.

All sanity left my mind. I opened my lips and let out a small gasp as his tongue brushed my lower lip. A tiny tingle clenched my stomach, right before I lost it for good.

I started unbuttoning his shirt as his lips danced on mine, a moan escaping from deep inside his chest. The sound was so eager, it made me lose my patience and I ripped the rest of it open—a button or two might've popped off and flown somewhere. I let my hands wander on his abdomen, feeling up the tight and toned muscles that were no longer hidden behind clothing.

Parting our lips, I moved on to press my lips on his jawline. He took a tiny step back, pulling me forward at the same time my lips landed on the side of his neck. I moved my hands up, over his broad shoulders with the goal of sliding off his shirt. Tae helped me before gathering the hem of my shirt in his fists in turn. He pulled it all the way up, with me only barely helping him by lifting my arms. The shirt was tossed to the side and Tae leaned towards my neck.

I was intent on making him lose control this time. I evaded his lips and pushed him against the fridge with a determined thrust. After everything that had happened, I was sick and tired of tender and soft. What I wanted was to be fucked so hard I'd see stars. A galaxy of them. And I knew that I'd get exactly that if I'd manage to drive Tae far enough over his mental restraints.

Who would've known having memories would turn out to be so useful from time to time?

I knew every single one of Tae's weak spots and made my first goal his overly sensitive nipples. When I twirled my tongue over one, he threw his head back with a satisfying sigh. That wasn't enough for me. I tore his belt open while tracing down the dip between his abs. Slowly like that, I made my way all the way down to my knees.

He let out a sharp breath when I yanked his jeans to his knees. And then another when I pulled his boxer briefs down, freeing his semi-erected cock from the constraints of the underwear. With a smile, I watched his abs clench when I brushed my finger softly against the underside of his tightening balls before I gripped the base of his now rock hard dick. I couldn't help but smile at the sight, glad to see I hadn't lost my abilities in this field.

Too worked up to only tease, I licked my lips and then laid a kiss on the underside of his shaft, then made my way up to his glans. Another groan escaped his lips when I took as much of the length as possible inside my mouth, my tongue pressing against a throbbing vein on the underside. I glanced up; Tae was already breathing heavily, his hands clenched in tight fists. Closing my eyes and bobbing my head up before twirling my tongue over the head of his member, I added a moan, sending vibrations through his whole cock.

"Oh fuck," he breathed. I locked my eyes briefly with his before starting to move up and down his length, listening to his deep grunts. Another throaty moan escaped me, sending another surge of vibrations on his cock. This time it made him suck in a breath through his teeth.

The moment I knew I was winning was when he fisted a bunch of my hair and pulled back, hard. The pain made the corners of my eyes water, but I didn't care. As I continued to slide my mouth back and forth while working my tongue against the underside, he pulled my hair harder and harder...and when his cock started throbbing, I knew he was getting close. But just when I was sure he was going to shoot his load down my throat, he yanked my head back so forcibly his cock slid out of my mouth, and I gasped.

"Why stop?" I asked, smirking, my eyes nailed on the gasping man that let go of my hair and gripped my hand instead.

"Because I was close and I still need to fuck you senseless before all that mess," he stated with his voice all worked up and husky. I loved it.

"Then take me to the bedroom," I said.

"Nah we ain't gonna make it that far," he replied with a smirk and tilted his head towards the drawers. "Bottom drawer right behind you. All the way in the back."

Intrigued, I turned around and pulled the said drawer open. Reaching my hand back behind the dividers that held the kitchen equipment in their places, my fingertips curled around a plastic bottle. I pulled the lube out and stood up, arching my eyebrows up at Tae.

"What? It's good to be prepared." He was grinning so wide even the dimple made an appearance. Snatching the bottle out of my hand, he added, "My turn."

"Yeah?" I wasn't too convinced I'd worked him up enough for my purposes.

He took my hand in his after laying the lube bottle on the counter. Slowly, he lifted it, laying a soft kiss to the back of my hand. "I've wanted this ever since I first brought you here."

"What? To kiss my hand?" I asked, admittedly a bit disappointed. This was not what I was after, like... at all.

With eyes burning with that dark fire and a smirk on his lips, he traced my stomach down with the back of his free hand. "No, dumbass. This—" he said, abruptly yanking my hand so I spun around. "—And this." He turned that same hand in a position behind my back. I had no other choice than to bend over the counter.

I gasped and tried to stay upwards by pressing my free hand's palm against the marble countertop. Tae wasn't having it and twisted my arm further up my back, literally making me bend down. All the way down. Despite my struggle, my chest was soon pressed against the cold surface.

"Now, you do remember the safe word, right?" Tae asked.

"Obviously," I said breathlessly.

"Good."

I didn't have any time or even a chance to think about the fact of how unsanitary this all was before Tae pulled my pants down. The lecture about hygiene could wait for another time. Tae smacked my ass so hard my whole body jerked against the counter, and I sucked in another surprised gasp through my teeth. Before the pain even fully registered, he had already massaged it away. It all happened so fast.

A cold drop of lube landed on my ass, dripping down the crack. Then another, and another, until some of it reached my tightening balls. Tae certainly didn't waste any more time—his fingers found my entrance and with a prompt push he had one inside, making me arch my back as much as possible in the highly uncomfortable, but oh-so-provocative, position. A long, harsh moan erupted from somewhere deep in my chest.

But Tae didn't stop there either. Swiftly, he inserted another finger. I squirmed as he worked my hole. As I struggled against his hold, to no avail whatsoever, more moans escaped my lips, and I threw my head back. My dick was already leaking, aching, rock hard, and twitching every time he hit my prostate with such a force it drove me wild.

Just as abruptly as he inserted his fingers inside me, he took them out. Suddenly empty, I craved for so much more I let out an involuntary whine. Again, Tae was ahead of me, his cock lining up against my hole, teasing it.

"Ready?" he asked with a breathless voice, sliding his cock up and down my ass.

My answer was a continuous whine because I was not even remotely able to form coherent words. The whine turned into a gasp and then a cry as he slammed his cock inside me with one firm push. My every sense exploded. The pain made me squeeze my watering eyes shut and arch my back. But the pleasure soon overpowered the pain, sending crazy tingles to the pit of my stomach. I was a total half-crying, half-moaning mess, so out of this world I didn't even care.

One might've thought Tae would've let me rest for a bit. Oh, how wrong that assumption turned out to be. He only pulled back some, slowly, giving more playroom for that famous false hope...before he thrust back, all the way inside, balls deep. It sent another surge of pain and pleasure dancing all over me, both feelings so intense I couldn't tell them apart any longer. My cry turned into a sob, which then turned into a moan, and then back to a cry—but this time more because of pleasure rather than pain.

Tae held my arm firmly against my back to make sure I couldn't move...as if even thinking about going anywhere was an option at this point. Then he fisted a bunch of my hair with his other hand and pulled, arching me like a bow. The next thrust was an out of this world experience as Tae's dick rubbed directly against the magic spot. Completely at his mercy, I tried to hold on to the edge of the kitchen counter with my only free hand for dear life.

The stress of the past couple of days, the anxiety over the memory loss, the struggle of trying to rearrange the regained memories, or even the irritation that the night's events had caused...none of it mattered. I couldn't care less if it was the pain or the pleasure that made me lose myself in the moment, I was grateful for all of it.

My feet shook, my throat grew sore, and my ass sorer, as we banged closer to the edge with every push and pull. Tae's cock got even bigger and harder inside me, right before he let go of my arm and I staggered a little, losing my balance. A little relieved, I grabbed the edge of the counter with the just freed hand for more support. The relief didn't last long though, as Tae pulled my hair even harder and grabbed my cock with his other hand.

With a scream, or a sob, or a cry—I wasn't even sure—I reached the peak. My aching cock fisted tightly in Tae's hand. I jerked as I emptied my load to the floor. The orgasmic waves that washed over me were like shockwaves, making my whole body tremble.

By far, it was the most intense orgasm I had ever had.

Tae followed me over the edge a few pushes later, causing a smaller jolt to go through my body as he hit my prostate one last time. With a groan, he unloaded his hot cum deep inside me. Tae barely managed to hold us both upright. My feet were useless; they totally gave up.

Almost like in complete contrast to his earlier actions, he let go of my hair and pulled his cock out of me, ever so gently. As I all but collapsed against the counter, he held me up effortlessly.

My eyes barely opened as he cupped my face and trailed his thumb across my cheek.

"Saranghae," he said with a soft voice, before picking my limp body up and carrying it straight to the upstairs bathroom. Even gentler, he washed me and himself up before tucking me under the duvet on the soft bed.

My mind was already drifting to the dreamlands when he suddenly turned his back on me and started to leave.

I grabbed his wrist. "Don't go."

He leaned down and placed one, perfect, soft kiss on my lips. "I would never. I just figured, as a cheesy blanket thief, it would be good for me to have my own duvet."

Epilogue: About Chris

"What are those?" Tae asked.

After jumping up startled and then getting over the mild heart attack, I turned around to face him.

The morning light poured from the gigantic window behind his back as he leaned against the doorframe leisurely with his arms crossed over his broad, muscular chest that its nakedness only emphasized. He was clearly fresh out of the shower, only a towel hanging low on his waist and hair still dripping wet. The sight damn nearly distracted me from my task of arranging my notebooks on one shelf of my—err—*our* walk-in closet.

"These..." I ran my index finger on one of the spines, "...these are notebooks. Filled ones."

"I see. What's in those if you don't mind my asking?"

Aish, what the hell. It wasn't like he didn't deserve to know after all we'd been through in such a short time. Besides, I didn't want to hide them anymore. It was time.

Tae made his way behind my back and wrapped his hands around my waist, leaning his chin on my shoulder, a couple of beads of water dripping from his hair to my collar.

"Remember that ancient track we did back in the day and threw on Soundcloud? The only one I've ever written lyrics to?" I asked, almost inaudible.

"Yeah... 'Savage,' was it?" he muttered, nuzzling his face on the nook of my neck. "I liked that song, by the way."

"Well, the lyrics are from this one," I said, trying to not get distracted by Tae's lips, which were wandering my neck, and grabbed a small, black notebook from the shelf. Quickly, I flipped through the pages to find the right one before smashing it to his face.

"Ouch," He let out a chuckle and rubbed his nose. At the same time, he picked up the book that had dropped to the floor with his other hand.

When he started browsing through it, I studied his expressions. They varied from surprise, to amused, and then back to surprise. "Wow, I had no idea you'd been hiding such good lyrics around."

"Yeah, well...thanks, I guess," I said, blushing all over again. Seemed like Tae had this effect on me with and without the memories…much to my disappointment.

When Tae continued flipping through the worn-out pages with a slight frown between his eyebrows, I started rambling. I just couldn't take the silence.

"Not all of it is lyrics, though. Some are kind of diary entries and such. I started keeping a diary for mom when she, uhh, passed away. I couldn't keep up with it long though, so the notes turned out to be this...mess. Eventually. Can I have it back now—"

"Oh shush, some of these are genius. Why aren't more of these lyrics in our music?"

"They're kinda personal," I said and snatched the notebook out of his hands. "I'd appreciate it if you'd keep their existence to yourself."

"Well, suit yourself. But I could get so many new track ideas by going through those..." he said softly. Then he turned towards the next shelf on the left, stroking the back of one of the pumps' heel. "And one day I'm going to rail you while you're wearing a pair of these."

Despite how tempting that sounded, I hit Tae's shoulder with the notebook softly before turning to put it back on the shelf. "Don't hold your breath."

Tae's hands wrapped around my waist again. "Oh, trust me, someday."

"Well, maybe," I said with that all too familiar heat rising up my cheeks. Still, I gave up and leaned my back against him.

We stayed that way for a while, hugging each other in the closet, ironically enough. Since we had decided, once again, that we were going to keep this—our relationship—out of the spotlight for the time being. Too much had happened lately to make any new headlines that had even the slightest chance to turn negative.

I didn't mind, though. What we had was already fine for me. More than fine. As long as he'd give me some awesome dick, and I could continue my career in the music industry, everything else could wait for better timing. No need to stress about it.

As I planned to turn around and take Tae to bed, he laid a short kiss on my neck and took a step back. "I should put on some clothes and head downstairs to make us some breakfast."

"Or we could have a quickie first," I said, turning around to face him with a smirk on my lips.

"Tempting, but we have to get to HQ within the next hour and a half," he stated, smirking right back at me before disappearing towards his—former—room, presumably to get some clothes. We hadn't had time to move those yet. Let alone figure out what we'd do with all the extra rooms we totally didn't need. *I* had a little playroom in mind, but I hadn't figured out how to bring that up with Tae yet.

My shoulders slumped a bit, but nevertheless, I arranged the rest of the notebooks on the shelf. When I was done, I made sure my outfit of tight fitted bright red jeans and black, loose button-up was still okay. Then I put on some accessories and took a final glance at the mirror, at least somewhat satisfied with what I saw.

I mean, the stiffness on my neck was still visible, and the dark circles around my eyes hadn't completely faded away. But other than that, I looked like myself. Even more importantly, I started to feel like myself. And that's one hell of an achievement, after all the shit that had happened.

Happily, I skipped downstairs. Tae was already frying some eggs sunny side up while humming out a tune and scribbling some notes on the piece of paper on his left at the same time. While he might've had a little stronger jawline than what was the beauty standard around here, and not very wide eyes, he looked absolutely perfect to me.

I walked across the large room and hopped to sit on the very counter we had banged against the other night. He had laid a small bowl of strawberries to the side, and I couldn't help but snag one

Tae's eyes snapped up to meet mine. "Hey, those are for later!"

I could see the small twitch on his lips as he tried to hold his smile at bay.

"Mmhm, come get it back," I said and placed the berry in between my teeth.

Tae couldn't hold the smile back anymore—it flashed on his lips in a fraction of a second. Dimple and all. I loved it. It didn't take him much longer to place the just fried eggs on a plate, turn the stove off and put the pan away before he was already standing in front of me. I pulled him between my legs.

"You're one evil bitch when left unsupervised, you know that?" he said, before leaning in.

Soon the strawberry was thoroughly consumed, but our lips remained in contact. Our hands started wandering. Mine, for example, made their way on Tae's hips, trying to yank his button-up from the hold of his pants.

That's when Tae's phone rang on the table, and we parted. With a deep frown, he picked it up and took a long glance at the name that was displayed on the screen.

"Huh," he muttered. "Sorry, I've gotta take this. It's Jae-beom."

The lawyer, that had lifted us from the shit that had been the Domino scandal. What could he possibly want? Likely…nothing good.

Tae all but ran into his study and yanked the door shut behind him, leaving me to sit on the counter dumbfounded. Never, not once, had he wanted that much privacy just to speak on the phone.

Not to mention the fact that Jae-beom called us, or Tae, directly, extremely rarely. If ever.

With a deep worry settling in my stomach, I hopped down and glanced around the kitchen. Desperate to find something to do with my hands, I started arranging the breakfast that Tae had almost finished to the dining table and brewed some coffee.

My mind went over all the possibilities a million times over. Surely Min and Do hadn't managed to flame another scandal? Though that was highly unlikely, because as far as I knew, they had been only transferring their stuff from the old dorms to their new place these past couple of days.

Maybe something happened at the amusement park, something I couldn't remember...something big? All I knew about that day was that Joe had shot Min-ho, and I had regained most of my memories. Well, except the memories of that day...which was annoying in times like this.

I placed the freshly brewed coffee in the middle of the table and sat down. At that moment, Tae emerged from his study, eyes cast down. His hands shook for the sheer force his grip placed on the phone.

My eyebrows knitted together. "What's wrong?"

Tae blinked a couple of times, before shutting the office's door behind him and let his eyes focus on mine.

"It's Chris."

"What about Chris?" I asked, already scared of what I'd hear.

Tae ran his hand through his hair and sighed, turning to look outside with an empty gaze.

"He's been arrested."

Author's Note

Thank you for reading the independent second part of the On Stage Trilogy! Liked it? If so, please consider leaving a review or even just a rating, it would be highly appreciated. In addition, please check out my website for the latest news:

www.namiartopit.com

xoxo Nami